THE
SEA
QUEEN

ALSO BY LINNEA HARTSUYKER

The Half-Drowned King

THE
SEA
QUEEN

LINNEA HARTSUYKER

Little, Brown

LITTLE, BROWN

First published in the United States in 2018 by HarperCollins Publishers
First published in Great Britain in 2018 by Little, Brown

Copyright © 2018 by Linnea Hartsuyker

Map © 2018 Laura Hartman Maestro

The moral right of the author has been asserted.

A CIP catalogue record for this book
is available from the British Library.

Hardback ISBN 978-1-4087-0882-8
Trade paperback ISBN 978-1-4087-0883-5

Printed and bound in Great Britain by
Clays Ltd, Elcograf S.p.A.

Papers used by Little, Brown are from well-managed forests
and other responsible sources.

Little, Brown
An imprint of
Little, Brown Book Group
Carmelite House
50 Victoria Embankment
London EC4Y 0DZ

An Hachette UK Company
www.hachette.co.uk

www.littlebrown.co.uk

The Sea Queen

ICELAND
Reykjavik

Faroe Islands

Norwegian Sea

Arctic Circle

Trondheim Fjord

Smola

Halogaland

Geiranger Fjord

Nidaros
Trondelag

Naustdal

Maer

Tafjord

Sogn Fjord

Sogn

Jordalo

Hardanger Fjord

Fossland

NORWAY

Modern day border

SWEDEN

Hafrsfjord

Shetland Islands

Hebrides

Orkney Islands

SCOTLAND

Vest-fold

Oslo Fjord

Skagerrak Strait

Jutland

Skane

Atlantic Ocean

North Sea

Ribe

Roskilde

IRELAND

Dublin

FRISIA

Kilometers

0   100   200   300   400

0   100   200   300

Miles

map © 2018 by
Laura Hartman Maestro

PLACES AND CHARACTERS

PLACES

Sogn—a district in western Norway, south of Maer, ruled by Ragnvald

    Ardal—Ragnvald and Svanhild's childhood home

    Sogn Fjord—the fjord in Sogn

    Kaupanger—a market town on the north side of Sogn Fjord, one of the few towns in Viking-age Norway

The Keel—the mountain range that runs the length of Norway, dividing east from west

Trondelag—a district in northwest Norway

    Trondheim Fjord—the fjord in Trondelag

    Nidaros—King Harald's northwest capital, modern-day Trondheim

Halogaland—a district in northwest Norway, ruled by King Hakon

    Yrjar—King Hakon's seat of power in Halogaland

    Smola—an island near Yrjar

Maer—a district in conflict, formerly ruled by Solvi's line

Tafjord—King Hunthiof's seat of power, at the end of Geiranger Fjord

Geiranger Fjord—the fjord in Maer

Naustdal—the seat of power in South Maer

Vestfold—a district in southeastern Norway, ruled by King Harald

Vermaland—a section of Vestfold

Faroe Islands—islands between Iceland and Norway, ruled by King Hakon

Reykjavik—Iceland's primary settlement

Dublin—the capital of Norse Ireland, ruled by King Imar

Uppsala—the capital of Sweden, ruled by King Eirik

CHARACTERS

Ragnvald Eysteinsson, king of Sogn

Vigdis Hallbjornsdatter, Ragnvald's stepmother and concubine

Einar Ragnvaldsson, Ragnvald's son with Vigdis

Ragnhild Hrolfsdatter, called Hilda, Ragnvald's wife

Ivar Ragnvaldsson, Ragnvald's first son with Hilda

Thorir Ragnvaldsson, Ragnvald's second son with Hilda

Hrolf Ragnvaldsson, called Rolli, Ragnvald's third son with Hilda

Sigurd Olafsson, Ragnvald's stepbrother

Arnfast, man-at-arms

Svanhild Eysteinsdatter, Ragnvald's sister

Solvi Hunthiofsson, Svanhild's husband

>   **Eystein Solvisson**, Svanhild's son with Solvi

>   **Tryggulf, Snorri, and Ulfarr**, Solvi's companions since boyhood

>   **Thorstein**, a young captain

Harald Halfdansson, king of Norway

>   **Guthorm**, Harald's uncle and adviser

>   **Asa Hakonsdatter**, Harald's wife, King Hakon's daughter

>   **Gyda Eiriksdatter**, Harald's betrothed, queen of Hordaland

Atli Kolbrandsson, an adventurer

>   **Bertha**, Atli's wife

>   **Aldulf Atlisson**, called Aldi, Atli's son

Hrolf Nefia, farmer in Maer

>   **Egil Hrolfsson**, Hrolf's son

>   **Ragnhild Hrolfsdatter**, called Hilda, daughter, Ragnvald's wife

>   **Ingifrid Hrolfsdatter**, another of Hrolf's daughters

Hakon Grjotgardsson, king of Halogaland

>   **Heming Hakonsson**, Hakon's oldest son, rules Maer

>   **Asa Hakonsdatter**, Hakon's daughter, married to King Harald

>   **Oddi Hakonsson**, Hakon's base-born son

>   **Geirbjorn Hakonsson**, Hakon's son

>   **Herlaug Hakonsson**, Hakon's son

THE
SEA
QUEEN

I

HILDA RESTED ON A ROUGH WOODEN BENCH THAT STOOD against the outside of the living hall at Sogn. She closed her eyes and tipped her head back so the overhanging roof shadowed her face, and the afternoon sun warmed her body. After a cold and rainy spring, the summer's heat made her feel almost drunk. She smelled the comforting scents of ripening hay, fertile earth, and smoke from the kitchen fire. Her youngest, Hrolf—called Rolli—mouthed at her breast. If she sat still, eyes half-closed, not moving, she could ignore her aches and exhaustion, the weariness that had plagued her since Rolli's difficult birth. At least Ragnvald's battles kept him and his men away this summer. She found it much easier to run the hall with only a few men around, her word obeyed without question.

A boy's shriek forced her to sit up and open her eyes. Einar, Hilda's stepson—Ragnvald's son by his former concubine, Vigdis—lay with his stomach on a branch of the tree that stood just outside the hall. He held his half-brother Ivar by the wrist so Ivar's feet dangled in the air. Ivar yelled and squirmed, and then swung once, twice, and hooked the branch with his other elbow. With Einar's guidance, he pulled up both feet and held on from underneath the branch with all four limbs wrapped around it. At the foot of the tree, their younger brother Thorir looked up enviously from his play. He was still too small to climb trees with them.

"Einar, be careful of your brother. You'll hurt his shoulder," said Hilda.

"I'm always careful," said Einar, with his usual sullenness. Whenever Hilda scolded him, he responded like a man whose honor had been challenged, as though he wanted to put his hand to the sword he would one day wear. Einar had Vigdis's golden coloring and her high cheekbones, which on him looked raw rather than beautiful. Ragnvald had named him for his foster-brother, Einar, who he had been forced to kill while reclaiming his birthright from his stepfather. "You have to swing," he said to Ivar. "Let go with your arms and swing."

Ivar did as his brother suggested, and then yelled in triumph as he caught the branch with his two arms wrapped around one side. He let his legs go and swung again, sending a stab of worry into Hilda's chest, and then wriggled his way onto the top.

"I did it, Mother, see!" Ivar cried. The two boys lay atop the branch facing each other, grinning. With Ivar's russet head and Einar's golden one, they made a perfect image of carefree boyhood: suspended in a green tree, against a sky of blue and white, two boys who loved each other as strongly as their mothers had hated. Hilda felt a brief twinge of guilt at depriving Einar of Vigdis. The boy deserved more mothering than Hilda could give him, but she hated Vigdis too much to allow her to stay for her son's sake.

By the time Ragnvald had brought Hilda home as his bride, Vigdis, his own stepmother, was six months pregnant with his son Einar. Pregnant, she looked even more like Freya, goddess of fertility and the harvest, a goddess who demanded sacrifices of honey and blood, sweet and bitter, life and death. Hilda could not compete with her beauty or the way she had enthralled Ragnvald. Finally, after Hilda had given birth to Ivar, and Ragnvald had accepted his son by laying a sword across Hilda's lap, which she would hold in trust for Ivar until he grew to manhood, Hilda had asked him for another gift: to send Vigdis away, and he had done it, though not happily.

"I see Uncle Sigurd," said Ivar from his perch. He squatted atop the branch now, testing his balance.

Einar crouched on the branch as well, looking like a forest cat about to pounce. "That's not Sigurd," he said. "That's . . . why are there so many?"

"We have enough food for dinner if Sigurd has brought friends," said Hilda. Sigurd spent little time at the hall during these long summer days, and Hilda did not begrudge him his leisure. Soon the harvest would bring too much work for Hilda to rest in the sunshine with her children, and soon Ragnvald would return as well, bringing news and demands she must satisfy.

"My lady, there were too many men in the field," said Einar. "It wasn't Sigurd that I saw."

Hilda stood, cradling Rolli more tightly. Einar could be exaggerating to make himself seem important, but he had keen eyesight. Hilda saw only waving grass beyond the fences, green and gold, rippling in the wind. "Where?" she asked.

"They're gone now," Einar replied.

"And I see Sigurd," said Hilda. She moved Rolli over to her hip so she could hold him with one arm and wave to Sigurd with the other. Sigurd waved back—an expansive, friendly gesture—and so did his companion, Dusi, a follower of Ragnvald's who had stayed in Sogn and married the daughter of a farmer with no sons.

"My lady!" Sigurd called out as he opened the wicker gate and walked into the yard. When he passed under the tree, Ivar jumped down onto his back so Sigurd could swing him around and then up onto his shoulders. Einar waited until Sigurd had carried Ivar a few steps away before dropping down from the branch and landing lightly on his feet. Sigurd would have carried him too, but Einar rarely liked to be touched.

"Any news?" Hilda asked, warming under Sigurd's smile.

Sigurd bent forward to balance Ivar against his head and raised his palms so Hilda could see the grime covering them, black dust and ash. "The house of Svein the Charcoaler burned down," he said.

"Again? Was anyone hurt?"

"Svein's hands are blistered and his wife has a black eye from a beam that fell on her," Sigurd answered.

"Svein is too foolish to be the charcoaler, I suppose," said Hilda. Dusi laughed as he fell into step behind them. Einar stepped forward to take his bundle of dead birds. He slung them over his shoulder so they dangled down his back, their heads just brushing the ground.

"Come," Hilda said warmly to Sigurd and Dusi. "Let us go inside. I will have Thora give you some ale. You can tell me more of Svein the Charcoaler's accident. What a fool!"

Hilda walked into the kitchen as Sigurd told the story. Her eyes adjusted slowly from the bright afternoon to the darkness within, where most of the light came from the cook fire in the hearth. The room was empty except for the young deaf thrall who kept the fire fed and floor swept.

"Thora," Hilda called out for the servant who should be over-seeing the kitchen and its thralls. "Where are you? Where is every-one?" The kitchen should have been full of women at this time of day. A droplet of sweat from Hilda's neck ran down her back, mak-ing her twitch. She bent down and gave Rolli to Ivar, and touched Thorir's lips to quiet his toddler's chatter. Ivar was too small to hold the baby easily, and Rolli began to fuss until Einar walked over and gravely stroked the baby's head. Even through her uneasiness, the sight caused Hilda another pang of guilt. She should be kinder to the boy.

In the quiet, Hilda heard low sounds of conversation from the hall's great room, where the household slept and worked in bad weather. Perhaps a traveling peddler had come selling trinkets cheap enough for even thralls to covet, and drawn all the women from the kitchen. Since Harald moved his court to Nidaros and installed Ragnvald in Sogn, farmers need not fear raiders as they had in years past. No one should be in the hall without her knowledge, though, and Einar had seen men in the fields.

Hilda pulled her eating dagger from the scabbard at her waist. It would do her little good against a trained warrior, but she felt better clutching the steel grip.

"What is it?" Sigurd asked loudly. Hilda flinched and put a finger to her lips. She crept toward the door. "Let me," said Sigurd, drawing his sword. "I will tell you if there is anything to fear."

Before Hilda could stop him, Sigurd burst through the door into the hall's main room where men's shouts greeted him. A warrior grabbed his shoulders and spun him around. Another shook Sigurd's sword from his grasp, while a third pressed him against the wall with a dagger to his throat. A Sogn man lay tied up and gagged on the floor near Sigurd's feet.

More men stepped forward and pulled Hilda through the door, bruising her wrists. They shoved her face-first over the long table. She froze. Her head scarf fell over her forehead, so she could see nothing except the stained wood of the table she was pressed against. She smelled the grease from years of meals eaten upon it, mixed with the sweat of these men. She had always hoped she would fight if raiders attacked, and choose death rather than letting a man rape her, but instead she was grateful she could see little, and only hoped it would be over quickly.

"Grab the boys," said one of them. Rage flooded through her, breaking her paralysis. She would fight for her sons as long as she lived, and she was ashamed that she had forgotten them in her fear, for even a moment. She raised her right foot, kicking her heel up between the legs of the man who held her. He grunted and shoved her face harder into the table.

"Let her up, let her up," said another man, this voice lighter and gentler than the others. Hilda's captor pulled her to standing and turned her around to face the newcomer. She sat back against the table, her heart pounding, her mouth full of a bitter tang, as though her stomach tried to crawl out through her throat. With her newly free hands she pushed her scarf back so she could see.

In front of her stood a slim man, with lean cheeks and bulging, colorless eyes that caught the lamplight. He wore rich clothing, and held himself wary and upright like a warrior.

"Greetings, my lady," he said. His was the gentle voice she had heard, a beautiful baritone, melodious and mocking. "I am Jarl Atli Kolbrandsson. And Sogn is mine."

2

RAGNVALD ROSE FROM HIS SEAT BY THE FIRE TO GREET ARN-
fast, who ran, panting, into the camp. He had seen Arnfast winded
after a scouting mission many times before, and knew not to ask for a
report until Arnfast's chest had stopped heaving, no matter how impa-
tient he was. Arnfast put his hands on the back of his head, drew a few
more deep breaths, and shook himself slightly. Aside from the sheen of
sweat on his brow, he now looked as fresh as he had when he departed
at midday. "King Vemund and twenty of his men have camped at the
foot of the cliff near the rock fall," he announced.

Ragnvald frowned, rubbing his thumb along the side of his beard,
over the scar by his mouth that gave his expression a sardonic twist no
matter what mood he wished to convey. "That does not seem right,"
he said. "Why would he camp at a cliff face with no escape?"

Arnfast shrugged. "I only know what I saw." He had been Ragnvald's
sworn warrior since the battle at Vestfold and understood his duty: to
act as Ragnvald's eyes, not his mind. Five summers of battle had kept
Arnfast fleet and slim; the passing time only made his face grow thinner. He shifted his weight from side to side. He was restless unless he
was moving, or watching in stillness. He always scouted alone.

"It is certainly a trap. But you say that King Vemund was there?"
Ragnvald asked, though he had never known Arnfast to be wrong.

"Yes," said Arnfast. "I saw his sharp teeth, with the ruby set in one
of them." King Vemund, styling himself a wild raider, showed his

bravery by enduring the pain of having his teeth filed into points, and set with jewels. Arnfast had seen truly.

"It is the first sure sighting we have had of him in a month," said Oddi, who was sitting by the fire, carving wooden nails, always needed for ship repair. He flung the wood shavings onto the campfire's coals, where they burst into tiny flames. Heming sat nearby, surrounded by his favorite warriors, feeding crumbs of stale bread to a squirrel by his feet. Ragnvald beckoned him over to hear Arnfast repeat his report.

While he spoke, Ragnvald looked out over the other men sitting around the fires. Harald's armies had been chasing their enemy King Vemund over South Maer all summer. Too many of Ragnvald's men had fallen to arrows that came without warning from thick stands of trees, and from the blows of warriors who appeared as if from nowhere, and disappeared as quickly, always refusing to meet in pitched battle. Ragnvald needed to win a victory for Harald soon, or this whole summer of battles would add up to nothing but losses on Harald's side.

Now, at least, Ragnvald knew the location of their most important enemy: a place he knew well, for his men and Harald's had marched over every patch of ground in Vemund's territory of Naustdal. The flat clearing at the base of the cliff formed an ideal camping ground in peace time, with a fire pit already dug and lined with stones. A tangle of rock fall and saplings rose to the east, which made approach or escape impossible in that direction. Only one path led to the clearing.

Vemund had started the summer with perhaps a hundred men loyal to him. But Ragnvald had killed his share, as had most of Harald's followers. Now Vemund set a tempting trap, one Ragnvald could not afford to ignore. Though if he attacked, Vemund would likely have another force ready to come and trap them there, against the wall. After the summer's fighting, he probably had no more than forty men remaining. An even fight against Ragnvald's forces on open ground; an uneven one in Vemund's forest. Still, if Ragnvald did not confront Vemund now, he would escape for another year, and Ragnvald would have failed Harald.

"Very well," said Ragnvald. "We will wait here and attack at midnight."

"And spring his trap?" Oddi asked.

"Yes, but we will separate, so it is he who will be trapped," said Ragnvald. "This is a desperate gambit for him—even if he tries to trap us, he is still up against the cliff wall." He explained how they should approach: well spaced for stealth but exchanging frequent signals. If any man missed a signal, it meant they had encountered attackers in the dark, and should retreat. "When we see their torches through the trees, Oddi, your half will hold back, and wait for the trap to close, then come to help us." He made Oddi, Heming, and Arnfast repeat his instructions back to him.

"You fret like a woman," said Heming. He tugged off his bright tunic and exchanged it for one of dark homespun that would fade into the forest's dimness. "My men are bold enough to win through without this trickery. You would have us tiptoe like mice."

"You're alive because of Ragnvald's trickery and you know it," said Oddi, testily. "If you walk into a trap, you must walk carefully." Ragnvald ignored both of them. Heming would grumble, and then do as Ragnvald asked. He would only worry about Heming disobeying him if he did not complain.

Ragnvald tugged at the padding inside his helmet—a reward from Harald for his victories the previous summer—to make sure it would not come loose during the fighting. It had a cap of unbreakable steel, decorated with gold filigree—a rich gift and a mark of favor that Ragnvald feared he had not yet fully earned. He drew his sword half out of its scabbard to ensure that nothing in his gear impeded his movements. Mist gathered under the trees. Droplets of water from the branches fell into the fire, sending up bursts of steam. Ragnvald could not count how many nights this summer had begun like this, in quiet preparation, and ended in mornings of laying out the dead and tending the wounded. King Vemund had refused to swear loyalty to Harald, and only killing him would end this fighting. His sons fought well but were too young to take his place.

After Ragnvald finished his adjustments he paced around the fire. The fire's heat made his clothes steam.

"How will we know when it is midnight in this weather?" Oddi grumbled.

"Does it matter?" Heming asked, just as peevishly as his brother. "You'll do whatever Ragnvald says, as you always do."

"Do you have a better plan?" Oddi asked.

"Solvi Hunthiofsson sends his ships to harass Tafjord, and I should be there," said Heming. "Not here."

"If you had killed Vemund like you promised, none of us would be here," said Oddi. True enough; Heming had a taste for the more enjoyable parts of kingship, but not the hard work of subduing districts and rooting out rebels.

"Keep telling our father that," said Heming, "and maybe he'll give you Maer. But if he gives you Maer, you will inherit all of my enemies, and one more besides." He put his hand on his sword. "Me."

Oddi laughed shortly. "I don't tell King Hakon anything. You're the one who goes crying to him whenever you think King Harald has treated you poorly."

Heming sprang to his feet. "I do nothing of the sort. I have endured all of Father's scolding while you hide from him with Ragnvald. *I* do my duty as a son should. Anyway, your precious Harald didn't give me enough men."

"I thought that was our precious father's decision," said Oddi.

"You shouldn't speak about him that way. You'd be nothing if he hadn't taken you from your mother. Ragnvald would be nothing if our father hadn't noticed him."

"Do you ever shut up?" Oddi asked.

Ragnvald sighed. Oddi did not care enough about Heming's words to duel him, and Heming feared his father's anger too much to force the issue. "Both of you be quiet," he commanded. "We are too close to King Vemund for this noise."

"I thought you set guards," said Heming. "You're always setting guards."

"Guards can be killed," said Ragnvald. Or bribed. Too many times this summer, Vemund's warriors had surprised Harald's forces.

As the talk quieted, Ragnvald heard nightingales calling to one another. He remembered watching them above the fields of Ardal during the long summer evenings of his boyhood. They dipped through the deep blue sky of a summer night in pairs, catching insects on every mirrored flight. Nightingales mated for life, the legends said. Like swans—and he could never think of swans without then thinking of his sister, Svanhild, whose name meant "swan-battle" and who had now mated with Solvi Hunthiofsson, perhaps for life, a life that would never bring her back to Ragnvald's side.

The sky turned a deeper blue and the nightingales fell silent. The only thing Ragnvald could hear beyond the breathing and shifting of his men was the chirp of insects in the grass. He looked at Oddi, nodded, and came to his feet, shaking out the tension in his arms. He felt nervous before every battle, no matter how many times he fought and survived. He feared his sword arm, which had always been strong, would fail him. He feared the gods might, without warning, take from him all that he had earned.

He and his men followed Arnfast through the woods on a trail that Arnfast had marked with signs only he could read in the dimness: a broken twig, a fallen branch placed against a tree trunk, a scrape in the pine-needle floor, which led over the softest ground, where their passing would make the least noise. He stepped where Arnfast did, watching the heels of Arnfast's shoes, hardly visible against the dark forest floor. Low birdcalls made by his men signaled that everyone in the attack party still lived, and kept pace.

Arnfast held a hand up and stopped. Ragnvald echoed the gesture and heard the wave of feet coming to a halt behind him. A campfire gleamed between the tree branches before them. Ragnvald averted his eyes from the brightness. He quieted his breathing to listen for a moment, and heard nothing but the sounds of snores, and the shuffles of men moving quietly as they kept a light guard over their sleeping fellows. Or seemed to. Vemund would bait his trap well. Ragnvald made the signal that would divide their force, and heard Oddi's answering call.

Another call told his men to block off the camp's available exits. Ragnvald slid his sword out of its sheath, and moved forward, trying to be as quiet in his own steps as he had been following Arnfast's. When he judged that enough time had passed for all of his men to get into place, he made the signal for attack.

Ragnvald drew his sword and ran forward, then stumbled when

Heming pushed past him, yelling out, "For Maer, for Hakon's sons!" as he swung his ax. Ragnvald followed a moment later, hoping that the yell had not given away the slim advantage of surprise his forces had against a foe who knew this land far better than they did.

Ragnvald's sword clashed against the blade of a stout man whose battered leather helmet tipped forward to half cover his eyes. His opponent retreated a few steps for no reason Ragnvald could see, and defended himself against Ragnvald's second blow a half second too late. Ragnvald's sword cut through the hardened leather armor protecting his upper arm. As Ragnvald swung his sword again, the man dropped his weapon and raised his hand in submission.

"Stop, King Ragnvald, stop! I'm Isolfur Arnbjornsson. I fight for Harald, like you. Why are you attacking us?"

Ragnvald checked his swing and looked around the camp. Everywhere he saw a bit of armor, the movement of a blade, and the set of a pair of shoulders that he recognized. "Halt! Halt!" he called. "These are Harald's men. Stop fighting."

Only a few heartbeats passed, yet his words took far too long to reach the ears of men in a battle rage. A young man bled from a cut that had opened his cheek from eye to jaw, shattering his teeth and leaving a flap of flesh hanging loose over his chin. He would have a terrible scar if he lived. The wounded man turned, clapping his hand to his face, and Ragnvald recognized him as Herlaug, one of King Hakon's sons. Arnfast stood over him, his bloody sword falling from his hand.

"Tend him," Ragnvald yelled. Oddi rushed to Herlaug's side. Herlaug's eyes, round and white above his dreadful wound, rolled up into his head and he collapsed onto the dead leaves of the forest floor.

Oddi pressed his hand to Herlaug's cheek, trying to press the flesh back into place. "We need a healer to sew my brother up." Oddi's face was pale even to his lips.

"Arnfast." Ragnvald made his voice harsh to cover his feeling of helplessness at seeing these wounds dealt by his own men. "I thought you said this was Vemund's camp. Did you see them?"

"Yes." He gave Ragnvald a pleading look. "I swear it. I saw King Vemund. He was in this place."

"Isolfur," Ragnvald said. "When did you arrive?"

"Late evening." Isolfur held a hand to his bicep. Blood leaked between his fingers, dripping dark in the firelight. "Guthorm sent us as an advance party. He wanted us to find a way to surround Vemund's force. There was already a fire pit here and we thought it would be as good a place as any to spend the night."

"Did you not think it would be a trap?" said Ragnvald. If Harald's uncle Guthorm had sent another attack party, that meant he doubted Ragnvald's sortie would be a success. "There is no exit here."

"We guarded the southern approach. It seemed good that it had few paths, and anyway, we only meant to spend one night."

This was a different trap from the one Ragnvald had foreseen, perhaps, or only terrible luck, a god's curse on this summer.

"Ragnvald," said Oddi, still looking pale. He knelt by Herlaug's side and held a piece of cloth to his cheek that was not enough to stanch the bleeding.

"Arnfast, run to the main camp, and come back with a healer and more guards. Many more guards, as fast as you can. This was a trap—I'm sure of it." Best to act sure now, to set a story in his men's minds. "Tell Harald that Vemund meant us to attack our own men. And now we are all here, all of Hakon's sons and me. Wounded. Come back quickly with help." Arnfast nodded and sprinted into the woods, fleet as a deer. For a moment, Ragnvald envied him the ability to run away from this, even if only to come back with help. But Arnfast would have to pay a mighty wergild for wounding the son of a king, far more than he could afford. If Ragnvald did not help him, Arnfast's entire family would have to sell themselves into bondage to discharge the debt.

Ragnvald turned and counted the men who were still whole. He found enough that if half of the unwounded stood guard, they would have good warning of any more attacks. Too many were injured to move camp, though. Vemund—and Ragnvald's folly—had trapped them here.

3

SVANHILD PULLED ON THE STEERING OAR SO HER SHIP FOL-
lowed Solvi's as closely as possible, carving the same line as his had
through the waves. It took all her strength plus the strength of a man
from her crew to turn the huge board against the force of the water.
She liked to have her hands on it, though, for through that contact she
could feel qualities in the water, as Solvi had taught her. A heaviness
told her of the strength of the rising storm, as did the wind blowing
her hair into her face. To the west, Hakon's pursuing ships faded from
view behind sheets of rain as the Faroe Islands themselves receded
behind that veil.

"Look, Eystein," she said to her son. "Your father has done it again.
The winds carry him faster than any other man." Eystein was tall for
his age, at six summers already past Svanhild's waist. Solvi's father,
King Hunthiof, had been of normal height and Solvi might have been
as well, if he had not been burned in childhood. Svanhild hoped their
son would tower over both of them.

"Whose ships are those?" Eystein pointed behind them, toward the
four trailing ships in their convoy.

"Those are our friends. Boddi is in one of those ships," said Svanhild. Boddi was Eystein's particular friend, a boy a year younger than
him who disdained the more boisterous children among Solvi's followers and had attached himself to Svanhild's quiet son. "And your
father is in front of us. He is leading us to safety." The wind, the mist,

every element of the sea bent to Solvi's will, and thwarted any who sailed against him. Svanhild had seen it often in the years they traveled together; from the great city of Constantinople, the capital of the Eastern Roman Empire, to the northern reaches of Iceland, the sea goddess Ran treated Solvi as her cherished son.

"The wind carries Solvi better because he's so light!" said Ulfarr. He had thickened over the years, growing bigger in the shoulders and stomach, so he could no longer climb up a mast. He rushed toward Eystein with his head down, as though he meant to scoop Eystein up in his arms, as he often did. Eystein hung back and hid behind Svanhild's hip.

"Don't let him, Mama," he said.

"It's only Ulfarr," said Svanhild, though she was glad that steering the ship meant she did not have to move to allow Ulfarr access to her son. Even though she was his king's wife, Ulfarr sometimes put his hands on her lewdly until she shook him off. She knew that Solvi would laugh if she said anything—after all, Ulfarr was one of his oldest friends—but she did not have to like him.

"Mama," said Eystein. "Look!"

A flock of dark birds flew toward them, tumbling, calling wildly, moving faster than their own wings should carry them. They passed just above the top of the mast. The blast of wind that had flung the birds forward hit the sail with a force that made the whole ship dip forward. A loud crack sounded: the breaking of one of the lines that held the sail in place. Svanhild prayed that her other lines would hold and adjusted her heading, spilling wind from the sail. The ship rolled toward the other side before regaining its balance. Before her, she saw that Solvi had done the same, and felt a swell of pride. He had taught her well; now she could steer a ship almost as well as he could, and perform any sailing task that did not require a man's strength.

She turned to look at the ships behind them again, holding Eystein against her leg so he would not fall as the ship rocked. The gust had also struck the other vessels in the convoy. The sail of one hung crosswise, as though its lines had come loose or been torn off. Another bobbed broadside to the wind when it should have pointed into the waves. Solvi had placed skilled captains in those ships, ships that

were filled with his followers and their families. Some had joined
Solvi for plunder. More, though, were refugees fleeing Harald's Norway, subjects, petty kings, and jarls from Hordaland and Rogaland,
Agder and Thelemark, who would not swear to Harald and pay the
heavy tax burden that went along with that oath. Still others Harald had not even given the choice of oath and payment, and instead
expelled them to make room for Hakon's sons and other allies who
wanted land to buy their loyalty. At least Ragnvald had only accepted
his birthright from Harald, and no more.

A yell drew her attention back to Solvi's ship. He gestured to her
and called out, "Reef the sail!"

Svanhild echoed the command to her own crew and Ulfarr am-
plified it. Men rushed to unwind the lines that held the yard, bringing it halfway down the mast and securing the small ties that would
decrease the sail's surface area. Now the ship could ride the strong
winds without putting as much strain on the mast.

Svanhild's vessel rested in a lull for a strange, brief moment before the wind hit again, stronger and harder, while in the distance,
the other ships shuddered and skittered across the waves. The ship
behind her heeled over on its side like a child's spinning top about
to fall over. Then, as a rain squall blurred the air between them, the
ship toppled and the sail disappeared from view. The next gust hit her
own ship, shuddering the wood in Svanhild's hands.

She scanned the horizon frantically for the capsized ship until Eystein's insistent tugging on her skirt forced her attention to him.

"The ship—is Boddi—are they dead?" Eystein asked.

"I don't know." Svanhild pulled him close without looking away
from the emptiness where the ship had been. "If you see the sail again,
they may be all right." She turned to face forward again; she could not
afford to split her attention, now that the storm had reached her ship.

"I don't see them," said Eystein.

"Then they are gone," said Svanhild. "Or will be soon." Eystein
shivered against her and buried his face in the folds of her skirt.

"What will happen to them?" he asked.

None of the ships could go to the rescue of their fallen brother.
Perhaps a few strong swimmers might be lucky enough to cling to

a rope flung from another ship—if one passed nearby. "They will drown," said Svanhild, "and then, I suppose, they will join the fleet of the goddess Ran, who sends ghost ships out all across the sea. They will feast in her golden hall." Svanhild shivered as well. She did not want to think of this.

"I hate the sea," said Eystein. "I don't want to be cold anymore. Will Boddi always be cold, then?"

Svanhild directed one of her men to hold the heading for her. She crouched down before Eystein. The sudden shelter from the ship's walls blocking the wind made her face hot, as if she stood before a fire. Eystein looked at her, eyes pleading for word from her that could make his friend live again.

"Boddi will crew a great ship," she said, "and when he grows up will marry one of Ran's beautiful daughters. Ran's husband, Aegir, has the finest drinking hall of all the gods, save Odin's Valhalla. When we are out of this storm, I will tell you the story of how Thor tricked the miserly Aegir into holding a feast. Now go in the tent and warm yourself." She could not give him more than a moment in the midst of this storm. "If you want to help, pray to the sea goddess."

The men in her ship mouthed their own prayers, wearing grim expressions as they carried out their tasks, lashing down barrels and tightening the lines that held the sail in place. Svanhild could not recall which other friends and acquaintances had been on the capsized ship. They had fled so quickly when Hakon's force arrived that surely some who usually traveled in the fallen ship had found other berths. Families would be torn in two.

"Mourn," she remembered Solvi saying to his men after a previous wreck, "but remember that they are beyond suffering, and you are lucky to be alive. Bless your luck, and keep on living." Svanhild could not face death so calmly, though she would gladly give herself to the sea to save Eystein. He became ill when ship-bound, and only grew healthy when he had solid ground under his feet. An ill-fitting son for the sea king Solvi Klofe, Solvi the Short, a man who wore his deficiencies as a badge of honor.

"Mama, I'm still cold." Eystein had gone into the tent—the ship's only real shelter—briefly, and come out again to cling to her, digging

skinny arms into the top of Svanhild's hip bones. The wind drove the
rain hard against her back, frothing the surface of the sea into stripes
of foam and deep green.

"I'm sorry, Monkey," Svanhild said. Svanhild had seen a monkey
once in Spain and thought Eystein, with his long limbs, big eyes, and
tendency to cling, could be one of those strange creatures who looked
at her with such intelligence. "It's warmer in the tent, and there you
can play with Katla." Katla was Svanhild's servant, a Norse-Irish girl
who feared storms.

"But I will not see Boddi again," said Eystein. His words made
Svanhild cold beyond the touch of rain and wind. He had walked
too close to death since the moment of his birth, when the midwife
had to breathe into his little mouth to start his lungs. Svanhild kept a
close watch on any sign that death stalked him still. She had named
him after her father, for though he had been killed when Svanhild
was only five, what she remembered most about him was how in-
tensely alive he had been. Eystein would benefit from a portion of his
grandfather's spirit.

"Look, the storm is passing," said Svanhild. The ship moved more
smoothly over the water as the waves subsided and the wind grew
steadier. Men sheltering under benches with cloaks drawn over their
heads began to unfold themselves. Ulfarr glanced at her, waiting to
see if she wanted the sail raised again. She shook her head. She would
keep it half-reefed until morning, or until Solvi ordered otherwise.
She looked over her shoulder and thought she saw the shapes of ships
in the distance, but did not try to count them, not yet. She did not
want to think about further losses.

✦   ✦   ✦

WHEN THE WIND slackened near dawn, the remaining four ships
drew together. Tryggulf's ship had torn off half its lines in the storm.
Solvi's men passed some replacement rope over to him. A good wind
carried them to the east coast of Iceland a few days later, past narrow
beaches of black sand, but it was not until late evening, the sun no
more than an orange glow on the horizon, that Solvi found a beach of
black pebbles wide enough to pull up the ships safely. A huge brown

stone, mottled with lichen and moss, stood alone a little offshore. In the dim light, it looked like a giant's head peering up, the rest of the body still buried in sand.

Svanhild stumbled down from her ship, light-headed from hunger and exhaustion. She did not notice Solvi approaching until he put an arm around her. He pulled her close and kissed her temple. "You did well, my sea queen." His arm pressed into the space between her ribs and hip. "You're so skinny."

She tried halfheartedly to pull away. On the voyage from Frisia to the Faroes she had lost what little fat she carried and did not have time to replenish her reserves before Hakon's forces pressed them on. She always lost flesh when they were at sea. "We must feed you well in Iceland," Solvi added.

"Yes," said Svanhild. "I remember the fat cows, and streams full of salmon. I want nothing more than to eat myself bursting every night and grow plump and happy and bear you another child." Solvi pulled her closer, though he said nothing. She knew he blamed himself that she had not carried a child to term since Eystein. If she could stop moving for a year or two, she would catch a healthy child again, she felt certain. Eystein would be better off if she could give him a younger brother, someone to protect and be bold for.

Solvi would like another son, one more like him. He loved Eystein, in his way, though Svanhild sometimes caught him watching his son in the same way that Eystein watched the little creatures of shore and grass, as if peering into a world that interested him, but that he could never understand. Solvi still thought that one day Eystein would love his ships, and crave adventure the same way he did.

"Who was on board that ship?" Svanhild asked.

"Besides Thorolf?" Solvi asked, naming a young captain who had shown enough promise for Solvi to give him a ship to command only a few weeks earlier. "His wife and children traveled with him. Some of Snorri's kin, I think."

"Perhaps they survived. They were nearest Hakon's ships," said Svanhild. Solvi did not answer. Svanhild knew what he thought of her hopes: she lived in a dream world, while he inhabited the true one. They had fought often enough about how she saw bright glimmers where he saw only shadow. "I need to make camp," she added. Eystein would not sleep well without his favorite blankets, and a tent on even ground. As she walked up the beach, her toes caught on small stones, and she stumbled. The ground swayed beneath her as she fought to maintain balance on a surface that did not move as she expected it to.

Eystein had fallen asleep against a rock by the time she had the tent set up. She had to drag him inside and settle him next to her under the wet, itchy wool of her blankets. It had grown still darker when she woke to the warmth of Solvi's chest against her back. Eystein's small body, curled in the hollow of her own, vibrated with his shivering, even in sleep.

Solvi pulled her close and buried his face in her hair. "I believed we would stay in the Faroes for the winter," he said to her. Svanhild longed to rest, but she knew that Solvi could only voice his doubts in the middle of the night, while she lingered at the gates of sleep. Perhaps some nights he told her sleeping form his secrets and she never heard them except in dreams.

"Hakon claims the Faroes," said Svanhild. "He has done so since your father's time." She did not mind returning to Iceland. The Faroe Islands had even fewer trees, only mountains and rocky fields where sheep grazed. The inhabitants built their homes out of turf, living low and in the dirt, in barrows even before their deaths. Many had fled there to escape Harald's taxes, only to find that Hakon's demands bit just as deep.

"Is there nowhere a man can go that Hakon or Harald does not claim?" Solvi asked. "Is not my Maer enough for them?"

"Hush, you will wake our son," said Svanhild. She did not want to speak his name for fear it would draw him from sleep. "Iceland is still free. It will be a good home for us."

"I do not speak of a home," said Solvi. "You and I have never had a home together, not since Hakon took my land for his sons."

"That is why we must make our own home together," said Svanhild. "We can claim land here in Iceland, and build a farm to pass on to our son." More quietly, she added, "You know he is no sailor."

"And I am no farmer," said Solvi. He had said the same when they

left Vestfold together, when Svanhild had been pregnant with Eystein, wearing a gown that was Ragnvald's last gift to her. She thought
of her hand around a cow's teat rather than the steering oar, of comb-
ing a sheep's wool until all the fibers lay straight in a well-ordered
cloud—the calming repetition of it, of all the little tasks that must
be performed to run a farm. Not so different from managing a ship.

"Promise me," she said. "Promise me that we will stop for a time
so our son can grow strong." She yawned; she could not help it. The
pebble beach had shifted under her body to make a cradle for her,
comfortable after days of sleeping on a narrow rowing bench.

"Sleep, my love," he said. "I promise you, our son will have his birthright."

"What does that mean?" Svanhild rolled over to face him. "Does
that mean we will stay in Iceland for a time?" Eystein stirred, woken
by her movement.

"Perhaps. I would rather he grow up in Tafjord."

Solvi had said that before, and each time Svanhild had tried to
turn his ambitions elsewhere. "I know, but that is not possible." She
reached out to touch Solvi's face. "We need to find a new land for
him."

Solvi pulled away. "There is a difference between what you think
is impossible and what you fear to attempt."

Eystein sat up. "Mother, is it—do we have to flee again?"

Svanhild turned again and pulled him back to her. "No. Hush now.
Sleep." She stroked his shoulder the way he liked until his breathing grew even. She would continue this argument with Solvi in the
morning.

✛   ✛   ✛

THE CONVOY RESTED for a day on the beach. Eystein chased shorebirds across the shallows and dug for clams that hid below the depth
of the birds' beaks. Svanhild showed him how to roast them open on
the campfire's coals. As she packed up the tent, Eystein came running
up to her. His fine russet hair was still rumpled on one side from
sleep, and his face was dirty at his hairline, though he had washed it.
He liked to be clean, and Svanhild looked forward to bringing him

to a hot spring once they reached the settlement. He had been too young the last time they came here to remember the bliss and lasting warmth that the waters provided.

"Mother, come, I have to show you something," he said. Svanhild had taken the tent down, and spread out all the items within it so she knew where everything was before she packed. She hated to leave her work now, when a gust of wind might scatter it all, but Eystein's eyes shone bright, and she did not like to resist him.

"Come on," he said again, rocking back and forth on his feet. Svanhild held out her hand to take his—gritty, cold, and clammy with seawater—and walked with him up the beach past the ships. On the marshy shore to the east, two white swans cast off into the water, with four gray cygnets between them.

"Swans," said Eystein. "Like you."

"Yes," said Svanhild, watching the stately birds. They swam in a perfect line, even the young ones, moving across the still water like ships in a steady breeze. "It is a good omen, Monkey, a swan family to welcome us home."

✧   ✧   ✧

THE NEXT DAY was mild, so Svanhild rode in Solvi's ship while his young apprentice Thorstein captained the ship she had guided through the storm. The ships hugged Iceland's southern coast. An arctic wolf lifted its head from a bloodied seal carcass and met Svanhild's eyes as the ships passed. The light from the low sun made its white fur look gold. Svanhild turned away, reminded of Ragnvald's prophecy that Harald was a golden wolf who would either burn up or burnish all he touched, a prophecy that had further buttressed Harald's claim to be king over all Norway. Ragnvald's golden wolf should stay in Norway. Iceland was a land without kings.

Fog filled the air as they approached the settlement at Reykjavik— Smokey Bay. Solvi ordered men to the oars and lowered the sail. He never liked approaching through a dense fog that could hide friend or foe, or simply a rock that might punch a hole in a ship's hull.

"It's a strange place," he said as the settlement emerged from the mist, a small collection of houses on plots of green farmland ridged by the stumps of the dwarf forest that had stood for a thousand years before the Norse arrived. Twisted stretches of black rock surrounded the strands of green. Above the farms, the mountains rose up sharply, snowcapped and smoking. Skalds said that gateways to the underworld of dragons and dwarves opened into those mountains, and Svanhild believed it.

"Rich farmland," said Svanhild. "And all of it for the taking."

"And clearing, and farming." Solvi laughed. "I don't mind the taking part."

A party assembled on the dock to greet them. Ingolfur Arnasson, who claimed to be Iceland's first settler, was the first to greet Solvi when he stepped down from his ship. Ingolfur had fled Vestfold when Harald outlawed him for murdering his neighbor in a feud that had lasted three generations by the time he inherited it. He had grown rich from trade and raiding, and set out with his family for the rocky shores of Iceland.

In the tale Ingolfur told, and paid his skald to repeat, he and his brothers threw the pillars of the high seat of their ancestral hall into the sea and decided to settle where they washed up onshore, which seemed to Svanhild the height of foolishness. The pillars stood behind Ingolfur in his hall, a reminder to everyone that no matter how many kings and jarls settled in Iceland, Ingolfur had arrived first.

"This is a lot of men you have here," Ingolfur said to Solvi as Svanhild climbed down the ship's ladder onto the stone dock. Ingolfur stood no more than average height but carried himself with such weighty dignity, his solid stomach leading the way through any crowd and his long mustache announcing how important he found himself, that Svanhild always thought of him as a tall man.

"Women too," said Svanhild.

"That is good." Ingolfur squinted down at her. "Still, you have many people, with winter coming on."

"The sun still shines for most of the night," said Solvi.

"And every day is shorter," Ingolfur replied. "Too short for clearing, planting, and harvesting enough food for your followers, even if you claim land."

Solvi gave Svanhild a look that she read well enough. Ingolfur wanted them gone, and Solvi would echo him later. When Svanhild frowned at Solvi, he turned back to Ingolfur. "Are you denying us hospitality?"

"Of course not," said Ingolfur. "Yet guests bearing gifts are the most welcome guests of all."

"When you give us welcome, we will give gifts." Solvi gave Ingolfur one of his sharp, dangerous grins.

"We have lost friends and family in this voyage," Svanhild added. "A funeral feast would show the gods they are not forgotten, even in this faraway land."

Ingolfur's mustache drooped. "Your woman has the right of it," he said. He put his hand on Svanhild's shoulder and left it there. "My wife would be happy to make a feast for your fallen friends—in two days' time?"

"The gods will be pleased," said Svanhild, "and we will show our appreciation for your generosity." She bowed her head, and slid closer to Solvi's side, freeing herself from Ingolfur's touch.

"I will send thralls to help unload your ships," said Ingolfur. He bowed and walked stiffly back up the beach.

Solvi watched him go. "We had already gifted for a winter's lodgings in the Faroes. This will beggar us."

Ulfarr stepped up behind them and Svanhild pressed herself against Solvi. "Send me to get more gold," Ulfarr said. "Iceland has too few women for my taste."

"There are plenty of Irish thralls," said Solvi. Svanhild had seen them among the curious who came down to the dock when she and Solvi arrived: short figures wearing homespun, with close-cropped hair that blurred the differences between men and women.

"Pah—all their men want to marry them—"

"And won't take kindly to you raping their future wives?" Solvi said with a laugh. "You can get us gold and punish Hakon too—you said Heming Hakonsson does not defend Tafjord well?"

"Not the last time I was there," said Ulfarr. "I stole his armband and his favorite concubine last year!" Svanhild remembered a beautiful, sad-eyed woman who had tried to escape in the Faroes and washed up, her corpse pummeled by the waves, on a beach a few days later. Svanhild had not asked where the woman had come from. She tried to think about Ulfarr's women as little as possible.

"Go back," said Solvi. "Hakon's gold is inexhaustible."

"His patience with raids against Heming may not be," said Svanhild. "Why tweak his tail? Hakon could easily follow us here from the Faroes." She spoke to the space between Ulfarr and Solvi, hoping not to anger either of them with her doubts.

"Let him," said Solvi. "Go, my friend, and tweak his tail as much as you wish. And if you kill Heming, I will give you a jarldom." Ulfarr grinned at him, ignoring Svanhild, nodded, and walked away to find his favorite warriors and plan their attack.

"I did not know you had sent Ulfarr to raid Tafjord before," said Svanhild. This was another thread to pick up from their abandoned argument. Solvi's followers came and went, exercising the freedom that would be denied them if they swore to Harald or his subject kings. Solvi shrugged and began directing the unloading of the ships. She did not know what jarldom Solvi could promise—he had always said that his kingdom was his ships and his subjects anyone who chose to sail with him for a time, in the way of the sea kings of old.

✜   ✜   ✜

SVANHILD OVERSAW THE setup of her larger tent, the one that she could arrange almost as a small house, and then took Eystein, along with a few of Solvi's guards, to visit her friend Unna, who had a farm on the hill above the settlement. Unna knew everything that happened in Iceland, better even than Ingolfur and his wife. She would know who in the settlement could shelter the families that traveled with Solvi, and who could not, and where the best farmland could be claimed.

Unna was a widow with iron-colored hair who had come to Iceland from Scotland after the death of her husband and son to a sickness there. She brought with her five stout thralls and a young man named Donall who had a shocking red beard, spoke a strongly accented Norse, and, it was plain, shared her bed. When he and Unna spoke together, it was in a language Svanhild could not make out. He

was at least fifteen years younger than Unna, and she was no beauty.
The planes of her face made Svanhild think of an ax carving, severe
and expressive. But Donall obeyed her every word and hardly looked
at the maidens of Iceland who were closer to his age. He did not give
Svanhild admiring glances, though songs of her beauty and the battles it inspired usually drew the attention of men in every land she
visited.

Unna's farm spread over a notch between two hills, and was full
of thick green grass that rippled with wind that carried cold and the
strange sulfur breath of the volcanoes down from the mountains.
Over the crest of a hill, the roof of another house spilled smoke from
a cook fire into the air. The scent made Svanhild's stomach growl.

Unna nodded when she saw Svanhild walking with Eystein across
the grass, as if she had expected Svanhild to come today, though they
had not seen each other for a few years. She suffered Svanhild's embrace and acknowledged Eystein's bow to her, and then looked Svanhild up and down. "You should stay this time, I think. You will not
bring a babe to birth unless you keep your feet in one place for a
while. Children like to be born onto solid ground, not a tossing ship."

"I hope to," said Svanhild. "I might convince Solvi. He said he
wants Eystein's birthright in Maer, but we could claim a new one for
him here."

She left Eystein with Donall so she and Unna could walk alongside
the rock wall that marked the edges of the farm. She told Unna of
her travels since their last meeting, while Unna, in her turn, related
the business of her farm and the settlement. Many new families had
arrived all summer, she said, fleeing Norse battles.

"This is the farthest reach of my claim." Unna showed Svanhild a
carved post, almost hidden in the lush grass. "A day's walk all around,
stretching up the mountain. This is what you must do: take your
whole household, and lead a heifer to pace out the edges of your land.
You will walk for as long as you can, while there is still daylight. Mark
out the borders as I have done, state your claim at the summer *alting*
meeting, and the land will be yours for your sons to inherit. This
land is fertile. As farmwives in Norway stir the ash from their cook
fires into their gardens, so did the gods of this place scatter ash from

the heavens to make the island bloom." Unna's voice held a note of motherly pride when she spoke of her land.

The path of the fence led them back toward her farm buildings. When they drew closer, Eystein came running up to Svanhild, clutching a handful of flowers. Svanhild thanked him and tucked a purple bloom behind her ear.

"I can claim land, myself?" Svanhild asked. "Even though I am married?" Eystein bounded forward, toward the farm. He had recovered his spirits since the voyage.

"At last count I heard there were two hundred families who claimed land, but this is a big island," said Unna. "If you make the claim and your husband does not repudiate it, I see no reason why it should not stand. Still, do not tarry. I want you to find land near mine."

Svanhild squeezed her arm. Unna only showed affection to Svanhild when they walked alone. Otherwise, she spoke almost as harshly to Svanhild as to any of her servants or Donall. She had to be sharp, she said, as a woman alone, or a man might try to take advantage of her.

Svanhild glanced toward her farmhouse, with its turf roof sloping down to the ground. Standing in the doorway to the barn, Donall waved his arm over his head to draw their attention.

"We must return," said Svanhild.

"I suppose." Unna released Svanhild's elbow. Donall greeted them with a bow. He was very handsome, even with his freckles, and had pale lashes that would have looked good on a woman.

"More ships have come, ladies," he said. "With kings and warriors."

"Svanhild and her sea king just arrived this morning," said Unna, in Norse so Svanhild could understand.

"These are new ships," said Donall.

Unna spoke a few words to him in their language, then turned to Svanhild. "We will go," said Unna. "Would you like to leave your son with my servants?" she asked Svanhild.

"No, I will bring him," said Svanhild.

"Then I will see you there. I think Donall and I can move faster." Unna walked past Svanhild, carrying herself as upright as a fireplace poker, with Donall half a step behind. Abrupt, and close to rudeness—

that was Unna, a law unto herself in a lawless place. She and Solvi had disliked each other on sight. Solvi preferred the company of those who could laugh sometimes, and Unna rarely smiled.

Eystein sat in the lee of Unna's house, looking east, over the pasture dotted with sheep. One of Unna's thralls churned butter nearby.

"More ships have come," said Svanhild, facing toward the water, which was too far away for her to see, though not too far to smell when the wind shifted. "Come with me."

He looked up slowly. "I like it here," he said softly.

"I know, and we will visit again soon," she said. "Now come with me. We must see who Donall thinks is more important than your father."

"I'm tired. Mother, will you carry me there?" Eystein asked. She could see the black silhouettes of the ships' masts against the gray sky. A wave lifted the prow of one briefly, revealing the curves of a sleek warship. Svanhild scooped Eystein up into her arms—he was still light enough for that, tall but very slender. His eyes looked enormous in his thin face, above sharp cheekbones that seemed as though they might pierce his skin.

"Who are they?" Eystein pointed toward the ships.

"I don't know, love. Let us go see."

4

RAGNVALD STOOD GUARD ALL NIGHT UNTIL ARNFAST RE-
turned with the dawn, followed by the best healer in Harald's camp, a
young woman who wore trousers like a man. Ragnvald showed her to
where Herlaug sat propped against a rock, holding his bandaged face.
The bleeding had slowed to a trickle. Oddi and Heming sat on either
side of him, their expressions of worry giving their faces a temporary
likeness.

The healer spoke low words to Herlaug and persuaded him to let
her look at the wound. When Ragnvald heard the sticky pull of fabric
from the wound, he looked away, feeling an echo of the wound in
his own cheek, a phantom pull of ripped flesh. The healer called for
wine to cleanse the gash. Ragnvald forced himself to watch as she
made small, neat stitches in Herlaug's face with a length of silk thread,
which was dyed a darker red every time it passed through Herlaug's
skin and left weeping puncture marks along the wound.

After she finished, she wiped her hands off with a rag and stood.
"There is a lot of tearing. The stitches may not hold," she said to Ragnvald. "I must burn the wound closed to prevent infection."

"Do you want my permission?" Ragnvald asked. "Do what you
must." Behind her, on the ground, Herlaug moaned and shook his
head. He tried to speak then stopped when the movement pulled on
his wound.

"He does not want to be burned," said Heming.

"He will die of fever otherwise," said the healer. "Heat your sword tip until it glows." Ragnvald was not used to being commanded in his own camp, even by healers, and he hesitated.

"He does not want it," Oddi cried. "Don't torture him any more." Heming touched his brother's face on the unharmed cheek until he parted his lips, then emptied a skin of spirits down his throat, and smiled grimly when Herlaug fell back into a snuffling sleep.

"His brothers say no," said Ragnvald. "Bandage him."

"He will die," said the healer. "Or wish he was dead. And you have wasted my time and my stitches."

"There are more wounded for you to tend," said Ragnvald, glad to turn away from Herlaug's disfigurement. "Finish here, and then come with me."

✢ ✢ ✢

AFTER ANOTHER NIGHT spent at the cliff-side camp, Ragnvald led his men back to Harald and the main force. Herlaug made noises of pain as he shuffled forward with his arms slung over the shoulders of his brothers. Ragnvald half hoped that one of Vemund's bowmen would pick him off to spare everyone his moans today and Arnfast the suit he would bring later. If Herlaug died in battle, he could not sue for an injury. Better to think of that than imagine Harald's disappointment in Ragnvald for falling into Vemund's trap.

Six years ago, Harald had fulfilled his promise to Ragnvald after the battle of Vestfold. He accompanied him to Sogn for Ragnvald's wedding to Hilda. At the Sogn *ting*, where all the families of Sogn gathered at midsummer for trials and games, Harald's skald sang of Ragnvald's deeds and his ancestry, of their origins in the loins of the gods. He sang how the bones of Ragnvald's forefathers had mixed with the soil of Sogn for so many generations that they were part of the bedrock now. Harald stood by Ragnvald's side as the men at the *ting* elected Ragnvald as their king. Everything Ragnvald possessed had come from Harald. Ragnvald had failed in Harald's war this summer, and when he was away from Sogn, he failed to make Sogn rich as well.

At Harald's camp a sea of wool tents with timber crossbeams

spread out over the bank of a fjord tributary. A sentry greeted Ragnvald and then ran to Harald's tent to tell him of Ragnvald's coming. Harald emerged, arms open to embrace him, while Guthorm,
Harald's uncle, sat in the open doorway of Harald's tent, his arms
crossed.

Harald had grown into the size promised by his youth, and lost
no grace as he grew from boy into giant. He stood half a head taller
than Ragnvald, who was taller than many men, and was half again
as broad in the shoulder. Since his oath to conquer all of Norway and
gain the hand of Princess Gyda, his hair had grown tangled, long and
wild. It made him look like something more than a man—a savage
and beautiful god, equal to his bloody *wyrd*.

"You seem in poor spirits," said Harald to Ragnvald. "But I have
good news. We cannot tempt Vemund into open war, and we cannot best him on his own ground, so only one course remains." He
gave Ragnvald a sly smile that sat oddly on features made for friendly
grins. "Treachery."

"That is what we have faced," Ragnvald replied. He gave a report of what had happened at the foot of the cliff. "My man Arnfast
grievously wounded Herlaug Hakonsson. I fear the wergild he will
demand." And that Harald would grant him, the son of his most powerful ally.

Guthorm came to his feet to join their conversation. "Vemund
leads you into worse and worse blunders with every step you take,"
he said. "More lives lost. I would have advised against this attack."

"No one died this time, and you were not there to advise us." Ragnvald looked longingly over to his own tent. The crossbeams, carved
into snarling hunting dogs, looked as tired as he felt, mouths open in
panting exhaustion rather than ferocity. "Perhaps if we had not been
there, King Vemund would have returned and ambushed Hakon's
younger sons. You cannot know."

"That's true," said Harald. He rocked back and forth on his feet.
"If no one died, that is good enough news for me. And I have better.
Two of Vemund's men have sworn to follow me, rather than risk end-
less war. Grai, Illugi."

Ill-fated names, Ragnvald thought, before he even saw the men to dislike them. They emerged from behind Harald's great tent, a small man with a puff of pale hair atop a round and too-pretty face—Illugi—and Grai, tall and doughy, with eyes that never seemed to focus in the right place, and a narrow mouth surrounded by a beard a much lighter brown than the hair on his head.

"Tell Ragnvald what you told me," Harald said to them.

"We were King Vemund's men," said Grai, looking over Ragnvald's shoulder rather than meeting his eyes. "He sent us—Illugi and me—scouting to find you."

"And we thought we'd like to back the winning horse," said Illugi in a voice like the twang of a bow. "Vemund was pleased with the trick he played on you. Seems like it worked. He's with his wife in their hall in Naustdal to rest. He took a wound and it's festering. You should attack him there."

"See," said Harald to Ragnvald. "The gods do still smile on us."

Ragnvald would have preferred a blessing that did not come with these two, who looked like they would stab Harald in the back as easily as they would their own king. "I did not hear that Vemund had been wounded," he said. From time to time, his men captured Vemund's scouts and questioned them.

"He broke his leg running through the woods," said Illugi. "No luck. I want a lucky king."

"You trust these oath breakers?" Ragnvald asked Harald. He usually refused the service of men sworn elsewhere. Ragnvald's own oath to Hakon had kept him from swearing to Harald until Hakon released him.

"We never swore oaths to Vemund," said Grai. "But we'll swear to King Harald."

"See?" said Harald.

"I'd like to ask Vemund that," said Ragnvald, "and hear it for myself."

"Ragnvald only trusts his own eyes and ears." Harald gave him a fond smile. "Come with me, Ragnvald. We will discuss this privately."

Ragnvald followed Harald into his tent, high enough at the roof beam for even Harald to stand with ease. A servant brought them each a cup of ale. The tent smelled like old, sweaty leather and damp wool. A cot covered with furs and discarded clothing stood in one corner. Harald sat down at the table in the center and gestured for Ragnvald to join him.

"I fear this is another trap," said Ragnvald. "Vemund is too crafty to allow these two to come to us. I'm sure he sent them. We should question them until they reveal how Vemund has tricked us so many times."

"He knows this land." Harald took a sip of his ale. "And you see traps and treachery everywhere."

"Not the right traps," Ragnvald muttered.

"Blaming yourself for last night?" Harald asked.

"Who else?"

"You may have saved that party from worse—as you told my uncle."

"You know that was only an excuse."

"I know you think so. Never mind that. Attacking Vemund now, in his hall, is our best chance," said Harald. "I will trust my luck. Can't you?"

"I trust your luck," said Ragnvald. "It's mine that has gone missing." He sighed. "Tell me what you want me to do."

"Take your men and follow Grai and Illugi to Vemund's hall. If they lie, kill them. I do not think they do, though. They are men who value their own lives above everything else."

"Even honor," said Ragnvald.

"Even honor," Harald agreed. "I need men like that sometimes."

"I still don't like it," said Ragnvald. "What does your uncle say?" He tried without success to keep the rancor from his voice. Guthorm doubted all of Ragnvald's plans after it was too late for his doubts to do any good.

"He has no advice," said Harald. "He thinks I should follow my instincts."

"That does not surprise me," said Ragnvald dryly.

Harald smiled and walked over to his bedroll, from which he pulled a small leather satchel. "My mother gave me a set of rune-bones she said would not fail to provide wisdom," he said. "We will ask them and see what they say." Harald opened the pouch and shook out the set of carved bone pieces into his hands. Each had a different rune upon it, the angular symbols carved deeply and colored with ocher.

"Do you know how to read them?" Ragnvald asked.

"Well enough," said Harald. "Tyr's rune is for betrayal—"

"Or a lawsuit," said Ragnvald.

"No one is likely to sue us here. Vemund would rather just kill us." Harald continued his recitation: "Heimdall's for loyalty, Odin's for battle, and Frigga's for peace, and so on. Simple." He crouched down, shook the bones in his hands while reciting a blessing, and then scattered them on the table where the pattern of their fall should give a hint from the gods of how they should proceed.

"There is Heimdall's rune," said Ragnvald. "And Odin's. And Frigga's. And this is Frey's crossed by Thor's. Are you sure you did it right?"

"You are supposed to be wise," said Harald. "What do you think it means?"

Ragnvald snorted. The scattered bones showed little more wisdom to him than if they had been rabbit droppings. "If I were a traveling fortune-teller, I would say that loyalty will lead to battle, and then peace." Ragnvald threw up his hands in exasperation. "And if Thor has put a leg over Frey, maybe that's why it hasn't stopped raining since midsummer."

Harald laughed. "Maybe that is why. They say Frey is the handsomest of the gods and even his sister, Freya, cannot resist his charms!"

"And you want to trust these traitors," said Ragnvald, trying to turn the conversation back to its purpose.

"It is the best chance we've been offered," said Harald. "Take a hundred men, and burn his hall to the ground. With Vemund and his family in it if possible. If not—harvesttime and winter are coming soon. Burn any grain you find, and let Vemund's people starve all winter. They will be happy then to accept my rule come spring."

Or they might hate Harald for starving them. A hundred men should be enough to overcome any resistance Vemund could muster, though, even if Grai and Illugi were leading them into a trap.

✛ ✛ ✛

RANKS UPON RANKS of Harald's men stood in orderly lines in the dim light of early morning. In silent columns, they boarded the ships, also stretched single file along the narrow fjord, so both ends of the procession disappeared into mist. Even Harald's berserkers, wild men with no fear who prided themselves on the chaos they brought everywhere, waited their turn. Only their tangled hair and outfits of mottled furs marked them out from Harald's other men.

Harald climbed up the beach to where Ragnvald waited with his own men, also arrayed in silent ranks. Here and there a man drooped on his feet, weak from an unhealed wound, and one of his fellows had to hold him up. A few miles away, a man who called himself a king slept with his warriors, exhausted and mead-drunk after months of hard fighting in the hills and valleys in South Maer.

Stay, Ragnvald wanted to say to Harald. Or leave your berserkers to do this deed. They revel in death, they court it. They have no more fear of it, and will not mind this task. Each of the berserkers had faced a battle against terrible odds, and had his fear and most of his humanity stripped from him by it. They went into battle without armor, and killed without remorse.

"You will finish this, Ragnvald, and it will add to your glory," said Harald. He clasped Ragnvald's arm. "And then come to me in Nidaros, and I will reward you. King Vemund sleeps yonder. The gods have told us this is true."

Harald's eyes were wide and guileless. Even after fighting together for six years, Ragnvald did not always know when Harald believed his own legends. He was a king now in truth, full of certainty that everything he did was good and right, even burning men alive.

"You know what to do." He squeezed Ragnvald's arm again before letting it go.

"Do you not want to witness this triumph?" Ragnvald asked.

"No," said Harald. "My mother told me there would be a storm before the new moon, and I must return home before then."

"She can calm the weather," said Ragnvald. She was a sorceress, a prophetess, half a goddess—Ragnvald had seen many easy tricks called magic to fool the simple, but Ronhild could truly perform wonders.

Herlaug would also leave with Harald, in hopes that Ronhild could use her magic to heal his face fully.

"Not this storm," said Harald. "She told me. Now, King Vemund must die, with all his men."

Ragnvald remembered what Ronhild had told him once, when he lay near death in Harald's service: that Ragnvald would sacrifice many things he held dear, and see Harald king of all Norway, before he finally sacrificed his life. He would hold the torch and burn Vemund's hall, because Harald asked, because the discomfort of doing this must be one of those sacrifices.

"Then go home and see your family—your reward will wait," Harald continued. "Give your wife a swollen belly, and bring your sons to celebrate Yule with mine." He gave Ragnvald a rough hug, and turned to walk down to the beach. The quiet scrape of rocky shore on wood followed as ship after ship cast out into the blanket of mist.

✢   ✢   ✢

GRAI AND ILLUGI led Ragnvald's forces toward Vemund's hall. From time to time, Grai gestured at a tree or a boulder, and behind it, Ragnvald found one of Vemund's sentries. He killed his share, while Grai and Illugi sent the signals—birdcalls and regular flashes of torchlight between trees—that would make Vemund think all was well.

Following Ragnvald, his men gathered bundles of dry wood and bound them with tinder on the outside so they would catch fire easily. Ragnvald himself carried the ember to light the flame that would end this summer of fighting. He had Harald's orders: burn the hall or burn the land. If Vemund did not want to die like this, he could have sworn to Harald, like other kings. Harald would at least have granted him exile for his surrender.

They reached the hall at dusk, when the dying light turned the mist between the trees blue. The hall stood in a small clearing. Smoke rose from holes in the roof, light shone between the planks, and sounds of habitation told Ragnvald Grai and Illugi had not lied.

Ragnvald's men placed bundles of wood leaning up against the hall at regular intervals. He gestured for guards to flank the door so none could escape. Arnfast handed him a torch, which he lit with the coal he carried. He passed the flame to Oddi's torch, and Oddi sent the flame around to each of the men in turn, until a wreath of lights surrounded the hall.

Harald's orders had been to fire the hall without warning, but Ragnvald hesitated. He had slept in this hall once when Vemund's force hid in the hills and left it empty. At least most of Vemund's women and children would still be in hiding. Vemund would not have felt safe bringing them back, even had his trap against the cliff face been more successful.

"You must do it," said Oddi.

"So their shades can haunt me? I need no more ghosts."

Oddi gave him a wry smile. "You cannot avoid that," he said.

Ragnvald raised his torch and knocked on the hall's great double doors. "I am Ragnvald Eysteinsson, king of Sogn. Men surround your hall, ready to burn it. Send your women out to be our slaves. Send your men out to die like warriors on our swords. The time to submit is past. I have come for your deaths." It was more mercy than Harald wanted to offer.

"You are not warrior enough to send me, King Vemund of Naustdal, up to Valhalla," came the reply. A loud voice, though muffled through the oaken door.

A woman's voice added, "You and your Harald are cowards. You cannot face us in a fair fight, so you burn us." So Vemund intended at least one of his wives to join him in the afterlife.

Ragnvald waited for more replies that did not come. He tried again. "All who wish it will be spared. Do not force your women to die for your stubbornness."

"Better they should die with me than end as slaves like you," said Vemund. "We stay."

"If I thought myself a slave, I would lie on your pyre with you," said Ragnvald.

Vemund laughed, a low rumble. "And I have heard you called wise," he said.

Oddi touched Ragnvald's arm as he began to frame some other

argument. He glanced down. His torch had burned down, and embers crumbled close to his hand.

"Harald sent us to burn him, not argue with him," said Oddi. "He is honorable to die rather than be enslaved. It is the decision any of us would make."

"He meant—"

"Yes," said Oddi. "But if he is to die, you can let him have the last word."

Ragnvald nodded. Vemund only echoed what every one of Harald's enemies protested, that Harald had turned kings into slaves. Ragnvald lowered his torch to the tinder, and his men followed. The fire caught quickly, flames traveling from twigs to sticks to larger branches, and finally to the hall itself. Fire leaped eagerly to the hall's gray, weathered wood. Ragnvald stood his ground as long as he could, until the gold of his neck ring grew hot and began to burn him.

The fire roared like an angry giant. In its hunger, it sucked the air of the forest toward it, bending trees, burning off the fog. Vemund and his household would be huddled in the middle of the hall. He had wanted none to leave, wanted his men, and even his wife and children, on his funeral pyre with him. The wood of the hall cracked and twisted, drowning out the screams that Ragnvald knew must be coming from burning throats. Ragnvald's father's hall had been burned, and though it had been empty, the remnants of charcoal on that patch of ground had given Ragnvald nightmares in his boyhood.

He felt Oddi's hand pulling at his arm. "The roof will fall soon—we have to get clear," he yelled. Ragnvald let Oddi tug him back to join the rest of the men standing in the cool forest. He thought Oddi wanted to say something, but in six years of battling together, he had learned that nothing could lessen the pull the dead exerted on Ragnvald in moments like these, nothing except the passing of time. Ragnvald stood and watched the hall burn. No one tried to escape.

By the following midday, all that remained was a pile of charred timbers. A skull, covered with blackened flesh like mold on a log, had rolled out at one corner. Nearby, a skeletal arm that still had a few black-fleshed fingers extended from the wreck.

"What do we do now?" Oddi asked. Behind him, a charred beam shifted and the arm disappeared. "It will be days before it cools enough to search for treasure."

It would be dirty, gruesome work to sort through the heap of charcoal, ash, and remains, and for what—the ruby in Vemund's tooth? Let him keep it, and his shade rest. Ragnvald closed his eyes and saw instead a round green hill covered with wildflowers, the bones tying the spirits of the dead to the land of Maer.

"No," said Ragnvald. "Let the dead have their burial mound. My men want to go home."

5

SOLVI REMAINED WITH HIS SHIPS AT THE REYKJAVIK HARBOR
as his men unloaded them. Once they had been emptied, Solvi would
make sure they were beached securely, so no storm could damage
them. These were his own ships, his treasure poured into their making.

He watched as Svanhild's small figure, hard to see in the brown of
her sailing tunic and trousers, disappeared over the hill. Even here, his
view filled by farmland dotted with sheep and timbered halls, Iceland
was an eerie place. The rocks came in shapes not found in any other
lands, the bay steamed, and smoke and strange smells came from the
mountains. He needed to tell Svanhild, and soon, that he had no plans
to join the brotherhood of dispossessed kings too cowardly to take
back their land. If Svanhild spent less times in dreams and fantasies,
she would know that already. She feared that Solvi would fight Ragnvald again if he tried to reclaim his land. Solvi feared that too—he
feared that Svanhild would choose Ragnvald over him if she had another chance. That fear had kept him from Tafjord for too long.

He watched men helping their wives out of the ships. It had been
the first sea journey for many of them, and they showed it in the slow
and awkward way they climbed down. Solvi made note of who had
survived: among them raiders like Ketil Flatnose, whose nose had
been smashed by a club in his youth and healed into a broad, misshapen thing, and members of families who had lost people in the
storm. These walked with stumbling steps along the beach, peering

at strangers they knew were not their loved ones, checking and re-checking faces they had already examined.

Some of the passengers fought over goods that had been hastily packed, and Solvi settled these fights brusquely, dividing the goods in half where possible, or keeping them for himself if he liked the look of them. The arguments grew fewer as word traveled of his method. In earlier years, when only men and boys crewed his ships, then he had known how to rule them, care for them, make them wealthy, and then send them back to their farms and kingdoms. Harald had taken that from Solvi as well: made him a nursemaid for the weak and helpless rather than a commander of strong men.

He looked up to see ships approaching, warships all, but none of the people onshore seemed fearful of raiders—Iceland's settlers craved newcomers to fill the lonely landscape: more wives, more gossip, more food, more protection. Any approaching ship could only bring good news.

Solvi recognized King Gudbrand when he climbed out of his ship, his figure unmistakable with his long legs, potbelly, and a stoop that pushed his head far in front of his shoulders. His sons, for those giants who followed along behind him could only be his blood, had a better configuration of similar limbs, closer to beauty, and yet they moved like him, leading with their chins. Solvi had once thought Gudbrand dead at the Vestfold battle against Harald that had claimed Solvi's father, Hunthiof, and kept Solvi from returning to Norway's shores since. That battle had returned Svanhild to his side, though, bearing their son under her girdle. Later, Solvi had learned that Gudbrand had escaped to his island fortress in Hardanger Fjord, and then fled Harald's forces a year later. He owed Solvi for abandoning him.

Another man came after them, walking slowly, bowed down, though not yet disfigured by age. A woman followed him a half step behind. She seemed familiar to Solvi, but from this distance, he could not see her features, only her ash blond banner of hair, blowing in the wind. Her serene gait seemed to float her above the uneven rocks on the shore.

"Make sure this all gets organized," Solvi said to Thorstein, waving his hand at the people and goods on the shore. "And Ulfarr is not to leave without speaking with me first."

"Yes, of course." Thorstein swallowed, his throat moving under the sparse down of his new beard. He would be nervous giving orders to Ulfarr.

Solvi cursed his short legs as he scrambled over the shore's stones. He never walked comfortably after a long voyage, and making his way across the rocks required climbing with his hands until he reached the ground on which Ingolfur held court with the newcomers.

"I've been here less than half a day," said Solvi, interrupting Ingolfur's long-winded welcome speech. "But I can bid you welcome as well." Ingolfur made a noise of protest, while Gudbrand's face registered surprise, followed by a moment of decision, and finally gladness.

"I thought you weren't coming until the spring," said Gudbrand. "I heard in Dorestad that you planned to winter in the Faroe Islands."

"Yes," said Solvi. "But Hakon's reach extends farther than I thought. It has brought us here together, so I cannot complain."

"Can you not?" asked the woman, stepping out from behind the bulk of Gudbrand and his sons. All the blood left Solvi's face at the sight of his former wife.

"Geirny Nokkvesdatter," he said. The old man next to her must be her father. Solvi had not seen him in a decade. "I had not thought to meet you again."

"I'm sure not," she said.

"Is your husband here with you?" Solvi asked.

"You mean other than you?" she asked. "My second husband died fighting Harald on my father's behalf. Harald killed the wrong one of my husbands, I think."

"Now, Geirny," said Nokkve. "It has been a long time."

Those years had made changes in Geirny, changes for the better, at least in her looks and spirit, Solvi thought. She had been very young when she and Solvi wed, and her pregnancies at Tafjord had kept her sickly. Now she held herself firm and upright, and had a more solid figure than the slender girl he had left behind. Her face still had strong, handsome planes, and her eyes had turned from vague to fierce, but were the same silver Solvi remembered.

To Ingolfur she said, "I need to bathe and have some refreshment. My servants are bringing my clothes. Have your wife show me to the bath-house." She left the party of men, carrying herself in the same upright way she had when she came from the ship. Solvi watched her go. From time to time she seemed to sag forward with fatigue, and in those gaps in her composure, Solvi saw glimpses of the girl who had been his wife.

"Now we can talk," said Solvi.

"Be courteous to my daughter," said Nokkve. "You caused her much pain from which she is only now recovering."

They had caused each other much pain, Solvi could have said, but to no purpose. He bowed his head slightly to Nokkve.

"We have brought great tidings," said Gudbrand. "And allies. With my friends from Sweden and your alliance with Frisia, we can finally mount a real attack on Harald."

"Sweden?" Solvi asked.

Gudbrand grinned, showing teeth almost as yellow as his mus-tache. He looked like an old walrus. Solvi hoped that this time he would be as deadly as that great beast, if he truly planned to fight Harald. "Yes, I have made us an alliance that cannot fail," said Gud-brand. "King Eirik looks out from Sweden and does not wish to see Harald control all of Norway any more than we do. He sends his envoy and another jarl to join our fight, and promises more if he likes our plans. Are you ready to join with us again?"

"You did not even know you would find me here," said Solvi. Over Ingolfur's shoulder, he saw Svanhild approaching across the farm-land. She walked too quickly for Eystein to keep up and then, with exasperation written in every line of her body, she hoisted him up, and swung him around so he clung to her back.

"Our meeting is a blessing from the gods, which tells me we are on the right course," said Gudbrand.

Eystein laid his cheek down against his mother's shoulder, as though he needed to absorb Svanhild's strength. He would never be a sea king, but if Solvi could raise him at Tafjord, with Svanhild as his mother, he would never need to become one. In Tafjord he could grow into a king like Solvi's father had never been, one who would care for the people of North Maer.

"I am still deciding my course," said Solvi, unwilling to expose his thoughts just yet. "I will hear more from your new allies, and speak with Svanhild. She will not like to send me back to war."

Gudbrand laughed. "She is your wife, is she not? Tell her what you're going to do—or simply do it!"

"I can see you have not been married in a long time," said Nokkve. Solvi looked at him in surprise that he should take his part.

"My sons take no trouble from their wives," said Gudbrand.

"That is because your sons married women as empty-headed as themselves," Nokkve snapped. To Solvi he said, "Solvi Hunthiofsson, you and I have had our differences, and if my daughter had asked it, I would have taken my revenge upon you. But your father and I were friends, and I know you for the best sailor on any water. We want your help—if you will give it. I know that when others fled from the battle at Vestfold, you stayed and fought."

"Thank you," said Solvi. He did not know until now how much he had hungered to hear that acclaim. He had barely escaped with his life and his woman, while Gudbrand and his other allies fled as soon as the battle turned, and paid little price for their flight.

"I think I can convince Svanhild and save my peace," he said. An idea, half formed, was coming to him—a trick, a lie with its roots in truth. "But I need you and your daughter's hatred, not your praise. Can you do that?"

Nokkve had raided with Solvi's father all over the coast of Norway and Frisia. He had made many daring ambushes, and burned kings alive in their halls. He was no longer that man, but Solvi thought he would enjoy pulling a small trick now. Nokkve's lips quirked as he nodded and said yes.

"Excellent," said Solvi. "Tell your daughter—I do not think she will find it difficult."

"She will not," Nokkve said dryly. "What should we do?"

"At some point, declare in my wife's hearing that you and your daughter will not consent to share Iceland with me. That you will only view me a true man if I take up a sword against this Harald who has put me out of my home. That if I can do that, then I may share Iceland or any other land between here and the northern lights with you."

"A true man should not be afraid of his wife," said Gudbrand.

"As Nokkve will soon tell you, I am no true man," said Solvi with a grin. Now was not the time to make Gudbrand feel the shame of his flight from Vestfold. Solvi would hold that in reserve. He made his expression more sober. "You have met her. I do not fear her, but I fear the unhappiness of one who has been as close to me as my own sword for these past years." He gave Nokkve a small smile. "She will see the rightness of this more if it comes from someone other than her husband."

Svanhild reached Solvi just as Gudbrand and the others left to follow Ingolfur to his hall. Ingolfur would not spoil Solvi's game with Svanhild, not after Svanhild had forced his hand in the matter of the funeral feast. Svanhild set Eystein down, and he jumped into the space between two of the rocks to examine the creatures that wriggled in the muck. He had brought his finds to Solvi until he grew discouraged by Solvi's lack of interest. At least the boy was no coward, judging by the things he was willing to pick up: the spiny, the slimy, the sharp-toothed.

"Was that Gudbrand?" Svanhild asked. "You looked pleased to see a man who abandoned you at the Vestfold battle." Solvi smiled at her scowl. A woman could hold a grudge more perfectly than a man ever could. Solvi planned to use his grievance against Gudbrand as leverage, and discard it when it no longer served him.

"He used his judgment, and saved himself and his sons," said Solvi. "He has lived to be able to bring battle to Harald again. As have I."

Svanhild narrowed her eyes. "There is no need to bring battle here. Unna told me Harald has given his permission—those that do not wish to live in his Norway may claim land here, as much as they can walk around in a day. She also says that he will revoke his permission and attack if anyone strikes against him from Iceland."

"That woman says a lot for one who was born in Scotland," said Solvi. "She has never set foot on Norse soil."

Svanhild shrugged, though her face remained obstinate. "Who was that with Gudbrand?"

"King Nokkve," Solvi admitted. "And Geirny Nokkvesdatter." Svanhild would find out sooner or later.

She frowned. "Geirny plans to settle here? Does she mean you harm?"

"I don't know that either." He and Svanhild had spoken little of Geirny in their time together. Solvi did not like to dwell on the past, especially the children who had died before being named, whose faces he had never seen, and Svanhild had not probed. Solvi wondered if she avoided the subject for the same reason he never asked whether she would choose his life over Ragnvald's, if she had to. Neither of them wanted to hear those answers.

☩ ☩ ☩

AS PROMISED, TWO days later, Ingolfur hosted funeral games for those who had drowned in the storm. Solvi bet on the footraces, which Thorstein won, after Solvi convinced him that tripping his opponents would not diminish his honor—it was expected, even. Ketil won an ax-throwing contest against Ingolfur himself, while Tryggulf came second at archery against Unna's servant Donall.

Ingolfur had built a fine drinking hall, in addition to his living hall, with torches lighting the path that led up to it from the bay. Low scrub brush had stood on this spot until recently, leaving the ground covered with bare stumps. An amputated forest, it seemed to Solvi. For the feast, Svanhild dressed in a rich burgundy silk that Solvi had bought in a Spanish market, and which a Dublin seamstress had made up into a dress. Silver brooches, as big as Solvi's palm, held up her overdress.

He too wore fine clothes in bright colors, befitting his wealth, with gold at his throat and waist, and in a thick band around his arm. If Ingolfur thought Solvi rich, he might accept a delay in the gift he would expect for feeding all of Solvi's followers through the winter. He need not know that Solvi had carried little gold with him from the Faroes, beyond his and Svanhild's personal jewelry.

A long fire stretched the length of the hall, ringed by benches. Nearly half of the free men of Iceland's two hundred families were here, lining the walls, waiting for the ritual welcome drink and greeting to begin the feasting. Solvi and Svanhild exchanged greetings with those they knew. Svanhild's attention seemed divided until she spotted Geirny sitting at the high table. She raised her chin and turned away.

"Can the two of you share this island? It is far bigger even than Streymoy," Solvi asked, naming the island on which they had meant to pass the winter. Perhaps Svanhild would refuse, and make his plans easier.

"You would jest? About her?" Svanhild asked. Solvi did not answer, unsure what response would serve his purpose best. Before Svanhild could press, Ingolfur and his wife took their places at the high table, and the room quieted.

"He is too pleased with himself," said Solvi to Svanhild. "If he was first, how did he know to come here?"

Svanhild gave him an amused smile and twined her fingers with his under the table as Ingolfur, standing by the famous pillars that had led him to Reykjavik, began to speak: "We have many great men here tonight. I do not know which king to honor with the first toast, so I will choose the oldest."

He looked around the room, and, not seeing the response he hoped for, quickly amended. "I mean the king who has had the most years in which to gather, ah, wisdom. King Nokkve of Romsdal."

"No longer of Romsdal," said Svanhild, still under her breath. Solvi tightened his grip on her hand warningly. Everyone here had suffered a defeat at Harald's hand. Could there be any ranking among the exiles? Nokkve stood, and raised his cup for the first draught, speaking the ritual words of welcome, and calling down a blessing upon their food and drink.

"I do not like always being a guest in another man's hall," said Solvi. Ingolfur's servants brought dishes of meat to the table, stewed seal with an intense marine smell.

"Then is it time to build our own?" Svanhild asked. "Some fine land near Unna's farm remains unclaimed."

Ingolfur introduced a skald from the court of King Eirik of Sweden, then, with the skald's prompting, added, "Skald Meldun trained on an island of Irish druids who study so long and rigorously that none can match the strength of their voices or the length of their memories. Is that right?"

"Bards," said this Meldun, in a voice that did sound well trained, for it carried to all ears in the hall. His pale skin contrasted with his dark hair and eyes. "But both druids and bards can do magic with their words. The Christians have tried to defeat the old magic, but it lives on." Then, seeing that his words held little meaning for his audience, he changed his tack. "My king, Eirik of Sweden, has sent me here to Iceland to see how far the bravest of the Norse kings have fallen." He waited for the aggrieved shouts to fade, and moved alongside the head table, where the long fire threw strange shadows on his face. He shook his head sadly. "The tyranny of Harald swells your ranks with men who seek freedom, who will bend the knee to no one. Some of you will claim new land and make Iceland your homes, and live in the old way, where every free man has a voice."

He waited through the toast that inevitably followed, led by Ingolfur, and echoed around the room. Solvi joined in the cheer, though halfheartedly, and then passed his cup to Svanhild.

"My lords and kings, free men and slaves, I have a tale for you of a war from long ago." Meldun paused again, this time to sip some ale to wet his throat, and began speaking his tale in the cadence used by skalds to help their memory. "In the time when gods and goddesses walked the earth, there was as much strife as there is now. Great was the struggle between the Aesir gods and the frost giants of Jotunheim, between the sons of light, and the sons of ice and darkness.

"The battle raged for a long time until both sides were weary of fighting, and finally the giant Jotun king offered his daughter Skadi to marry one of the Aesir. Skadi was a fierce girl, and also a beauty. She skied the upper reaches of the world alone, with only her bow on her back. She made sport with the ice bears, and hunted wild reindeer to bring back to her father's feasting hall. She was wild, and she desired a wild husband to hunt by her side.

"Now crafty Odin, drinker of the wine of wisdom, agreed to this, for Skadi would make a fine wife for any of the Aesir. Their children would be gods. But none of Odin's warriors, the Aesir, wished to be married to a giant girl, despite her beauty. When Odin asked each of them to marry Skadi, each of them declined in turn.

"Heimdall said, 'I cannot marry her, for I cannot abandon my post.'

"Baldur said, 'I cannot marry her for she is a huntress, and I am gentle and a lover of all beasts.'

"Tyr said, 'I cannot marry her for I have only one hand, and a hunter needs both of his hands to hunt.'

"Odin could not fail to find a husband for her, though, for he knew that such an insult would cause the Jotuns to take up arms against him again, and so he persuaded the gods to assemble so that Skadi might choose her groom. Then he caused a fog to cover the gods from their heads to their waists.

"'You may have any one of the Aesir's warriors to be your husband,' said Odin, 'but you must make your choice from seeing his legs only.'"

"Was it their legs she was looking at, or did she glance a little higher?" called out one of Ingolfur's guests, prompting a laugh from the crowd.

Meldun the skald smiled, and waited for the crowd to quiet. "Skadi walked up and down the line of gods, trying to peer through the fog, but even a Jotun, a daughter of the foggy northern wastes, could not pierce Odin's veil. Finally, she chose the strongest, most elegant pair of legs she could see, hoping they belonged to Baldur, for after a life lived among frost giants, she valued gentleness.

"Odin caused the fog to lift, and Skadi saw that she had chosen Njord, a god of the sea, whose legs were fine and long for swimming, whose waist was lean and trim, and whose broad shoulders might make any maiden weak with delight.

"She could not find a fault in him that would let her refuse the marriage, and indeed, he was her choice, but they made an ill match and began to fight immediately. Skadi loved the mountains, the sharp tall peaks and the scent of snow. Njord loved salt and sea. He draped himself in seaweed, and on him it looked as fine as the costliest silk. They resolved to spend part of the year in the mountains, and part of the year in the sea, and yet neither was ever truly happy, each always yearning for the home left behind."

Meldun's voice died out and the room grew silent. He waited for long enough that Solvi grew uneasy, though he knew this was simply a skald's trick, and when someone else shifted as though they might break the silence, Meldun continued.

"Now, I have heard some versions of the tale where Skadi divorced Njord after a time and married Ull, the hunter god, and together they lived in the far north, under the dancing northern lights with an ice bear for their children's nurse. I do not think this is the true tale, though. There are as many mismatched marriages as good ones, and as many men taken from their homes by duty as those whose *wyrd* lets them follow the path of their desire. Instead I believe the tale that tells how Skadi and Njord grew bitter with each other, each missing home, and when Skadi bore children they bred true to their giant mother, steeped in hate. She called them Ice and Storm, and they will be among the giants who overtake the earth at the end of time."

A smattering of applause greeted the end of his tale. Meldun bowed his head to acknowledge it. This was not a tale intended to make happy a land of exiles—or any married person—and perhaps that was its purpose. Around the table, men looked into their cups before draining them, as if searching for an answer within. Svanhild's hand felt clammy in Solvi's.

"Why that story, do you think?" Svanhild asked.

"Dissatisfaction will help his master," said Solvi. "Meldun has given us the poetry. King Eirik's emissary will give us the prose." At the high table, Meldun consulted with the giant man sitting next to him—Rane, King Eirik's emissary.

"I'm glad you didn't have to choose me by my legs," said Solvi in Svanhild's ear. She touched his knee under the table where he had whole skin between his scars.

"No, I chose you for your handsome face," she said, smiling. "That is what made me weak with delight." Her words and her smile made him feel some weakness himself, a tide of desire, mixed with sadness that this warmth was not enough to bridge the gap between her hopes and his. The tale was a reminder that the world was bigger than the two of them.

6

SVANHILD SHIFTED, UNEASY AFTER THE SKALD'S TALE OF SKADI and Njord. At the high table, Geirny's face was pensive. Svanhild hoped she had heard this story as a reminder of how poorly suited she and Solvi had been. She leaned against him, touching her thigh to his, hungry for his warmth like a cat lying in the summer sun, dreading winter's bite.

Rane, the Swedish emissary, rose. "Thank you for that tale, Meldun. You told it even better here than you did in the court of my king." Rane was a mountain of a man, with a huge, apple-red face sitting atop a barrel-shaped torso. His wide shoulders and back tapered to a surprisingly small waist draped with a heavy belt. He walked toward the open space before the high table. "I've not come here to tell you what to do. I am a simple man. I was a jarl in Vermaland, until Harald and his father pushed me out. I'm not one to sit around and complain, so I became a warrior for King Eirik of Sweden. He gave me a farm, and I've a wife who's borne me sons. For myself I only want to be an honorable man. But I've failed my sons—they should be free men, who live on the same land where their fathers and forefathers ruled. How can I deny them this? Harald of Vestfold has taken that from me, and from you."

Svanhild looked at Solvi as Rane spoke these words. This was what he wanted for Eystein, or thought he should want. Ragnvald had killed Olaf for Ardal. Men killed and died to claim crowded lands, when farmland in Iceland lay fallow.

Rane continued. "Men of Iceland, many of you were kings before Harald demanded unlawful oaths and stripped you of your lands. And now you are here. It is a beautiful land, but is it home?" He clenched a huge fist. This sort of rousing speech did not seem to come naturally to him, and his rehearsed gestures made it seem more honest, not less. "My king does not want a tyrant for a neighbor. He will swell your ranks with tested warriors, and bring you to battles in well-made ships, as long as you sail them against King Harald."

Ingolfur had been looking less and less pleased by Rane's speech and now he banged his fist on the table and stood. "What is wrong with settling in Iceland? We will be a mighty land one day and the farmland here is free and fertile. A man can make himself rich in a generation here."

Rane nodded a couple times, and resumed his walking to and fro. "Good. Good. You should be proud of your new land—even if you still have to follow Harald's rules. I have heard it said that every man is a king in Iceland, even if they are only kings of ice and rock. But if every man is a king, then no man may be. Yes, Ingolfur is right. This is a fine land. Fit for all of your younger sons, to make it a great nation. It will be, of that I am sure. But are you all so ready to live the life of an exile?" Svanhild raised her estimation of Rane. He mixed insult with his praise and fed the uneasiness that Meldun's tale had sparked.

Gudbrand stood. "Harald has the mightiest kings of Norway with him, and Loki's own luck against his enemies. I have learned that—as has my friend Solvi Hunthiofsson, the craftiest man who ever fought a sea battle." Solvi shifted in his seat. Svanhild glanced at him side-long to see how he liked the flattery. He looked bemused, pleased against his will.

Rane clenched his fist again. "If you unite, you cannot but defeat him. Harald's friends are fewer than they seem. Hakon of Halogaland claims far more land than one king can govern, and his sons are no help. The king of Hordaland is old. Harald makes a new home in Nidaros, leaving the southern districts unprotected. Now is the time to draw him into battle and take back what is ours."

"What of Ragnvald of Sogn?" Solvi's man Snorri asked. Svanhild nodded. Ragnvald should have been mentioned among that list.

"It is said he is a mighty leader, though young," said Rane. "But I have also heard that he burned King Vemund alive in his hall rather than face him on the field of battle. This is the sort of man that Harald calls to his side: betrayers and oath breakers."

Solvi's fingers tightened on Svanhild's forearm as she half rose from her seat. He leaned over and said into her ear, "You will do little good by defending him. This Rane did not mention him at first because he knows he cannot say much ill of Ragnvald. Take joy in that, if you must." Solvi's words both pleased and troubled her. She wished these ships had never come. Even this news of Ragnvald was no blessing; hearing his name pained her more than no mention at all would have. Six years had passed. She knew he had married Hilda, and had children by her—and she would never meet them, nor he Eystein.

"Now is the time?" Solvi asked loudly. "Why not six years ago? Could it be because now Harald's Norway is strong enough to frighten the king of Sweden?"

"Oh no," said Rane. He turned slowly so he could fix each guest with his gaze before ending by facing Solvi. "If you call it that, you have already lost. 'Harald's Norway.' No, it is your Norway. Your kingdoms, and you should rule it."

"You haven't answered my question," said Solvi. "King Eirik wants Norway weak. He would send Norsemen to do this work for him."

"I don't know what he wants," said Rane. "His mind is too subtle for me. But he sends help to you. Do you want to turn it down?"

"If it turns to betrayal in the middle of a raid, I might," said Solvi, quietly enough that Rane could pretend he did not hear.

"A king offers you friendship," said Rane. "He offers you your land again. I have said what I came to say." He sat and emptied his cup of ale.

Meldun took up a small Irish harp, and began a song to fill the lull, telling a simple, tragic story of brothers torn apart by feud, but after his earlier tale, this one had a troubling resonance. When he finished, King Nokkve rose to his feet. His face had the same fine bones as his daughter's, with a white beard that furred the hollows under his cheeks.

"I would speak," he said.

"Speak. We are all equals here," said Rane, further annoying In-golfur, Svanhild could see. He had lost control of his feast.

"Gudbrand and I have pledged to Rane and the king of Sweden that we will fight Harald to regain our lands. Do not think that joining this fight will deprive you of your land in Iceland. I mean to claim land here for my daughter, Geirny, and set her up with a great farm that will help feed all of you through lean winters, and prove to you all that ambition in Iceland is no bar to honor at home." Nokkve paused and licked his lips. His eyes lighted briefly on Svan-hild and Solvi, and then he continued. "Iceland should be a land for men of honor. So I will not allow my daughter to share it with this Solvi Hunthiofsson—who did not have enough loyalty to remain my daughter's husband."

Solvi sprang to his feet. "Your daughter could not give me sons," he said.

Gudbrand's son rose next. "Who is to know that isn't because of your own weak seed?" Nokkve shoved Gudbrand's son back hard as Solvi's hand went to his sword.

"I have a son now," Solvi cried. "And I do not want to share land with your daughter either. I have a home in Norway—even now one of my men sails toward it. I have no doubt I will find him there feast-ing when we attack in the fall." Some confused cheering sounded around the table then quieted.

"Husband," said Svanhild, her voice catching in her throat. Her plans had come to ruin so quickly. "You cannot mean this—Nokkve cannot forbid us to claim a farm in Iceland."

"A farm?" he said, looking down at her. "I am a sea king, and the son of sea kings, not a slave to the land. No wonder Nokkve ques-tions my honor." Svanhild recoiled. She knew Solvi was playing a part. Usually, though, she could tell his heading, and steer to follow him. And usually his tactics did not set her up as his adversary.

Rane shoved his way in front of Nokkve and Gudbrand's sons. "I know there is much to discuss," he said. "Not everything must be decided tonight, but I am glad to hear such clamor for battle."

That settled the room generally. Solvi shoved his sword back into its scabbard and stepped back from the table. Svanhild grabbed his arm. "You are your own man—free to make your own choices. Nok-kve of Romsdal cannot tell you what to do."

"I am going to get an apology from Gudmar Gudbrandsson and King Nokkve," he said grimly. "That insult cannot stand." Svanhild watched him go. She knew he would avoid dueling Gudbrand's son—he fought well enough in raids and sneak attacks, but his small size and weak legs hampered him in individual combat. The whole feast had witnessed the insult, though, so Solvi would probably force a public apology and a gift to restore his honor.

He did not return for a long time. The skald Meldun sang other songs that were not so pointed, songs about battle, songs about adventuring, songs about drinking, and finally a song about a witch queen that made the hall ring with laughter, for she had, when her paramour spurned her, made his phallus too large for him to penetrate any woman. Svanhild drank more than she ought, until she saw Unna and Donall preparing to leave, and decided to return home herself.

Solvi came to her side as she wrapped her cloak around her shoulders. She gave him an angry stare through eyes made bleary with ale and exhaustion, and pushed his hands away when he tried to tug her cloak more tightly around her shoulders. "No, you should stay with your new allies. If you come home, you will only lie to me."

"It is not decided yet," said Solvi. "Though the weighting on the scale has changed."

"Do I not get a voice in this decision?"

"In what I choose to do?" Solvi asked. He seemed less drunk than she, and had a dangerous edge in his voice.

"No, husband," she said, bowing her head so he would not see the sudden tears in her eyes. She felt too muddleheaded from drink to form an argument. "You usually at least ask my advice, though."

"And I shall," said Solvi.

"Come back to the tent with me if you like," she said, softening somewhat. Better he should come with her than stay with Gudbrand and Rane, who would fill his head with visions of battle. Gudbrand lurched over to them, nearly tripping over a man who had fallen asleep near where Svanhild had been sitting.

"Do you not want to stay and plan our conquest?" he asked.

"It is too late for politics, my lords," said Svanhild. "There will be time tomorrow."

"Yes, tomorrow," said Solvi. "We will go sailing to the north of the island. You have only seen Ingolfur's settlement—there is much untouched wilderness, and a mountain that belches fire. And we will have privacy from all but the seals."

✢ ✢ ✢

THE NEXT DAY began late as Gudbrand's men, staggering from the previous night's feasting, made their way to Solvi's camp. Svanhild served them bread and cheese to soak up the remains of the drink in their stomach, and light ale to settle them further. Gudbrand arrived last, with his sons Gudmar and Ogmund, who squinted at the bright sky.

"Wife, we will return in a day or so," Solvi announced to Svanhild after the men had eaten their fill.

"I'm going too," said Svanhild. She had no plan but knew that she did not want Solvi speaking with these men outside her hearing. Had she not helped him countless times, in foreign courts, to get what they wanted?

Her guests exchanged glances. Gudbrand's sons were as tall and broad as their father, though Svanhild did not see the intelligence in them that she had marked in Gudbrand. "Yes, of course, you as well," said Gudbrand. "Your husband says your counsel is wise."

Eystein was quiet this morning, having had his sleep disturbed by Svanhild and Solvi's late return the night before. Svanhild told him she would return in a few days, and put him in the care of her servant Katla. She packed a bag with blankets, since they would almost certainly sleep out of doors that night.

Gudbrand had borrowed a small vessel from one of the settlers, and they set out in the mild afternoon winds. White clouds chased one another across the sky. Wind and sea both flowed toward an arch of rock in the distance. Svanhild watched the shoreline go by, enjoying the freedom of traveling without worrying about Eystein. She had not realized how much his dislike of sailing had curdled her pleasure.

"We should go there." Gudbrand pointed at the arch.

"It is far," said Solvi. "We will not be able to return by morning."

"That is where I want to go," said Gudbrand. "I want to make sure we can speak without witnesses. Even your servants may be spies for Harald."

"How do you know your own men are loyal?" Svanhild asked. Solvi gave her a warning look.

"It is said that Harald's mother is a sorceress who can look out through the eyes of other men," said one of Gudbrand's sons. Svanhild snorted with disbelief.

"If you don't believe in his magic," said Gudbrand, "believe that Harald has spies. His captain Ragnvald is crafty and puts eyes everywhere." Svanhild could not help but feel pleased, both at the praise and the idea that Ragnvald might see her through these spies.

The sun hovered just above the horizon when the boat reached the arch of rock. They camped at the beach just to its south. Svanhild heated water from a barrel to boil some rye and dried fruit, and the men passed a skin of ale around the fire while she worked. She had just passed around some bread and cheese when Gudbrand stood. Svanhild followed his gaze and saw another boat approaching.

"Good, it is Nokkve," said Gudbrand.

All of Svanhild's ease faded. "Why did you bring us here?" she asked Gudbrand. "Is it not enough that Nokkve should humiliate my husband in public—now you have some ambush planned in private as well?"

"You did not have to come," he said. "Get back to your cooking."

"I'm sure he means us no harm," said Solvi. "And we do need to talk privately."

"Talk of what, how you and Nokkve will duel over who may settle here?" Svanhild asked.

"Let us wait and discuss it with him," said Solvi. He gave her another pointed look, which Svanhild added to her list of grievances. She could not help him if she did not understand what he planned. As the ship beached, Svanhild saw that it contained not only Nokkve, but also Geirny as well, attended by two female servants, who held up the hem of her dress to keep it out of the surf.

When she saw Svanhild, she turned to her father and said, "You did not say she would be here."

"It does not matter," he replied. "Pour the wine I brought, and we will discuss things."

Nokkve's servants unloaded a large tent and set it up. They started another fire, as if the one that Svanhild had made did not suit them somehow.

When the sun set, Nokkve's servants served a meal full of delicacies brought from Frisia: salt beef stewed with raisins, cured fatback, and cake of honey and nuts for dessert. Svanhild wished she could refuse the food, but when Solvi accepted, she did as well. The wine was Frankish, tasting of a sun that burned hotter than Iceland's ever would.

"You trust this Rane?" Solvi asked as the fire settled into coals. "His Swedish king will outfit an attack against Harald?"

"He will do so if it suits his interest," said Gudbrand.

"Which will only be if we do not grow too powerful," said Solvi.

"Not a great worry right now," said Geirny tartly. Svanhild glared at her.

"My daughter is right," said Nokkve. "Harald is powerful and we are weak, unless we bind together."

"Like you did last time?" Svanhild asked. "You left Solvi in Vestfold to face all of Harald's forces alone."

"We were trapped by your brother and his ships," said Gudbrand. "No one expected his coming. We had to fight our way out."

"If you could fight your way out, could you also have fought your way forward and come to my aid?" Solvi asked. "I've chewed over it for five years. Sometimes I think it shows that Harald is wrong and his kings will never be united under him. Look how poorly we fared. Perhaps it would be best for each man to follow his own will, to sail and settle where the wind takes him."

"I told you he was no man to join us," said Nokkve to Gudbrand. "You know how he treated my daughter—she does not want to be in the same land with him."

"Yet you brought her here to meet with him." Svanhild rose to her feet. She should not have to listen to this.

"In hopes that she might convince him to be a better man, if I could not," said Nokkve.

"Sit, wife," said Solvi. Then to Gudbrand: "What does this attack of yours look like?"

Gudbrand shrugged. "Band together, and attack where Harald is weak."

"And where is that?" Solvi asked.

"Jarl Rane says he has abandoned Vestfold," said one of Gudbrand's sons.

Solvi turned to look at him. "Rane was an upland jarl, a farmer. He doesn't know the coast," said Solvi.

"You are the sea king among us," said Nokkve. "Do you not know Vestfold?"

"I saw more of it than my allies did as they fled," said Solvi.

"If you continually throw that in my face . . . ," Gudbrand warned, his hand moving toward his sword.

"Why shouldn't he bring it up?" Svanhild asked. "Why should any-one want to ally with you again?"

Solvi spoke over her. "I would begin my attack in Tafjord," he said. "Not only because I know it well, but also because Heming Hakons-son is weak and will not hold it. When my father held it, none could pry him loose. It would be a protected base from which to launch at-tacks on the rest of the western coast—our old lands that each of us knows well."

Gudbrand shook his head. "Jarl Rane wants us to get Vermaland back for him first, and for that we must attack through Vestfold."

"Tell him that when Harald is distracted by multiple attacks on the western coast, he will be able to take Vestfold even if his only army is boys with wooden swords," said Solvi. "He should like that."

"Then you will fight on our side?" Gudbrand asked.

"If you agree to bring forces against Tafjord first, I will . . . con-sider it."

Svanhild felt as though she were back on board the ship that had brought her to Iceland, beset by storms, but without even a steering oar this time. She could not argue with Solvi in front of these men who might be allies or enemies, so she walked away from the campfire and sat down on a fallen log that let her look out toward the western sea. No one knew what lay over that horizon, though rumors of warm green lands filled the tales of Iceland's skalds. Back at the fire, Geirny drank from a jeweled goblet while everyone else had only sewn, leather cups. All of this was her fault, her coming the gust that had knocked Solvi off course. He did not want to stay in Iceland with her any more than she with him.

Eventually the discussion around the fire dwindled, and all retired to their tents. Svanhild lay awake in the dark, next to Solvi, who breathed deep and even in his sleep. She had feigned sleep when he entered the tent—she did not know what she could say to him that would not cause an argument loud enough to wake the camp. She did not care about Tafjord, and Solvi had never seemed to either, except when his pride was pricked. She would say all these things to him and more, but not when so many could hear, for she knew she would cry and rage if she spoke even one word.

Nokkve and Geirny were the problem—if Nokkve withdrew his words, if Geirny decided she did not want to live in Iceland after all, then some of the pressure on Solvi would lift. Svanhild felt at the pile of clothes by her side for the dagger she usually wore about her waist. She pulled it over to her, taking care to make no noise. She sat up slowly. Solvi did not stir. He slept on his back tonight, his brow furrowed by his dreams.

Svanhild pushed the flap of the tent aside. The waves lapped quietly at the shore. Little breezes shivered the grass, and the coals in the campfire gave out a steady orange glow. Svanhild walked gingerly toward Geirny's tent over sand that made a quiet sigh under her footsteps. She sliced through the fabric without a sound and glanced around to make sure that she was not observed before stepping through the opening she had made.

Geirny slept alone in her cot, with her hands drawn up under her chin. She would disturb no one when Svanhild forced her to stand. Svanhild looped a length of rope loosely around her wrists. Geirny stirred as Svanhild did her work, but did not wake. Svanhild wadded up a sock in one hand, pinched Geirny's nose, and when she opened her mouth, shoved it in and pulled the rope tight. She put her dagger to Geirny's throat.

"I will kill you and risk the feud with your father," she said to Geirny. "Or you can come with me."

7

ON THE MORNING THAT RAGNVALD PLANNED TO LEAVE NAUSTDAL for Sogn, he found a boy he did not recognize at his cook fire, stirring porridge. Ragnvald stared at him for a long moment without saying anything. He had slept poorly, awoken early from another nightmare of Vemund's hall burning. The day before, Oddi had followed a path leading away from the burned hall that ended in a cove sheltering five broad-bellied ships. They resembled trading vessels more than warships, though they did have oar ports. Ships were wealth and, unlike gold, could create more wealth in their use. Ragnvald would have to spread his forces thin to sail all of these ships to Sogn, and then on to Nidaros for Harald, but they were well worth the difficulty.

"You're not my servant," said Ragnvald.

"Didn't think you'd notice," the boy replied.

"You should have joined one of the other warriors—I might not have noticed then." Ragnvald put his hand on the boy's shoulder and turned him around.

"You're the one with the most servants." The boy shrugged out of Ragnvald's grasp and went on stirring the porridge.

"Who are you?" Ragnvald asked.

"My mother said the king was my father, but he didn't acknowledge me. I didn't want to burn. You said any who didn't want to burn you'd make into slaves."

Oddi emerged from the tent he shared with Ragnvald. He yawned and rubbed his eyes. "Who's this?" He jerked his chin at Ragnvald's visitor.

"Vemund's bastard, he claims." Ragnvald turned back to the boy. "What's your name?"

"Alarr." He met Ragnvald's eyes this time. He had a plain, dour face, and the flat eyes of one resigned to every blow of fate.

"Who else escaped? Was there anyone with you?" Ragnvald asked.

The boy's shoulders jerked, as though he might throw up. Ragnvald stepped back. "Just me," he said, looking at the ground again. "I was hiding. From him. The king."

"And you want to be my slave? Why?" Ragnvald asked.

"Better than dying."

"You could have run away."

"Who'd feed me?" the boy asked.

Oddi laughed. "Food triumphs over honor."

"And freedom," said Ragnvald.

"Are you going to keep him?" Oddi asked.

"Do you want him?"

"Why?" Oddi replied. "Because I've a soft spot for bastard sons of kings? No more than you." He gave Ragnvald a sardonic smile.

"Do you want him?" Ragnvald asked again. Oddi so rarely asked for anything, even obliquely, that Ragnvald wanted to grant him this. "I'll keep this Alarr for you at Sogn and train him among the local boys—then you can free him if you wish. He'll never overcome the stain of letting himself be enslaved, though. It might be better to sell him south."

"No," said Oddi. "It would not be better to send him among foreigners. Bring him up, train him, and he can guard my old bones when I can no longer fight."

Ragnvald was not sure he wanted to put a sword in this child's hands, for the boy might one day decide he wanted revenge for his father's murder. Yet he had won his stepbrother, Sigurd, to his side, even after killing his father. He found it darkly amusing: the idea that he should lead an army composed of the sons of men who had met their deaths at his hands. Let the skalds sing of that, not of hall-burnings.

✛　✛　✛

RAGNVALD LOOKED BACK at the convoy of ships for the tenth time that afternoon, the hundredth time that day, the thousandth since they had left Naustdal. He scanned the horizon for a ship that might be Solvi's, and might bear Svanhild among its passengers. It seemed strange, with so many rumored raids by Solvi and his men, that he had never seen either of them, as though a strand of his fate had gone astray. He had heard that Svanhild had a son, a son that should have been a foster-son to him, for a sister's sons should be as close to a man as his own.

On the other side of the ship, Arnfast watched the horizon. Ragnvald knew he feared the cost of Herlaug's wound, and what it would mean for his family, though Ragnvald had promised to defend him. Ragnvald wished Oddi sailed with him, to raise Arnfast's spirits, but with so many ships, he needed Oddi to captain one of them. The convoy stretched behind him, swelled with Vemund's ships.

Grai and Illugi sat playing dice near the mast, ignoring the passing islands. Their company made a poor substitute for Oddi's; they only reminded Ragnvald of the bad advice he had given Harald. Grai and Illugi had been right about Vemund's hall, and the ease of trapping him there. Harald valued Ragnvald's cleverness above all other things, and Ragnvald could not let himself make mistakes like that, not if he wanted to remain one of Harald's close advisers.

Oddi rejoined him that night when the convoy beached on a grassy island at the mouth of Sogn Fjord. Yellow and green striped the pastures on the cliff tops. Harvesttime had almost arrived, a good time to return home. Ragnvald had never spent a full autumn as king in Sogn, celebrating the harvest with blessings and sacrifices as a king should, without Harald calling him away.

"Remember we won, even if you don't like how it happened," said Oddi. He sat by Ragnvald's side, watching the evening sun play over the fields. "And my brother Heming should have stopped Vemund's rebellion. Maer was his to subdue and defend."

"Perhaps it is too big for one king," said Ragnvald. Better to think of politics than Vemund's hall, all those who burned alive, drowning in flames. In his dreams, Ragnvald heard the screams that the roaring of the fire had covered. If he told Oddi his dreams, Oddi would understand, or claim to. But Oddi would also tell Ragnvald that a willing bedmate and a skin of ale would put such things out of his head, and Ragnvald should try it for once.

"Neither my father nor Harald would agree with that," said Oddi. Hakon and Harald had managed to remain allies since the battle of Vestfold by spending as little time together as possible. As long as Hakon thought Harald would keep his promise to give kingdoms to Hakon's sons, he made his warriors available to fight Harald's battles.

"Oh, they agree about something?" Ragnvald asked, amused.

Oddi chuckled. "My father and Harald agree that Heming has disappointed them."

"It was Solvi's father, King Hunthiof, who let Maer become a haven for sea kings and bandits," Ragnvald reminded him.

"Yes, and Heming was supposed to clear them out. That is why Harald gave him Maer to begin with."

"Heming failed in that. Now we can all agree."

Oddi raised his cup. "I will toast to that. Agreement among all of Harald's allies. May it last longer than this ale stays in my belly before I have to piss it out."

"Indeed," said Ragnvald, draining his own glass. "It may even last twice that long." Hakon never stopped pressing Harald to give Geirbjorn and Herlaug districts of their own, but Harald wanted to delay until they reached manhood at age twenty. This year, Harald must make good on his promise for Geirbjorn, or see Hakon turn into an enemy. Oddi had stayed out of the conflict by swearing brotherhood with Ragnvald at the same Sogn *ting* when Ragnvald became king, an oath that placed his loyalty to Ragnvald above even family.

When Ragnvald asked him why, he said that he would not strive with his brothers for his father's favor. "I chose the brother I prefer," he added sometimes, when ale made him affectionate. Ragnvald had pledged his brotherhood as well but was glad that friendship with Oddi did not hamper his ambition. He could not set that aside as easily as Oddi had.

✤   ✤   ✤

AS RAGNVALD'S SHIP passed the final bend the green slopes of Sogn rose in the distance. His new hall, gleaming golden in the sunlight slanting through gaps in the clouds, sat halfway up the hill. White sheep dotted the meadows, eating the rich grass of summer's end. Two small figures became visible as the ships drew closer. His sons were old enough to play within view of the hall without a nurse to mind them. They sat next to each other on a rock, one head brown and the other gold.

He waved from his ship and they waved back. They grew larger with each gust of wind that carried the ship forward until Ragnvald could see them perfectly: Einar, with Vigdis's red-gold hair and his own severe features, and Ivar, Hilda's first son, with her even, serious eyes, Ragnvald's dark coloring, and a beauty that owed more to the gods than to his parents. He was, in Ragnvald's estimation, a boy without fault—except perhaps his attachment to his half-brother, Einar.

As soon as Ragnvald's ship touched the shore, he leaped out and splashed through the shallow water to pick Ivar up in his arms. He kissed Ivar's cheeks and touched his silky hair. Ivar smelled of sweetgrass—perhaps he had come from the barn where new-baled hay made an enticing fort for a young boy. Oddi greeted Einar, giving him a bow that bent his head almost to the ground. Einar did the same with an ironic slant to his lips, a strangely adult expression on his young face. Oddi and Einar had a bond that Ragnvald noticed from time to time, composed of rituals like this, and exchanges of looks that Ragnvald did not trouble to understand.

"Father," said Einar, tugging at Ragnvald's shirt. "Something has happened." Ragnvald ignored him and tossed Ivar onto his shoulders. Ivar's fingers tightened in Ragnvald's hair, a sensation that finally drove thoughts of Vemund's hall from his mind. Here was Ivar, future king of Sogn, for whom Ragnvald fought and strove.

"Something happened, Father," Einar repeated.

"He told us not to tell," said Ivar.

"Father should know," said Einar. Ragnvald was usually inclined to take Ivar's side, but Einar's words concerned him.

"What is it?" Ragnvald asked.

"Men came," said Ivar. "They took over the hall. They are having a feast tonight to welcome you."

Ragnvald looked up at the hall, which still seemed as peaceful as when they had arrived. "Who came?" he asked.

"He says he is Atli Mjove," said Einar. Atli the Slender. Atli had been in Ireland at the Norse court in Dublin when Ragnvald wintered there on his first raiding voyage, in Solvi's service. Atli was a jarl, wealthy from raiding. Ragnvald had only seen him from afar in Dublin; one of Solvi's young followers would not have reason to speak with such a wealthy man. He had heard of Atli's exploits since and thought him another sea king without a home, king of waves and the rocks and the gold he carried, the slaves he sold, the men who fought by his side.

"What happened?" Ragnvald asked.

"Men—they had swords. One said—" Ivar began.

"Atli said that Sogn was his, and that he was here to take it back," said Einar, defiant now. He sounded pleased that he should remember this and be the one to tell Ragnvald.

"What of your mother? Your brothers?" Ragnvald asked roughly.

"They are alive, Father," said Einar. Ragnvald wanted to shake him for more answers, but it was useless to try to get information from barely weaned children.

On the hill above, a curl of smoke drifted up from the hole in the hall's roof, showing white against a sudden patch of blue sky. In the fields, the sheep's minder, a lanky boy in blue trousers, picked slowly between the rocks, two reddish dogs at his feet. All seemed to be as it should. Though more people should be out of doors on an evening like this, with no rain and winter soon coming to lock them all inside.

"No one has come to greet us," Oddi agreed, then touched Ragnvald's shoulder. "Except your sons. It cannot be very bad if they still live."

"Hide yourselves among the rocks here," Ragnvald instructed the boys. "Do not follow me up to the hall."

Ragnvald assembled his men on the beach. After the long journey they looked weary. Ragnvald did not want them to have to fight again this summer. Oddi stepped forward and spoke: "We have been gone longer than we hoped, and now your king faces a threat at home." He glanced at Ragnvald, waiting for him to continue.

"You fought for Harald," said Ragnvald, "who wants a Norway free of bandits, where men's homes are safe. You fought for me in Maer, and you deserve your reward. Now come with me and free my hall from this interloper so I have a place to feast you and toast your accomplishments." The words sounded hollow to Ragnvald even as he said them. A king should be able to keep his home safe, at least, if nowhere else. Still his men cheered for him, and followed him, their steps thunderous as they climbed the hill behind him.

When his force reached the hall, Ragnvald gestured for men to fan out and surround it to prevent anyone from exiting through other doors, just as they had done at Vemund's hall-burning. He banged his fist on the great doors that, when opened, allowed five stout men to enter abreast. Carvings of wolves and dragons, made by Harald's master wood-shapers, adorned them.

The doors swung open, and a tall, slim man stood at the head of a group of warriors—Atli the Slender. He lowered his shield to reveal the silver mail of his armor, and the bright silk of his tunic. He had ash-colored hair, and an ill-favored face: narrow with bulging eyes and lips too full and red for a man.

"Ragnvald Eysteinsson," said Atli in greeting.

"King Ragnvald of Sogn," said Oddi, standing at Ragnvald's side. "Whose hall you trespass."

"Trespass? I greet him under the laws of hospitality. His lady has prepared a feast so we may welcome him home."

"Who are you to give me welcome?" Ragnvald demanded. "You have not given me your name."

"This is Atli Kolbrandsson, called Atli Mjove, rightful king of Sogn," said Atli's second, a burly, thick-bearded man.

"You have no claim to Sogn," said Ragnvald. "The bones of my ancestors are buried here. My father, grandfather, who was king of Sogn, and his father before him, also king, and great-grandfather all the way back to Odin himself are buried in this ground."

"Odin's bones are here?" Atli asked with a smirk. "I must have a look around for them."

"Where are your family laid?" Ragnvald asked, annoyed that Atli did not show fear.

"Here and there," said Atli. "I am told your grandfather left some of my grandfather's bones here when he betrayed his king and took his place."

Ragnvald lunged forward, but Atli parried him easily. He wore a sardonic smile and moved in a graceful, sinuous way that made his slenderness into beauty. A man who moved like that would be a dangerous swordsman, impossible to predict. And Ragnvald was tired.

"King Ragnvald," said Atli, still holding his sword at the ready, "thank you for building a hall for me. I'm sure King Harald, who thinks so highly of you, will find you another kingdom and another hall. He has promised this one to me."

"That is a lie. I have two hundred men," said Ragnvald. "I do not need to trade insults with you. You can die here if you like, or quit my hall and live."

"Funny," said Atli. "Those are the same words I said to your brother." He still held his sword up, its tip perfectly still, as though the blade weighed nothing to him, while Ragnvald's arm grew tired.

"Where are my wife and children?" Ragnvald asked. "If they live, then you may live." He did not want to pour out his men's blood, or anyone's, on his own hearth. His hall had only seen peace until now.

"They are well—I am not a killer of women, children, or womanish men." Behind him, Ragnvald's men stirred. The insult was aimed at his stepbrother, Sigurd, though, and Ragnvald would not be facing Atli now if those words did not have some truth in them. "Come and feast with us," Atli added.

"You will not offer me hospitality in my own home. You will leave tonight. My men's swords have tasted blood recently, but they are still thirsty."

Atli looked unconcerned. "Your men look weary to me. Come and rest. If I cannot give your men hospitality, then you can give it to mine, and in the morning you and I can travel to King Harald, and let him decide who has rights to Sogn."

"The man who holds it," said Oddi hotly. He advanced forward to press his shoulder against Ragnvald's.

"That would be me then," Atli replied, though he gave Oddi a wary glance.

"Very well," said Ragnvald tightly. "You and your men may eat and rest here tonight, and in the morning you will be gone, or my men will wet their swords again."

"May the gods smile upon your gracious hospitality," said Atli. He made an ironic bow. "No man can know his fate."

Atli dismissed his men and they retired back to places within the hall and tents outside. They had passed enough time here to make themselves at home. Ragnvald sheathed his sword. He felt as though Atli had somehow won their confrontation by maneuvering Ragnvald into letting his men stay the night and feast. Behind them stood Hilda, her face shadowed in the hall's dimness. Ragnvald stepped forward and let his eyes adjust to the light.

"Welcome home, husband," she said, bowing her head. "A great feast has been prepared for you and your men." Ragnvald had seen the meanest farmer's wife rush to embrace her husband when he came home from raiding, yet he and Hilda remained frozen.

"Come into the—what is wrong, Hilda?" Ragnvald asked. "Come to me."

She stepped forward, her face still downcast. When she raised it, he saw a purple bruise on her cheek, marked in the middle with flesh burst like a star, now knitting together. Her eye was swollen as well on that side.

"The silver mirror you gave me does not show a face that a husband would like to see," she said.

Ragnvald put his hand to his sword again. "I'll kill him," he said.

"You have given him hospitality," she replied. "And besides, it was not Atli Kolbrandsson who did this."

"Who then?" Ragnvald asked.

"One of his men. And Atli killed him in punishment. All is well, husband."

From behind him, Atli said, "No price is high enough for the wounding of your wife."

Ragnvald whirled to face him. "Leave Sogn now and abandon this baseless claim. Will you pay that price for my wife's bruises?"

"That I cannot do," said Atli. Ragnvald had already grown to hate his cheerful, ingratiating voice. "I owe my followers a home."

"You caused my wife's injury," said Ragnvald. "No matter which of your men did it."

"Husband, I am well. It will heal," said Hilda. She still hung her head down.

"She is more than well," said Atli. "She stood before all of my men, daring them to kill her, so your brother could get your sons away. You have chosen a fine wife."

"I do not need you to tell me that," said Ragnvald. His anger felt cold and clear. "I am inclined to kill you anyway, and ask Harald to pardon me for breaking the laws of hospitality." He heard Atli's men moving behind him, forming up to protect their leader.

"Harald might, though he and I are friends of old, but would the gods?" Atli asked.

"Ragnvald," said Hilda. "Please."

"Get out," said Ragnvald to Atli. "Let me greet my wife without my enemies as witnesses."

"I am not your enemy," Atli said over his shoulder. Ragnvald wanted to argue, but from the short time he had spent with Atli, he already knew that for a fool's errand. Instead he turned to watch Atli and his men leave the hall to him and Hilda alone.

"I am sorry," said Hilda. "This is not the welcome you deserve."

"And you deserved better than this," said Ragnvald. He reached and she flinched at the touch of his fingers, gentle on her cheek.

"He told me to hang back," she said. "He said that you would kill him if you saw my face first."

"I would have," said Ragnvald. "And I will, but not today, not if you do not wish it. The gods will have their hospitality. Atli did not offer you any other insult?"

"He scared me, that first day," said Hilda, "but since then he has been a good guest and set his men to help with the harvest." She still looked down until Ragnvald touched her chin and forced her to look into his eyes.

"Truly?" he asked.

"Truly," she said. "It has been humiliating, sometimes, to wait on him, but he has done no harm."

"He has done some harm," said Ragnvald, "and I fear he will do more. How did it happen? How did he come here?"

She told him of being surprised in her own hall, Sigurd and Ragnvald's guards overwhelmed by Atli's quick action against them. "Then he told me that he would not hurt us—his men would not even touch our thralls, if I did not sanction it." Some angry tears shone in her eyelashes. "And I did not." Her fierceness lent her beauty.

"How long has he been here?" Ragnvald asked.

"Ten days. I thought about poisoning him," said Hilda, with faint humor. "But he is not so bad as that. I would not mind him as a neighbor like I do as a master."

"What of the children?" Ragnvald asked.

"They are well enough. Einar hates Atli. Ivar likes him," she said.

"Ivar could learn more sense," said Ragnvald. "But it is not a bad thing to try to make friends with an enemy." A small boy must do that, lacking any other power. Ragnvald had other options.

8

SVANHILD PRODDED GEIRNY UP OVER THE DUNES UNTIL THEY had gone far enough that the sound of the waves and the wind in the grass would hide any noise from their speaking. She pulled the sock from Geirny's mouth, still holding the dagger at her throat. Geirny jerked her chin away and sank to the ground so Svanhild had to sit down with her to keep the blade against her skin.

"I have you at my mercy now," said Svanhild. "So let us discuss the terms of my letting you go alive."

"You are as cruel as he," said Geirny. She raised her tied hands to wipe the tears from her face. "You suit each other well."

"You threatened me." Svanhild's unsteady hand had made the skin under Geirny's jawline red, a series of little scratches on her fair flesh. "You threatened my family."

"This has nothing to do with you."

"We need to stay here in Iceland. I will let you go if you convince your father that Solvi may stay here."

Geirny laughed, hollow and wild, sounding as mad as she had when Svanhild met her in Tafjord, as Solvi's first wife. Perhaps she was, and could not be convinced of anything that did not originate in her fevered mind.

"Why did you come here today?" Svanhild asked. "Do you want to force him into taking you back?"

Geirny laughed again. "No. If I had known he was in Iceland, I would never have come. When he divorced me, my father scolded me for letting the daughter of a dead farmer take my place as the wife of a king's son. As though I wanted a place with that deformed little dwarf. Your face is pretty enough, but perhaps you are as twisted as him under your clothes, and together you will bring forth dwarf children. Freya knows that he could never get whole children on me."

"Daughters," said Svanhild. "Daughters are still whole. And you murdered them."

"You don't know what it was like," said Geirny. "I once thought I wanted your dwarf to suffer, but now I would rather not be reminded of him at all."

"What did he do that was so terrible?" Svanhild asked.

Geirny craned her neck around so she could look at Svanhild, hardly flinching when the movement caused Svanhild's knife to cut her. She stared at Svanhild until Svanhild had to meet her eyes. "You love him," she said.

"Yes," said Svanhild.

"Then you are a fool. You saw what Tafjord was like. What it was. There were no women except slaves who Hunthiof's and Solvi's men raped every day. I hated that place, and I hated giving my body to him. When I had my first daughter, I gave her to a wet nurse because I could make no milk, and I cried. All I did was cry. Hunthiof came to me and said that Solvi would be happier if I let him expose our daughter so I could try for a son, so I let him do it. I hated myself after, but at least, I thought, I had done what my husband wanted. Then when he came back, he was furious with me. I never fell pregnant again. I hated him, so I told him that I'd killed his daughters. But I would have killed them rather than let them be brought up there." She was sobbing now.

"Be quiet or I'll hurt you again," said Svanhild. She could see all too clearly what Geirny had endured, the underworld that Tafjord had been.

Geirny continued in a harsh whisper. "Would you want a daughter to grow up in a place like that, Svanhild, truly? What if Solvi had left you there instead of taking you with him?"

"I would have left on horseback, or on foot, or hired a ship. I would have gotten away," said Svanhild truthfully.

"And what if they came to drag you back?"

"Is that what they did to you?" Svanhild asked.

"No," said Geirny. "I thought they would have, though."

"It is easy for one person to hide," said Svanhild softly. She did not want to feel any sympathy for this woman.

"I would envy your certainty that everything will always go your way, if I weren't sure the gods will teach you differently one day," said Geirny bitterly.

"Why are you here then?" Svanhild asked. "Why don't you go back to Norway?"

"I told you. My last husband died, and I am under my father's control again."

"Not if your husband had money, land."

"He was a younger son. I—it's complicated. My father needed me."

"And now, though you did not need to be here, you are trying to upend my life," said Svanhild.

Geirny laughed. "You are so naive. Ask your husband why my father wants him gone."

"It was you. It's because of you," said Svanhild. "Tell him you don't care and he'll let us stay."

"Your dear Solvi"—she said his name as though it tasted bad—"made a deal with my father. My father wants him to fight Harald. Solvi asked him to make these objections so it would be easier to convince you."

Svanhild sat back, taking her knife from Geirny's throat. She still held the rope around Geirny's wrists, though if Geirny wanted to, she could rip it from Svanhild's hands. She did not doubt the truth of Geirny's words. Solvi thought like that, in twists and turns. He had often told her that if you felled the right tree, it would bring down the whole forest.

"I'm glad he did," said Geirny. "You should know what your husband is. Anyway, I do not want to share a land with him any more than he wants to share land with me."

"Then go home," said Svanhild quietly. "I will spare your life and let you go, if you ask your father to bring you home."

"We don't have a home anymore." She slipped back against Svanhild's leg, and Svanhild grabbed her by the shoulder to make her sit up. "My father came here to find allies, and I will help him in that."

"If you hate my husband, then why do you want him by your father's side?"

"He will help my father win."

Svanhild felt panic begin to grip her again. She was all alone here, acting against even her husband. Nokkve could demand a payment for the wound and insult to his daughter. Svanhild dragged the point of her dagger over the scratches already on Geirny's throat, slowly, in a way she hoped was as frightening as it was painful. "You will stand on the top of this dune and make an oath for all to hear that you are willing to have me and my family stay in Iceland. That you do not want Solvi to fight by your father's side. Then I will let you go," said Svanhild.

"You should let him go fight his war," said Geirny. "Then he will die, and you will be a rich widow."

Svanhild gagged Geirny's mouth again, shoving in the sock until Geirny choked and whimpered, and then sat down next to her in the sand. She pulled tighter on the rope securing Geirny's wrists, so Geirny could not break away. She listened to the surf, the crawling of little animals around the sea grass. The sand of the dunes stayed cool even as the rising sun began to heat Svanhild's shoulders. Her eyes became gritty with missed sleep.

She heard the stirring of men in the camp, and then yelling when they discovered that Geirny was missing. They would find Svanhild soon enough, unless she did something first. She dragged Geirny up to the top of the dune so she could look down on the camp, and before the exertion could make her winded, she forced Geirny to her feet, and put her knife against her neck again.

"Solvi and I have as much right to settle in Iceland as anyone," Svanhild said. "We do not need to fight your war." Men arming themselves turned to look up at her. One of Gudbrand's sons rushed forward and Nokkve put an arm in front of him to hold him back.

Solvi gestured to the other men to stay where they were, and stepped forward, looking up at Svanhild, his eyes beseeching. "Come down here. You are doing yourself no good."

"I am doing this for us!" Svanhild cried. "You want to put our family in danger. Tell them, Geirny."

"She told me to say—"

"No, you have to swear it," said Svanhild.

"How much do you trust an oath given with a knife to my throat?" Geirny asked.

"Women's oaths don't matter," said Gudbrand. He gestured at his sons, who began to climb the dune toward them. Svanhild pressed her knife deeper into Geirny's throat.

"I hate Solvi Hunthiofsson. I don't want him fighting on my father's side," said Geirny. "Now let me go, you harridan." She swung her bound hands to the side to elbow Svanhild under the ribs. Svanhild coughed, her knife slipping from Geirny's throat for a moment. Geirny took the chance to pull herself loose from Svanhild's grip.

She had spoken the words though, so Svanhild did not chase her. Geirny stumbled down the dune and into her father's arms while Gudbrand's sons advanced on Svanhild. One of them grabbed her wrist and squeezed until she dropped the knife. The other picked her up, slung her over his shoulder, and carried her down the hill.

He dropped her at Solvi's feet. "You need to keep better track of your woman," he said.

"King Nokkve," said Solvi. "I apologize on behalf of my wife. I will pay your insult price, and I will certainly fight Harald with you."

"You should have told her the truth," said Nokkve to Solvi. "This was contrived so you would not have to face your wife, and my daughter has paid for your cowardice. I thought it harmless fun. Now I have to question your judgment."

"Don't be hasty," said Gudbrand. "Solvi can recruit raiders from every shore, and win any sea battle. We cannot succeed without him." He gave Svanhild a cold look. "He would not be the first man made foolish by his wife."

✛   ✛   ✛

SVANHILD FOUND NO one willing to talk with her on the trip back to the Smokey Bay settlement. She sat on a rowing bench with her back against one of the boat's knees—not comfortable, but it let her lie still, dozing with her eyes half-closed. Solvi, with a man's pride and the need to appear undiminished, walked around the boat, commenting on the boat's construction, which had shorter strakes than he was used to because Iceland grew few trees taller than a man's height. He spoke to all on board, save Svanhild, and especially engaged Nokkve in conversation about how Nokkve might rule Romsdal when he won his kingdom back.

Gray clouds moved swiftly across the sky, and a shifting breeze kept the sailors busy trimming the sail, altering the course to catch it. Again and again, the wind failed to fill the sail and it hung slack and tired until Solvi took the steering oar and began calling out commands to Gudbrand's men.

"Truly you are the best of sailors," said Gudbrand when Solvi increased the speed of the boat, and the Iceland coastline flew by on their left. Gudbrand glanced at Nokkve. They had been carrying out this argument during the whole return voyage, more and less overtly, with Gudbrand praising Solvi, and Nokkve insulting him. Svanhild thought Nokkve would give in soon. Gudbrand had been correct—Solvi was widely respected. The king of every Norse outpost she and Solvi had visited for the last six years wanted to know what Solvi's plans were against Harald.

The boat reached the settlement in the late afternoon. Solvi helped Svanhild down onto the shore rocks, and walked with her, holding her arm, up to their campsite. With the tent empty—Katla and Eystein at Unna's farm—the hanging fabric made Svanhild think of a shroud. Both were made of the same weather-bleached homespun, and both enclosed a dead thing. No work was done in Svanhild's tent, no craftsmanship, no farming. It was a body without a spirit; a tent, not a home.

"I am tired and dirty," she said to Solvi. "I am going to take a bath."

"Svanhild, we need to talk," he said. He called her many things, "wife," "love," and other pet names, but rarely by her given name. It made him sound like a stranger.

"Bath first," she said. "We should find more servants if we intend to stay," she added as they walked up toward Unna's bathhouse.

Solvi did not speak again until they were both in the bath: a small building made of birch harvested from Iceland's dwarf forests. In the light from the bathhouse brazier, Svanhild started to help Solvi strip off his clothes. He stopped her when she came to his trousers. "Svanhild, you cost me today, in reputation and likely gold."

"You deceived me." She continued to work on the knot in his waist-cord.

"I knew you did not like the idea of my going to war again."

"I do not," said Svanhild. "The man I married is king of waves, not land. He takes what he wants."

"And yet you would tie me to this strange place, and make your sea king into a farmer."

"For Eystein," said Svanhild. "He is no sailor, and he never will be."

"That is why I would give him a kingdom," Solvi replied. "His inheritance should be a kingdom, and not a farm. As my father tried to leave for me."

"Now? He is a boy." She pulled her own dress off and sat down next to him on the dry wood, waiting for the bloom of sweat to clean her.

"He will grow into a man," said Solvi.

"Gods willing," Svanhild added.

"Gods willing," Solvi echoed. "A man with more ambitions than farming."

They were both naked now as newly formed humans, the bare branches into which the gods had breathed life. Svanhild stood, ready to berate him, to vent her anger with words, bow down his head with them. Sweat and lamplight made Solvi's beard glisten like gold. The pull she felt toward him was as much a part of her as her own skin, as their child. His ambitions were not Eystein's; they were a knife that would cut their family apart.

"You may die," said Svanhild simply. "I would rather have you living."

"All men die," said Solvi. "The fates have already measured out my life. Between now and then, I can only do what I must."

Svanhild remembered when she had first married him, she had feared that he had no honor, for he did not mind lying or cheating, and he broke his word when it suited him. Then she had found he did have honor, though he steered himself by his own star, and the words of other men did not sway him. She should have remembered that when Nokkve insulted him, then perhaps she would not have been fooled.

"What are we to do?" Svanhild asked.

"You could come with me," said Solvi. "You are very useful in a battle, and you can take care of yourself. As you have recently reminded me."

Svanhild flushed. She could wield a knife as well as any man now, though she would always be clumsy with a heavy sword. She had a good mind for battle tactics, and Solvi valued her advice.

"And what of our son?" Svanhild asked. "He would not be useful in a battle."

"Svanhild . . . ," he said. He would not be the one to say it, she knew. He kissed her instead, ran a hand up her arm. She and Solvi had not been parted for more than a day since Svanhild, pregnant with Eystein, bid Ragnvald farewell. When she had asked, with no hope of success, if Ragnvald would come with them. The thought of watching Solvi sail off and leave her for a year or more, perhaps heading toward his death, made Svanhild feel as though she were drowning in the hot close air of the bath. He was here now, flesh pressed to hers, but in a day, or a week, he could be gone, never to return.

"I don't want you to go," she said.

He stood and embraced her, and then pulled her down so she straddled his lap. He kissed her as she took him into her, and only moved a little, not seeming to want his release or hers, only to stay like this, joined, forever.

"I will miss this," she said as she moved slowly. "Will you miss this?"

"More than anything." He breathed. "So much I fear I cannot do without it."

"You must keep yourself safe so you can come back to me."

"Svanhild," he said again, burying his face in her neck, and moving in time to meet her. He made her cry out, and afterward she cried in truth against his shoulder. He held her until she stopped.

"I cannot," she said. "Eystein cannot travel with us."

"Wouldn't your Unna foster him? If you asked her?" Solvi asked. He reached out and caught her hand. "I cannot . . . do not make me leave you behind."

A breeze stole between the slats in the bathhouse. Unna might, and Svanhild could shed the shackles of motherhood the same way she had shed her earlier chains. Leave Eystein behind and let others mother him as best they could. She saw before her Ragnvald's face when she left, betrayed—but he had been a grown man, and Eystein was a child.

"I cannot leave him," she said. "And if you think on it, you will not want me to. The tides of battle are too uncertain."

"I know." He looked down at the floor of the bathhouse and sighed heavily. "I know—it is too dangerous. You may stay with Unna while I bring war to Harald. I will send for you when it is safe."

9

ATLI'S MEN AND RAGNVALD'S GATHERED AROUND THE COALS of the long fire in the Sogn drinking hall, as the evening sun shone through the open door. Servants poured ale for all and offered Frankish wine at the high table. Atli allowed himself to be seated below Hilda and Ragnvald without complaint, below even Oddi and a few of Ragnvald's other captains. Ragnvald watched the border between the two groups closely, to see if a fight would erupt. A bloodied nose did not break the laws of hospitality, and would make Ragnvald feel better even if he could not throw the punch himself.

Sigurd was still absent. Hilda had told Ragnvald that he had run off after Atli's coming. Ragnvald did not know if he wished that Sigurd had stayed—then he might have a companion in his shame, for both of them had failed to protect Sogn, in his way—or glad that he need not take responsibility for Sigurd's weakness. Ragnvald's mother, Ascrida, had been brought to the high table as well. She had become simple in her old age. She went where she was bid, and could perform easy chores, though she also had moments of stubbornness when she behaved like an angry child.

Atli complimented Hilda on setting a good table. "But then, I have grown to enjoy it often," he added, nodding at her. Hilda flushed, making Ragnvald wonder how much she had minded her unexpected guest.

"You have had great success, I think," said Atli, "judging by the ships in your train." His beard shone with the fat from the meat. He wiped it off with the sleeve of his shirt—a gesture that any man might make, but it annoyed Ragnvald. Sogn thralls must wash that shirt. Atli had brought only men to consume his resources, and no women to replenish them.

"We defeated Vemund," said Ragnvald.

"You spin a tale fit to pass a long winter's night!" Atli exclaimed. "I will send you a skald to accompany you on all your battles, if this is the type of story you tell."

"Ragnvald does not like to boast," said Hilda. "I have told you this."

"Your deeds have spoken for themselves," said Atli. "Far and wide, and beyond Norway's borders." His expression turned inward, at odds with the forced cheer in his tone. Perhaps this was a glimpse of Atli's true feelings, his jealousy that his name was less famous. "It is fitting in a king," he added, still grandly. The flattery pleased Ragnvald, against his will. Too often Harald and his other captains mocked Ragnvald for his short speech. He frowned at Atli; he did not want to like the man even a little.

"Yet it is not fitting that your men should go without praise," Atli continued. "Are you so closemouthed about their deeds?"

"Odd—Oddbjorn Hakonsson will call out their deeds if my own praise falls short," said Ragnvald. He did not want to give up any ground to Atli, even the freedom of Oddi's nickname. Atli took too much as his due already.

"Then let him praise your men tonight. They have come too far not to be feasted and rewarded properly."

"After we have set your ships on the whale's road again, it will be time to feast properly. Then we will have more to celebrate."

"Can you not be generous with your entertainment as you have been with your food?" Atli's voice grew louder. "I am your guest. My men and I both would benefit from the example of your fine company and their deeds. Let us hear them."

Ragnvald could see no way of winning this petty battle. He would indeed look churlish and ill-tempered if he refused to gift his men with their gold, and call out their deeds. Let it be done and let Atli see what fine men followed Ragnvald, heroes from all over Norway and farmers that he had forged into warriors. He glanced at Oddi, who shrugged. Ragnvald stood. Men around the hall grew quiet, set down their eating daggers, and held cups between their hands, ready to toast. These men would do what he asked and wished for his recognition above all things. It was a headier draught than any Frankish wine.

"Atli has asked for my generosity, and reminded me of my duty to a guest. He has asked to hear your deeds, and I would not let your praises go unsung," said Ragnvald. "Oddbjorn Hakonsson, your able captain, will begin. But"—he glanced at Atli—"there is much more to tell. I wish for each man among you to stand and give an accounting of the deeds of you and your fellows. Even a king cannot have eyes everywhere, and I know that deeds of valor large and small have taken place this summer. Let no man be silent if he has a tale to tell." Tonight Ragnvald would not need their swords to best Atli, only their words.

✢ ✢ ✢

OF THOSE SEATED at the high table, Atli nodded off first, followed by Oddi. Then Hilda gathered the children from where they lay dozing among the sleeping dogs and tucked them into their beds, behind curtains at the hall's perimeter. Atli's men began to droop after ten of Ragnvald's had stood to relate the tales of their small skirmishes. The snores of Ragnvald's men soon joined Atli's. Ragnvald had to pinch his thigh to keep himself awake as his warriors told their stories. If the talk flagged, Ragnvald roused himself to question the speaker and extend his tale. He pushed on through a haze of fatigue, finding that he did not want to sleep, even though his body craved rest. These tales told him parts of the battle he had missed.

Frakki had fought side by side with his best friend from childhood at their first stand against Vemund and saw him die three days later of a stomach wound.

Malmury, one of the few women among Ragnvald's fighters, had lost her right eye. Ragnvald decided to compensate her with a large chunk of an armband, hacking it to pieces on the table with an ax, and startling Atli awake for a moment. Malmury declared that she would rather have the gold than her eye, since she had never been a beauty. Those who remained awake toasted Ragnvald as ring breaker.

"Ring melter, rather," said Slagvi, a grim-looking man with a mean, twisted mouth. "It takes a hard man to stand by while other men burn," he said. Slagvi claimed that he had kept the fire burning all night, while other men withdrew. "I watched, just as you did, my lord." Ragnvald was loath to reward him—the fire had not needed tending, not that Ragnvald remembered. Yet reward him he did, for following orders, for not flinching from the fire's gaze.

At length all men slept, including Atli and his warriors. Even the last man to speak, Bergvith, who had saved his scouting party from certain ambush, sat down after his tale, dazed, and was asleep with his head on the table a moment later.

Ragnvald crawled into bed next to Hilda. Still asleep, she turned over to make room for him. He wished to wake her, not to satisfy himself on her, but to see a more pleasant sight than the rough faces of his men, still not washed from their journey. Ragnvald was finally home, and wanted to be wrapped in its embrace. He listened to Hilda's breathing until it finally sent him to sleep as well.

✢   ✢   ✢

WHEN RAGNVALD WOKE the next morning, Hilda's side of the bed was cool. Ragnvald felt relaxed and alert—better than he ought to after a late night of drinking. Today the hall would be his alone. He knew he must follow Atli to Nidaros to make sure Atli did not use his silver tongue to persuade Harald he had some claim to Sogn. Harald would never favor Atli over Ragnvald, but if Ragnvald were not there to defend himself, Atli could use his tale of taking over Sogn for ten days to his advantage.

Still, there would be time enough for Ragnvald to have some meals with his wife, play with his sons, and see how Sogn had fared this summer without him before rushing back to Harald's court. When Harald had made Ragnvald king of Sogn six years earlier, Ragnvald thought that the whole of his duty was to protect his subjects from raiders, collect taxes, and hold the year-turning feasts. He would let none of his subjects starve, of course, and if he succeeded in those aims, he would be remembered as a better king than his grandfather, and far better than his father, who had not even been acclaimed king by the Sogn *ting*, had only managed his own estate, and that poorly.

Ragnvald had hosted a harvest festival in his first year as king, and attracted only a few of his subjects, though he sent messengers in every direction carrying his invitation. The food he asked Hilda to cook had spoiled without enough guests to eat it, and thralls fed it to the pigs. Ragnvald assembled a band of warriors and set out to collect the taxes he owed Harald, which at least some of his subjects should have brought to the festival in the form of livestock, grain, and cheese. He would, in turn, give his taxes to Harald as silver, timber, or furs. Ragnvald's first stop was at the farm of Lief Liefsson. He had visited Lief's farm with his father as a boy—the elder Lief had a herd of cattle that dwarfed the herd at Ardal. When Ragnvald became king, his son Lief had twenty cows, which still made his one of the richer farms in Sogn.

"What happened to your fine herd, Leif?" Ragnvald had asked him. "I thought to borrow one of your bulls to service our cows at the hall."

"Starved," said Lief. "Another bad winter like the last, and the herd will not survive."

Ragnvald had not thought it a particularly bad winter. Then, he had spent it with Harald at Vestfold, where the weather was milder. "How did you come to such a pass?"

"Too many raids from other districts—carried off all the good stock, and what is left breeds sickly. They don't give much milk, the calves don't survive. My brother Leiknarr thought he would fare better in Iceland, so off he went. Also, he fought for King Gudbrand in Hordaland and feared Harald would not like him here."

Harald might care about the allegiance of Leiknarr and once-rich farmers like him, or he might not. Probably not, as long as none of them decided to call himself king and take a king's privileges. "I will send my men to borrow your strongest bull as your season's tax," said Ragnvald. "I will ask for no more than that."

He found the same or worse at most of the other farms he visited on that first circuit. The farmers on poor land owned no livestock at all except some stringy chickens that rarely laid eggs. At many farms, the damage had been done by earlier raids that were never answered in kind. The farms that had held on to their wealth boasted many sons who grew to manhood and could wield a sword well enough to raid the livestock back from their neighbors. That was as it should be—raids of neighbors were for sharpening the skills of high-spirited boys, not draining away Sogn's prosperity.

Ragnvald could not give Harald taxes from Sogn that year, or any year since. He spent all of his first winter in Sogn making plans, and in the spring, he began to use the gold he had won fighting at Harald's side to gift all of the farmers who attended his feasts with calves and sheep. He took Lief with him to visit other districts and buy livestock from them, for Maer had fared better over the last few years. Though Maer's farmers raided one another, King Hunthiof and Solvi had been too fearsome for raiders from outside the district to trouble them. Each year Ragnvald poured what he won from Harald's wars into Sogn's farms, and each year they grew a little richer.

Now Sogn farms produced as much as they had before Ragnvald's father died. In another three years they could sell cows, sheep, and goats to the kingdoms that had first supplied them, and begin to replenish the gold Ragnvald had spent. Would Atli have done that as king of Sogn, or would he have taken what little Sogn's farmers still possessed?

Atli's was the first face Ragnvald saw in the hall after pushing back the curtain that hid his bed from the common area. He sat dicing desultorily with one of his men and pushing his spoon around a bowl of steaming porridge. He grinned when he saw Ragnvald. "Good morning, Ragnvald Eysteinsson. In wakefulness, at least, you are a hero without peer!" If Atli's head pained him, it did not show. Well, he had slept longer than Ragnvald, if less comfortably.

Ragnvald put his hand to his sword. "My hospitality extended through the night, and I slept late enough to give you plenty of time to be gone."

"Come, you kept us up so late, I was certain you had changed your mind and wished to extend our stay." Atli ate a spoonful of his breakfast.

"Were you certain of that? Truly?" Ragnvald asked. "I promise, I have not."

"Do you withdraw your hospitality, then? Is it to be a battle?" Atli spoke the words as a jest, his red, too-full lips opening over half-chewed food and making Ragnvald's stomach unsteady. A servant appeared at that moment with some light ale and a bowl of porridge. The smell of food settled his queasiness. He was only hungry.

"If you like," said Ragnvald, imitating Atli's jesting tone with an edge. "Since your men cannot move with enough speed to have cleared out by morning, and there are fewer of them than mine, I will let you be the one to decide."

"My brother king," said Atli, "can we not stop this bickering until we have a judgment? I have been promised Sogn as you have."

"You are no king to call me brother. I cannot believe that Harald promised you Sogn," said Ragnvald. "Tell me truthfully what you were told, and I may hold back my men's swords."

Atli took another bite of his porridge, chewed, and swallowed it, and wiped his mouth with his shirt again, leaving a smear upon the fabric. "It was not Harald but his closest adviser," said Atli. "Lord Guthorm told me that you were so often absent from Sogn on his nephew's behalf that it needed a true king."

Ragnvald had long felt Guthorm's animosity, and if Atli spoke truly, now he had proof. "And he thought that I would hand over Sogn to you without a fight?"

"He thought I should see what needed doing here, and I found you absent, just as he said."

"I can't tell which of us is being misled," said Ragnvald, "and I don't care. Sogn does not need you for a king. You have tangled Guthorm's words to your own ends."

Atli shrugged. "Perhaps. The way I see it, the only thing to do is go to Harald, this most just of kings, and let him decide. Together. I could have run off and stolen a march on you, yet I did not. I want this done fairly."

"I would gladly agree to meet you there in a few weeks," said Ragnvald, "and let you pour whatever you liked into Harald's ear in the meantime. I do not need that advantage."

"We are both for Harald," said Atli, "so we should be friends, and arrive as friends. You are cleverer than I expected, though. Guthorm told me you were a solid fighter, but too quick to anger, and to take offense. Last night you proved that you can make a joke as well as any man. I slept well, though, so the joke is on you—"

"You do chatter on," said Ragnvald testily, trying to discern insult from flattery in Atli's cascade of words. "I have been long from home. I must oversee the harvest. Remove your men from my hall. I do not care to where, but leave Sogn." Atli's style of speech was catching.

"My men are farmers too," said Atli. "Farmers without homes. Now that Harald has made Norway safer, he invited us home. We will help with your harvest and travel together to Nidaros in plenty of time for Yule."

Ragnvald did not want to do murder under his own roof, or order his battle-weary men to another fight, not when they all ached to go home to their own farms. Atli had done no damage here, except to Ragnvald's pride, and even then, he had given no outright insult. He had punished the man who had harmed Hilda.

"Very well," said Ragnvald. "Your men may camp in my fields. If they help with the harvest, they will be fed."

"Excellent," said Atli.

"I expect your men to behave themselves. If any of them commit a crime, all will be counted guilty, and punished."

"I will fill a basket with their severed hands if any of them are caught stealing," Atli agreed cheerfully. Ragnvald could not frame an adequate response to that, so he shooed Atli off. Atli ordered his men out of the hall. They moved with impressive speed, even with aching heads, and made camp on the sunny side of Ragnvald's hall, while Ragnvald went to tell Hilda what he had agreed to. He had been bested again, though he was not sure exactly how it could be an advantage to Atli to arrive together—perhaps Atli wanted them to be friends, to gain whatever advantage he thought Ragnvald's friendship could bestow. Or perhaps he could not approach anything directly, but must tack after it, missing, and aiming again, blown from his goal by his own contrary spirit. But no, Atli seemed more like a cunning man who had gamed this out many moves ahead.

+ + +

RAGNVALD WATCHED HILDA run her boar-bristle brush through her hair, counting out the strokes under her breath. When she reached a hundred with one handful of hair, she moved to the next. Unbound, her hair puddled around her as she sat on the bed. It glowed in the candlelight, as smooth and inviting to the touch as tallow-finished oak. She bent, and the candle behind her showed the outline of her breasts through the thin fabric of her underdress. She had grown heavier with the bearing of each of the children, and looked forbidding when fully clothed, solid as a fence post. Here, in private, Ragnvald saw her beauty again, the soft curves of the woman he had married.

He had spent the day visiting the farmers in his district whose lands bordered his own, to find out how their summer had passed. Sigurd should have been here to report to him. He sighed angrily, and Hilda turned to look at him.

"No, continue," he said. "I do not want to disturb such beautiful work."

She smiled, the curtain of her hair hiding her bruised cheek. She held the brush out to him, a little hesitantly. Sometimes in the winter he did this for her. He rarely had the time or patience when he was home in the summer, after a long day doing whatever work Sogn's rulership required. He took the brush and sat behind her, noting the part she had made to divide what was done from what was undone. He worked out the tangles from the bottom first, thinking of Svanhild carding wool, the task that she spent most of the winter doing, since her spinning did not live up to their mother's standards. Hilda's hair was autumn, not winter, a deep brown with the golden highlights of a long harvest afternoon.

"What are you thinking of?" Hilda asked, carefully keeping her head still as she spoke.

"You'll make me lose count," said Ragnvald.

"You're not counting," said Hilda. "You've gone past a hundred already."

Ragnvald reluctantly set aside the handful of hair that he had been brushing, letting it slide over his hand before picking up the next.

"Where is Sigurd?" Ragnvald asked.

"Atli's men made him the butt of their jokes," said Hilda. "They did not harm him. Or any of us. Yet . . ."

Ragnvald could see it. Sigurd had grown up into a warrior of surprising physical talent, and little sense. His pride was like a boy's, innocent and easily wounded.

"You know him," said Hilda. "He goes up to stay with my father sometimes. You know he and my brother are friends."

"Your father makes him feel important," said Ragnvald. Of course Sigurd would go there to lick his wounds. Hilda let him finish the rest of her hair. When he was done, she took the brush from his hands, and began plaiting her hair into the long tail she left it in while she slept, a rope thick enough to tie a warship to shore even in a gale. After she finished, she took his hands, and lifted them to her lips, kissing each, one at a time.

"Atli is still here," she said.

"He told me he means to stay until I will go with him to Harald so each of us can argue our case."

Hilda let go of his hands. "And you agreed? Do you fear that Harald would give away your land? Does he hold your loyalty so cheaply?"

"No, Harald would never do that," said Ragnvald.

"Then why would you go?" Hilda asked.

"Atli won't leave unless I go with him," said Ragnvald.

"You've only just returned," said Hilda. She took his hand again. "Your sons miss you."

"I missed them." He pulled her closer to him. "And you."

"Atli is still here," she said again, with different meaning. She pushed at him weakly.

"So you refuse my bed?" Ragnvald picked up the end of her braid and brushed it over his fingers. She could not object to this touch. "Perhaps I should kill him after all. Then he could not spread tales to Harald."

"No," said Hilda. "Not under our roof."

She yielded to him then, and unbound the hair she had just braided so she could lay it across his body, but when she spread her legs she said, "Be careful. I do not want to be pregnant again so soon."

He stopped before they could join and rolled on his back on the bed next to her. "We only have three sons, and no daughters. A man who is rich in children is wealthy no matter what else befalls him."

"It is too soon," said Hilda. "Rolli is not yet weaned."

"Being careful is how we got Rolli," said Ragnvald. Hilda had not wanted to be pregnant then either, and then he had agreed and tried to spill his seed on the ground whenever they lay together, but still she became pregnant.

"He is a joy. But you must be more careful."

"Another one might be a joy as well."

"His birth nearly killed me," she said with a shaking voice. "If you cannot be careful, then take one of the thralls instead."

He looked up at the ceiling. He had been away in Nidaros for Rolli's birth, and had returned to find his wife quieter, more inward-looking than she had been before—the marks of a confrontation with death. It had been a year, though. He felt her heat beside him, and wanted to be in it, part of it. He never liked rutting with thralls. A thrall had no choice but to submit, and, in the best case, seemed to accept it as a duty. In the worst, well, some men seemed to like a crying woman, but Ragnvald did not. "I do not want a thrall," he said.

Hilda turned onto her side to face him. "A concubine, then."

"You sent Vigdis away," Ragnvald reminded her.

"Yes. Do you want her back?" Her voice grew cold.

"I want more sons. And daughters to marry Harald's sons."

"Then you need a concubine younger than your stepmother," said Hilda.

✢ ✢ ✢

RAGNVALD PASSED THE next day doing harvest tasks, making sure Sogn was ready for the coming winter. He had just finished counting and inspecting his cattle, newly returned from the shieling, the high pasture where they grazed during early summer, when Oddi fell into step with him, Einar bounding after them.

"Tell your father what you told me," Oddi said to Einar. He lifted Einar up into his arms, Ragnvald's little son who did not like to be touched by anyone. He sat in the crook of Oddi's shoulder as though it were a hall's high seat.

"What?" Ragnvald asked.

"He overheard some of Atli's men—"

"Eavesdropping?" Ragnvald asked.

Oddi gave Ragnvald an irritated look. "Paying attention. Listen to him."

Ragnvald looked at Einar. His son resembled Vigdis too much for Ragnvald's comfort, and reminded him of his conversation with Hilda the night before. Ragnvald had gone out to sleep among his warriors, leaving Hilda to her empty bed.

"One of Atli's men said that your grandfather killed his grandfather by treachery," said Einar. He scowled. "He told a long story. I don't remember all of it."

"That's what Atli said to me," said Ragnvald. "It doesn't make it true."

Oddi set Einar on the ground, and he ran off to where Ivar played near the open kitchen door. "Yes, but he's trying to convince your men of it. And your son."

"Of course." Ragnvald sighed. "This is why he wanted to stay for the harvest. I should have known."

"Yes, you should have," said Oddi. Ragnvald looked at him sharply. Oddi rarely criticized him so directly. "And you should be kinder to your son. He is a very clever boy. He could be a great credit to you, or he could stab you in the back."

"It's the latter I fear," said Ragnvald. A child so cool and watchful unsettled him.

"He fears you and worships you," said Oddi. "You may not see it, but if you treat him as your stepfather did you—"

"You compare me with Olaf?"

"Yes," said Oddi. "I don't think you mean him harm, but you will make him cruel and fearful if you are not kinder to him. It is not too late. If your Ivar is to be king of Sogn after you, Einar will be his right-hand man, as valuable to him as you are to Harald."

"I am not so valuable to Harald," said Ragnvald. "He sent this Atli to me."

Oddi gave him a sardonic smile. "Maybe he wanted to get rid of him and trusted you to do it."

✛ ✛ ✛

WHEN RAGNVALD INQUIRED about the behavior of Atli and his men, Fergulf, the steward of the farm at Sogn, told Ragnvald that Atli's men were always the first to wake and go out to the fields, and the last to come in and eat at night, but lacked skill. Hilda told him they had blistered hands from scything the grass for hay, and came to her for salves of precious beeswax.

During harvesttime even men who had their own cottages came to the hall to eat. Atli stayed out of Ragnvald's way. He ate with his own men, and slept with them in tents that ringed the hall and made it look as though a *ting* had sprung up there. Ragnvald joined them that evening, bringing with him a servant who carried a bowl of rich, sour *skyr* fermented from the farm's best milk to add to the men's meals of stewed meat that had been stretched thin with porridge and onions to feed all of the hungry mouths at the hall.

Ragnvald brought his plate to Atli's end of the rough, outdoor table where they all ate. "Your men work hard," he said.

"Thank you," said Atli with a quick and insincere smile.

"Have any of them ever helped with a harvest before?" Ragnvald asked.

"No, but there is nothing they won't do if I ask them," said Atli.

"It shows," said Ragnvald. "They work hard, but they are not much help without knowing their craft. From now on, they will be paired with my men, who can better show them how to put their remarkable strength and loyalty to better use." He stood, taking his untouched trencher with him, and turned back after he had left their circle. "Unless you would rather go. I would gladly meet you in Nidaros in a few weeks."

"Of course we will stay and help," said Atli, without a smile this time.

Behind the table where Atli and his men sat, a party of men approached across the field, leading a number of ponies laden with baggage. As they drew closer Ragnvald saw among them his father-in-law, Hrolf Nefia, his son, Egil, and, by Egil's side, Sigurd. The ponies would carry furs, then, for Ragnvald to trade in Nidaros. Ragnvald waved a greeting and walked across the field to meet them. The situation with Atli and his men was volatile enough without bringing Sigurd back into it, at least not before hearing what he had to say.

"Well met, Father," said Ragnvald when he reached Hrolf's group. "You are welcome here. My hospitality is open to you as always, though my hall is rather crowded right now."

"Greetings, King Ragnvald," said Hrolf. He wore fine clothes in many bright colors, and a giant silver belt buckle that Ragnvald had gifted him. Ragnvald's generosity had improved his fortunes over the past five years. When Ragnvald went to Hrolf's home to take Hilda back as his bride, he had arrived with Harald, Oddi, and Sigurd by his side, all in their finest imported silks. Harald bought a number of the fine ermine furs that Hrolf traded from the Keel's trappers, and promised to send his agents to purchase all of the rest so they could be sold in his new capital. Dazzled, Hrolf had happily given Hilda in marriage the next day, celebrated by Harald's men and all of Hilda's sisters. And Ragnvald had always made sure that Hrolf did not regret the match. He had paid for the new outbuildings that housed the mountain ponies that Hrolf used to bring furs down to Sogn.

Ragnvald felt Atli's presence by his side, and introduced him before Atli could say anything. "This is Atli Kolbrandsson from Dublin. Do not trust a word he says."

Hrolf laughed. "Very well, I won't."

"Atli, this is my father-in-law, Hrolf Nefia, his son, Egil, and you know my brother Sigurd."

"Your brother?" Atli asked. "I thought he was only your stepbrother."

"He has been a brother to me, so he deserves the honor of that title," said Ragnvald. "If he is so much as scratched while you are both at Sogn, you will suffer for it."

10

IN THE WEEKS THAT FOLLOWED SVANHILD'S ATTACK ON GEIRNY, Solvi and his men spent most of their time in negotiations with Gudbrand and his allies. The argument over whether to attack Vestfold or somewhere on the west coast of Norway seemed interminable to Svanhild. She hoped they would argue long enough so that winter would prevent any ships from departing. Solvi brought Svanhild to Geirny's tent, outside a half-built turf hall, and required her to make a humiliating apology, along with a gift of jewels to pay for the offense. Svanhild felt the sting of embarrassment keenly and avoided the company of all Icelanders save Unna and her family.

"You must claim your land before Solvi leaves," said Unna as she and Svanhild walked out to the edge of Unna's land, searching for one of Unna's ewes. "If you claim land, Solvi will be forced to hire men to farm it, and to defend it. If he leaves before you do it, you will have nothing, only his gift to me to feed you and your son through the winter."

The sulfur in the air was strong today—rotten egg with a tang of metal in it—a choking scent that rolled down from the smoking mountains and cooled, so the air seemed thick and viscous when it reached the lowlands. Some days Svanhild could not smell it, and she wondered if it had become part of her skin and her breath, the way a fisherman always smelled like his catch. Or how Solvi smelled of sail wool and seawater, even when he was far from his ships.

Unna gave Svanhild a knowing look when she hesitated in reply-
ing. "You must secure Eystein's inheritance. What else do you have to
give him?" If Solvi did not return from the coming war, then Eystein's
inheritance would be a handful of treasure cached all over the Norse
and Irish coasts. Solvi had a magpie's love of bright objects, and as
little idea as a magpie what he should do with them.

Svanhild took Unna's elbow so they could steady each other over
the uneven ground. "Solvi is a good father," she said. "He will do right
by Eystein."

"Where is he now?" Unna asked.

For a moment, Svanhild did not know if she meant Eystein or his
father. She had left Eystein behind with Donall, who Eystein liked,
even if they had trouble understanding each other's words. Donall
had a knowledge of livestock that surpassed most of Iceland's other
farmers, and many of them called on him to heal their sick animals.
Svanhild thought Eystein would like to learn these skills from him.

"Solvi is speaking with . . ." Svanhild waved her hand toward the
dwellings near the bay. Everyone in the settlement knew of the battles
brewing and each had a differing opinion. Some feared that attacking
Harald from Iceland might bring his forces down upon them. Some,
mostly nobles who had left Norway rather than swear to him, hoped
for the allies' success, even if they would not go themselves. Many did
want to go, and every day more promised to sail with them. Svanhild
found it restful that Unna had not yet shared her own opinions about
the planned attack.

Unna made a skeptical noise and tightened her arm in Svanhild's.
"Every man will fail you eventually," she said. "Look to your own
future."

"Solvi is not every man," said Svanhild, though without conviction. If only Eystein could stand sailing better, Svanhild would take
him and join Solvi. She need not fear violence; she and Eystein were
both ransom prizes too precious to harm, equally valuable to Solvi
or Ragnvald.

A droplet of rain fell on Svanhild's arm. She looked up the slope,
into the wind. She did not yet know Iceland well enough to tell which
clouds brought weather and which came from the volcanoes that

expelled their smoke and ash into the sky. Eystein loved this land already, the flowing green grasses that rippled over the hills like another ocean, and the black rock on the sides of mountains that met glaciers of searing white. He loved the plants and growing things, and often brought her butterflies and ladybugs that she let crawl over her hands. A few days earlier, he had brought her a small vole, its fur as soft as the hair on his head had been when he was a baby. He had sat all afternoon, he said, with a crumb of bread in his hands, waiting for it to lose its fear of him. In Svanhild's grasp, the vole shuddered and trembled, as though it might shake to death, until she released it among the grasses to find its own kind.

A crying noise stopped Unna, and Svanhild with her. Unna crouched down and listened. The bleat came again from a hollow in the grasses, and Svanhild saw a tuft of wool caught in a thistle nearby.

"Help me," Unna commanded. A small ewe, younger than most of Unna's flock, was kneeling on its forelegs hidden by a tuft of grass. "Hold her," said Unna. Mud pulled at Svanhild's feet. She looked down at her shoes: fine worked, embroidered in crimson and gold floss. Solvi would drape her in gold for the seagulls to admire if she let him.

"Well?" said Unna. Svanhild took her shoes off and walked down into the water barefoot. She expected cold, but it warmed her chilled feet. A hot spring must run off here. No wonder Unna grew such lush crops.

The ewe rolled its head, wild and frightened, and showed the whites of its eyes. It tried to find purchase with its forelimb and then cried when the broken bone collapsed beneath it. Svanhild crouched next to it, and petted its head, oily with lanolin and matted with mud.

"No, hold its hindquarters," said Unna. Svanhild moved farther back and did so, while Unna looped the ewe's head under her shoulder and, with a hard stroke of her dagger, cut its throat. The blood warmed the water further, and dyed Svanhild's toes pink.

"I'll send Donall out here to fetch it for supper, or it will draw wolves," she said, wiping her dagger in the grass. "Too bad—I liked this one's wool, though she never had enough sense to stay out of the nettles." Unna touched the stem of the plant with the tip of her dagger, and stepped carefully around it. "Sweet, but only if you can grasp them."

"I used to be good at this," said Svanhild. She pulled her own dagger and used it to cut low on the stems of the nettles while she wrapped her hand around the leaves so they protected her from the barbs. These would make a flavorful stew.

"What will you do if you do not claim land?" Unna asked. "Solvi could be gone for years."

"Stay with you, if you will have me," said Svanhild.

"I would," said Unna, "but we are strong-willed women to share a household for long. Better you claim some land—you can stay with me for the winter, and in the summer hire men to build you a house of your own. Perhaps your Solvi will win and can send you timbers from his district, and you will have the finest house in Iceland."

"I don't think Ingolfur would like that much," said Svanhild.

"He will always have his chair posts," Unna replied, with a quirk of her lips.

Still, Svanhild hesitated. Solvi did not want her to take this step. They had visited many places where Solvi might have been granted the land of the conquered. Islands in the Hebrides were as fertile and green as this. With the Irish subdued, they might even have taken land outside Dublin, if Solvi had been willing. They had little to bind them to Iceland—no one here did, except exile.

"What if he wins and I have to go back to Norway?" Svanhild asked. She looked up at Unna.

Unna shrugged. "I will run it for you while you are gone—for a portion of the output. Do not worry about that."

"Solvi won't like it," said Svanhild. The peace between them these past few weeks was fragile and hard-won. If she did nothing, and waited until he was gone to make her claim, she would avoid another argument—but Unna was right, she needed him to buy slaves, and pay laborers to work it for her. Her jewelry, fine as it was, would not buy the years of hard work that turned scrub forest and heather into farmland.

"It is easier to ask for forgiveness than permission," said Unna.

"That is a boy's reasoning," said Svanhild.

"And I heard that sometimes you wore trousers and rubbed dirt on your face pretending to be a boy in Solvi's service," said Unna. Svanhild smiled—she had done that at the battle of Vestfold to secure Solvi's freedom. "You must do this to secure an inheritance for your son. He will not want his father's ships."

Svanhild told Unna she would do it the next day. That morning, Solvi seemed pleased with himself, saying that he had not formed an agreement but was bending Gudbrand and Nokkve to his way of thinking. Only Rane, backed by the Swedish king, preferred to start his conquest in Vestfold.

"I told Rane I would go to the court of Eirik myself and make him see that he will get more for his investment this way," Solvi said to Svanhild in their tent, that morning. "Then we'll attack in the spring. Eirik will listen to me. Rane is only a minor jarl."

"What of Ulfarr? You sent him to Tafjord," Svanhild asked. She cared little for Ulfarr himself, but he had protected Solvi well since boyhood. If he must be anywhere, Svanhild wanted him by Solvi's side.

"Yes," said Solvi. "I had meant it for a raid only, but if Ulfarr draws Harald's forces to Tafjord . . ." He trailed off, then kissed Svanhild on the lips excitedly. "Yes, you are right. They will certainly follow me to Tafjord if I tell them Harald will come. Thank you, my sea queen." Svanhild watched him go, bemused. She had not wanted to make this war any easier for him.

Svanhild brought Eystein and Katla to meet Unna at the edge of her land just before sunrise the next day. The ritual required her whole household, all who planned to work the land and profit from it. She would begin her homestead with herself, Katla, and Eystein, and add to it later: servants and thralls, bought now with plunder and later with lengths of wool cloth woven from her own sheep. In exchange for Katla's participation in the ritual, Svanhild had promised her a dowry so she could make a good marriage, and if she had sons, Svanhild would give them portions of land on which to live. Katla's usually truculent expression became more open at Svanhild's offer.

"If you live up to the trust I have placed in you," Svanhild said to her, "you may even be housekeeper and oversee all of this land, to be trusted to make all of the decisions I would make when I am gone."

A man could make a claim by lighting bonfires in sight of each other, and all the land within their perimeter at the end of the day would be his. A woman's portion was smaller: she could claim the land around which she could lead a heifer in a day. This close to fall, the day was not much longer than the night, and Svanhild must walk quickly, pulling a plodding cow. Unna had gifted her a sprightly young heifer, barely older than a calf, who often galloped in Unna's fields for its own pleasure.

Unna knew the prayers well enough to act as priestess. She spoke the blessings to Freya while Donall, in his strange accent, gave the responses of Frey, the god of fertility. Unna placed a flower crown on Svanhild's hair and draped a garland around her wrists. She put the cow's lead rope in Svanhild's palms, and draped another garland around the cow's neck. Hops, barley, rye, and wheat, braided with the grass that fed the sheep. As soon as Unna spoke the blessings and bid her go, Svanhild took her first step.

Her pockets bulged with carrots and packets of grain sweetened with honey, as many inducements as she could carry to keep the cow moving. Katla carried a bronze dish that contained hot coals, bright with little licks of fire. With every step Svanhild declared herself the land's mistress, showing her household's mastery over livestock and fire. That was what Unna said: with the right blessings, this magic would bind the land to her and her line for all time. Donall followed, keeping watch over Eystein, and marking the edges of Svanhild's land with sticks thrust into the ground.

A few days earlier, she had paced out this land, to see how far she could walk between sunrise and sunset. The blessings worked best if she completed her circuit ending where she began, enclosing the land as the garland encircled her head. The cow half led her at first, thinking the walk a game, but as the day wore on it became weary. Svanhild saw the land differently today, when every footfall claimed it for her. At the first turn of the path, she stumbled and almost dropped the cow's rope. Stones would follow in each of her footsteps, and grow into a fence that marked off her land with cairns, blessed by fire and prayers to the fertility gods at each turning. Now the path took her upward, up the slope of the smoking mountain. Svanhild had to pull on the heifer to make her climb.

In the afternoon, Eystein grew tired of Donall's company and walked quietly by Svanhild's side. Small creatures ran over the bare, volcanic sand among the explosions of grass. Crickets jumped away from her feet, brown and silent, though Svanhild remembered hearing their song in the spring and summer. Winter and death would come for them soon. She would make no mark upon this land except by the invisible signs left by the ritual until the coming of spring. Over the winter Svanhild would need to prepare everything she could to be ready for the short growing season. She sensed Eystein becoming ever wearier, his shoulders drooping, but concentrated all of her attention on coaxing the heifer forward. If she stopped, it would be very hard to get the animal moving again.

By the time she neared the end of her circuit, she could think of nothing else except the aching of her legs. She heard Unna making encouraging noises, and plodded forward, keeping tension in the rope, and sometimes turning to hold forth a carrot for the cow.

"Svanhild," said Unna sharply, cutting through her concentration. "These are the last few steps. You must make the final prayer, and then this land is yours and your descendants'. Do not worry about him."

In her haze, Svanhild thought Unna meant Eystein, silent and pensive a few paces behind her, until she glanced up and saw Solvi standing, watching her, his face still as a carven figurehead. He was not happy—she read that in every line of his body—but she could not think of that now. She crossed the last few steps, to the same patch of earth where she had begun this journey. It was strewn with the petals of the flowers Unna had decked her in. Along her journey, the garland around her wrists had slipped off, and the wreath around her head fallen apart, so only straggling twigs clung to her hair.

She spoke the words as Unna prompted, again beseeching Frey and Freya for fertility in her land and in her body. Only then did she let go of the cow's rope. It shook itself and gave an irritated moo before putting its head down in the grass.

"What witchcraft is this, woman?" Solvi asked. In her exhaustion, Svanhild could not tell if he addressed her or Unna.

"I have claimed land here for our sons," said Svanhild. Solvi's face twisted slightly. Svanhild had not meant to say sons. They had one son, and by unspoken agreement, neither blamed the other for the lack of others.

"His land is in Maer," said Solvi. "But now you have bound us—" He cut himself off. "Is this business done now?" he asked Unna.

"Yes," said Unna, her voice hard. She crossed her arms over her chest.

"Return home with me then," said Solvi to Svanhild. "We have much to discuss." She followed along after him, feeling like a scolded child again, but in no way sorry for her deed.

"I did what I thought was necessary," she ventured, after they had walked in silence for a time. Eystein did not speak either. Svanhild glanced down at him. He had been so good today, with few complaints about the long walk. He must have felt the weight of this ritual, the bindings that she had laid upon both of them.

"We will speak of it later," said Solvi.

Svanhild stopped. "Why? So your men can hear us argue?" At her side, Eystein flinched away from the anger in her voice. "Go on ahead to our tent," said Svanhild to Eystein. She leaned down to push back his hair and kiss his forehead.

"They can hear us now well enough," said Solvi. "Sound carries over this plain. Women, alone, making a procession over the fields—it was bound to be noticed. Did you think I wouldn't see?"

"Would you have done it with me?" Svanhild asked. "You are sailing away from me, perhaps to your death. Battle is uncertain. What am I—what are we supposed to do without you?"

"Trust me, and the gods," said Solvi. "I thought you did not want to be tied down."

"I am tied," said Svanhild. "I cannot escape it. I am tied down by you, by our son, by a future that you will not face."

"What do you propose to do with this land?" Solvi asked scornfully.

"I will farm it," said Svanhild.

"You alone?"

"No, I will need to hire men to help me clear the land and build a house. You can bring me timber from Norway."

"I can, can I?"

"Do you mean for me to live in a tent all winter? To wait and depend on others' charity until you return?"

"No," said Solvi. "It is you who seem to think that I would leave you with nothing, so much that you had to grab this land for yourself."

"What would you leave me with? Gold that will run out while you are gone? Should I hire a ship to find your other treasure? I mean to sustain myself—sustain our family—until you return."

"You have bound yourself to this land," he said. "What if I return, and tell you Tafjord is ours, and that is our home now? Will the gods allow it?"

"I think they must," said Svanhild. "Men are always coming and going from here. Go win back Tafjord and then we will see."

"What if they do not let me win now—what if you have forced their hand and bound us here?"

Svanhild was taken aback. She had known Solvi was superstitious, as all sailors were, but she had not thought about this, that he might feel as though the gods would deny him another blessing, having given his family land in Iceland. "Then it is well you did not participate in the ritual," said Svanhild. "The land is mine, not yours. It passes to my line. You are free."

"I don't want to be free of you," he said. "You are the one fleeing from me."

"Tell me, which of us is sailing away?" Svanhild asked.

A spill of hot, sulfurous air swept away her words, rushing across the plain, making her eyes and her throat taste like blood. She looked for Eystein where he walked toward their tent, and saw his spindly form weaving among the tufts of grass. And slowly, like the capsizing of a ship, she saw him lose his balance and fall.

II

WITH ATLI, HROLF, AND SIGURD ALL SHARING THE DINNER
table that night, Ragnvald feared an outbreak of hostilities, or at least
arguments he would have to settle. If only Atli had not come, he would
be enjoying his homecoming with his family, sharing the spoils of his
summer of war, and settling in for a winter of peace. Instead his hall
was too full of men, all at odds with one another. It was no better than
being at Nidaros in Harald's court.

Before preparing to leave, Ragnvald visited a few nearby farmers,
hoping that a summer away would be enough time to notice a change
in them: middling farms becoming rich, poor ones climbing out of
bare subsistence. He looked everywhere for signs, happy when he
rode past a field with all of its grass close clipped by the teeth of sheep
right up to the base of the stone wall. A goat walked along the top of it,
keeping pace with him for a while, and Ragnvald smiled at its insolent
curiosity.

When he returned in the late afternoon, Hrolf was waiting to speak
with him. Ragnvald was surprised—Hrolf liked to be waited upon,
not to wait for others. Hrolf caught the bridle of Ragnvald's horse and
held him steady while Ragnvald dismounted.

"Sigurd came seven days ago," said Hrolf. "He said he wanted to
walk the trapping lines and learn that trade, so he and Egil went up
into the mountains." Ragnvald sighed at their folly. While Egil was
more of a farmer than a trapper, living at the margins of the moun-

tains he had learned some of that craft. Sigurd was far too old to begin the trade. Of course they had returned to the hall at Sogn instead.
"They brought back more than furs. Your brother has convinced my
son to leave Norway and claim land in Iceland."

"Sigurd is not apt to convince anyone of anything," he said to
Hrolf. "More likely it is the other way around."

Hrolf grabbed Ragnvald's arm. "You must persuade Egil not to go."
He gave Ragnvald a pleading look that kept Ragnvald from reminding
him that as a king, no one except Harald told him what he must do.
"Find a place for him in Sogn. You cannot still blame him for what he
said or did not say at the *ting*."

"What you pushed him to say," Ragnvald reminded him. Hrolf
looked abashed. When Ragnvald had needed his friend Egil to testify
on his behalf at his *ting* trial, to get payment after Solvi tried to kill
him, Hrolf had pushed his son to lie. Now when Ragnvald gave Hrolf
and his daughters gifts and arranged fine betrothals, he did it as much
to remind Hrolf of how wrong he had been as to please Hilda.

"He is my only son," said Hrolf. "So he will inherit my farm and
the trapping rights. But it is a small, poor farm, and he wishes for
adventure."

"I remember a time when Egil feared doing anything you did not
sanction," said Ragnvald. "But if he wants a place in Harald's army, I
will ask for that favor."

Before Hrolf could reply, Egil fell into step beside them, making
Ragnvald's horse shy to one side. "I heard my name. What are you
saying about me?" he asked.

"That I will ask Harald for the favor of giving you a place in his
army," said Ragnvald. "Warriors may grow wealthy in his service."

"Taking land and gold from rightful kings," said Egil scornfully.

"If they swear to Harald, he does not take their gold," said Ragnvald.

"He takes it in taxes if they stay, and their every possession if they
leave. How does that make him lawful? No assembly voted him king."

"Who have you been talking with?" Ragnvald asked. "Sigurd did
not put these ideas in your head."

"Men of Sogn," said Egil.

"See what I have to contend with?" Hrolf asked.

Egil could do what he wanted, but Ragnvald felt an odd disloca-tion at the idea of Sigurd sailing away from Sogn. "Leave me," he said to Egil and Hrolf. "I will speak with him."

Ragnvald found Sigurd at a small stone table a short walk away from the hall. He was scraping bits of dried flesh off a tattered pelt. As Ragnvald watched, he made an impatient motion that further ripped the skin, and then flung it away onto the muddy ground. He stood when he saw Ragnvald. He had grown tall and well favored, and though his face was not handsome in repose, a smile could turn it winning.

"So you are going to Iceland now?" Ragnvald asked him. "What of Sogn? I need you here. You cannot flee whenever something goes wrong."

"Why, because people will call me a coward? They should. I am ashamed."

"You are not a coward," said Ragnvald, irritated. "Hilda told me that you wanted to attack them and she kept you from it—that is not cowardice. Tell me—why were so few men guarding Sogn?" Rag-nvald had spoken with his guards Dusi and Fergulf, but he wanted to hear what Sigurd had to say.

"They all wanted to go back to their farms," said Sigurd. "It's harvest-time. And Atli and his men came overland, not down the fjord where you have your scouts." Ragnvald had expected raiders from the sea, since Sogn Fjord was the only road that could carry enough men to threaten his hall at Sogn. Or so he had thought. "Why did you let him stay?" Sigurd asked plaintively. "Atli—I thought you would kill him, and then I would never have to see him again."

It was a fair question. But if Ragnvald killed Atli, then some might later say his claims had merit. Ragnvald had given Atli hospitality, which Atli had exploited to the utmost, but he had given it. Atli claimed Harald's friendship. Atli was too slippery to kill. Ragnvald had a dozen reasons he could tell Sigurd, but the truth was that he had arrived home too weary of death to seek Atli's.

"Things have passed beyond that," he said to Sigurd.

"Brother, I am sorry—Hilda said it was better to live than to fight—

they would have killed me quickly. I've never even killed a man, but I would have fought if I thought you wanted me to. I would have died to protect this hall, even if it were in vain. I—"

Ragnvald held up a hand to stop his speaking. "You did—your best. You could have signaled to the scouts to come and help . . ." He stopped. He would have time enough later to lesson Sigurd about all the ways a smaller force could best a larger one, if their leader knew the territory and the interlopers did not. And as soon as Ragnvald settled his business with Atli, he planned to spend some time at home and command Sogn's guard himself. Let someone else fight Harald's wars for a season.

"You should come with me to Harald's court and join his army," said Ragnvald. "You have done a fine job guarding Ardal, and then Sogn for me all these years. It is your time for glory."

Hope leaped in Sigurd's eyes for a moment, but then his shoulders slumped forward again. Ragnvald realized he should have made this offer long ago. Sigurd might not be a clever man, but he was good enough with a sword—he could serve Harald well. Ragnvald had kept Sigurd at home when he should have been fighting battles and winning treasure.

"Who will guard Sogn while you fight for Harald?" Sigurd asked.

"I can find someone," said Ragnvald. Arnfast would be a good choice for now—he could not fight by the side of Herlaug Hakonsson until the boy's face healed, if ever. "You deserve your reward."

"Don't," said Sigurd. He looked away from Ragnvald, down the slope where sheep grazed, white puffs on green. "Egil is going to Iceland, and I am going with him. You gave me a home when you could have killed me. I was a coward and I took it. And I let Atli take Sogn without even fighting him. I don't know why you don't kill me for that now."

"Because you are my brother, or as close as I have to one," said Ragnvald. "Because no man can choose his father or we both might have chosen differently." Without Sigurd, he would have no one at Sogn who had shared his boyhood with him, who had seen all that he had done and still stayed by his side. Svanhild was gone with Solvi. Ragnvald had killed his foster-brother, Einar, and his stepfather. He had driven off Vigdis, and his mother's mind was all but lost. "Harald will give you all you could desire. And I will give you a farm when you return."

"You are too generous," said Sigurd. "Egil is right—I need to discover what I can do on my own."

"It is a king's task to be generous, and in that I have failed you," said Ragnvald. "Let me do something for you."

"Everything I have comes from you," said Sigurd. "I have to know if that's all I am." He gave Ragnvald a brave smile, though his eyes shone with unshed tears, and Ragnvald decided to argue no further. Most men fled the truth of their weakness; Sigurd fled to confront his. Ragnvald could only admire him for his choice.

✝ ✝ ✝

PAIRING ATLI'S MEN with Sogn men served its purpose, and soon the harvest was finished. Ragnvald grew eager to leave, for with Atli present, Sogn felt like a trap. Sigurd and Egil left on overnight trips to nearby farms to recruit other settlers for their journey to Iceland. Ragnvald tried to pay their plans as little attention as possible. They would likely become discouraged when they realized they would never find a ship to take them before winter prevented passage across open sea, and Sigurd would stay.

The night before the harvest festival, Ragnvald was able to join Hilda in bed before she had fallen asleep. All of the men at Sogn were too weary to fight this evening.

"Husband," said Hilda with a smile. Ragnvald felt almost grateful that he was too tired to desire her. He could avoid that fight, and accept her sleepy affection.

He climbed under the blankets and curled himself around her. Her height meant that each of her curves fit into the space he made.

"Come with me to Nidaros," he said. "I will leave Arnfast here to guard our hall—no one will want him in Nidaros after he laid open Herlaug Hakonsson's cheek to his molars." He felt her flinch at the description. It was just as well Atli was forcing him to Nidaros early. Ragnvald needed to plead Arnfast's case for him and ensure he had to pay the wergild for only an accidental wounding. "You will see

Harald's new halls," he added more gently. "He is building a town full of artisans who craft wonders. And what he cannot make there, he will trade for, so there will be nothing that cannot be bought. Come with me."

"We need some new field slaves," said Hilda. "Two of them ran off over the summer—I think they sold themselves onto a ship for Iceland."

"Harald will give us some. Come with me." Ragnvald wanted to see the wind blow her hair about, to see her occupied with things other than the running of a household, the cares that had bound her for their whole marriage.

"The children . . . ," she said, wavering. She wanted to be convinced.

"Bring them too. They should know the sea, and Harald should meet the boys who will be his own sons' closest companions."

"Is it safe?"

Nowhere is safe but the grave, Ragnvald almost said, but did not want to make Hilda think of death again. "It is hardly autumn yet. It is as safe as staying here."

Those words still seemed to trouble her. "Yes, nowhere is truly safe for our children, is it?"

"I would enjoy having them with us," said Ragnvald. He stroked her shoulder until he felt her relax again.

"Then you shall," she said. "When do you—when do we leave?"

"As soon as possible," he answered. "While the sailing is still good."

✝ ✝ ✝

IT TOOK A few days to ready the traveling party. Hilda had endless questions about what the boys would need, not only on board the ship but also at court in Nidaros. Atli too wanted to negotiate with Ragnvald about which of his men he should bring with him, and which he should leave in Sogn. Ragnvald told him that since he depended on Ragnvald for transport, he should count himself lucky Ragnvald did not require him to walk back the way he came. Atli and his men had come from Nidaros by land, a journey Ragnvald could hardly imagine through dense, trackless forests. Atli looked as though he was tempted, and closed his eyes in fear when he stepped onto the ship.

"If I haven't killed you yet, I won't do so at sea either," said Ragnvald, enjoying Atli's uncertainty.

After most had boarded the ships, Ragnvald bid good-bye to Sigurd. "I will see you when I return after Yule," he said.

"We mean to be gone by then," Sigurd told him.

"Do you have a ship?" Ragnvald asked.

"Egil says we will find one."

Ragnvald doubted that, but he did not know what was in Egil's mind. He looked at Sigurd, and for a moment thought he could see through him, as though Sigurd were already a ghost, or departed, never to return. He reached out to grip Sigurd's forearm and made sure Sigurd met his eyes before he said, "You are always welcome at my hearth. Tomorrow or ten years hence."

"I will always count you a brother." Sigurd stepped forward and gave him a firm embrace.

Strong emotion made Ragnvald's throat tighten, and he pitched his voice low to hide it. "Thank you, brother." He held Sigurd's arms for a long moment before letting him go. As he turned to leave, he glimpsed the grove of trees beyond his hall where he held the district's sacrifices and rituals. As king, Ragnvald was priest of his Sogn, elevated in the eyes of the gods as well as men. He turned back to Sigurd and put his hands on Sigurd's head. "Odin give you wisdom, Thor give you strength, and Njord protect you at sea," he said. Then, as a cool breeze from the fjord made him shiver, he added, "And let Ran's eye pass you by."

Sigurd bowed his head, and Ragnvald turned away and went down to the shore to board his waiting ship.

✤   ✤   ✤

THE WIND BLEW hard against Ragnvald's ship as he tried to depart from Sogn. With every difficult tack it felt as though the gods were advising against this journey. Hilda sat at the stern holding Rolli. Ivar and Einar were together, as always, climbing over everything, and racing around the ship. Ragnvald's men made space for their play;

they were both graceful boys, and, while loud and underfoot, they rarely caused real trouble. Thorir, only a year younger, tried to chase after them but could not keep up.

Ragnvald had elevated Malmury and Frakki to be his personal guards, for they had impressed him in their battles with Vemund's forces. He chose Malmury initially because he thought she might annoy Atli, but she acted much as a man would, including pissing against a tree with her pants down at their first campsite, and so Atli treated her as one. Soon Ragnvald forgot that she was any different from his men, just as he had in Naustdal. With the seamed red scar that creased the eyelid of her missing eye, she seemed far more akin to one of his warriors than to Hilda or even Svanhild.

Atli tried to play with the boys, but they preferred Oddi above all other adults, and wanted little to do with him. He went to talk with Hilda for a time, and it appeared a pleasant enough conversation. Hilda had adapted well to shipboard life. Ragnvald had hardly been able to picture her away from Sogn, making her daily progress from cooking to cloth making to caring for their children and back again. That night she turned the camp into a small version of her kitchen, pounding and boiling dried fish into an edible meal at night, and spinning while she watched the boys play in the shallows after dinner.

Atli sat next to Ragnvald when they ate dinner. Though Ragnvald had allowed Atli to bring some men, Atli had left most of them in Sogn, still clinging to the idea they would become Sogn farmers. "You have a handsome family," he said.

"You would know," said Ragnvald. "You have seen more of them than I have lately."

"I've a wife, but I need some land to plant her on, and my sons too."

"Where are they?" Ragnvald asked.

"My eldest, Aldulf—called Aldi—is in Nidaros, and the others are in Dublin, or thereabouts. It's been a few years since I saw them."

"Perhaps you should ask Harald for some land that is not already taken, and bring them there," said Ragnvald.

"Perhaps that land that you took from King Vemund when you

burned him alive," said Atli brightly. He must have known that memory troubled Ragnvald; he had a nose for such things.

"Tell me again what Guthorm said to you when he was giving
away land that isn't his," said Ragnvald.

"I reminded him that my grandfather was king of Sogn," said Atli.
"My father always told me this." He sucked at the bones of the seabird
he ate for dinner, smacking his lips too loudly.

"My grandfather was king of Sogn," said Ragnvald. "I do not wish
to hear more of your lies."

"You asked." Atli seemed quieter here, subdued by the sound of
wind rushing down the fjord, blowing the smoke from their cook fire
back toward Sogn. "And Harald did tell me that there was land for me
in Sogn. When he and Guthorm visited Dublin looking for allies."
Before Ragnvald had even met Harald.

"Why did you take so long to come and claim it then?" Ragnvald
asked.

"I was raiding. And my wife likes the court in Dublin. She need do
no work other than embroider fine cloth, and share cups with great
warriors at the feasting table. I brought her gold, and took my sons
raiding with me when they were old enough. There was no reason
to leave."

"Why now, then? Why should there ever be a reason to leave such
bounty?" Ragnvald asked with heavy sarcasm. Atli had lived as Solvi
did, depending on his gold and other men's generosity for a place to
sleep.

"I made the crossing in the spring, from Dublin to Nidaros. I meant
to see Harald's new court, offer my ships for his wars, and see if any
of the gold that flocks to him wanted to fly to my hand instead." He
looked carefully at Ragnvald. "You have made that crossing, I think.
I hear that is when you became Half-Drowned, and gained that scar."

Ragnvald touched the scar that tightened his right cheek, a ha-
bitual motion, one that he never realized he was making until his
fingers traced the ridge of skin. The scar that pulled at his mouth
made his smile into something mocking—he knew, for he had tested
it many times in Hilda's silver mirror.

"It is a long journey," Atli continued, "around Scotland, and through the strange currents of the Orkney Islands. The winds nearly blew us onto those cliffs more than once. But that was not what changed my mind. We became calmed in the middle of the North Sea. Hard to imagine, I'm sure—that place always seems to be blowing in one direction or another. It was a misty morning, or afternoon, or evening—I don't know, but there was fog all around us, and no difference between sky and water. The calm lasted perhaps two days, summer days, with neither sun nor dark. It was a strange time for my men as well. We thought we had sailed into one of the elf-lands."

Ragnvald became aware that Malmury and Frakki, who had been noisily cracking the bones of their own fowl, had now fallen silent and listened to Atli and Ragnvald's conversation with interest. Ivar slept, with his head pillowed on Hilda's lap, while Einar stood behind them, listening. Hilda too, raised her head from where she bent over Rolli at her breast.

"A gale blew us out of the calm, and at first we were glad for it, sailing before the wind as fast as we could go. Then the waves grew larger, some nearly as tall as the mast. We reefed down the sail, and used oars and the steering board to head into them. It was hard, punishing work, and I thought I would die of fatigue before the storm blew itself out.

"All at once the wind died, and I felt a moment of relief. Short-lived though. Out of the distance reared up a wave, the likes of which I have never seen before—three times the height of the mast." Atli smiled slightly. "I can tell you do not believe me. Few to whom I have told this story to do. Except those who have seen such sights themselves and know that out in the sea where land is hidden, the sea goddess sometimes sends these waves to bring her treasure. You know her—can you really doubt her, Ragnvald?"

It seemed that it was not Atli who spoke at that moment, but Ran, the cruel goddess of storms and shipwrecks, calling again to Ragnvald from the deep. But when he tried to picture Atli's wave, instead he saw Vemund's hall, capped with fire, burning up into the sky, as though it were a wave that would crash upon him.

"I do not doubt her," said Ragnvald gravely.

"Of course, we all thought we were going to die. Men said prayers.

One dived into the water—perhaps it was his sacrifice that carried us through, or perhaps he was only out of his head with fear. Either way, we did as we had done before, and steered the wave up the face of this monster. I thought it would flip us over and we would all go tumbling down to Ran's realm.

"When we made it over the top, I saw another, just as huge headed for us. In the moments before it came, I said we needed another sacrifice, and I would do it myself, if it came to that, but instead we drew lots, and though Logi did not want to die, in he went.

"The third wave was just as big, and we had to push Mani into the water. He clung to the side, and I hacked off his fingers with my ax to make him let go. We survived that wave too, and I was resolved to throw myself in if another came, but while the rest of the night was difficult, nothing like those three waves hit us again.

"I cannot doubt now that it was a message from Ran. What else could it be? Three is a number sacred to the gods. She said that she would have me if I ever ventured into her realm again. So I have lost my taste for sailing, for raiding. I will send a message for my wife to join me if she will, but I will never make that crossing again."

He poked at the fire with a stick, sending a burst of sparks up into the air. "That is my story, Ragnvald Eysteinsson. Is it a good enough story for you?"

"Harald will judge," said Ragnvald gruffly. "It is not reason enough to hand over Sogn to you. The goddess Ran did not promise you that."

The story affected Ragnvald when he tried to sleep that night, little though he wished it to. How small his own adventure in the fjord at Solvi's hand seemed now, though he had seen his vision then, of Harald as the golden wolf he must follow. He dreamed uneasily and woke in the dimness before dawn with his cloak sodden by a thick fog.

+ + +

IN THE MORNING, as Ragnvald took down the crossbeams of his tent, Oddi pointed to two dragon ships traversing a narrow channel between two islands and then turning to sail up Geiranger Fjord. They looked far away, bent on other prey, but Ragnvald ordered all men to make ready to fight, in case the raiders saw them. The vessels passed by quickly, though, taking advantage of the morning's landward wind, which would turn by midday and slow their passage.

"More raiders from Solvi," said Ragnvald grimly. He did not know for sure—every raid on the western districts was attributed to Solvi these days—but he could see these ships had come to plunder, and had crossed open sea to do so. "We could leave Hilda and the children here, and sail to help Heming, if you want," Ragnvald suggested. Sigurd's farewell had made Ragnvald resolve to treat Oddi better; Oddi was his friend, his sworn brother, not merely a retainer, bound to Ragnvald's will.

Oddi laughed shortly. "No," he said. "Not unless you command it."

"Your father would want us to," said Ragnvald.

"And Heming would not. Let him prove himself or fail. I want to keep my neck far from Heming's sword."

"You do him wrong," said Ragnvald. "He is only jealous."

"His jealousy is dangerous," said Oddi flatly. "You saw how he killed Harald's captain Thorbrand, and before that my father's favorite jarl—what was his name?"

"Runolf," said Ragnvald, remembering the dark-haired man whose death he had witnessed at the Sogn *ting* that had so altered his fortunes. "His name was Runolf."

"I would be forgotten as easily," said Oddi. "My father would mourn for a time, but he would never avenge me."

"I would—"

"He would never allow anyone else to avenge me either."

"What do you want?" Ragnvald asked. "What can I do for you?"

"Keep me by your side," said Oddi. "When I can't fight anymore, grant me some land and a plump pretty girl to tend me and give me some sons in my dotage."

"I don't believe that's all you want," said Ragnvald, though he was gratified. "I think you want glory. What if you had other brothers, better brothers? Would you then want a kingdom of your own?"

Ragnvald could hardly read the emotions that crossed Oddi's face, pain and longing, quickly followed by dismissal, and then good cheer again.

"It matters not—I have the brothers my father gave me," he said. "It was only my good fate to find a better one."

✛ ✛ ✛

RAGNVALD'S SHIP PASSED the island of Smola at midday, before entering the fjord system that led to Nidaros. Ragnvald remembered the eeriness of Smola's treeless plains at dusk, lit by summer lightning. He wished they had come at evening, so he would have an excuse to stop there, and again walk the ground on which he had fought the dead man, the *draugr*, plaguing Smola. Where he had won King Hakon's admiration, and Oddi's. In the time that passed, it had ceased to bother him that the *draugr* was only a witless man, stumbling around his old haunts until his wound killed his body as it had already killed his mind.

He wondered too if the sorceress Alfrith, the *draugr's* sister, still lived there, brewing her remedies and depending on the generosity of many men rather than binding herself to one. If she kept her beauty, he might take her as a concubine and finally settle the debt he had incurred in killing her brother.

By evening, the wind had carried Ragnvald's ships within view of Harald's town, which lay on a bend in Trondheim Fjord. The polished wood of new buildings gleamed in the settling sun, dazzling Ragnvald's eyes before he picked out the high carved crossbeams of Harald's mead hall, the one that could seat five hundred warriors at its long tables.

The breeze whipped the water's surface into whitecaps. Ivar stood at the bow with Einar, both of their mouths open like excited puppies, watching the shore fly past. Atli fared less well. He had been nervous even on calm portions of the trip, gripping his seat too tightly, never able to cross from one part of the ship to the other without a firm grasp on something. Once, Ragnvald had almost been driven to the deck by Atli's heavy hand on his shoulder when he had nothing else to cling to.

These choppy waves made even the sleekest of dragon ships shudder like a cart on a rocky trail. Atli sat on one of the rowing benches facing the water, clasping the gunwale with both of his hands. He looked down at his hands, the knuckles white. Ragnvald wondered if he was thinking of the sailor whose fingers he had severed before sending the man to his death. A small part of Ragnvald did not relish the ruin of Atli's courage. Atli had been a mighty warrior and raider, and had been undone by a wave. Three waves, goddess-sent. So little—no more than a quarter of a day between the time when Atli could count himself a man, and was then turned into this. What was a Norseman who could not sail?

Atli regained his composure when the ship drew near the docks at Nidaros, visibly shedding his anxiety, and pulling his shoulders back. "I have seen you," Ragnvald said. He stood at the steering board himself to guide the ship into the harbor at Nidaros. "I have seen you frightened."

Atli fixed his eyes at Ragnvald's hand on the board. "But Harald has not," he said. "I will sit in the high seat of Sogn's hall yet, you will see."

"You have—for ten whole days. I hope you enjoyed it," said Ragnvald.

As soon as he turned his ship into the small harbor, the wind fell off, but the ship's momentum carried it up next to the stone dock as easily as if a giant's hand had given it a push across the calm water. Ragnvald flung a line to a waiting guard, who caught it and wound it around a piling.

Ragnvald leaped out of the ship with Atli a half step behind him. He walked quickly, hoping in vain that Atli would stumble on legs that did not transition easily between sea and land, but Atli managed, keeping pace with Ragnvald, so when they reached Harald's guards, they were both half running.

"King Ragnvald of Sogn," said Oddi, racing up behind them, out of breath, "and his followers. Let us pass. Ragnvald, I will bring Hilda and the boys." Ragnvald flushed, angry that Atli had caused him to neglect his wife.

"Atli Kolbrandsson," said Atli, announcing himself. His men had not yet caught up to him either. "You know me, Ulf, I was here in the summer."

This Ulf, skinny, with a scraggly beard, and high, narrow shoulders, cracked a grin that showed many of his teeth missing.

"'Course I remember you," said Ulf. "Come in."

Ragnvald knew Ulf as well, and had never received a smile like that from him. He resolved to see if any of Harald's servants might be willing to be his eyes and ears in Nidaros when he was absent.

✢ ✢ ✢

THE EVENING MEAL had already started when Ragnvald and his family entered the feasting hall. Harald had made Nidaros into a Valhalla for the living, where his men sparred every morning, patched up their bruises in the afternoon, and drank together every night. At times they hunted as well, though the animals replenished themselves less well than the warriors did. Ragnvald heard grumblings that the woods around Nidaros had run out of deer this fall.

Harald sat at the high table with his uncle Guthorm, King Hakon, and Hakon's middle son, Geirbjorn, and, Ragnvald noted, Atli had been seated with him as well. Nearby a dark-skinned man in odd dress spoke with one of Harald's warriors. This must be an explorer from the south. The table was so fully laden with cheese, breads, fruit preserves, and stewed meat that what little planking could be seen between serving dishes glistened with spilled fat. Only men dined here tonight; the women ate separately in their own hall with the children.

Every night, Harald fed his household and guests with a feast that would beggar Ragnvald if he hosted it even once. One day, Ragnvald promised himself, he would make Sogn flow with the same bounty he saw here, to repay Harald, and to show him what a rich district Sogn could be with him as king.

Still Ragnvald was gratified to see Harald rise to his feet as soon as he entered, setting down a spoonful of meat so that he could come to greet Ragnvald with a back-pounding embrace.

"I had not thought to see you so soon," said Harald.

"Me either, but you sent a plague to me, and I have come to bring it back," said Ragnvald wryly.

"A plague?" Harald asked.

"Atli Kolbrandsson."

Harald stood too close, and Ragnvald had to crane his neck to see

Harald's face. His expression darkened. "Oh him. Yes, he has asked me for a formal hearing, a few days from now. What other news do you have to tell me?" he asked with a growing grin, and a voice that stilled other conversation.

"Much news—but later," said Ragnvald, more quietly. Harald should hear of Sigurd and Egil's leaving, not because they were important, but because they followed others, a tide of free men who liked their chances better abroad than in Harald's Norway.

"I hear Vemund is finally dealt with," said Harald. He cracked his knuckles.

"Dead and burned." Ragnvald tried to match Harald's hearty tone. "He will trouble us no more."

"I will raise a toast to that, and tell of your deed," Harald promised.

"Please do not," said Ragnvald. He moved his hand toward his scar, but let it fall again before he could make the gesture and show his discomfort. In his vision of Harald as a golden wolf, Harald had burned where he touched. This deed was his.

"A man should boast of his triumphs," said Harald more quietly as conversations resumed around them, "or how else will others know of them?"

"I would rather boast of battles," Ragnvald said. "I have brought his men, the betrayers Illugi and Grai, back to you."

"Why?"

Ragnvald shrugged. "What else could I do with them? I do not trust them."

"They helped you defeat Vemund."

"They helped you," said Ragnvald. "But they are oath breakers."

"They swore they were not," said Harald. He gave Ragnvald a sly look and shrugged. "I am certain I can find use for them."

"What of Atli Kolbrandsson—can you find a better use for him?" Ragnvald asked. "He claims Sogn. And your uncle encouraged him in this."

Harald put his hand on Ragnvald's shoulder. "I'm sure it is a misunderstanding," he said. "I cannot discuss it now, though. This must be done before witnesses. You understand?"

Ragnvald nodded. He knew better than to argue. He would have his chance later, so Harald could make an example of his fairness and generosity. This must be witnessed so all would know Harald's decision, and there could be no more temptation for men like Atli.

"I will hold court to settle disputes in a few days, and then I will hear the arguments and make my decision known. In the meantime, enjoy my table—there is none better in all of Norway."

"As I well know," said Ragnvald, bowing his head.

He returned to sit next to Oddi. "He will hear our dispute later," Ragnvald told him.

"Did he give you hope he would decide in your favor?" Oddi asked.

"I cannot imagine he would decide against me," said Ragnvald, though even as he said it, he found that he could. Harald claimed that he never broke a vow and treated all men fairly, but Ragnvald knew that he had killed or outlawed Norse kings without giving them a chance to swear to him when he wanted their land for his allies—kings who had as much right to their land as Ragnvald had to Sogn.

"It was Guthorm who sent Atli to Sogn," Ragnvald added. "Do you think I should fear him?"

"You have always had to fear him," said Oddi.

Ragnvald watched the high table, trying to read the faces and interactions of the men: Hakon grew harder and leaner with the years, and Guthorm's golden hair had faded to a dull yellow, matching his stained teeth, though he still had broad, powerful shoulders and a face like a mountainside. He had sent Atli to Sogn with bad information, hoping to spark a fight. Ragnvald had always found Guthorm unforgiving but fair, willing to follow Ragnvald's advice if it helped Harald, though he had grown both more cautious and more critical of late, as Harald grew out from under his shadow. When Atli saw Ragnvald watching them, he gave him a slight smile, a self-satisfied widening of his greasy lips.

"Perhaps you are right," said Ragnvald.

12

SVANHILD RUSHED TO EYSTEIN'S SIDE, COUGHING FROM THE searing wind. She put her sleeve over her mouth. It hardly helped; the air burned her throat, tasting of the sulfur that suffused everything in Iceland. Solvi had to walk more slowly over the uneven ground, and by the time he reached them, Svanhild had already picked up her son. She could not rouse him; his eyelashes only fluttered when she tapped his cheek. His legs dangled on the ground as he slipped down in her arms. Solvi helped lift him up so she could get a better grip and then arranged his legs around her waist and his arms around her neck.

"He is ill," she said. Even with Svanhild's face burning from the overheated air, Eystein felt hotter still.

"Yes." Solvi stood, still as a block of wood.

"Go find Unna—she is a great healer," said Svanhild. Unna had walked away when he arrived to scold Svanhild. Solvi did not move. "Go," she said more forcefully. "I will take him home."

She could carry him easily enough on an ordinary day, but after the long land-claiming ritual, her arms had far less strength. "Hold on to me, Monkey," she said. "Please. We will be home soon and you can sleep and get better."

He murmured something against her shoulder. He's only tired, she told herself. He had walked far today for a child. Too far without enough food. She should have fed him more, given Unna bread to feed him while her hands were occupied leading the heifer. She would take Eystein back to the tent and tuck him into bed. Willow bark tea would bring his fever down, and broth would give him back his strength. It was only a passing ague, the sort that happened to all children.

She tucked Eystein under his blankets in his cot, and made him the willow bark tea. She set a spoonful against his lips, and tipped it in when he opened them. After a few spoonfuls he refused more. Not enough. She lay down next to him on the narrow pallet and put her arm gently over him, in hopes that if he grew chilled from the breeze that blew through the tent he could take some warmth from her.

She tried to think of the children she had grown up with at Ardal. She remembered a boy she played with when Ragnvald had no time for her, a boy named—her memory failed her. His face was suddenly very vivid to her, gap-toothed, with an overbite, and a head as round as the pig-bladder ball that they had kicked around in play. He had not been particularly sickly, but a fever had still carried him off in his sixth year, turning him from an active child to a glass-eyed doll, and then a gray-skinned corpse. He had been healthy until then, though. A fever might take a child at any time, with no warning. Svanhild clung to that: if a healthy child could die, then might not a sickly child live? And she wished she could remember the name of her friend.

She must have dozed off next to Eystein, for she saw the blond boy from her youth coming to her across a field covered with the same mist that often lay in the hollows of Iceland's fields where hot spring water met cold air. He spoke to her it seemed, though she did not hear his voice, and asked her why she did not remember his name.

"I was young," said Svanhild.

"The age that your son is now," said the boy, only now he was Svanhild's mother, face ravaged and back bent over with age. "Do you think he will remember your name in the lands of death? Or is he too young?"

"I am his mother," Svanhild cried, feeling as though she barely had breath to make the words, and hearing only silence instead of words. "He will remember me. And he will not die until he is an old man."

She woke to Solvi shaking her shoulder. He knelt by the side of her pallet, and glanced down at her, then quickly away. "Svanhild, you were calling out." As before, her name sounded false on his lips, a stranger speaking through him.

"I had a dream," said Svanhild. "A boy I knew . . . Ingmar. See I remembered his name."

"Yes, you did," said Solvi. "That is what you kept crying out. I worried I had a rival." He gave her one of his mischievous smiles, a smile that Svanhild could not bring herself to return.

"We must give his name to Eystein. Eystein Ingmar. I did not do well to name him for my father." Her father had died young, shamed, and murdered by his friends. She had thought she followed in his footsteps, for he was an adventurer, but she had only borrowed his ill-luck for her son. Perhaps if Svanhild honored Ingmar's memory, his spirit would guard Eystein from death.

+ + +

WHEN SVANHILD WOKE again, Unna was sitting by Eystein's side. Pillows propped up his head. In the shadows cast by the lamplight, he looked far too thin, his skin no more than silk stretched across the frame of his bones.

"How long has he had a bloody cough?" Unna asked. She looked very worried, so much that Svanhild wanted to send her away, to keep her from infecting Eystein with her fear. "Svanhild, did you hear me?" Unna asked again. "How long has he been coughing blood?"

"I . . . he wasn't. He didn't. He's not." Svanhild sat up and rubbed her head. Her mouth was dry.

Wordlessly, Unna wiped a finger along the spittle that ringed his mouth, and held it under the lamp to show how it painted her skin red.

"I think—a few days?" Svanhild said. "I thought he cut his mouth. Did you see him coughing blood? When we visited before?" She smoothed his lank and sodden hair back from his forehead. Fever had made his cheeks and lips vividly pink, giving him a false look of health.

"No," said Unna. "He spent more of his time with Donall, remember. I can ask him."

"Ask the boy," said Solvi. "He has not lost his wits, he is only sick."

"Eystein, my son." Svanhild looked down at him. "How long have you been coughing blood?"

He seemed to struggle to make his eyes meet hers. "I don't know."

"Think," said Solvi. He stood behind Svanhild and put his hand on her shoulder. "Was it before we left the Faroe Islands?" Eystein looked at Svanhild, pleadingly, tears in his eyes. He nodded. "What does it mean, this coughing blood?" Solvi asked Unna.

"I have seen it before," said Unna. "Please." She gestured for Svanhild to give her space to examine Eystein.

Unna pulled up his shirt, exposing his thin white chest. His ribs made Svanhild think of the bones of a whale she had seen washed up on a beach. How had she missed his failing health? She should have forced him to drink broth thickened with bull's blood until muscle and flesh covered those fragile bones. Unna put her ear to Eystein's chest. "Take a deep breath," she bid him. He did so, raising Unna's head with the movement. "And another."

This one made him cough again. Svanhild could not deny it now: the spittle ringing his mouth was red with blood, making him look like a little wolf that had been at its prey. If only he were as healthy as that.

"His lungs are crackling," said Unna. "He will have been weak for a while, if it has come to this point. Did you not notice?"

"You did not notice," said Svanhild, trying to cover her panic with anger. "He kept up with me today."

"He is not my son," said Unna.

"I do not need your reproach," Svanhild cried. "Help me. Help him."

"What do you know of this illness?" Solvi asked Unna, his voice harsh.

Unna did not answer for a moment. She pulled Eystein's shirt back down and his blanket up to his chin. "I know that it spreads easily and it usually ends in death."

Svanhild wanted to rush forward to cover Eystein's ears. He would be so frightened—Unna had no children, otherwise she would know that some things had to be hidden from them.

"Get out," said Solvi. "I too heard I would die at his age, and I did not. I will not have you ill-wishing my son."

"Wait," said Svanhild as Unna gathered her basket of herbs so she could leave. "How can we make him better?"

Unna wrapped her shawl around her shoulders. "Keep him warm, give him willow bark tea to keep his fever down, and keep him fed. No matter what, you must keep him warm." She looked pointedly at the fabric walls of the tent. "He is already far too thin." Her words twisted in Svanhild's stomach like a blade.

"What causes this sickness?" Svanhild asked.

"Some think sorcery," said Unna. "Some think bad air."

"You have brought both of those with you today," said Solvi. "Get out, or I will make you leave."

"Svanhild, come and see me," said Unna. She opened the tent flap to let herself out.

"She is trying to help," said Svanhild to Solvi. She could not bear to look at him, to take her eyes from Eystein for even a moment.

"She is a part of the poison of this place," said Solvi. "If she did not cause his illness, be sure she did nothing to prevent it. And yet she tries to blame you. I know of no better mother than you, Svanhild."

"You did not know much of any mothering," cried Svanhild. "How would you know?"

"As you like." His voice was grim. "You cannot stay here now."

"What? Our son is ill. Where should I go?"

"Back to Norway—the air here has poisoned him, Unna said. It is the only way. Svanhild, come, leave with me tonight."

"What of your war?" Svanhild asked, still watching Eystein. He had fallen asleep as they argued in tones that usually sent him into hiding until his parents had made peace again.

"This is more important than that."

"Don't lie to me again. You want to use his illness as an excuse to drag me and my son into your war, when he needs stable ground beneath him to become healthy again."

"I mean to give him stable ground—a stable kingdom," said Solvi. "Svanhild, look at me." Svanhild turned toward him. She saw in the gold of his beard glinting in the lantern's light and the laugh lines near his eyes, one half of all she loved in the world. Then Eystein coughed again and she turned back toward her son.

"Go away, husband," she said. "I do not want to hear of moving him. He is too weak as it is, and sea journeys have never agreed with him."

"It is being away from his home that disagrees with him."

"And where is his home? You have never given him a home for more than a season at a time."

"That is what I mean to change," said Solvi. "I will give him a few days to become stronger, but do not mistake me, Svanhild. We will bring him back to Tafjord, and he will be healed there."

☩   ☩   ☩

THROUGH THE SECOND night of Eystein's illness, Svanhild lay in her cot next to Solvi, listening to every sound that came from Eystein's bed: a painful cough, the sounds his rush mattress made when he turned over on it.

In the first two days Solvi tried to order her to leave Eystein's bedside and prepare for their journey, but she refused, and eventually he left her alone. He seemed a stranger in those moments, an enemy to whom she never should have joined herself. As the endless time passed, marked within the tent only by the lightening and darkening of the hanging wool of the walls, Eystein began to eat more, and eventually sit up. A night passed when he did not cough at all, and Svanhild began to hope that Unna had been wrong. She put her ear to his chest when he breathed and was not sure if she heard crackling or not. It could be the wind moving over the sand, or the shifting of his mattress.

Finally, ten days after Svanhild had claimed her land, Eystein said he felt well enough—and was restless enough—to get out of bed. He wanted to go outside. He stood unsteadily, clinging to Svanhild's hand, and took a few halting steps to reach the door of the tent. Svanhild lifted the tent flap, and they both squinted at the harsh gray light of the overcast day.

"Are you feeling better, son? Truly?" Svanhild asked.

"The light makes my head hurt," he said. "But I am hungry."

Tears burned in her eyes. She had spent the last ten days begging him to swallow bread soaked in broth, only to have him cry and push it away, saying it hurt his throat. Her stomach growled in answer to his words. She had eaten little but his leavings, and her body cried out for meat, vegetables, food of the living, not the sickbed.

"Let us fix you some food then," she said brightly. She fought her own dizziness, watching stars dance in the blackness that overtook her vision. "What are you hungry for? Some soft bread and cheese?"

"With honey?" he asked.

She laughed and hugged him to her. "Of course. As much honey as you want until you grow fat as a little round bear cub." She took a moment, listening to the cries of the gulls, to gather her strength so she could stand and greet Solvi, who crossed the beach and walked toward the cottage.

"He is better," she said as soon as he was within hearing distance.

"That is good," he said grimly. He wore a stern expression that Svanhild had rarely seen on his face before, except the night that she gave birth to Eystein and he left her chamber even though she begged him to stay. He had insisted that his presence interfered with the women's magic of midwifery. She had not forgiven him for a month afterward, for she believed having him by her side would have taken away her pain in a way the Frisian women who had attended the birth could not. Her anger rose, surprising her with its intensity. Eystein had been birthed from sickness to wellness again, and as before, Svanhild had to do it on her own.

"I am glad," he said. "But in growing well, I fear he has made you ill. You look terrible." His face softened into a tender look that made Svanhild's throat tight. She looked away again. She needed all her determination for Eystein. She touched her hair, which was oily and dirty from so long without a bath.

"I had more important things to do than to be beautiful for you," said Svanhild.

"It is not your beauty I am worried about," said Solvi. "You are pale and your eyes are dark. You are skinnier than when we were trapped in the Hebrides for ten days and we had to live on limpets."

Svanhild had always remembered those days with a fierce joy, and measured every other peril against them. She had been so hungry she felt like a wild animal, and feared every night that Scottish tribes might find them and kill them. They had slept in a low tent, making a nest for Eystein between them, the soft noises of Solvi's sentries keeping watch their lullaby. Each sunrise, Svanhild began the day's work that kept Solvi and his men fed, and sewed up rents in the sail, while Solvi's men hunted for a straight tree to serve as a new mast. When they finally set sail again, the preceding misery made their victory all the sweeter.

Now she also recalled that she had held Eystein against her breast every day and found her milk growing thinner, and smelling of the shellfish that was all she had to eat. The memory had become a happy one, but only because she and Eystein had survived. Now Solvi had poisoned that memory too—what if those days, and others, less memorable but still full of hardships, had made Eystein weak now?

"I have been caring for our son," said Svanhild. "I will eat now that he is better."

"I would not lose both of you," said Solvi. "The witch said that this sickness spreads easily. Tell me truly, Svanhild. Is it only hunger or have you become ill as well?" He moved toward her as Svanhild came to her feet. Svanhild held up a hand to warn him off.

"It is only hunger," she said, standing upright. She held herself still while the spots before her eyes receded.

"Good," said Solvi. "Be ready to sail tomorrow. The winds and tides will be good for us to depart for Norway."

"What? We are not going anywhere," said Svanhild. "He is only now well enough to sit up and venture outside, not to take a sea voyage."

"I will not argue with you, Svanhild. If my men must bind you and the boy to get you in the ship, we will." As she scowled, he added, "And do not think of hiding. You can only go to Unna's. If you go elsewhere, I will make her tell me—and neither she nor her man will enjoy that."

"If she is a witch as you say, don't you fear her vengeance?" Svanhild asked angrily.

"Not as much as I fear staying here," said Solvi. His voice changed, growing desperate. "Svanhild, do not fight me. Can't you see this is for the best?" He reached out to her again.

"No, it is only for your pride that you want to go back to Tafjord."

Solvi set his jaw. "Do you want to be bundled on board the ship like a bolt of cloth, or do you want to step onto it with dignity? I have spoken, Svanhild, and I will not argue this further."

He turned away from her and walked back toward the ship. Svanhild stared after him. She could recall loving him, longing for him, but could not find that emotion within herself now, not after his threats. She could take a bath, comb out her hair, make herself sweet smelling and soft for him, and after rekindling his tenderness, beg him to let her stay. The thought made her feel weary and as old as death. Solvi would do this thing, no matter how much Svanhild protested. He wanted his war, he wanted Svanhild with him, and he had convinced himself that it would be better for Eystein as well.

How could he think of subjecting Eystein to a voyage where the tossing of the ship would make him worse, where he could not drink fresh milk every day unless—yes, Svanhild would insist that they bring a goat for fresh milk. Katla would know which one was young and biddable, and calm enough to give milk even shipboard. But that was giving in to Solvi—she could not let this happen. Eystein would not survive a sea voyage, and what would they find when they reached Tafjord? A hall occupied by one of Harald's allies, well provisioned, with an army to defend him. She and Eystein would live in a camp in the woods all winter rather than a snug hall.

She said as much to Solvi when he returned and found that she had done no packing, only combed out her hair and tucked Eystein, full of bread and honey, back into bed. Solvi sat down on their bed and pulled her onto his lap. He was clean and well dressed, as if unaffected by all that Svanhild had gone through at Eystein's side these past days. Svanhild touched his cheek, running her thumb along the soft fur of his beard.

"Can we not stay?" she asked simply. How could this man have become her enemy so quickly?

"I believe Ulfarr has already taken Tafjord," Solvi replied. "And it is too late in the year for Harald to bring war against him. By the time the winter comes, we will be well provisioned there, and defended by the king of Sweden."

"You are so certain, but Harald has beaten you every time you've faced him," Svanhild cried, standing up and backing away from him.

"One time." Solvi's voice grew cold. "Make ready."

"Ulfarr might be dead," Svanhild suggested. "A sea journey could kill us all." Solvi would not be drawn into an argument, though. Svanhild might escape him for a time, but not with Eystein in tow. Her son could not travel quickly over land, and his sickness would frighten anyone who might give them shelter. She packed without thinking, her hands guided by the practice of years. If she refused to pack, Solvi would only send his men to do it, and tie her up as he promised—and whoever packed hers and Eystein's things might forget something that could mean the difference between life and death on the open sea.

The next morning, when they were to leave, as Svanhild handed Solvi his breakfast of porridge, she said, "I wish to say good-bye to Unna. If you want to prevent me, you can tie me up now." She proffered her wrists toward him, and looked at his hands, callused by hauling on a ship's lines, his joints thickened by cold nights at sea.

"Svanhild," he said, his voice pleading, "you will see this is right."

She wanted to scream at him. What will you give me if you are wrong? Will you give me another son? "Are you going to tie me up or not, husband?" she asked, still holding her wrists out. "Or may I speak to my friend?"

"Take Thorstein with you," said Solvi.

"If either of us deserves this little trust, it is you," she replied.

The air up on the slopes where Unna lived chilled Svanhild's nose, a bite of winter, which came early to Iceland, even earlier than in the mountains of Norway. A light frost left its crystals on the tops of the grass.

Unna gave her a warm smile that sat awkwardly on her severe features. "I am sorry I spoke so harshly to you about your son." She held her arms open for Svanhild's embrace.

Svanhild accepted the contact gladly, and found herself crying against Unna's shoulder for a long moment, tears whose source was a well of hopelessness she could not drain, though Unna's pats on her back did give her a moment of peace.

"I thought you did not apologize," said Svanhild, wiping her eyes on her sleeves.

"Donall has told me that I should, and he is usually right about these things," said Unna.

"I wanted to say good-bye. You have been good to me, no matter what Solvi has said to Ingolfur or the other settlers."

"He can do little damage to me," said Unna. "The people here trust me more than they do him. They know I will stay, and that my magics will help them in hard times. What do they know of him? That he will take advantage of their hospitality and be gone before he can be asked to return it?"

Svanhild felt an urge to defend Solvi that came more from habit than true conviction. "We will give you hospitality in Tafjord," she said.

"Will you?" Unna asked, returning to her customary brusqueness. "I was born in Scotland and would have stayed if there had been anything for me. Norway is nothing to me."

"Nonetheless, if you come, you will be welcome."

Unna pressed her lips together and gave Svanhild another quick hug. "And you will be welcome here," she said. "I will never begrudge you hospitality. I will guard your land as if it is my own."

"If I return, I will make a fair arrangement for it," Svanhild said. Perhaps Unna could keep it until her death, and then will it to Eystein, for she had no living children of her own.

"Be safe and brave and free," said Unna, a blessing said sometimes by wives sending their warrior husbands off to battle. Svanhild smiled sadly. She was Solvi's captive, her battle already lost, bound to defeat by marriage and by her son.

The ship set off from the harbor, and the black and white bulk of Iceland retreated into the distance. In the past, sailing away at Solvi's side had always filled her with hope; now she had left her hopes for Eystein behind in the land she had claimed.

13

HILDA EDGED AROUND THE ROOM HARALD HAD GIVEN TO HER and Ragnvald in Nidaros. Heavy curtains divided it from the rest of the living hall. A soapstone lamp full of oil spilled a rich scent along with its light over the bed. A private space, even one barely bigger than the down-filled mattress on its raised platform, was a luxury that surely no other king in all of the Norse lands could boast for his guests. When Harald came to Nidaros, she and Ragnvald gave up their room to him. Harald could provide a king's chamber for all of his important visitors.

"Surely Nidaros must rival Constantinople," she said to Ragnvald, who was putting on a homespun shirt. She examined the fine carvings on the bedstead, the silver mirror resting on the table next to a comb of walrus ivory. She touched the gold on the comb's spine lightly. Ragnvald had given her treasures that approached these, gifts from his plunder to mark the birth and first tooth of each of her sons, and she guarded them jealously. Harald's wives had set these prizes out the way Hilda might give a guest a ewer of water at her bedside.

"I am told Constantinople is far bigger," said Ragnvald.

"I cannot imagine." Hilda touched a silver hair clasp inlaid with blue and red enamel. "There are so many buildings and people here."

"Harald would have it larger. It may one day rival Dublin. Even that is bigger, though much dirtier." Ragnvald moved closer to her so she backed up with her legs against the bed frame. "Should I take you there someday?" he asked.

The luxury of this room was such that they might indulge in mid-day lovemaking. She wished to pull him to her, to welcome him into her as she had not since his return home. It troubled him, she knew, to show his care for her, his desire for her, and to have it rebuffed.

"No," said Hilda softly. "I am content at home." She swallowed and put her hand on his chest, though without the pressure to push him away. "I do not know why Harald needs so many people together in one place. How can he feed them all?"

"He buys food or takes it in taxes from the districts, and the men and women who live here are artisans who can ply their craft all day long," said Ragnvald.

"It cannot be safe. What if there is a fire among all these build-ings?" She stretched out her fingers again and this time Ragnvald covered her hand with his. If he pressed her now, she would yield to him, and then sleep the day away. If her life were as easy as a Nidaros woman's, perhaps she would not dread bearing endless children.

"I'm sure it is as safe as anywhere else." Ragnvald sounded impa-tient. "Ask a thrall where the women's chambers are. You can meet Harald's wives and see their handwork." He patted her hand and then let it go.

"I don't know," said Hilda. "They can invite me if they wish."

"Why all this fear? You were brave enough when Atli came to Sogn."

Hilda could not meet his eyes. She had not told him that she had given up and hoped for death, even before Atli's man hit her. He liked to think of her as brave. She was spared from making any reply by Ivar rushing into the room, followed by Einar.

"They have the littlest ponies, Mother," Ivar cried, "and they said we could ride them. Can we? Can we?"

Ivar bounced on his feet, and Ragnvald caught him up in his arms. "I'm surprised you even asked," Ragnvald said.

"King Harald said we must," said Ivar.

"He said—he requests that you join him in the practice yard," said Einar to his father.

"Very well. I shall join him." He echoed Einar's formality. "Meet the women," he said to Hilda. "Perhaps we can find a new waiting-woman for you."

Ivar tugged on Ragnvald's trousers. "Come on, Father."

"King Harald is waiting," said Einar.

"As are the ponies." Ragnvald nodded farewell to her.

Freed even from her family's company, Hilda sat down on the bed. Ragnvald would want to know that she had met the other women, the wives and daughters of kings. They could not be so different from her. They would still embroider fabric, weave on cards—of ivory, not wood, with silken thread, not woolen—even spin, perhaps. Hilda had brought her spindle and a sack of finest black lamb's wool to spin into yarn for a cloak for Ragnvald. He avoided the bright colors that some of his fellow kings wore, especially on his summer battle excursions. He had praised the cloak she made him for a wedding gift, which hid him against dark tree trunks, and had worn it threadbare.

Hilda walked outside and quickly became lost among all of the buildings. On a fine day like this, she thought the women might sit in the sun, perhaps even near the practice ground so they could watch their men compete. Hilda liked watching Ragnvald, at least when he won with no trouble. She flinched whenever he took a blow, even from a wooden sword.

She rounded the corner of a building and saw Atli. He waved to her, so she could not avoid him. "Hilda Hrolfsdatter!" He swept a bow, so deep that it seemed mocking. "How do you like Nidaros?"

Everyone asked her that and she did not know what they wanted to hear from her—probably praise of Harald. "It is big," she said.

"So it is," said Atli. "Not as welcoming as your cozy hall at Sogn."

As often with Atli, she could not tell if he insulted her or not. "It is much finer," she said. "I had thought to meet some of Harald's wives, but this place is very confusing."

"I will show you, my lady." He walked with her toward another hall, as new and gleaming as the one that held her bedroom. As Atli took her elbow to help her over some uneven ground, a woman came toward them, clad in a fine brown overdress that set off the blue of her shift and the honey of her hair. Hilda wondered if she could wear those colors—the simplicity might suit her better than patterned silks. The woman pulled her hair over her shoulder in a very familiar way, and Hilda realized, with a feeling of helplessness, that this was

Vigdis. Hilda hoped never to see her again after she left Sogn. But of course Vigdis would find her way to this concentration of powerful men, rather than end her days alone in the mountains.

Vigdis looked at Hilda and then at Atli and then nodded at both of them as Atli swept a bow neither as deep nor slow as the one he had given Hilda. Hilda wanted to look away. Sharing Ragnvald had always made her feel uncomfortably intimate with Vigdis, as though Vigdis had looked upon Hilda's nakedness. Vigdis's eyes seemed to catch on Atli, then on Hilda, and Hilda had a flash of intuition: there was something between these two connivers, something both of them wanted hidden, that augured ill for Ragnvald.

Hilda moved to block Vigdis's path, forcing her to a halt. "Vigdis Hallbjornsdatter," Hilda said, inclining her head politely. "I am so glad that you have found another protector in Atli Kolbrandsson. And now you wish for him to have Sogn so you can return to the site of your former triumphs. It is a compliment to my home that you liked it so much."

Vigdis glanced at Atli, and then back to Hilda. Hilda bared her teeth slightly, waiting for Vigdis's response. The smile Vigdis gave her in return was warm and false, one that Hilda remembered well from her welcome home to Sogn after her wedding to Ragnvald. Vigdis had put her hands over her pregnant belly, swelling with Ragnvald's son, and smiled in just this way.

"Yes," said Vigdis simply. Hilda would have preferred to watch Vigdis flounder, but she had still won her victory in that admission.

"My dear," said Atli, "Hilda is looking for the other women. Can you please show her where you are sitting today?"

"Of course," said Vigdis. She offered her arm to Hilda, who looked at it until Vigdis let it fall to her side again. "Follow me."

Ragnvald had come to marry Hilda even before he let Harald make him king of Sogn. Hilda had been dazzled by his gold and his friendship with the most important man in Norway, until they returned to Sogn and she found Vigdis pregnant. She had denied him her bed in anger on that first night in Sogn, and he had punished her by seeking Vigdis's every night after that. At least he had made Hilda pregnant before they left her father's house, and once the pregnancy began to show, Hilda found her voice. "It is wrong," she had said. "She is your stepmother."

"It would be wrong if I married her," said Ragnvald. "But she can be my concubine. My stepfather married her young."

"It is incest," said Hilda.

"We share no blood. She and my mother had the misfortune to share a husband, that is all."

By his scowl, Hilda knew he agreed with her, at least a little—it was wrong, and he was ashamed. "If my child is a boy, promise me you will send her away," Hilda said.

"If your child is a boy," Ragnvald promised, "I will get rid of Vigdis." And he had done it. By the time he set a sword in Hilda's lap to welcome Ivar, two of his men were escorting Vigdis into the mountains where her father lived. Now she was back, to reopen a wound that had hardly healed between them, and use Atli to do it.

Hilda walked a half step behind Vigdis between two smaller buildings. The years had treated Vigdis far too well: her waist slimmer than when Hilda had seen her last, when she was still recovering from Einar's birth. Hilda felt like a solid old heifer next to a doe, wild and lovely, glimpsed in a spring forest. Ragnvald would think so too; he might hate Vigdis for taking up with Atli, but his eyes would follow her everywhere, and when they did not, his body would still be turned toward her. It had been that way at Sogn as well.

✛ ✛ ✛

RAGNVALD FOLLOWED EINAR through the hall's warren of chambers. Curtains made up the walls between them, and Ivar, still held against Ragnvald's chest, laughed when they brushed against him. A few clay lamps hung from the ceiling, burning whale oil and casting their light and shadows over the hangings. He emerged at the rear of the building, where a fenced-in field held six hairy ponies whose backs were no higher than Ragnvald's hip.

Harald stood at the fence, talking with the ponies' handler. Next to the ponies, Harald looked even more like a giant, his tangled blond hair providing its own sunlight against the overcast sky.

"He breeds them small for children," said Harald. "Makes me wish I was a boy again."

"You could never have been small enough to ride them," said Ragnvald. He pushed his sons toward the open gate. The handler let Ivar and Einar into the paddock, and whistled for the ponies. He set Ivar on a white one, and would have helped Einar onto a dappled gray, but Einar wrapped his arms around the pony's neck and swung up onto it himself, giving the man a defiant look. The ponies walked gently at the handler's urging, making a slow circle around the inside of the fence. When he saw that the boys could stay on, he gave a low whistle and the ponies picked up speed.

Ragnvald heard a rush of chatter behind him and was almost bowled over by a gaggle of larger boys. They climbed the fence quickly, and began running after the loose ponies, trying to frighten them. Their minder looked at Harald, who smiled and shrugged. All of the boys were tall and a few years older than Ragnvald's sons. Ragnvald saw Harald's wide-set eyes and big, prominent teeth, crowded on these smaller faces.

"Your sons," said Ragnvald.

Harald grinned. "Yes, they're all mine." He had been making sons far longer than Ragnvald—since his fourteenth year, with half of the noble daughters of Norway.

"Are you trying to breed up an army all by yourself?" Ragnvald asked.

"I want as many sons as Odin," said Harald. "I never had brothers. I want my sons to lack for nothing. Not kin or anything else."

"Sometimes fewer brothers may be better," said Ragnvald, thinking of Hakon's brood. Then, to change the subject: "I brought furs from the Keel for you for taxes. Sogn has returned to self-sufficiency, but is not producing surplus yet."

Harald waved his hand to interrupt Ragnvald. "You are more useful to me in battle than as a Sogn farmer."

"Sogn will be able to pay you full taxes in a year or two, but I know you do not want to starve us," said Ragnvald.

Harald turned away from the chaos of boys and ponies in the paddock. "You fret over nothing, my friend," he said. "You bring me land and new kings to pay me taxes every time we ride to battle together. I cannot forgive your taxes without inviting excuses from every king in Norway, but you may wait until these boys have white in their beards before you pay them."

Ragnvald leaned on the fence, feeling the same mixture of shame and pleasure as he did when Harald praised him for deeds of which he could not be proud, like the burning of Vemund's hall. In the paddock, Ivar and Einar had both kept their seats, though their mounts skittered nervously as the other ponies, frightened by Harald's sons, jostled around them. The tallest grabbed the tail of Ivar's pony. It spun around, nipping, and tossed Ivar into the dirt. Ragnvald started forward, ready to break this up.

"You should let them settle their own business," said Harald.

With five of Harald's sons to his two, Ragnvald hardly thought this an even match, but he did not want to make his sons look weak by intervening. Einar slid off his pony and ran toward Ivar, putting himself between Ivar and the other boys. The largest of Harald's sons stood in the fore. This was Halfdan Kvite, red-haired and ill-tempered, Harald's big features raw and unfinished on his boy's face.

Einar, two years younger and a head shorter, snarled at Halfdan. "Fight me first," he said. "I'll fight any of you."

Harald nodded approvingly. Halfdan rushed toward Einar, and shoved him in the chest, knocking him over. Harald's other sons circled him, hiding Ragnvald's sons from his view. His face heated with anger. King or no, Ragnvald would not let his sons be beaten while he stood by.

"Halfdan, one at a time," Harald yelled, bringing Ragnvald back to his senses. "Only a coward hits a man when he's down." Halfdan gave his father a sullen look. He pushed his brothers away so Ragnvald could see Einar standing and brushing dirt off his clothes. Ivar waited uncertainly behind him.

"Try that again," said Einar.

"Let your little brother fight," said one of the other boys, this one black-haired and with the tilted eyes of the upland families.

"No," said Einar. "You beat me, then you can fight him."

"I already did," said Halfdan.

"You pushed me. You didn't beat me," said Einar. His self-possession was unsettling in a boy so young, but Ragnvald had to admire the purity of his will.

Halfdan rushed Einar again, and this time Einar flung a handful of dirt from the practice ground into his eyes. As Halfdan tried to brush off his face, Einar grabbed his shoulders and kneed him hard in the crotch. The boy screamed and collapsed. Einar pulled Ivar over to the fence and helped him over it, onto safe ground between Ragnvald and Harald.

"He can fight," said Harald approvingly, though with an unsteady laugh. "This is Vigdis's son?"

Ragnvald nodded. The boy had fought viciously, in a way Ragnvald had never taught him. Einar would do anything for Ivar, even if he made himself the target of a similar attack later. In the paddock, Harald's sons now rode as fast as the tiny, docile beasts would carry them, jostling for the lead. "You let them run wild," said Ragnvald.

"They are just boys," said Harald. "There's no harm in it. They have to learn to fight."

"They are just boys today," said Einar.

"Ha," Harald barked. "I see he is your son and no other's. I'd wager you were like this at his age. A serious little law-speaker."

"He is his mother's son," said Ragnvald, stung by the comparison. "I don't think I ever fought like that."

Harald liked this subject, though. "If you are Einar, who does Ivar resemble? Is he much like your grandfather for whom he is named?"

"I never knew my grandfather. Ivar is Svanhild, perhaps," Ragnvald said, half to himself. He saw the truth of that comparison more, in Ivar's beautiful russet hair and deep-set eyes. Ivar was sweet tempered, though, where Svanhild was sharp. Perhaps he was like Svanhild when she was a child, when Ragnvald was still able to protect her. Harald looked carefully at the boy, reminding Ragnvald that he once had hoped for a match between Svanhild and his king.

"I hope he serves you better than Svanhild did you," said Harald.

"Yes," Ragnvald agreed. He hoped for that as well. He looked down at Einar, whose face had already begun to purple from the other boy's blow. "Let us find someone to put a cool cloth on that bruise."

Einar looked up at him curiously, almost as he had at Halfdan, before that first shove, as if he did not know whether to count his father friend or foe. Ragnvald extended a hand to Einar, who took it gravely, and his other hand to Ivar. He asked for Harald's leave to go, and Harald waved a hand at him while cheering on his sons as they raced the ponies around the ring.

"You will have to fight those boys again," said Ragnvald to his sons. "Make some friends here, or stay in my sight unless you want them kicking your balls in."

Ivar laughed at that. Ragnvald glanced down at Einar, who nodded seriously. "If they do, I will hurt them worse," he said.

"No, you can defend yourself, but don't hurt them. They are Harald's sons," said Ragnvald. He pushed the kitchen door open.

"What does that matter?" Ivar asked.

Einar peered around Ragnvald to look at his brother. "There are some people who can only hurt you," he said to Ivar. "You can't hurt them."

✛   ✛   ✛

THE KITCHEN SERVANTS directed Ragnvald to Hilda where she sat with Harald's wives and the other important women of Nidaros. They sat outside in the afternoon sun on logs rough-hewn into seats, arranged in a double circle. Servants sat in the larger, outer ring ready to wait upon their mistresses. Hands rose and fell as the women teased out fiber between their fingers and let the weight and motion of their spindles turn it into yarn. There was a beauty in all of those clever female hands, each with a length of roving wound around her wrist, and the thread held between thumb and forefinger. Ragnvald was loath to interrupt.

Asa Hakonsdatter, Harald's first wife, saw him first, and wound the yarn onto her spindle before setting it down in a wooden bowl by her side. She was Hakon's oldest daughter, and had the same sort of beauty as her brother Heming, blond and clear-eyed, with high cheekbones. Ragnvald caught something of Heming's dissatisfaction in her face as well. Next to her sat Hilda. On seeing Ragnvald she tilted her head slightly toward Vigdis, who was braiding a narrow cord. She must be furious that Vigdis was here, though she covered it well.

"Ragnvald," said Asa, "we heard yelling, and were wagering what the trouble was."

"Only some boys fighting." Ragnvald pushed Einar forward so the women could see the swelling around his eye. "I was looking for Hilda to help tend this."

Vigdis rose slightly, then sat again. It was her son who had been hurt. Hilda raised her head and gave Ragnvald an opaque look. She too wound the roving carefully around the spindle, set it on her seat, and stepped out from between the chairs. After bending down to look at Einar's face, she said, "Mafa, please take care of this."

Mafa, a round brown girl with a long narrow braid down her back, took Ivar and Einar by their hands and led them away. As soon as Ragnvald had walked Hilda out of earshot of the women, he turned to her and said, "I didn't know she was here."

"I know," Hilda replied. She gave Ragnvald a tight smile. "She has become Atli's mistress. I believe she sent him to Sogn, or at least encouraged him."

"Truly?" Ragnvald asked, relieved that this was Hilda's reaction.

Hilda described how Vigdis had come upon them, a note of pride in her voice. "It was something about the way they looked at each other," she said. "And she did not say anything until I did. I think she would have said something if . . . anyway, she admitted it. I do not know if it can help you to know this, but at least you will not be surprised."

"That is very good for me to know," Ragnvald replied. He took her hands in his. "I am glad to have such a clever wife." He glanced back over his shoulder at Vigdis. She met his eyes briefly, and then laughed and turned to say something to the woman sitting next to her. So Atli had come to Sogn even better informed of Ragnvald's weaknesses than he had realized. His face grew hot as he imagined Atli lying with Vigdis, laughing at him. She could have revealed anything, from embarrassments in bed to Sigurd's lax defense of Sogn.

"It would be better if you did not stare at her so. She is a poison. Everything she touches withers. I hate her." Hilda's vehemence surprised Ragnvald. She usually spoke to him in such measured tones that he sometimes wished for more passion from her.

"She is a poison, you are right," Ragnvald agreed. A part of him had always known that, no matter what else came between them. Perhaps at times, as a boy, he had foolishly thought that desire meant affection, but the having of Vigdis erased that illusion. "I do not want you unhappy," he added.

"I will be as you request, then," said Hilda. "Happy. Or not unhappy."

That was not the response Ragnvald wanted. Hilda set traps, much as Vigdis did—Vigdis with her looks, her presence, and Hilda with a mire of words where every step Ragnvald took was wrong. "If I can help in any way, to find you excuses to be away from her, I will," he said. "That is what I meant. The boys . . ."

Hilda seemed to soften slightly. "Thank you, but no. I can manage her, if you can manage Atli."

✢   ✢   ✢

IT WAS RAINING steadily the next morning, so Harald held his court in his great hall rather than outside. He had many lamps lit, and the doors flung open to keep it from growing too hot. Sitting before his huge, carven seat posts, his face was cast into darkness whenever he sat back in his chair.

Men had come from the surrounding areas to have justice done, as they did in Ragnvald's hall, but in far greater numbers here. Women attended as well; Ragnvald saw Vigdis standing near the fire and, as far from her as possible, his own Hilda, her chin higher than other women's heads. Between them he noted Harald's upland princess Gyda, her beauty like a knife blade. They had not yet married, for Gyda had said she would not marry him until he had put all of Norway under his rule, causing Harald to swear that he would not cut his hair, nor trim his beard, until then. Harald had gotten a son on Gyda's sister, though, whom Gyda had adopted to raise as her own.

"How does he have time to do this so often?" Ragnvald muttered to Oddi. Ragnvald had not yet determined what Vigdis's presence might mean for him, except to put him more on his guard. He and Oddi sat close to Harald, in chairs that flanked the dais. On one side of Harald sat Guthorm, looking as Harald might when he aged forty years, down to the way he leaned on one elbow and rested his temple against his knuckles. On the other side sat Hakon, hiding his impatience poorly.

"The more justice a king gives, the more justice there is to give," said Oddi dolefully. Ragnvald suspected he quoted a proverb; he had a store of these, and Ragnvald often could not make out whether he meant them in jest or not.

"I will hear the complaints of kings first," said Harald, breaking through the chatter. "And not too many others. Sitting inside on a day like this is more tiring than any battle."

The crowd laughed dutifully. Ragnvald looked at Atli, who sat across the hall from him. Ragnvald decided he had no complaint, now that Atli was gone from Sogn. Let him be the first to speak.

"Do any kings have complaint?" Harald asked. "Ragnvald, I think you have a complaint."

"None," said Ragnvald. "I am pleased to be here, and ready to forgive any slights against me."

"I have a complaint," said King Hakon. Harald's shoulders sagged slightly and he glanced at Asa, who avoided meeting his eyes. King Hakon was leaving middle age behind, Ragnvald thought, and would soon have to put down his sword, let his sons lead his battles. Hakon and Harald had never become friendly again since Hakon's son Heming killed Harald's favorite captain, and Hakon had never warmed again to Ragnvald either after Ragnvald transferred his loyalty to Harald. Hakon still had power, though, and the loyalty of many lesser kings and jarls.

"Very well," said Harald, and gestured for him to speak.

Hakon walked out into the open floor before Harald's seat and began to speak. "I have lately returned from the Faroe Islands, where I found Solvi Hunthiofsson treating my land as if it were his own. I do not bring a complaint about this today, though King Harald swore to defend my lands as I defend his. I have a more pressing matter."

As Harald sat back into the shadows, Ragnvald thought he saw a roll of his eyes.

"You know my son Geirbjorn," Hakon continued. "He will tell what has passed, and then you may judge."

Geirbjorn and Ragnvald had been friendly during the brief time when Ragnvald stood high in Hakon's affections, but of all Hakon's sons, Ragnvald knew him the least. He was a bird of good camouflage, blending into any company, neither as tall nor handsome as his brother Heming, or as ill-favored as Herlaug was even before his wounding. Now he hesitated before stepping forward and speaking. "My brother Herlaug was grievously wounded in the face by one of Ragnvald Eysteinsson's men," he said. He turned to look at his father, who nodded for him to continue. "We ask for this man's death—"

A commotion interrupted him until Hakon held up his hand for silence. "The man's death, not King Ragnvald's," said Hakon. "Continue, my son."

"As for the king of Sogn"—this Geirbjorn said with a sneer—"he must make certain that the man's family pays a penalty."

"His name is Arnfast," Oddi called out. "You were once friends."

Geirbjorn shrugged. Harald sat forward and turned toward Hakon. "Death and a penalty payment—your son must be an important king indeed."

"Arnfast is an oath breaker," said Geirbjorn. "He used to be my father's man, and now he is Ragnvald's."

"So now you remember his name," said Harald. "This man whose death you desire—did he swear an oath to your father to serve him for life?"

Geirbjorn glanced at his father, Hakon, who stepped forward to speak. "Arnfast betrayed me to him"—Hakon pointed at Ragnvald— "and Ragnvald of Ardal also turned my son Oddi from his duty to his family. I have held my peace for the sake of King Harald, but now he has done my son Herlaug a terrible injury that has disfigured him for life."

"I am not aware that you or your family have ever been betrayed by my friend Ragnvald Eysteinsson, king of Sogn," said Harald. "Who is it you bring suit against today?"

Hakon and Geirbjorn exchanged a few low words with each other.

Ragnvald would have found this amusing if it targeted someone other than himself.

"Arnfast," said Geirbjorn finally. "We bring suit against him for this wound."

"Shouldn't Herlaug Hakonsson bring his own suit?" Harald asked.

"My son lies in fever with half his face gone," said Hakon. "Someone must pay for this. I demand nothing less than death for Arnfast and three measures of gold for his injury."

"I am sorry for your son's injury," said Harald. "A payment is just; death is not. If we would answer injury with death, then let us answer death with death, and condemn your son Heming for the death of my friend Thorbrand." His voice was cold. A murmur sounded in the hall. The death of Thorbrand in an ill-fated duel with Heming was a subject that Harald had not mentioned publicly since forgiving Heming after the battle of Vestfold. Harald waited for the talk to quiet and turned to Ragnvald. "My friend, you were there at Herlaug's wounding. Perhaps you can tell us what happened."

Ragnvald stood forward and spoke of the trap that Vemund had led them into and how, in the confusion, Arnfast had wounded Herlaug. He tried to put equal weight on Arnfast's report of the campsite, his own decision, and the precautions he took. "This wound was done by misadventure," Ragnvald finished. "As for Arnfast, he is a Sogn man. He served Hakon as a boy, and now he serves me, his king."

"King Hakon," said Harald, "here is my decision: you may choose a fine that I will decide, a fair wound-price for a king's son, or three years' outlawry for Arnfast."

"I will not choose," said Hakon. "I will agree to a lifetime's outlawry for Arnfast, and . . . double the usual fine." He glanced at Geirbjorn, and Ragnvald suspected their intention. If Arnfast was outlawed, his life would be forfeit if he remained within the bounds of Norway, and Hakon would make sure he was found and killed before he could leave.

"Neither the injured party nor his injurer are present to agree to a punishment or fine," said Ragnvald. "What if both would prefer to duel?"

"I have outlawed dueling," said Harald.

"Unsanctioned duels," Ragnvald reminded him. "If all parties agree and you sanction it . . ."

"My son will agree to anything I accept," said Hakon.

"And I will do my best to convince Arnfast of the rightness of what is decided here," said Ragnvald. "He is his own man, though."

"And my sons are not?" Hakon asked.

Ragnvald shrugged.

"This is purposeless," said Harald. He banged his cup on his chair. "Here is my verdict: I agree to the double injury fee, for my ally's son has been disfigured." This caused a murmur among the crowd. No one but a king was usually compensated so greatly for an injury, even a disfiguring one. Harald continued: "Arnfast is outlawed for three years from all districts controlled by King Hakon and his sons, as well as my own."

"So he is confined to Sogn?" Ragnvald asked. Arnfast could not afford the price, and so Ragnvald would have to pay it, or put Arnfast and his family into indenture for the next three generations. Better Ragnvald should be in debt to Hakon than force his retainer's family into slavery.

"Yes," said Harald.

"You promised kingdoms for all my sons," said Hakon. "So far Heming only has North Maer. I will agree to this . . . justice if you make a place for my son Geirbjorn, and Herlaug as well if he recovers."

"My ally has been given all he asks for, and still he wants more," said Harald to the crowd. "Your son Heming has not defended Maer as he promised, and so I spent the summer fighting there. I should see if his brother can succeed instead. Geirbjorn may try his luck in North Maer."

"That is not what I meant," said Hakon. "I will not be satisfied with this."

"When are you ever satisfied?" Harald asked. "You try my patience. Here is my last offer, and then you may do what you will, with no fine, no outlawry, and no kingdoms either. Geirbjorn may go to Vestfold and lead my defenses there. I had planned to send my uncle Guthorm, for I fear the king of Sweden has designs upon our southern shores, but let your son prove himself there. If he does well, he shall have his district."

Harald stared down Hakon until he nodded and said, "I agree to this."

"Good," said Harald. "Make sure your sons do as well." He touched his forehead briefly then stood. "I am done giving justice today. Any with other matters may wait until tomorrow."

Harald walked over to Ragnvald as the hall began to clear. "From what I know of the skills of Hakon's sons, I might believe that Herlaug cut himself on his own blade, not Arnfast's." He laughed.

"That is not fair," Ragnvald answered, trying to hide a smile. "They are all good swordsmen, only—"

"How useful is Hakon as an ally, truly?" Harald asked. "My uncle insists that we cannot hold the west coast of Norway without him, but I cannot see how it will end between us except in war. I would rather bring it now than wait for his betrayal."

Ragnvald looked around. Hakon and Geirbjorn had already retreated. Anyone might report this conversation to Hakon, but that was probably what Harald wanted—to make clear that his patience grew thin.

"Your uncle is right," said Ragnvald. "Cheer up, though—Hakon is old and will be dead someday soon."

"Not soon enough," said Harald, but he grinned at that, and clapped Ragnvald on the shoulder. "Come spar with my men and make them better. You will forget all about this."

Ragnvald could not easily forget the gold he now owed Hakon for Herlaug's wounding, but he could remind Harald of his skill in battle before he had to argue with Atli tomorrow.

14

EYSTEIN HAD CRIED AS SVANHILD BROUGHT HIM ON BOARD
Solvi's ship, and then fretted himself into exhaustion. Now he slept
in a fur bag on a bench out of the way of the crew. He had dozed for
long stretches at a time, leaving Svanhild with no other company than
Katla, who did not trouble to hide her resentment that she had been
taken from Iceland so soon after putting her feet on solid ground. She
had no sympathy for Svanhild, and seemed to regard her as much the
cause of her distress as Solvi.

The ship moved swiftly, and Solvi kept its bearing with the aid of
the stars. "We must stop and rest when we can," said Svanhild to Solvi
warily, three days after leaving Iceland. She felt as though every time
she talked to him, he rejected her words. His anger had grown, as
she put all of hers into keeping her energy up to care for Eystein. The
route took them to the Faroe Islands, then the Shetlands, offering a
night or two of respite from the rocking of the ship, and the constant
wakefulness that overnight sailing demanded.

"Hakon's forces chased us out last time," said Solvi.

He had not dismissed her suggestion immediately so she pressed.
"There are many deserted beaches here. Eystein needs a night or two
of good sleep, and the warmth of a fire."

"All he's done is sleep," said Solvi. He glanced back to where Eystein
lay swaddled in his sleeping bag like a newborn.

"Because he is sick," said Svanhild. She could not stop herself from adding, "You are killing him with this voyage."

Solvi said nothing but turned the ship toward the green islands rising in the distance. The islands were tilted, tipped down toward the west as though pressed down by a giant hand, and rising to cliffs in the east. As Solvi's ship drew closer to the archipelago, he veered around to the south. Svanhild went to Eystein, who had opened his eyes and was struggling to sit up.

"See, we are nearing the Faroe Islands," she said to him. "The islands all wear clouds like woolly hats to keep them warm." Eystein smiled at the image. They had sat together this way many times so they could watch the approach of a new shore together, and speak about what they saw.

A small boat sailed east from the southern island, and Solvi steered the ship behind a point of land that would hide them. They made landfall on a narrow beach, ringed on all sides by high cliffs. Solvi's men dragged it up onto the sand, and then moved the stern so the whole of the ship nearly filled the beach, while Svanhild set up a tent in the dim alley between the ship and the cliff.

She sent Thorstein to climb for eggs hidden in the cliff above while she harvested wild lovage that grew in the narrow band of soil that had accumulated at its base. The plant's roots added starch and flavor to the eggs of seabirds, which otherwise tasted like the fish they ate. Eystein could not stay here long.

The wind blew unceasing against the beach, filling Svanhild's ears with a rushing sound that made it difficult to hear anything else. She slept that night in a tent with Katla, nestling Eystein between them for warmth. Overnight the wind shifted, and Svanhild woke in the dim predawn, her body sodden and frigid from rain that had been forced in through a gap in the tent's roof. She was shivering, teeth chattering in a way she thought she should be able to stop, but every time she did it turned into a deep shaking in her chest that felt as much like fear as cold. Eystein—she reached down to touch him, dreading that she would find him as cold as she. Instead, his rain-slick skin was hot with fever.

"Katla, help," Svanhild cried. "My son, his fever." She had let herself believe his illness had passed, even though Solvi put him at risk again. He had seemed better. She sat back on her heels crying, shivering, swatting at the raindrops that still came in through the gap in the tent. No one stirred; she had not spoken loudly enough to be heard over the storm.

"Katla," she cried again. "He is dying, my son is dying. Help me please, Frigga and Freya, goddesses, help me. I cannot bear it, I cannot bear it, I cannot bear it." She rocked and cried until finally Katla woke, and sat up, squinting and stretching. "Help him," said Svanhild. She shook Katla's shoulders. "Do something."

"What should I do?" Katla asked.

"He is burning up from this fever, and there is rain in the tent. Don't be a fool, Katla. This is dangerous."

"The rain will probably help keep his fever down," said Katla.

"Do as I say," said Svanhild. "Or at least fix the hole in the tent and find him some dry clothes."

Katla pawed through the wool bag at the foot of the tent. "They're all wet," she said.

"Then go wake the men. One of them must have some dry clothes—or you can fetch some from the ship."

Katla moved slowly, so slowly leaving the tent that Svanhild screamed at her. "Go. If he dies I will blame you."

"I thought you blamed your husband," Katla said sullenly. Svanhild rose up on her knees and slapped Katla across the face, hard enough it made Svanhild's hand hurt. Katla choked off a cry. She brought her hand to her face, stared at Svanhild for a long moment, and left the tent.

Svanhild lay back down next to Eystein. She cradled him against her chest, and he flopped against her, murmuring in his fever. His breath smelled oddly sweet, a sweetness that made Svanhild think of decay, but no dying thing could give off so much heat. Unna had said that fever burned out the evil that caused illness, like a furnace that smelted iron to remove its impurities. The body did its work, as long as it had the strength to keep up the heat, though a fever could burn out his wits. She would accept that if she had to, even if Eystein should live a fool. Perhaps then Solvi would stop trying to make him into a king.

She stopped those thoughts as swiftly as she could. She might tempt the gods to take that bargain. No, she wanted his wits, his sweetness, everything that made him her beloved son. "We are on a new island," she said to him, hoping he could hear her. "When the sun rises, you will see it better. It has black sand and high cliffs with birds living on them, and green grass above."

When Katla returned with blankets, Svanhild commanded her to fetch Solvi. He arrived after an agonizing wait as Svanhild fussed with Eystein's blankets.

"Well, wife," he said. He stooped to enter the tent. "What is it now?" He looked down at her.

"Your son is very ill," said Svanhild. "I know the men of these isles are not our friends, but we must remain here until he improves."

"He only became sicker when we made landfall," said Solvi. "We must press on."

"That is foolishness! Fevers ebb and flow—you know this. If you make us leave, you will kill him," said Svanhild.

Solvi left the tent without another word. In the morning, when his men packed the ships again, he came back to find her. "The tide is with us," he said. He picked up Eystein and slung him over his shoulder. "Shall I leave you on this beach, Svanhild?"

How tempting, to watch all her cares sail away. She could walk to the north end of the island, to the settlement at Sandvik, indenture herself as a servant, lose herself in a new life, and never think of Solvi or Eystein again.

"No," she said, the words choking in her throat. "No, I will not leave my son."

✢   ✢   ✢

THE FAROE ISLANDS faded from view at midday. The weather was blustery, with cloud cover that parted occasionally. After so little sleep, the brightness of those stabs of sunlight hurt Svanhild's eyes. Eystein did not wake, even when Svanhild pulled him against her. His fever was breaking; he grew cooler as the day wore on. His breaths came slowly, until Svanhild could hardly detect them at all. She held him closer, breathing with him, as though the constant filling and emptying of her own lungs should prompt his.

When she paused for a moment, feeling faint from breathing too hard, he seemed colder still. She pulled up his tunic to listen to his breath as Unna had done, and thought she saw a bruise spreading over his chest as though his heart had begun bleeding. His pulse gave a flutter in his neck, like the beating of a bird's wings, and then stopped. Svanhild held him, then shook him, willing him to wake again, but his body grew chilled as the spirit left it.

She recoiled and thrust him from her so he fell off the bench. When she saw what she had done, she cried out and reached for him again, but she could not make herself take the empty doll of his body back into her arms. Instead she composed his limbs so he lay peacefully against the curved floor of the ship. The beads of water that forced themselves in between the seams of the boards could not trouble him now.

"He is dead," she said. She knelt on the bench above him. She spoke at a normal volume, which was too quiet to be heard by anyone around her. Solvi, at his post by the steering oar, had stayed as far away as possible from where she held her dying son. She leaned down over Eystein and pulled his blanket up to his chin. She should cover his face, she knew, though she could not bear to do that yet. He was so thin, the ridges of his skull pressing through the skin of his forehead, making him look as much like an old man as a boy.

She stood, and stepped deliberately over coiled rope, around barrels of ale and fresh water. She watched herself take these steps as though from the outside. I am walking across the deck, she told herself. I am stepping around this barrel. I am going to my husband to tell him that our son is dead. I am a body doing these things and nothing more. What animates me no longer animates him.

"Our son is dead," said Svanhild, when she stood an arm's length away from Solvi. He seemed not to hear her at first, and then he went white and stumbled back. A swell pitched him forward and he crumpled to his knees, grabbing Svanhild's skirt. Svanhild sank as well, her chest so tight and pained she felt she would break in half.

She pulled Solvi to her breast and held him while he shook silently. She wished for someone she could cling to as he did, someone who could comfort her. Her mother, perhaps, as she was when Svanhild was a child, before tragedy stole her spirit. There had been a time when Svanhild knew that no matter how long or hard she cried, her mother would stroke her hair and console her.

She could not bring herself to stroke Solvi's hair the same way, and soon grew weary of holding him. Eystein needed her—to wash his body, prepare it for burial in a mound on the land she had claimed for him. Solvi must agree to that now; it was where Eystein had been the happiest.

✣ ✣ ✣

WITH KATLA'S HELP, Svanhild wrapped Eystein in another shroud that covered his face, and laid him flat on the floor of the ship. Otherwise, said Katla, he would stiffen sitting half upright, and be harder to bury. Solvi's men averted their eyes and found excuses to look away from the place on the ship now marked with death.

Solvi would not hear of taking Eystein back to Iceland to bury him. "No, we must continue to Tafjord. We are bringing war there, remember," he said. He would not look at her either, only at the horizon beyond the sail, scanning for signs of land.

He seemed to have aged in the half day since Eystein's death. The laugh lines at the corners of his eyes that Svanhild loved had been erased; only the stern furrows between his brows remained. He looked like a carving of an old king, with a pointed beard and empty eyes. He looked like his father.

"Where will our son lie then?" she asked dully.

"He will burn on a pyre as my father did. It matters not where, only that the ashes carry his soul to heaven," said Solvi.

"What heaven is for him?" Svanhild asked. "I want to be buried next to him so we can be together for all time."

"He is no warrior, but he can find a children's heaven, a broad field where he can run," said Solvi.

"We have a field back in Iceland," said Svanhild.

A spasm crossed Solvi's face, some very strong emotion that Svanhild could not read. "He was my son," said Solvi. "My line does not spend the afterlife buried under the ground. Put him in the sea if you prefer."

"No," said Svanhild. "I could not bear that." Her ancestors lay in mounds, guarding their land in death as they had in life. To burn Eystein was to destroy him. To put him in the sea was to abandon him. "Our son died of fever and now you want him to burn. Fire maimed you." Solvi set his jaw. "Do you want your body burned as well?" she asked.

"Yes," said Solvi shortly. "One day the fire shall finish its work."

"If you burn him, you should burn me too," said Svanhild. "You have stolen him from me twice. You will not take him a third time."

✝ ✝ ✝

SVANHILD HAD SPOKEN truth when she said she meant to burn herself with her son. She struggled against Solvi's men, who held her back as they lit the torch for his pyre, yet when shrouds began to burn away from Eystein's face and expose the blackened flesh underneath, she turned away. The wind blew the ashes into her face, and still hot, they made little stinging welts on her skin.

Then she sobbed, sinking to the ground, crying at the slight injury to her skin, crying that she had not forced herself to endure more. Eystein had been too weak to survive as her and Solvi's son, and she had been too weak to follow him into death. He had weakened on their sea journeys and grown stronger on land. He was never meant to be the son of a sea king who would burn his dead. The fates had sent him to the wrong family. They should have sent him to a priestess, to bring him up in the service of Frey. Svanhild should have given him over to them, to learn the magic of plants and the fields. The figure that seemed to writhe in the flames would never do any of those things.

Her crying slowed, and now she felt ill, and vomited up the little food she had eaten that morning onto the sand. She stood, and Solvi's men immediately grabbed her arms again. "I will not," she said, hating herself. She would not die today; she had not loved Eystein enough. "I want to rinse my mouth."

One of them poured from his ale skin into her cupped hands, and she splashed it into her mouth, onto her cheeks, washing away the tear tracks. Svanhild breathed slowly to steady herself. She knew this roiling in her stomach. It was not grief alone that wrenched her breakfast from her. Nor was it some delayed sea sickness. She was with child again. It had been a long time since she had reason to hope. A few times her courses had been late, but then they came, so if Solvi's seed had taken root, it had not stayed very long. This might come to nothing as well. She hoped it would pass early, so she did not have to worry for long about another of Solvi's children dying.

✜   ✜   ✜

THAT NIGHT, SOLVI came to their tent. He had avoided it since leaving Iceland. "Svanhild, are you in there?" he asked.

Svanhild looked up at the roof, shrouded in shadows. "Where else would I be? I am wherever you put me. I obey you, and go where you say, even when it means the death of my son."

"Good," he said. He blew out the lamp and came to her pallet. He pulled her blankets from her, and tugged up her nightgown. She wanted to turn him away. She was too full of her grief, of another child that she would likely mourn alone, to take him into her as well. She felt outside her body, as she had on the ship, as he pushed in between her legs, slicking himself with spit to ease the way. She did not expect to feel pleasure from it, and she remained detached until the end when sensation grabbed her as though she were crushed in a giant's hand, and wrung a sob from her. She clung to him. If he said one kind word to her, she would cry, scream out her grief. He pulled away.

"Stay," she said. "Please. Let it not be this way between us. I am . . ." She hesitated. She did not want to tell him of her pregnancy this early, but if it could forge a link between them, she must take that chance. "I am pregnant."

"You are?" he asked, sounding half skeptical, half hopeful. "Are you sure?"

"It is early, but I was sick on the beach . . . ," said Svanhild. He stiffened at the reminder of their son's funeral.

"Keep better watch of this one," said Solvi. "You let the first one die."

His words cut too close to her fears, that she should have guarded Eystein better, insisted on dry land for his bed before it became his pyre. "You're the one who made him sail when it weakened him," she cried.

"It was the air in Iceland."

Svanhild set her jaw. "Do you deny that sailing made him weak?"

"He was always weak," Solvi yelled, and then quieted to a whisper. "If anyone killed him, it was you performing that ritual in Iceland with your witch."

"You hate me," said Svanhild, crying. "Everyone—Geirny, my brother, said you were cruel, they told me of your father's death-worship, and said you were the same. I thought you a living man, but you are dead. Your seed is dead. You died as a boy, and I am married to your shade."

He slapped her, hard enough to stop her speaking. "If you were more of a woman, you would have kept him alive. You said he hated being on board a ship—but you didn't. A good mother would have made a home for him."

"You had a proper wife before, and you hated her," Svanhild cried. "Many children die. Your children die."

"Yes, and you should kill this one too—if it is even born. Better than letting it be our child."

"If you felt that way," said Svanhild quietly, "you should have divorced me."

"So I should have," said Solvi. "Then I wouldn't have had to watch you kill my son."

"Get out," said Svanhild. He hesitated, seeming aware that he had gone too far; they both had. Svanhild held herself motionless, waiting for his decision, willing him to defy her now, as he had so many times before. He cast his eyes down, and then turned and left the tent.

Svanhild only delayed for a moment before gathering her belongings. She kept her jewels with her at all times, in a bag that she wore tied around her waist. Solvi had been generous with her and always gave her gold, so she could carry the most value in the smallest volume. She had some silver as well, worked up into beautiful rings, brooches, and necklaces she had chosen to remember the lands they visited. It made a heavy package, stuffed with wool to keep it from jingling. Solvi trusted his men, usually, but a thick package of gold might be enough to tempt them. Her tent also contained a skin of watered ale, and the cakes that she had been feeding to Eystein, soaked in goat's milk to keep his strength up. It had not helped Eystein. Nothing had.

Svanhild tied her knife onto her belt, pulled on her cloak, and left her tent, walking out onto the beach on the edge of Trondheim Fjord. She could still stay with Solvi. She knew that his words had been a cry of pain, poorly masked by his anger. She might comfort him once the rawness of his grief passed, but she could never forgive what he had said. Without Eystein, she had nothing to bind herself to him. Ragnvald had offered to take her once with Solvi's child growing inside her. She hoped he would accept her six years later, in the same condition. He must. Ragnvald would count her return as a victory over Solvi.

The moon was big, though waning, and clouds shadowed it from time to time, plunging the beach into darkness. The tents of Solvi's men made dark shapes against the lighter background of the sand. None kept watch tonight. Who would suspect that one of Harald's enemies had washed up on this abandoned beach, next to rocky ground and a thick forest?

Svanhild trusted herself and her sense of direction from years of adventure with Solvi. He would hate her for leaving, she knew. But he already hated her for Eystein's death. This night, he had taken her body the same way he did early in their marriage, when he had hated her for her rejection of him almost as much as he hated her now. She did not want to win him back this time, though, with nothing to gain but more misery, more lost children.

When they came this way the day before, Solvi's ships had passed by a broader and more welcoming beach, with a slope that led up to a smallish hall on some farmland. Every day traders sailed these waters, as well as fishermen whose catch kept Harald's court fed. Svanhild set off through the trees toward that hall, moving slowly, from one tree to the next. It would only take half a night of walking to reach the farm, and someone there would bring her to Harald, then to Ragnvald, to safety.

The moon set well before dawn, leaving her in full darkness, too dark even to feel her way from tree to tree. She wrapped herself in her cloak and covered herself with a blanket of leaves for shelter. Her grief too kept her insulated. With this pain in her chest, how could cold or hunger hurt her? If Solvi came and found her, she would endure it; if someone else wanted to harm her, she would endure that too.

15

RAGNVALD COULD SPEND MORE TIME WITH HIS SONS AT NI-
daros than he did at Sogn, where he always had other work to do, disputes to settle, and farm business to oversee. Here his sons provided
a welcome distraction from the endless games of power and favor at
Harald's court, so after a breakfast where it seemed to Ragnvald that
every petty noble in Norway wanted him to use his influence with
Harald to better their position, Ragnvald brought his sons to see Harald's new stallion.

"Pretty," said Ivar. The stallion danced around its paddock, tossing
its glossy black mane. Compared with shaggy fjord ponies and their
crossbreeds, it looked delicate.

"Maybe too pretty for Harald," said Ragnvald. "It might want a smaller
rider."

"You, Father?" Einar asked.

"Not me. That gift would be more trouble than it's worth." Like
much of Harald's generosity.

"What kind of horse is it?" Ivar let go of Ragnvald's hand and pressed
himself up against the fence, looking between the slats. Einar followed
him, watching the horse warily.

"I've heard it's an Arab," said Ragnvald.

"What is that?" Einar asked.

"It is from a faraway land," Ragnvald answered. The horse was
beautiful and had a wild freedom to its movements, even in the pad-

dock, that made Ragnvald's chest tight with longing, not to ride the horse, but to free it, or to be it, in its native land of sand and sun. "Where it never snows and men have dark skin. They are like us though—great explorers and merchants. Sometimes their explorers come here. And a few Norsemen have gone to their great cities. When we are friends, we trade things."

"Like this horse," said Ivar.

"Like this horse," Ragnvald agreed.

As Ragnvald shepherded the boys toward the women's chamber to leave them in the care of Hilda or one of their servants, a woman overtook them. Her blue silk overdress caught the sunlight as she moved and Ragnvald knew her to be Vigdis by the shape of her hips and the way she moved, even before he saw her face. Golden hair tied back by a narrow band of the same blue snaked down her back in a long, complicated braid. She knelt down to greet the boys.

"Einar Ragnvaldsson," Vigdis said in her honeyed voice. "You look just like your brother Hallbjorn." That was her son by Ragnvald's stepfather, Olaf, named after Vigdis's father. When Ragnvald became king of Sogn, he had sent Hallbjorn to his grandfather, along with a wet nurse, so he would not have to raise up his enemy in his own household.

"Vigdis," said Ragnvald in a choked voice. "What do you want?"

"Do you remember me?" she asked Einar, not turning or acknowledging Ragnvald. Einar's eyes flicked up at Ragnvald, who remained carefully impassive. He wanted to know the answer as well. Ivar moved closer to his brother.

Einar nodded, once hesitantly, then again more emphatically. "You used to be one of the king's women."

"One of?" said Vigdis with a low laugh. Now she turned to look at Ragnvald. "I did not know there were so many."

"There were not—I mean . . . ," Ragnvald trailed off. He should have known better than to respond to her question. He had learned, when she still shared his bed, to keep silent when answering could not help him.

She looked satisfied at having flustered him, and turned back to

Einar, though her words were still for Ragnvald. "Should I hate you?" she asked. "For making my son forget me?"

"I remember you," said Einar coolly. Vigdis's face tightened.

"Einar, this is your mother. Vigdis, what are you doing here?" he asked, feeling helpless. "Did you not return safely to your brother?"

"Yes," she said with a hint of bitterness. "Safe and sound." Vigdis had grown up in a trapper's family in the mountains east of Stavanger Fjord.

"Did you miss the sea?" Ragnvald tried for sarcasm, yet to his ears his voice sounded as though he yearned for her still. "Why are you here?" he asked more roughly. He wanted her to reveal something that would help him against Atli. As much as he might wish it, that business would not be over until Harald gave his judgment, and perhaps not even then.

"I am a widow," she said, tossing her hair over her shoulder. "I may go where I wish."

"I wish—" Ragnvald cut off his thought. He wished she were anywhere else. He wished that Hilda had not forced him to send her away. She smiled up at him past a veil of hair that had come loose from her braid. The silk of her dress rippled against her thigh, over the curve where hip met waist. Ragnvald tried to think of Hilda's instead, pleasing and golden in candlelight, as if she spent all day sunning them instead of hiding them under her skirts. Hilda had no dress of such a vibrant blue. Ragnvald did not think such a bright color would suit her; it would make her look brown and worn.

Vigdis seemed to see all of this pass over his face. Ragnvald could not tell if it pleased her or not, to know that she still moved him. He had been unable to satisfy his craving for her in those early days, greedy for the feeling of her skin under his hands, her legs parting for him, the pleasure she gave him and the pleasure she sometimes took.

"I am glad I am here, though I am sure you are not." Vigdis stood, moving well away from Einar. "And your wife is not. I did not think you would bring your wife here." She smoothed down her dress over her waist. "She did not seem as though she would happily stir from Sogn."

"You hoped to find me alone? Ready to fall into your bed again?" Ragnvald asked. The boys watched silently, eyes round with interest. They could hardly understand these adult concerns but must sense their importance. "I would rather not see you at all. If more payment will make you leave, you shall have it."

"You cannot buy me off this time," she said. "I will stay clear of you, if I can. If that is what you wish." Her gaze dropped from his face to his belt, and Ragnvald had to grit his teeth to keep from putting his hands there, to adjust his tunic to make sure his clothes fell well, that he looked as trim and strong as when Vigdis had left.

"It is," said Ragnvald.

"Very well. I will do my best, if you grant me some time with my son." Her eyes finally left him. She looked down at Einar.

"What of the son you left behind in Stavanger?" Ragnvald asked.

"It is not Stavanger," said Vigdis, showing a rare irritation. "It is forests and nothing more. The river there is called Hel. But my son is well cared for."

"So is Einar," said Ragnvald, taken aback at the bitterness in her words. She must have been desperate to leave her brother's household.

"He is bruised," she said. She reached down to caress Einar's face, but he ducked her touch like an unfriendly cat.

"Boys fight," said Ragnvald. "He is fine."

She nodded her head and walked by him, leaving plenty of room between them so not even the hem of her dress touched him.

"Do you remember her truly?" Ragnvald asked Einar when she was out of earshot.

Einar glanced at Ivar, who had remained quiet throughout. He was a happy child who did not often react to the tensions between his elders, unlike Einar.

"I don't know, my lord," said Einar. "I think so."

"You may see her," said Ragnvald, "but tell me if she asks you to do anything." If he had said such things to Ivar, he would not have understood, but Einar seemed less a child than a small man standing before Ragnvald, one whom Ragnvald must meet on his own terms. "If you do not want to see her, you do not have to," he added.

"What do you wish of me?" Einar asked.

For you to behave as a child, thought Ragnvald. "For no more questions," he said brusquely. "Do as you please."

Ivar twisted his hands together. He plainly felt left out, and disconcerted by the conversations he did not understand. "What about me, Father?" he asked. Ragnvald looked down at both of them. Einar, six months older, a head taller, and years older in his spirit, still deserved better than to face Vigdis and her manipulations.

"Help your brother and be kind to your mother," said Ragnvald. "Things are strange for all of us here."

＋　＋　＋

A COMMOTION NEAR the water drew Ragnvald's attention away from the boys. Beyond the paddocks and shore buildings, he saw the mast of a ship drawing near. The sail, striped blue and white, hung at a slant, poorly trimmed. Dirt streaked its edges, and decay darkened the holes that ropes passed through. Halogaland kings—Hakon and his sons—used blue and white.

Ragnvald ran toward the shore, then slowed when he realized he had left his sons behind. He waited for them to catch up as Heming Hakonsson emerged from between two of the buildings. When he came closer Ragnvald saw he had dried blood streaked across his clothes and a cut above his eye.

"Are you hurt?" Ragnvald asked him. "Do you need a healer?"

Heming tugged at his shirt of saffron silk, and drew his fingers absently across the brownish spatters. He flexed his hands, which were streaked with blood and mottled with bruises on his knuckles. "No," he said after a moment. "Most of this is not my blood."

Heming's men, no more than ten, assembled behind him. A sorry lot, all young and richly dressed, but looking ashen, and bearing wounds and stains similar to Heming's. "I do not have time to greet you, Ragnvald. I must see Harald."

"He is usually at the practice ground at this time of day," said Ragnvald. "I will lead you."

"I know the way," said Heming. He pushed past Ragnvald.

"Go find your mother," said Ragnvald to his sons. "My lady," he added for Einar, who was very conscious of titles. "I want you both safe."

He followed Heming to the practice yard. A wooden fence enclosed an area big enough for a hundred men to spar without danger to any but their adversary. Harald stood at the top of the gentle slope, instructing Oddi and another man, whom Ragnvald recognized as Atli's son, Aldi. Hakon stood talking with Guthorm, in a low voice. Something in the way Hakon's eyes flickered at Ragnvald when he approached made Ragnvald think that he was the subject of their discussion.

Ragnvald never grew tired of seeing Harald fighting, either in practice or in battle. His ability with the sword seemed inborn, natural, but he also had the wit to be able to break his skill down and teach it to other men, and it was in these moments that he was most kingly. He forged bonds with his men this way, and made them into a force of warriors who would pour out their blood and effort every summer to build his kingdom. Six years of fighting by Harald's side and sparring against him had improved Ragnvald's swordsmanship until few could withstand him.

Harald stood, holding a practice sword in his hand, and beckoned his two attackers. As soon as they rushed him, he disarmed Aldi with a quick, hard parry, and then he turned and rammed his sword's pommel into Oddi's wrist, who dropped his blade and shook out his hand.

"How do you guard against this?" Aldi asked.

"Tighter grip," said Harald. "Practice carrying one of these oblong stones in your hand as long as you can." Harald picked up a stone about half as long as his thigh and as big around as his palm. "Walk about the yard with it, to measure off distance. Whatever distance you can do today, work until you've doubled it by next month, and again two months after."

"Don't fight a giant," said Ragnvald, giving Oddi a sideways smile. "That is even better advice."

"Ah, Ragnvald, this is why you are better than me at strategy," said Harald.

"You don't need strategy," said another man to Harald. "Strength and size—"

"King Harald," said Heming, interrupting. "I have come from Tafjord where Solvi Hunthiofsson's ships have attacked."

Harald took a ladle of water from one of his servants and tipped it into his mouth. It spilled over his snarled golden beard, and he shook himself off like a hound. "This is the only tale you ever come to tell me, even when I loaned you warriors and it turned out to be no more than local brigands. I hear that Solvi is in Iceland, and he and his wife have taken land there. Is he in two places at once?"

"It was not him, it was one of his men," said Heming. "But he used Solvi's colors and told me Solvi would follow soon after."

"Solvi Klofe? Solvi the Short?" Harald laughed. "This little man sent his little warriors to plunder your little hall, and you come running to me? Can you take care of nothing for yourself?" Heming's face went white. Harald baited him often in the years since the death of Thorbrand, and his taunts had been growing worse.

Hakon strode across the grounds to stand behind his son. "I came to see if any of your fine warriors wanted to help," said Heming, "or if they are better at burning halls than they are at protecting them." He clenched his fists.

Ragnvald had felt some sympathy for Heming as he bore up under Harald's taunts. Now he stepped toward Harald, in case Heming's anger broke into violence. He could disarm Heming with the move that Harald had just demonstrated.

Harald stepped forward to loom over Heming. "When you took Tafjord, you said that you could protect it, you and your father. You descend from the mightiest line of kings in western Norway, as I am always told." He looked at Hakon. "Why does your father not help you? Why did you come to me?"

"It is for you that Heming holds this land," said Hakon. "You should help him defend it."

"I think Heming did not want his father to know of his shame," said Harald. "He did not expect to find you here."

"One day, I will fight you," said Heming. "You cannot insult me forever."

"I do not want to kill you," said Harald. "So I withdraw my words—no shame, no dishonor. I am sure your men fought well."

Heming glanced at Oddi, then down at the ground. "Yes," he said. "I brought the fight to them in our ships and—well we escaped at least."

"Yes, thank the gods for that," said Harald with heavy sarcasm. "I'd rather have you than Tafjord, I suppose. Come before me tomorrow. I have many warriors here. Most of them wished to stay until Yule, but they will grow bored before long, and you are generous to come and share your troubles with us. I will find some willing to fight on your behalf. My servants will give you clean clothes and tend to your wounds."

Heming nodded his agreement to this and went off with his father. He would surely want a bath; he did not allow himself to look messy for long. Ragnvald watched them go. He worried Harald would provoke Heming and Hakon into war with him before he was ready to face them. A king must control his emotions, not vent them like a petty child, especially if he wanted to rule a land as vast and divided as Norway.

✛   ✛   ✛

THE FOLLOWING DAY a fall storm lashed Nidaros, making the practice ground into a mud slick, and hiding the far shore of Trondheim Fjord. Without better prospects for entertainment, Harald decided to hear more cases. Ragnvald suspected Atli had been pressing him, which seemed like a good sign. Ragnvald would win this by showing himself to be entirely indifferent to Atli, so much that he did not even see Atli as a real threat.

The hall was even more crowded than before, since the weather had lured no one outside. Leading women sat in rows near Harald's high seat, each with handwork in her lap. As soon as Harald sat down, he dispensed with ceremony, and said, "Atli Kolbrandsson, Ragnvald Eysteinsson, I know there is some matter between you. Let us settle it, and quickly."

"There is no purpose in airing dead grievances," said Ragnvald. "Atli has quit Sogn, so my quarrel with him is over."

"Good," said Harald. "I am done with kings and jarls then. Let me hear some simple disputes between farmers."

Atli stepped forward. "What Ragnvald Eysteinsson will not say is that he could not hold his land this summer," he said. "I sailed in and took it with twenty men."

"Sogn is a land at peace," said Harald. "What right had you to take it?"

"He did not take it," said Ragnvald. "He might have kept my seat warm with his unwelcome backside, but that is as far as it went." Harald smirked.

"I have a claim to Sogn," said Atli. "And your uncle Guthorm said I should go and guard it."

Guthorm shifted in his seat, glancing quickly at Ragnvald before turning his eyes to Harald. "I said that if you had a claim you should guard it," said Guthorm. "Only if."

"I have not heard of your claim to this land," said Harald. "You should have told me when you visited before. I am king, not my uncle." He gave Guthorm a warning look, and Guthorm surprised Ragnvald by shrinking somewhat under it. Guthorm had long led Harald, or at the least they moved as one, like a pair of oxen hitched to a plow.

"My apologies, King Harald," said Atli with a bow. "I can tell it now." He stood aside a little, and in a tone for storytelling said, "I heard it from my grandfather."

"You said that my grandfather killed him, so how did you hear it from him?" Ragnvald asked. "Scattered his bones on my land, you said."

"Yes," said Atli, his strange, protruding eyes round and wide, as though he had never thought of speaking anything but truth. "My grandfather came to claim what was rightfully his: the lands of Sogn, and your grandfather Ivar killed him and scattered his bones so his shade can never rest. It was my great-grandfather who was king of Sogn before Ivar came and took it from him. It is known." His claim had changed, Ragnvald noted, from grandfather to great-grandfather.

"We have a skald here who knows the ancestry of every leading man in the Norse lands," said Harald. "Perhaps he will know your ancestors."

"It does not matter," said Ragnvald. "A king must hold what he would keep."

"As you did?" Atli asked. "I took your land with twenty men."

"And here we are again," said Ragnvald. "You would have lost those men just as quickly had I not stayed my hand. Harald, are you going to listen to this upstart?"

"Upstart?" said Guthorm. "He has twenty years of fighting on you. Ships and swords, experienced warriors and sailors he can call from Dublin, enough to turn the hard-fought battles of this past summer into routs had he been with us. Surely Ragnvald the Wise can see the benefit of that." The byname stung, as it was meant to. Guthorm only used it when he wished to remind Ragnvald of his youth and lack of experience compared with Guthorm's many years of battle. "Let us see what this skald has to say," Guthorm added.

The elderly skald was summoned, and he began his song, naming Ragnvald's family tree, Ragnvald's father, Eystein, his father, Ivar, and his father, Halfdan, before him, into the mists of legend, and the loins of the gods. It was a litany Ragnvald knew well and repeated silently along with the skald.

Then he began Atli's: his father, Kolbrand, his grandfather Asleif before him, from whom Atli had taken his full name, and then his great-grandfather Halfdan.

"It is a common name," said Ragnvald. But the litany continued, naming the same men as in Ragnvald's line back to Fjornot the Giant, though at thirty generations back, the skald had skipped a few names to get there.

"You are kin," said Harald.

A movement caught Ragnvald's gaze, and he saw Vigdis's hand curling around the arm of her chair, her body angled forward. He looked at Atli, and then at the skald. Something passed between them, a recognition. Gold had changed hands to purchase the skald's words, Ragnvald would swear to it before the gods. He saw Vigdis's hand in all of this.

Ragnvald could not swear to it here, though, not without better proof than a glance. "My king," he said to Harald. "I have sworn to you and you have sworn to me to help me regain my father's lands. Which you did, and I bless you for it. Would you now strip them from me?" Harald hated nothing more than an oath breaker and would never allow himself to be called one.

"Of course not," said Harald. Vigdis sat back in her chair.

"I have nothing but reverence for Sogn, and its land, and its people," said Atli. "Remember, when I came, I did not injure anyone."

"One of your men beat my wife, Hilda—she can testify to it."

"And I punished him with death," said Atli. "I want to protect your family and lands. If I can be of value to Ragnvald while he helps Harald fight his battles, I would be honored. Ragnvald already introduced me and my men to all of the leading farmers of Sogn during the harvest."

"What?" Ragnvald exclaimed. Atli had pivoted like an expert swordsman.

"I thank you for that excellent introduction to Sogn and its people," said Atli.

"How can you say no to such a generous offer, Ragnvald?" said Guthorm.

"Indeed Ragnvald, how?" Atli asked with infuriating innocence.

"What would you have me agree to—handing over Sogn to this interloper?" Ragnvald asked.

"You fight so much on your king's behalf," said Atli, "and with your brother Sigurd as your land's only protector—"

"King Harald," said Ragnvald, speaking over him. "If Atli is such a brilliant fighter, with men who will follow him anywhere, why not enlist him to fight in Maer for Heming, and expel Solvi and his men once and for all?"

"Would he be better than you at this task?" Guthorm asked.

If only Ragnvald could get Harald alone, they could talk about this without the audience to whom Ragnvald must play, putting double and triple meanings in every word of his speech. He met Hilda's eyes across the room and let her calmness soothe him. Let Atli talk himself into trouble. In his glibness, he could easily put a foot wrong.

"Don't ask that," said Harald with a laugh. "Ragnvald is too modest to answer truly." To Ragnvald he said, "You command far more men and you are a proven leader. Atli has been gone too long and has what—thirty loyal men?"

"I have more in Dublin," said Atli. Ragnvald wanted to ask how useful they would be to him, if Atli could not cross the sea to bring them back to Norway, but that would not help his case.

"How many can you raise from Sogn?" Harald asked Ragnvald, though he knew the answer.

"At least five hundred," said Ragnvald, his heart sinking.

"Then it is settled," said Harald. "Atli will guard Sogn for you, while you bring North Maer back under our control."

"My king," said Ragnvald, "by the friendship you bear me, let us discuss this privately. Later. It is not now a matter of justice, but of strategy." He did not like to invoke Harald's friendship before witnesses unless he had to. He already owed Harald so much, and with Herlaug's wounding had gone even deeper into debt. It seemed too likely that one day Harald would find his requests too expensive, and withdraw his friendship rather than pay them.

"Of course!" said Harald. "You are right—this deserves more discussion. I would have peace between my friends, and both of your good swords bloodied in my conquest, not each other's throats. We will decide how best to situate both of you after Yule."

Ragnvald glanced at Guthorm, who looked satisfied enough by this. As Ragnvald left the audience chamber to refresh himself, he heard the swish of silk behind him and Vigdis seized his arm.

"Is this your doing?" he asked.

"You took me away from my son," she said. "If Atli is guarding your family and hall, then perhaps . . ."

"You never cared for Einar when you were with us," said Ragnvald.

"How could I, when your wife hated both of us so much?" said Vigdis, her voice rough, as though she truly felt pained. "Any affection I gave the kitten, I feared she would punish him for it."

"True motherhood is difficult, I am told," said Ragnvald dryly. Vigdis had never called Einar her kitten before, not in Ragnvald's hearing or anywhere else. If Einar resembled a kitten, it was a fierce forest cat, as likely to scratch as to curl toward its master's hand for affection.

"So it is," she replied. "Give me Einar to raise, and I will turn Atli from this course."

"Does he truly think he can get Sogn from me in this way?" Ragnvald asked.

"He already has," said Vigdis. "You saw what Harald's decision will be—he will not change his mind. And you do not have a better plan. If you did, you would have voiced it."

Ragnvald might think of a better plan if he had some time to read the currents and set a new course. Harald had given him until Yule. He could thwart Atli yet.

"The wind changes quickly," she said in a whisper, as though she knew the drift of his thoughts. Perhaps she did. She had known him longer than anyone else in Harald's court. "Best move with it."

He could give her Einar. A strange boy, little wanted by anyone except this woman. And his half-brother. Ragnvald could not do that to Ivar—the child would rather lose a limb than be parted from him.

"I will speak to Harald before I decide anything," said Ragnvald. "But I have made my last bargain with you. I've thought of fostering Einar in the Orkney Islands to strengthen our alliances there. As it stands, you may see him at some year-turning feasts, but if he goes across the sea . . ." He shrugged. "If you want to see your son again, you had better try to change Atli's mind."

16

SVANHILD SLUMPED AGAINST THE CAPSTAN OF A SHIP PI-
loted by Floki, warrior of Harald, king of all Norway. She had hailed
the ship as it passed, told Floki who she was, and that she wanted to go
to Nidaros. He helped her into the ship with a sort of frightened deference that made her wonder if he thought her a heroine or a villain.

She felt like a tapestry that had its ties cut. She did not even look at
the fjord passing by. She was limp, boneless, a sensation that brought
relief along with emptiness. Eystein was gone, that tether cut. She was
no longer Solvi's wife—that thought caused a tug in her breast. She
knew very well the pain that had caused his ugly words. Her pain
came in a different flavor, too bleak for anger, but she had said terrible
things to him, things she did not mean. She could not return after
those words had been said, flaying his manhood as surely as if she had
used a knife. He would never forgive her.

Now she had fallen to the ground, to the bottom of this unfamiliar
ship, the lowest point, where she could rest. And rest too upon Ragnvald's old promise to her, that he would take her in no matter what.
She had no doubt of his loyalty, and so she must do nothing now except let this ship bear her toward Nidaros.

She pulled herself up to standing when the ship made a broad turn
and slowed. It approached a muddy beach crowded with boats of all
sizes pulled up next to each other. A collection of houses beyond them
reminded her of the market town Kaupanger, though Nidaros was

more orderly. Newer and richer too, every building made of fresh-planed wood, kept well oiled. The seams between the turf bricks that made up the roofs were still visible. In another year or two, grass would grow to cover them.

She allowed Floki to set up a ladder for her to climb down from the ship. She had no desire to show off here as she did with Solvi's men, to make sure they knew that she could jump out of a ship as well as any of them.

"King Harald will want to see you," said Floki. "He speaks of you sometimes." Floki was young and dazzled by her legend. He could not see past it to the tired woman in a grubby dress, stained from weeks of travel, who reeked of sweat and vomit.

"That is flattering," said Svanhild, her voice dull. She tried to put the force and charm into it that had won men's loyalty before, and could not do it. "I have lost my son and my husband in one day, and I want the comfort of my brother Ragnvald. Please take me to him. I will be presented to King Harald when I am bathed and better dressed." Floki looked uncertain. Svanhild put her hand on his forearm again. "I will tell him how you found me, do not fear."

That was what Floki wanted to hear. He gave Svanhild an eager smile and then escorted her through the warren of buildings to a long hall where, he told her, Ragnvald had a sleeping room he shared with his wife. Floki said she might wait there, and he would fetch her brother.

Svanhild sat on the neatly made bed, wishing for nothing else but to lie down in it, dirty as she was, and escape her misery in sleep. She felt she could sleep for days, weeks, retreating to where the weight of Eystein's death and Solvi's betrayal could no longer touch her. To keep herself awake, she examined the treasures on the low folding table, and found among them a polished silver mirror. Even in the low lamplight she could see her face had grown thin and drawn from her weeks at sea tending Eystein. Unna had warned her that she would not carry a child to term unless she gained some weight. She put her hand over her womb—she had not felt the sickness since Eystein's funeral. A seer Solvi had met on his travels, before marrying Svanhild, had told him that he would have only one son, so if this child lived, it must be a daughter.

She had not experienced daily sickness during her pregnancy with Eystein either—it had come and gone depending, Svanhild sometimes thought, on the direction of the wind. Its lack might be no more than her body's natural pattern. Or Eystein's sister might have died with him, and was waiting only for Svanhild's body to expel her. She remembered Solvi holding her after she lost an early pregnancy, speaking no reproach, saying nothing at all, only letting his warmth soothe her sadness. How could that be the same man who had taken her child from her? A daughter would not tempt him to regain his ancestral land. For a daughter he would only try to amass a good dowry and find a worthy husband.

If he had been pleased to hear the news of her pregnancy, she would have stayed. She must cling to her anger, or she would throw herself at Ragnvald's feet and beg him to bring her back to Solvi. No, Solvi had denied her any choice when he dragged her and Eystein from Iceland, sent attackers to Tafjord, played her for a fool along with all of the other targets of his cleverness. She would make her own choices now.

Her face in the silver mirror twisted with these thoughts, turning as ugly as their parting words, so she put the mirror away. No wonder Floki thought her a sorceress. She would let Harald's cooks feed her up until she was plump again, and perhaps let Ragnvald marry her off to a new husband. She would make herself rich and happy and placid and take no more sea journeys except pleasure trips.

She heard swiftly moving feet, a rustle of curtains, and then Ragnvald was there.

"Svanhild," he said, staring at her dumbly. "You're . . . how? You're so thin."

She felt a rush of pleasure so strong at seeing him that it almost wrenched tears from her. She covered the force of her emotion by tossing a pillow weakly at him, which he caught and held in one hand. As he came toward her to put it back in the bed, she rose, threw her arms around him, and clung to him. He held her and when he would have let go, she held on tighter, until she was crying against his shoulder, hardly feeling it—no sobs, only tears that would not stop, a river she could not dam.

He maneuvered her so that he sat next to her on the bed and could hold her less awkwardly. When she finally released him, he pulled the scarf from her hair and gave it to her so she could use it to dry her tears.

"What are you doing here?" he asked as she dabbed at her cheeks. "Floki said you had run away from your husband. Can we expect Solvi at any instant? Or is he dead? Floki did not know."

"No, he's—" She cut herself off. If Solvi was no longer her husband, she could tell Ragnvald where he went, what he planned, but she could not take that step yet, not so quickly. She was not yet ready to imagine him dead on Ragnvald's sword. She would rather think of him at the steering oar of one of his ships, narrowing his eyes and looking at the horizon.

"He's sailing for Tafjord," said Ragnvald, half to himself. "Yes, he must. He will join his man there. And he expects reinforcements, or he would not bring his force into the heart of Harald's territory." At her expression, he added, "Do not worry, I would have guessed this. Harald has already planned to sail against him. Did Solvi think that we would ignore him all winter until he could dig in more? No, he is expecting to force a battle when the weather will make it all the more dangerous. But Harald's mother, Ronhild, is a better weather-witch than any he could have."

"Do you need me to answer any of your questions or do you know everything already?" Svanhild asked him crisply.

"Tell me why you came, Svanhild," he said, putting his arm around her again. "I do not need the whole story, only—did Solvi mistreat you?"

"No more than—no. He has been a good husband until . . . just now. And he was trying. Oh Ragnvald, our son . . ." She could hardly speak for crying again. "Do not make me say it." He pulled her close until she lay her head on his shoulder, and he stroked her hair until she stopped crying again. Hilda entered at that moment. Svanhild saw a flash of anger on her face followed by recognition.

"Wife, look—my sister has returned to me," said Ragnvald. "She is too ill and heartsick to be in much company. Please help her bathe and find her clothes. Keep her out of the way of Vigdis if you can."

"Vigdis?" Svanhild cried. "What is she doing here?"

"That is a long story," said Ragnvald, "and I'm sure you will hear the parts of it that flatter me the least from Hilda." He gave Hilda a look that mixed affection with annoyance. "I think no one would want to face that woman at less than their best. Once she hears of your coming she will seek you out. I will say you are ill as long as I can, but then you must make ready."

"Leave us, husband," said Hilda. "Svanhild needs to rest."

Ragnvald gave Svanhild one of his rare smiles. The scar across his cheek had cut one of his childhood dimples in half—Solvi's doing, she remembered. She returned it, though her smile felt brittle.

"I want a bath first," she said to Hilda. "And then rest, yes. Thank you, sister."

"You make Ragnvald sound like a boy again," said Hilda. "I have not heard him so carefree in a long time." Svanhild wondered what that meant, either about Ragnvald or his marriage to Hilda. Perhaps both of them were too serious to make a happy marriage. When they reached the bath, Hilda spoke a few words to the old woman attendant. "She will find me when you're done," said Hilda.

"Bathe with me," said Svanhild suddenly. She did not want to be alone. She had felt alone on her voyage, and now even more in this strange new town, though Ragnvald's welcome was like a warm blanket: her big brother, ready to take everything in hand. He did not need her to do anything but bathe and rest. If he fought Solvi—well, Solvi had always been sure, with some fey, inborn understanding, that he and Ragnvald would not be the cause of each other's deaths, and she was willing to comfort herself with that.

Hilda gave Svanhild a shy smile Svanhild remembered from their girlhood together. "Of course," she said. She hesitated, and added, "Sister."

In the bath, Svanhild leaned her head back against the dry wood and let the cleansing sweat pour from her body. It smelled of the sea, a marine tang that rose to Svanhild's nose. She washed off Solvi with this sweat and the frigid water she poured over herself. The cold drew tears to her eyes, from some bottomless source. She wondered if she would ever be done shedding them.

✧ ✧ ✧

SVANHILD SPENT HER first few days in Nidaros resting in Hilda's room with no will to leave the bed. When she slept, her body felt light, as though it scarcely existed. During the terrible times when it would not sleep, it was unbearably heavy, full of aches that had no source or end, that made even turning over into an ordeal.

Hilda joined her at night, to sleep next to her, and otherwise made no demands on her time. The children—Ragnvald's children—who she alluded to in conversation with Ragnvald, slept elsewhere, so they did not trouble Svanhild. Hilda took care not even to mention them to Svanhild, knowing her loss was raw, until Svanhild became annoyed and tried to bait her into talking about them. Hilda's avoidance was as cruel a reminder as hearing about them.

Ragnvald visited her sometimes, but even then she spoke little and had trouble staying awake. Neither he nor Hilda were the same people she had known when she left. Svanhild supposed she was not the same either, but she also did not know who she was now, no longer Solvi's wife or Eystein's mother. Ragnvald wore his new rank well, thicker of shoulder and solid and smooth through the waist, dressed in rich, dark clothing.

Hilda wore her years less well. Her clothes, though finely made, did not fit her well. She had a heaviness to her, not only of body, but also of spirit. She seemed years older than Ragnvald, dim where he was vital. She bore herself hesitantly, except when she had to deal with physical realities, like helping Svanhild out of her dress on that first night. Then her touch was firm and confident, and Svanhild wished Hilda would take charge of the rest of Svanhild's life with the same ease she had in manipulating Svanhild's limbs.

Svanhild only found peace in the moments between sleeping and waking, when she drifted in a dream state. At those times, she knew of her losses, but could pretend that they had happened to someone else, or to herself, but a long time ago. Like the loss of her father, experienced, mourned, and worked into her memories, no longer an open wound.

✤ ✤ ✤

EVENTUALLY SVANHILD'S LETHARGY faded enough that she grew tired of sleep and breathing the stale air of the hall. She wanted a freshening breeze on her face, and to see something other than the wooden ceiling of the room where she had spent the last seven days. She wanted to bathe again, this time to wash off the mustiness of lying too long abed. Hilda would surely prefer sharing a bed with her if she smelled better. She washed Svanhild's face and hands with a cloth in the morning, as though Svanhild were a child or an invalid.

Svanhild wrapped her hair under a wimple and added an extra hood to protect herself from the weather, then made her way through the maze of hangings to a door that led outside. The air that touched her face was pure and cold, more refreshing than a drink of spring water, though the light from the overcast sky seemed to stab her eyes. She chose a direction that paralleled the fjord, and began walking that way. If she did not find the bathhouse before she reached the edge of the town, she would turn around. It did not matter, as long as she had something to do.

Bare trees stretched toward the sky like hands reaching for one of the heavens. Crows roosted in the highest branches; at some unspoken signal a flock of them took to the skies, flying up and up until Svanhild lost them in black spots before her eyes.

She turned her gaze back to earth and saw a steaming, naked man run from a small building, followed by servants holding towels and a mug of something hot. The man whooped as he broke through the lacework of ice near the river's edge. Svanhild walked closer and saw him throw a mass of tangled blond hair over his head so the water from it streamed down his back.

He scrambled up the slope with a few athletic bounds, and ran back toward the bathhouse, his servants following him. He was very tall. Svanhild would not even come to his shoulder. His size and the striations of muscle along his back and flanks, the powerful symmetry of his shoulders, and his long white legs furred with golden hair, made him look a god—Heimdall, the white god, must glow like this when he came from the gods' bathhouse.

One of the servants walked directly toward her. "You cannot gawk at the king," he said. "Begone, old woman."

She turned away, slowly. She should not be ordered about by a servant. Was she not a sea queen in her own right?

"Who is this?" Harald asked, standing to be wrapped in a towel. Svanhild's gaze traveled down his naked torso. The muscles of his stomach moved in and out as he caught his breath from the cold.

"I am Svanhild Eysteinsdatter," said Svanhild. Her voice, long unused, cracked. She pitched it lower. "Sister of—"

"Sister of Ragnvald," said Harald. He seemed not to feel the cold, or his brightness was proof against it. "I am pleased to see you are feeling better. You came to bathe?" He gestured at the servant who had scolded her. "Send for waiting-women to attend the lady Svanhild in the bath."

He was definitely bigger than when she had seen him last in Vestfold, grown into his full potential. Svanhild flushed, annoyed and amused by her own lust, half pleased to feel life flowing through her again, and half angry that her body had forgotten its grief so easily.

"Thank you, my king," she said, lowering her head.

"If you are better, come to dinner tonight. You can sit at the head table if you like—or not, if it is too much."

"Thank you," she said again. "I will do as seems prudent." Her embarrassment made her speak formally. A throng of women servants came upon them then, saving her from saying more. They were young girls who reacted to Harald as Svanhild had, though they troubled to hide it less. They swept Svanhild toward the bathhouse where their chatter kept her from thinking of Harald or anyone else.

✟   ✟   ✟

HILDA WAS WAITING in the room when Svanhild returned. "They are taking battle to Tafjord soon," she told Svanhild. Svanhild had become accustomed to the dull, rough way that Hilda reported anything about which she was unhappy. She had said a few words about Vigdis in the same tone: how Ragnvald took her as a concubine, fathered a child on her, and then sent her away. It had shocked Svanhild. That Vigdis would seek his bed was not so surprising, nor that he would allow it, but that it would go on, with him acknowledging the child, seemed shameful. She supposed a king and ally of Harald might do what he liked. He had at least sent Vigdis away.

"Ronhild—Harald's mother—she wants all the women at dinner

tonight to remind the men of who they are coming home for," said Hilda, still diffident. "Will you join?"

"Please, yes, if you will help me prepare myself," said Svanhild. "I have been used to the company of rough men these many years past, and I do not want to shame Ragnvald."

"I don't know if I can help with that," said Hilda. "But I will braid your hair." She handed Svanhild a comb. "Brush it again and I will dress it for you."

Svanhild looked neat, at least, after Hilda finished her ministrations, and Svanhild examined herself in the silver mirror. Hilda had loaned her a dress of golden green covered by a bright gold overdress, and made a hasty hem so Svanhild would not trip on it. Amber beads hung between the bronze brooches that held up the outer dress. Hilda wore a dark burgundy dress with cream piping that suited her coloring, and a necklace of rubies and gold. Svanhild felt at her belt for her package of jewelry. She had worn it even in sleep in Harald's town. Too many people lived in Nidaros for Svanhild to trust them all. She did not want to adorn herself with Solvi's jewels, though—all would know from where they had come. Better Hilda's borrowed adornment.

Her hair looked severe the way Hilda had done it, with two braids keeping it back from her face. She was too thin; her protruding cheekbones made her look like a crone. Her eyes were deeply shadowed. She tugged at the hair around her face, trying to soften the lines.

"You are beautiful." Hilda's tone made it sound like less of a compliment than a rote phrase. She probably spoke to her children like that: it's not time for dinner yet, wipe your nose, stop hitting your brother.

"Thank you," said Svanhild. "I am scared." She had said it partially because she knew Hilda would like to hear Svanhild echoing her own fear of this place, but she found it was true. She could face Harald again, naked or not, and know what to say to him. She knew how to talk to a bold man like that. She did not know what she would say to the crowds of his supporters who knew her for Solvi's wife.

"Come," said Hilda, sounding pleased for the first time since Svanhild's arrival. "We will go together."

"Will your sons be there?" Svanhild asked. "I want to meet my nephews."

"Yes," said Hilda, still with warmth in her voice.

"Tell me about them." Svanhild linked her arm with Hilda.

"Ivar is my oldest," Hilda said as they walked, "and he is the sweetest, most handsome boy in all of Norway. Thorir is younger, and he always runs after his older brothers, trying to play with them, but they never let him unless one of them is sick or being punished. Rolli—Hrolf—is my youngest, named after my father. He's still at the breast, and he is as loud and demanding a child as ever lived. Nothing is too good for him." The pride in Hilda's voice made Svanhild smile in answer. Here was Hilda's joy.

"Older brothers?" she asked.

"Vigdis's boy is here too. Einar—guilt named. My husband killed his foster-brother, Einar, and hoped to placate the gods by making a new Einar." Svanhild had nothing to say to that. She remembered lame Einar, with his big shoulders and rough hands. He had flirted with her, hoped to marry her.

The high ceilings of Harald's feasting hall danced with light cast by stamped tin lamps that threw shards of brightness over the walls and ceiling beams. The food had not reached the table yet, but its aromas had: the rich smell of meat stewed in milk, the sweetness of fruit sauces, the sharp tang of leeks. Before today, Svanhild had eaten only the bread and cheese that Hilda brought to her, and more from a sense of duty than from hunger. It often took half of the day for her to finish her portion.

Floki bounded up to Svanhild. "I am glad you are well, Lady Svanhild," he said. "Please, let me introduce you to Harald. He is eager to meet you, as is his chief skald, Thorbjorg Hornklofe." Svanhild had heard of this skald even in Iceland. His poetry of Harald's deeds had reached them. Eystein had puzzled over bits of kenning, turning them over in his mouth, while Svanhild hoped that if he could not be a warrior, he might command men with his words.

Not now, though. She thought it deliberately, to test how the words stabbed pain into her breast. And they did, bringing with them the memory of Eystein's body burning on the beach, Solvi's face severe behind him. She closed her eyes tightly. When she opened them again, Floki was peering at her, concerned. "King Harald is not here yet. He usually likes to join the hall when all are ready for toasts."

And to make an entrance, Svanhild guessed.

"Let me show you to your seat," said Floki. He took her by the arm and brought her to a bench near the head of the hall. "I will have some wine brought to you."

Very good—she might sit with her cup and watch the people around her. Strange to be so shy when she had visited every kind of foreign court by Solvi's side, and had never minded when they saw her as a wild princess from the far north. The wine Floki brought was smooth and sweet, tasting of the apples of summers gone by. The apple trees in Iceland had not been old enough to bear anything but the tartest fruit that needed long stewing and the addition of honey to be palatable. This wine was a soft, sunlit day upon her tongue, golden light distilled.

"Svanhild, it is good to see you up," said Ragnvald as he approached her.

"Yes," said the dark-haired man next to him. "He has smiled more in the past three days than I have seen him do in six years of marriage! And I thought I must see you again too. You were only a girl when we met last, and now you are a beautiful woman."

Svanhild rose to greet Oddi Hakonsson with a bow. The poems she had heard never related Ragnvald's deeds without mentioning his best friend Oddi by his side. He had grown into his broad mouth and wide-set eyes, which Svanhild had thought made him ugly as a boy. A beard made his face look friendly, and not so broad, and he too moved with a warrior's grace.

"Thank you," she said. She feared she looked as though she needed Oddi's reassurance.

"It is sad to see you only to leave again on the morrow, but we will bring back treasure in time to celebrate Yule, I think." Oddi smiled ironically. "I should not mention our departure, your brother entreats me. How foolish—you know why we are all gathered here tonight. But I hope nothing we do tomorrow brings you sorrow."

With that he inclined his head, and he and Ragnvald left her stand-

ing alone. Svanhild supposed she would have to get used to conversations like that. All of these men were Solvi's enemies. If he did not
come for her within a year she could claim a divorce at the next *ting*
assembly. Harald might pronounce it sooner if he liked.

Svanhild knew Harald had entered even before she saw his head
above all the others, for suddenly the hall hushed and all of the guests'
heads turned like fish schooling in a current. His wild hair was bound
back with a leather tie, showing his broad forehead and wide blue
eyes. His beard, which had been unkempt when she saw it before,
was in three short braids.

She did not truly think he would ask her to sit at the high table with
him, with so many other demands on his attention, but he looked
around until his eyes found hers. He beckoned her over, and when
she reached his side, he led her up to the table, where she sat among
the family of King Hakon of Halogaland: his daughter, Asa, by Harald's side, and two of his sons, blond and handsome boys, dressed in
bright finery.

Svanhild sat quietly for a time, picking at her food. She could not
stomach the rich meats and cheeses, choosing instead a dish of stewed
berries. When Asa noticed her eating them, she said, "I will call for
more of those, if you like."

Svanhild looked at Asa's narrow, handsome face, so like her
brother Heming's, and her long fingers where she grasped her spoon.
She wanted to ask Asa questions that could not be asked of a near
stranger, like how she managed as one of Harald's several wives. Did
she like to share him or hate it, as Vigdis and Svanhild's mother had
hated to share a man they detested? Svanhild sensed that a similar
reticence held Asa back, but what could Svanhild be asked, save questions about her enemy husband and dead child?

Servants came and cleared the dishes. "Are you sure you don't
want more berries?" Asa asked.

Svanhild smiled and shook her head no. A servant refilled her cup,
and a skald stepped forward with his drum to keep the time and meter of his tale. His chosen tale was the Death of Baldur, which made
Svanhild wish all she had to face was awkward silence with Asa.
Her chest grew tight the moment he began to speak of the dream

of Frigga, the god's mother, whose prophecy showed her that some ill fate came for her son. Later, the whole world would grieve for him, all save for the evil trickster Loki, who had compassed his death. Svanhild understood Frigga's grief, and it was her trickster husband who had hastened her son's death.

King Hakon stood from his chair while the skald recited and moved behind Asa and Harald. "King Harald," he said. "I need to speak with you."

"Did you ask the skald to recite this?" Harald asked. "It is not fitting on the eve of battle."

"It suits me," said Hakon. "Baldur was killed by mischance, directed by another's hand, much like my son was injured."

Svanhild had not heard the whole story of Hakon's son, though she knew enough to see where he would find parallels. Indeed, the skald reached the part of the tale now where Loki directed the blind god Hod's arrow against Baldur, and it found its mark. Hod was killed for it, though he did not intend death, and Loki pursued through all of the nine realms for vengeance for Baldur, the most beloved of the gods.

"Have I not given you enough justice?" Harald asked, his voice suddenly chilly. That switch from warm to cold in the space of a heartbeat reminded Svanhild of Solvi.

"I must take my leave," said Hakon. "You do not need me in Tafjord tomorrow, and I have heard word that I am needed in the Faroe Islands, for Solvi has made a claim there."

"Solvi is everywhere!" said Harald. "He must be magical. Do you think he is lurking here? In this very hall?"

"You mock me," said Hakon. "His wife is here, let us ask her."

"Svanhild," said Harald, "where is your husband?"

"I do not know." Svanhild could not tell what he wanted from her, and decided on the barest version of truth that she knew. "But he traveled toward Tafjord when I saw him last. And he can go to Hel's realm for all the care I have of him."

"I have said what I heard," said Hakon. "Would you prevent me from protecting my holdings?"

"While your son's holdings go unprotected?" Harald asked, then

continued before Hakon could reply. "You may go, if you leave immediately. You have spoiled this feast enough. Does that suit you?"

Hakon sneered. "Better than you could know." He turned and left.

The feast's attendees seemed so used to Harald and Hakon's arguing that none marked it except Hakon's sons. Heming looked at his
father's back with fear and hunger on his face. Oddi's expression was
less easy to read. Svanhild sat quietly picking at her food as the skald
finished the tale—quickly now, with his patron gone.

When a lull came in the conversation, Svanhild turned to Asa and
said, "My lady Asa Hakonsdatter, can you please ask the king if he
would allow my brother to be seated with me. I have not spoken with
him as much as I would like since my return."

Asa agreed, pleasantly enough, and Harald beckoned Ragnvald to
join them. He and Harald spoke briefly about the departure of Hakon, agreeing that the lack of his forces would not harm their fight
against Solvi.

"Who knew I could simply ask him to leave?" Harald asked, grinning. Ragnvald glanced at Hakon's sons, who looked less annoyed at
Harald's words than Svanhild would have thought. He sat down next
to Svanhild, and she laid her head on his shoulder. "Please give me an
excuse to depart the feast early. Even if it is rude. I do not wish to hear
any songs sung of me tonight."

"You won't," said Ragnvald. "No one wants to praise Solvi Klofe
tonight, even in his choice of wife." Svanhild forced a smile at that. "I
am glad you are feeling better," he added, hesitantly.

"Am I?" Svanhild asked. "I do not know. I suppose I must go on living,
that is all."

"I hate to see you so sad, yet I am glad you have returned, more
than I can say," said Ragnvald. "Before we leave to fight, will you give
me your blessing?"

He sounded young when he asked, as if he desired the bond between them to be rebuilt. It was common for a wife to bless her husband, to call down the favor of the goddess Frigga on one she loved,
so if Odin marked the man for slaughter, his wife might intervene
on his behalf. Svanhild was not his wife, but a woman who wanted
Ragnvald to return. To succeed even, she thought—yes, she could

hope that, hope for Solvi's defeat. Not death, though. The idea of his death hurt her as though she herself were spitted on the very sword she imagined for him.

She put her hands on his head and entreated Frigga to spare him to come back to his family. He remained with his head bowed, and so she placed her hands on him again.

"Let his *wyrd* not be to kill my husband Solvi. For I have left him, and I hate him, but I love him still," said Svanhild, her voice breaking.

When he looked up, Svanhild saw this was as he had intended. He touched her chin where a teardrop was about to break free and fall to the floor. "I promise, I will not kill Solvi unless I must do it to save myself or another." He gave her a tight smile. "I would rather capture him anyway. I will come back to celebrate Yule with you, my sister." He kissed her forehead. "Now go to bed if you wish."

17

THE DAY AFTER EYSTEIN'S FUNERAL WAS CLOUDY AND BLUS-
tery. The wind filled the fjord with whitecaps and kicked the dull
water into spray. Solvi walked around what had been Eystein's pyre,
careful to stay outside its margin. The tide had risen and fallen overnight, sweeping away much of the ash, though the grayness still remained. Until they returned to their original color, Eystein's shade
would linger.

A glint of silver near the water's edge drew his eye, and Solvi
crouched down and picked up a pebble that looked like it had been
dipped in metal. A shadow of the pattern from the original silver remained, the knotwork that had traced over the boar's head amulet
Eystein had worn as a pendant. His son had chosen it himself, pre-
ferring Frey, a farmer's god, a bringer of rain, to the gods of sea and
treasure to which Solvi gave his allegiance. Even Eystein had stayed
with him longer than Svanhild, who had been missing from her tent
that morning. Katla slept through her going and had nothing useful
to say, even after Solvi shook and slapped her.

"We need to leave," said Snorri. Solvi flinched. "Harald will find out
we are here."

Thorstein, Snorri, and Tryggulf had been in conference since
dawn. Solvi could easily imagine their conversation, the decision that
had sent Snorri, with his damaged face and blurred speech, to be the

one to speak to him. "He listens to you," Tryggulf would have said. "You have to tell him."

"You think that's where she went? To Harald?" Solvi asked.

"You know she did," said Snorri.

He did. Where else? Years ago, Harald of Vestfold had come to Tafjord and declared his intention of expelling Solvi and his family from their ancestral lands, leaving no room to bargain, but Svanhild could betray and bargain again and again, and her brother would always forgive her. When Solvi woke and found her gone, a part of him finally felt satisfied. He had never entirely believed that she would stay with him, and now she had proved him right. If he had not half-expected it, he would have found forgiveness easier.

He walked down to the shore and splashed some water on his face, then dried it with a sleeve that gaped at the wrist—Svanhild had not sewed it closed as she had every morning before this one. "Yes, we need to go," he said. "Harald will send us a welcome we do not want. Ulfarr will have a better one for us in Tafjord."

Why did he need to go to Tafjord now, with Eystein dead and Svanhild run off? He had wanted the land for them, to turn himself into a king like Ragnvald, and give them better shelter than they could find between the walls of a ship. He looked at Thorstein, who stood a few paces away from him, waiting for his command. Thorstein was young and eager—he loved battle and the sea as Solvi had at his age. He would follow Solvi wherever he went, into endless wandering and pillaging. So would Snorri and Tryggulf. They had already proven this. But Ulfarr awaited Solvi at Tafjord; he had made his bargains with Rane of Vermaland, now of Sweden, and with Gudbrand and his sons, with Ketil Flatnose and his followers, who wanted war and plunder. Svanhild thought he had no honor, but he could not break this promise, not if he ever wanted allies again.

Solvi bowed his head one more time, the silver rock clutched in his hand. He thought of his gods again, gods of sea and wind, the gods Njord and Ran, gods of the life-giving sea, and the destructive sea. Of Thor, who brought thunder and storms to fields and coastlines, and Frey, who brought gentle, nourishing rain. He had no prayers for his son. Who would welcome Eystein into the afterlife? Where was the child's god, the gentle god, to make up for his harsh life? For once, Solvi saw the use of the Christian god, who, it was said, loved the weak and poor, though not enough to save them when Solvi's raiders came to take their treasures. For a moment a cringing monk in Solvi's memory wore his son's face, and tears sprang to his eyes. He had not given his son what he needed in his life. Perhaps some god would in the afterlife. Eystein had loved growing things, burrowing animals, shorebirds, small creatures that lived within the sphere defined for them and did not venture beyond. He would have made a good farmer. Frey then, the mystic, the god of fertility.

Solvi knelt on the rocks, and touched the water again. One of Solvi's earliest memories was his father acting as priest after his mother's death. He did not remember her as a living woman as vividly as he did that moment: when her body was consigned to flames, and Hunthiof stood by as she burned. Solvi had not recovered from his own burning enough to walk without a stick, so he reached the pyre after the torch had already touched his mother's body. He remembered her hands turning black as the shroud burned away, and panic in his throat, a fear that the flames might reach him, and beneath that, a fear that his legs might suddenly regain their strength, that the pain, which was sometimes all he could think about, would leave him, and he would run toward the pyre and throw himself on it. He remembered pressing the half-healed flesh of his thighs with his palms, riding the edge of pain and panic and grief, crying tears that no one noticed.

Now he prayed that Frey would find a home for his son, and that Solvi's mother would welcome him there, to warm fields, to her hearth, to the peace and comfort that Solvi had prayed for himself as a boy. Eystein would always be a boy now, and never hold a sword, never take a wife, never love his own children. Solvi's face was streaked with tears when he rose. None would think less of him for it. A boy's tears might be mocked. A man's tears showed his depth of feeling. Indeed, he saw he was not alone in his grief. Thorstein, on the cusp of manhood, who still feared being thought weak, wiped furiously at his own.

"We will sail for Tafjord on the next high tide," said Solvi. "Harald is a tyrant, and there are none who can stop him except us. We go to defend the homes of our ancestors." When Harald was dead, and someone of Solvi's choosing controlled Trondheim Fjord, he would establish a priesthood of Frey here, give them thralls to clear their land so they could farm and prophecy and mark the grave of his son with more than an ash-covered beach that would be washed clean by the following morning.

✛ ✛ ✛

SOLVI HAD NOT seen Tafjord in many years, not since departing to attack Vestfold. The old living hall looked the same, though perhaps its turf roof overhung the eaves more now. His father's drinking hall, constructed of upright staves, had been newly rubbed with fat, and many old boards replaced with gleaming new ones, so it looked trapped between some ancient age and a new one. Smaller half-built structures surrounded it, added by Heming.

Ulfarr strode down to the dock to greet Solvi's ships, and to ensure there was room for it among the others that had already come, the ships of Gudbrand and his sons, of Rane and his allies. Seeing so many ships lashed to one another against the shore reminded Solvi again of taking battle to Vestfold. This time he would find a way to spring the trap on Harald, not the other way around.

"You had no trouble taking the hall?" Solvi asked him.

"Heming took some ships and sailed out to meet us," said Ulfarr. "When the battle went against them, they fled."

"Fled to Harald in Nidaros?" Solvi asked.

"So I assume," said Ulfarr. "I see you left your wife in Iceland." He sounded pleased.

A rushing noise filled Solvi's ears, as if from a wave only he could see, a mass of losses that bore down upon him. He turned to Thorstein. "Tell Ulfarr what has passed. I need to go piss."

He walked away quickly as Thorstein began his tale. Let his men unload the ships. Let them find their own way to the hall—it was obvious, and they should not need his guidance. Let everything proceed without him until dinner.

"You there, thrall," Solvi called to an unfamiliar slave who fed the fire at the bathhouse. "Make this ready for me, and make sure I am not disturbed. I am Solvi Hunthiofsson, lord of this place." When that was done, he dozed off in the hot confines of the bathhouse, and woke feeling even more tired than before.

Dinner was well under way when he returned to the hall. The men were teasing Thorstein about one of the girl thralls who made eyes at him. "She's a hot one," Ulfarr was saying. "She might like you—if she's had enough of a man and wants to try a boy."

"Can't the boy have a girl who is not one of your leavings?" Solvi asked. Rane moved his vast bulk over to the side to make room for Solvi at the high table with Gudbrand and his sons.

"Not likely," said Ketil around a mouthful of bread. Ulfarr had another woman now. This one was a beauty, or would be without the fear in her eyes and tension thinning her lips. She had pale skin, red lips, and bright gold hair. In the dim hall, her vividness kept drawing Solvi's gaze back to her. She sat next to Ulfarr and opened her mouth dutifully when he fed her bits of his food. He had his left hand between her legs, while his right hand rooted around in his trencher for other things to feed her. She squirmed away from him as much as she was able, wedged in beside him and the warrior on his left, while he kept pulling her back.

"Few enough of those, but maybe that one"—Ulfarr pointed his grease-covered hand at a serving woman with gray hair and a pronounced hump on her back—"I don't think I've had her yet." He turned toward the woman by his side. "What do you think, should I ask her to join us?" Svanhild had always hated to see Ulfarr humiliating a woman, and would not have allowed a spectacle like this at her table. Though Solvi would not forbid Ulfarr many of his pleasures, he had backed her in that.

"We should toast your son," said Snorri, when Solvi had been silent for too long. He spoke slowly and loudly, to make himself understood.

"Thorstein said you did not have time afterward," said Ulfarr. Solvi glared at Thorstein until he shrugged uncomfortably.

"He was a young boy," said Solvi. "Few deeds to boast of." At this moment, stupid with grief and exhaustion, Solvi could remember nothing of Eystein except his end. He had been his mother's son, always by her side. He had not enjoyed sailing. He had been frightened of Solvi, as Solvi had been of his own father. He might have grown into a man, someone that Solvi could meet as a man, with his own strengths to make up for his weaknesses, but Solvi would never get to see Eystein's strengths now.

He rose to his feet. "Toast him if you wish," he said. "I do not want to hear his name again."

+ + +

WHEN SOLVI WOKE in his bed the next morning, he felt a dislocation, a sliding across time and space that he had never experienced before, no matter how many strange shores he had visited. It took a long time for him to remember why he was in Tafjord. Harald's forces would come to Tafjord now—they must, or they would have to wait until spring to attack. Svanhild—would she have told Harald of Solvi's alliances and plans? Best to assume she had.

He went outside and, through the morning mist, heard the sound of chopping wood, and followed it to where Rane split logs with a massive ax. With his weight behind the blows, Solvi was surprised the logs did not explode into splinters.

"Do you want a turn?" Rane asked. He swung the ax again and it became embedded in a knotty log. Solvi shook his head. Rane raised the ax and log together overhead and crashed both down. The log flew apart and the ax bit deep into the block. "It's hard losing a son," he said. "You must make a new son as soon as you can. Then it will hurt less."

Rane's simple words caused grief to flash through Solvi again, stealing his breath and bringing tears to his eyes. He had made a new son—or daughter—with Svanhild and then thrown the child away.

"It is hard," Rane continued. "Every night you will forget, and every morning you will feel it again." He picked up another log, his huge hand palming one end.

"Is that why you're doing a servant's work this morning?" Solvi asked.

"I got into the habit," said Rane. Solvi looked about at the scattering of log halves on the ground. He had not gotten into the habit of stacking them.

"Leave this for now," said Solvi. "We need to talk of the battle to come."

He gathered his allies and chief warriors outside. The fog did not lift as the morning went on, only eddied about the fjord and perched just above the top of his father's drinking hall.

"We need ships scouting to watch for Harald coming from Nidaros," said Solvi. "He might take any number of routes, though a few are the most likely." He sketched out his understanding of the coastline in charcoal upon a wide flagstone. Distances in the drawing troubled him, for when he sailed a span of coastline grew or shrank depending on the wind. But he knew he had placed the islands right, and marked which stretches of water could be seen from which vantage points. With his own forces recombined with Ulfarr's, and now Gudbrand's and Rane's, they would be able to defeat Harald.

"You've already taken Tafjord," said Rane. "And with it you control North Maer. What about my land in Vestfold?"

Solvi sighed. He thought they had agreed upon a strategy before leaving Iceland. "We agreed to make Tafjord the foothold of the resistance in the west," said Solvi. "Once we defeat Harald in battle, we will be established here, and we can take war to Nidaros, or lure Harald to Vestfold and make war on him there." Rane looked as though he wanted to speak again, and Solvi cut him off. "What does Harald offer?" Solvi asked Rane. "What does he give the jarls of Norway so they are willing to share taxes with him, and even give up their inheritance to him?"

Rane shook his head. "Nothing. He doesn't give, he takes. That is why we must take it back."

"Taxes?" Thorstein asked. "He takes our—your kingdoms from you, and gives over the taxes to the remaining jarls, so they have more gold."

"But he takes even more for himself," said Solvi. "No, I think he offers them safety in return for their freedom. A coward's bargain, bought with oaths and with gold and with land, but mostly freedom from uncertainty. And who among us can truly be free from uncertainty?"

"Only death is certain," said Ketil.

"Yes," said Solvi. "If they do not believe Harald can make them safe, then they will rise up against him. Harald's power rests on the belief that he will never lose. All we need to do is make him suffer one defeat. One defeat and men will no longer believe the gods favor him. One defeat and his kings will start to question whether it is worth paying his taxes. His heavy, punishing taxes that no king before him has ever required."

"Very well," said Rane. "But my men are not good sailors. I want them resting for the battle, not scouting."

"The battle will come to us with no warning if we do not have scouts," said Solvi.

"I thought you knew these lands well," said one of Gudbrand's sons. Solvi wished Gudbrand would send them away, for they had nothing useful to say. Rane did not either, but at least he had forces he could commit.

"I do," said Solvi testily. "That is why I know we need scouts in these places. We will have relief scouts for them so none are spending too long sleeping rough. All will be rested for the battle, I promise you."

"They won't be rested, they will be stranded!" said Rane.

"Some of them," said Solvi. "What is your suggestion?"

"Rest and feed ourselves"—Rane patted his broad belly—"until Harald brings battle to us, and then defeat him. You would split our forces."

"And you would give him an avenue to escape," said Solvi. "With scouts in these places"—he pointed them out again—"we will have time to get into position and trap him between two fleets."

"I still say we have enough ships to trap him here no matter what," said Rane.

"What if he sends scouts to see how many ships we have and does not even come here?" Solvi asked. "I am trying to give us the greatest chance of success."

"If he does not come here, then we can retake Vestfold in the spring," said Rane.

Solvi stood up from his drawing, rubbing his forehead between his eyes. His patience was fraying.

"What if we put it to the men and ask for a vote?" Ketil Flatnose asked. Solvi had used votes before to keep unity, though he only allowed them when he already knew what the outcome would be.

"You cannot command an army with a vote," said Rane. "Do you think Harald calls for votes?"

"We can discuss it more tonight," said Solvi. In the meantime, he would speak with Gudbrand privately, and Ketil as well—the suggestion of a vote was a foolish one. If Svanhild were here, Solvi could have put her by Rane's side, to flirt and charm him. She would challenge him, work him around to Solvi's plan until Rane thought it was his own idea.

✛   ✛   ✛

DINNER THAT NIGHT was overcooked, spitted goat—poor fare. Svanhild had once wanted to make Tafjord into a fine hall, a hall of which she could be proud. He grew angry with her again when he looked around at the faces of his men, picking at the stringy meat. Nothing prevented the food from being better except laziness and there being no one to command the servants to do better. She could have managed this place. Solvi did not know if he was more angry with her or himself for failing to give this to her. Tafjord needed a woman, and Solvi needed a woman's touch in these negotiations, if not Svanhild—he glanced at Ulfarr, who sat with the woman from the previous night. She had fresh bruises on her wrists.

"Ulfarr, come tell me again how you took Tafjord from Heming Hakonsson," said Solvi. "I want to make sure I understand all there is to know of him, for he will surely sail against us again."

Ulfarr rose, wiped his hands off on his tunic, and came to sit next to Solvi. "He is a foolish whelp," he said. "He did not set a guard, or—it was not a very good one, since we killed what scouts we could find, and the remaining did not pass the message along. He killed only a few of my men."

"How did he escape?" Solvi asked.

Ulfarr scowled, his heavy cheeks pouching out. "He was on a ship that slipped through our grasp. We captured four of his ships, and the men on them—well, some of them used to be your men, and plenty were happy to join me rather than face the sword. The others we killed and burned so they wouldn't stink up the place."

"What of his women?" Solvi asked.

Ulfarr grinned and jerked his head in the direction of the woman who still sat at his place, rubbing her wrists under the table. "I have his concubine now," he said. "She's a beauty, though she has no spirit."

"Do you mean to say you are growing tired of her?" Solvi asked. Ulfarr was always loyal, and unless he had fallen in love with the girl, he would give her over. "I have never seen you stay with one woman for very long." He gave her a long, appraising look, thinking of Svanhild to make his expression soften. The woman moved a hand to her belly. Solvi wondered if Ulfarr, or perhaps Heming before him, had made her pregnant, and that gave rise to the expression of disgust on her face, or perhaps it was her fear of Ulfarr's touch. Thinking about Svanhild with child, he felt as though a bowstring ran from his throat to his stomach, and suddenly stretched sharply.

"Yes," said Ulfarr, bringing Solvi's attention back to the woman. "I'm tired of her. You can have her." He said it with an ill grace that made Solvi wonder how true it was, but not for long—Ulfarr would find another woman. He stood up and walked over to her, and said a few words in her ear. Her eyes widened in a look of wild relief before she settled her face again, and rose gracefully from her seat.

Solvi made room for her next to him. "Ulfarr said you were Heming's mistress," he said.

She put a hand on his thigh and began sliding it upward. "Yes, and I know many tricks, tricks that could please a man as beautiful as Heming, who had his pick of women."

"Why did he not take you with him, then?" he asked. Anger crossed her features, as before, and again she settled them into a pleasant mask.

"He made the escape he could," she said. "And has left me free for other men."

"Free," said Solvi. "You are passed around like a gold armband. Is a piece of jewelry free?" He wanted to see if he could make her truly angry, for if Ulfarr or the men before him had broken her spirit too much, then she could be of no use to him.

"What woman is ever free?" she asked bitterly. "I thought you would humiliate me less than your captain, but instead I find you worse."

"Should I send you back to him?" Solvi asked.

She lowered her head and shook it. "No. I lied. You are not worse than him, at least not yet. And you might be better."

"Yes, tell me how I can do better," said Solvi. "I want truth from you."

"Truth? You have not even asked my name," she said.

"What is it?"

"Tova," she said. "What else do you want from me?"

"Just Tova?" Solvi asked.

"My mother had many men, and the man she called my father refused to give me his name."

"And so you follow in her footsteps?" At her angry look, he shook his head. He needed to control himself better. Tova was not Svanhild. "You need not answer that."

"Then what do you want of me?"

"Sit by my side. Tell me what you know of Heming, and his father, and anyone else you met while warming his bed."

"So you can defeat them?"

"Are you still loyal to Heming Hakonsson?" Solvi asked, more curious than angry.

"As loyal as I will be to you when you are gone," said Tova.

"So no," said Solvi. She held herself rigidly away from him, now that he had moved her hand away from his leg. He thought this the more honest posture. "I do not expect loyalty from you, only your service. But if I think you have served well, I will . . ." He hesitated, wondering what could she want from him, what could buy her service now, and perhaps keep her from betrayal later. "When this battle is done, I will reward you with gold, or send you where you wish. I will find you a husband, and give you a dowry, or make you my housekeeper. I will give you a choice."

"If you live," she said. "You may not. But I will answer you. Heming is a man of good intentions, with little ability to enforce his will. His father is a bully. His younger brothers are something of both."

Solvi had guessed all of that, for though Hakon and his sons had their deeds sung widely, only Hakon's achievements had been done without help, and lasted longer than a year or two. None would sing of Heming taking over Solvi's empty hall, especially now that he had lost it. "I need you to talk to Rane," Solvi said to her. "Find out what he fears and what he wants. Make him think that he should follow my lead in all things."

Tova sighed. "Do you want me to join him in bed?"

"If you wish," he said. "If you think it will help and it does not . . ." He did not know how to put it, only he did not want to see her bruised and flinching more than she already did. Her battered spirit made him feel hopeless. She stood again, and tugged her sleeves down over the bruises on her wrists. Within a moment of speaking to Rane, she had him laughing, his cheeks apple-bright. Good, at least he would be in a better mood when Solvi came to argue with him again.

When he judged that Tova had done her work, Solvi brought his drinking cup and a bottle of spiced Frankish wine over to him. He poured a glass for himself and one for Rane.

"What if I send my men as scouts?" Solvi asked. He had held this possibility in reserve, for it would stretch his forces thin, and put some of his best sailors out of the way for the battle. "And perhaps any of yours who volunteer? Will you then agree to my plan?"

"You may send your men," said Rane. Solvi tamped down his annoyance at Rane's assumption that he gave Solvi permission for anything. But Rane had the ear of the Swedish king. Solvi needed him. "Mine will do as I command," Rane added.

"But will you agree to my plan?" Solvi asked. "Yes," said Rane. "As long as my men are well rested before you send them out to close the trap."

"Agreed," said Solvi. He nodded his thanks at Tova, for whatever she had said, and toasted with Rane, who shared his cup with her.

On the following day, Snorri and Tryggulf organized shifts of scouts, both on foot and in boats, stationing them close enough to one another that they could pass signals: smoke, fire, piercing whistles from flutes carved out of hollow bird bones. Fishing boats patrolled every inch of Geiranger Fjord's shores, and Solvi promised a handful of silver to the family of whoever spotted Harald's ship first.

Every few days Solvi visited one of the closer scouts to make sure that signals passed correctly.

Then one day the message came that ships arrived from the north, bearing Harald's colors and Heming's. The wind carried Solvi quickly back to Tafjord. Rane took his eight ships to the bend in the fjord called Solskel to hide while Harald's forces passed. Solvi planned to sail out at first light. Between Solvi's ships and Rane's, Harald's force would be crushed and he could no longer claim to be undefeated. That night Solvi could not sleep for visions of what he would do to Harald when he caught him. He would not ransom him, no matter what his family offered. For Harald's dream to die, he must die too.

18

TWO WEEKS AFTER LEAVING THE NORSE COAST BEHIND, SIG-urd and Egil's ship had run low on drinking water. Arguments broke out between families and Sigurd feared outright mutiny until he finally sighted black shapes on the horizon that resolved into green islands when the ship drew closer. Even knowing little about sailing, Sigurd had not formed a very good opinion of their captain Dyri's skills. He had scarcely been able to find his way out of the Norse barrier islands, as the air grew colder and winter storms threatened. He seemed not to know how to handle his small ship, though he had claimed it was his own.

Sigurd noticed a plume of smoke coming from a hummock half-way up one of the island's hills. When the ship passed into the channel between the two islands, he saw that the hummock was a house made of stacked turf, as only the poorest families in Norway used. A harbor opened up before them, with a rocky beach that rose up to another grass-covered hill. At the top of the valley, a proper hall reached its crossbeams to the sky.

"That will be the most important man on the island," said Egil, who stood by him. "We should go there first and announce ourselves."

"Is this Iceland?" Sigurd asked. "We have been traveling long enough that it should be."

Egil shook his head. "I have not seen Iceland, but I think these are the Faroe Islands. Iceland is far larger and has already made room for many of the kings that Harald expelled. The Faroes are only a way station for us."

"Dyri, is that true?" Sigurd asked. "This is not Iceland?"

Dyri muttered something, and Sigurd did not press. If he exposed Dyri's ignorance, it would frighten their passengers.

"We will find out," said Sigurd. "You brought us safely to land."

Dyri nodded. "I did, yes, and the gods know you could not have done it."

"Exactly," said Sigurd. He had seen Egil chafe at these little slights, but Sigurd did not mind them; he had never sailed farther than a half day from Sogn before.

"You are the leading man among us," said Dyri to Sigurd. "You and Egil should go to the owner of that hall. Maybe they will give us food."

And if they do not? Sigurd wanted to ask, but he remained quiet. A leader should keep his doubts to himself.

✛　✛　✛

SIGURD AND EGIL climbed to the hall, while Dyri and the passengers unloaded their baggage onto the beach. The hall was weathered, though not too old, and long enough to shelter a large household. An armed man opened the door, asked their names, and, hearing nothing to worry him, conducted them into the hall's main room. Some men of middle age sat dicing at a table by a fire pit. Sigurd recognized the one dressed in bright colors, with gold at his waist and shoulders, from the Sogn *ting*. He looked as Sigurd thought a king should look, old but with the strong build of a warrior, upright and wary even sitting. Odin might look this way sitting in his high seat that overlooked the nine worlds of creation.

The fire flickered, and an image of the sacrifices at the Sogn *ting* sprang to Sigurd's mind, the night before his father took him to murder Ragnvald. Sigurd looked again upon Hakon Grjotgardsson, king of Halogaland, father of Oddi.

"I am Sigurd Olafsson, and this is my friend Egil Hrolfsson," he said, wondering if Hakon would remember him as well.

"Sigurd of Sogn," said Hakon. "I know your brother Ragnvald very well. What brings you to my shores?"

"This is your land?" Egil asked.

"My grandfather discovered these islands," said Hakon. "They have always been held by the jarls of Halogaland." Egil knocked his elbow into Sigurd's and Sigurd glanced at him. He could not read Egil's face, and so turned back to Hakon.

"We have stopped here on the way to Iceland to seek our fortune," said Sigurd. "Among us are many looking for a better life."

"And Ragnvald let you go?" Hakon asked.

"I am a grown man," said Sigurd, flushing. "I go where I wish."

"And there is no place for you by Ragnvald's side," said Hakon. "Good. I can welcome you and your men. There is porridge and sheep-cheese enough for all of you, and you can trade for more provisions here."

"Thank you," said Sigurd. "We are hungry and thirsty." He did not know what they had to trade for provisions. He had some treasures from Ragnvald: bits of hacksilver, a narrow gold arm ring, a penannular cloak clasp of brass and carnelian, though looking at Hakon's rich dress, with no metal less precious than gold adorning him, he wondered if Hakon had any use for these trinkets.

"How many are you?" Hakon asked.

"Thirty adults, and some children," said Sigurd.

Hakon smiled. "You are near enough to kin that I should be generous. Do not worry about payment—I will give you what you need. I am hungry for news, and feeding your followers is a small enough price to pay."

✢   ✢   ✢

HAKON COULD NOT feast Sigurd and the settlers very richly, but after weeks of dried fish and hard bread, his hall's stewed onions and herbed oat porridge, flecked with bits of goat meat, tasted nearly as good to Sigurd as the best cut of beef. Hakon bade Sigurd sit next to him and tell him all he could from Norway.

"What are you doing so far from Norway?" Sigurd asked Hakon. A few glasses of Hakon's mellow golden wine had emboldened his tongue.

"I always have to keep an eye on my holdings, and my sons are all busy."

"Did you hear of your son Herlaug's wounding?" Sigurd asked. "I heard that Ragnvald's man Arnfast cut open his face, and he will be scarred for life." As soon as he said it he saw that he had spoken out of turn.

"That is no way to tell a man of his son's injury," said Hakon. "Do you come here to bait me? There are many who would like discord between me and Harald's men."

Sigurd glanced at Egil, and found no help. He looked down at his plate. "I didn't, my lord. He is—he lives, I have heard. He will be scarred, but many men are scarred. I thought it was news you would want to know."

"Do not fear, young Sigurd," said Hakon, looking satisfied now. "I have seen my son, and he will live, with the good healing of the sorceress Ronhild, and he will take his revenge upon the men who disfigured him."

"I heard Harald outlawed feuding."

Hakon snorted. "Might as well outlaw breathing. How else can these matters be settled? The law courts? Only when the judgment is not tainted."

"Ragnvald said that feuds destroy districts and families," said Sigurd, carefully deferential. He did not want to feel Hakon's disapproval again.

"Ah, I see. You wonder if you will be able to strike against your brother," said Hakon. Sigurd was startled by his assumption, and opened his mouth to correct him when Hakon continued, "Do you have a son who can carry out your revenge for you if you fall?"

This was not what Sigurd meant at all. He had been relieved when Ragnvald offered him friendship and took the burden of vengeance from him. But he did have a younger half-brother whom he rarely thought of, Vigdis's son by Olaf, called Hallbjorn. He would now be a great boy of seven or eight. Old enough to learn to fight. Vigdis's kin might want him to challenge Ragnvald, with land like Sogn at stake.

"I have a half-brother," said Sigurd carefully. He wondered if Hakon meant to trap him into betraying Ragnvald. "I do not want to fight King Ragnvald."

"But you do not want to fight for him either," said Hakon. "Otherwise, you would not be here. Is it another land you seek, or only the freedom to make your own way, I wonder?"

"I seek another land," said Sigurd. "I have not made a success at home, and thought I might do better abroad. I am sorry, King Hakon, I think you want me to say something, and I do not know what it is."

"No," said Hakon. "I only want to hear what you think—what all men of Norway think. It is all very well for kings to make war on each other and take taxes, but we take them to protect our people."

"I had not thought of that," said Sigurd. When he gave these matters any thought at all, he remembered the stories skalds told of the gods, that they made some men to rule, and some men to serve, and those who ruled held land and were owed taxes as the gods were owed sacrifices.

"Well, I am glad to hear the news of home," said Hakon. "Your stepbrother, though you esteem him well, has risen too far, too fast." His mustache moved in a smile when he saw Sigurd's expression. "Do I surprise you?"

"I knew—I knew that you and he were no longer close."

"No longer close, ha. I suppose that is true. He is an ambitious one, stepping on many as he rises. Your father was one of them, my sons and I are others. If you see him again, you should punish him for so much ambition."

"I would not—" said Sigurd.

"No, I don't think you would," said Hakon. "He is lucky to have you so loyal. But remember—you were not loyal enough to stay. And you told me yourself that you are your own man. Do not forget that."

Hakon's words haunted Sigurd as he tried to sleep that night on a bed of dried grass that smelled like dog, and with Egil's sour breath in his face. After so long at sea, it felt strange not to have the swaying of the ship to rock him to sleep at night. In Sogn all loved Ragnvald, and none questioned Sigurd's choice to follow him. Perhaps he should not have left.

⁜   ⁜   ⁜

SIGURD AND THE settlers spent five days resting in and around Hakon's hall, relying on his generosity to stay fed and dry. Sigurd traded
some of his trinkets for provisions to feed their party for another four
weeks at sea, for the journey could take that long. With Egil's help,
he directed the loading of the ship, making sure that it was evenly
weighted, with the heaviest baggage along the keel.

They had no help from Dyri, who had made a place for himself
at Hakon's hearth and seldom stirred farther from it than to visit the
outhouse after drinking ale all day. Sigurd and Egil sat by him one
afternoon when the rain had been falling steadily all day from the low
clouds that hid the tops of the islands.

"The ship is packed," said Sigurd. "When can we leave?"

"After you build your own ship and learn to sail it," said Dyri. "I
will stay here."

It took a moment for Sigurd to realize what he was saying. He
already felt uncomfortable about the generosity that Hakon had extended them for this long, and now Dyri proposed relying on it further. "You need to look at the tides and tell us when we should be
ready," said Sigurd.

"I'm not going," said Dyri.

"Why?" Egil asked.

"Winter is coming on and the seas will only grow more dangerous," said Dyri. He had been playing knucklebones, and he turned his
back to Sigurd. He made another throw and caught the ball on the
back of his hand while he took the bones into his palm.

Sigurd kicked his leg. "You promised all of us a journey to Iceland.
You're saying we should hire a new pilot?"

Dyri kicked back at him. "No, I am keeping my ship and I am not
going any farther," he said. "There is land here to claim."

"No trees," said Egil. "Are you going to live in a turf house where
you can never stand up? Do you know where King Hakon got the
wood for this hall? He sailed it across from one of his Halogaland forests. You won't be able to do that."

"I have a ship," said Dyri with a shrug. "I can make that into a
house."

Egil snorted. "No you can't. The wood is too thin, and it will blow over in the first storm. And you will have many storms here. See how the houses are only in the valleys. I would wager it blows for months at a time in the winter."

"Turf will keep out the wind, then," said Dyri. "I go no farther."

✤   ✤   ✤

AFTER TALKING TO some of Hakon's men, Sigurd discovered that no other ship was likely to take them on to Iceland at this time of year, and that Dyri's refusal was not as strange and unmanly as he had thought. Hakon's most experienced pilot spoke of waves many times the height of a mast, which came crashing into the islands with the heavy storms that had, in the days when the gods walked the earth, blown all the trees away. He said he had hoped not to travel again until the spring, but Hakon would travel south to the Shetland and Orkney Islands, and then, hugging the Scottish shore, make his way to Dublin. Of course, the pilot added darkly, the sea could do anything it pleased. Many men had drowned in sight of land, and would continue to do so until the world serpent rose up out of the ocean and drank it down to the dregs.

"Would it be so terrible to remain here?" Sigurd asked Egil. "I might not like living under turf, but we can stay in Hakon's hall for now."

"Turf or wood, that is not my concern," said Egil. "Dyri is mistaken. All of the land here that is flat enough for building or farming is claimed. Perhaps he plans to beg his food off Hakon all winter. You may do as you please—I will find a way to go on to Iceland, if I have to make a raft and row there myself."

Rain lashed the outside of Hakon's hall, making the air inside close and damp. Steam rose up from Sigurd's clothes on the side closest to the hearth fire. "I don't know what you want me to do," said Sigurd. "I'm not going to force Dyri to sail us at sword point. Ragnvald says that men make poor decisions when they're threatened."

"Does Ragnvald have any other way for us to leave?" Egil asked, testily. Sigurd stood, fuming, and left Egil alone at the fire. Egil always reacted with annoyance when Sigurd mentioned Ragnvald.

He collided with Hakon's steward in the lee of the hall, as he directed the carrying of barrels of salt-fish from the hall's stores. Sigurd offered to help. He had found, in those terrible, frightening days after his father's death, that hard work kept him from thinking. Exhaustion quieted his wish to be someone different, someone who could have driven Atli off, not someone who looked like a man but was still a boy in his deeds.

On the evening before Hakon was set to leave, he held a feast for men of the island and asked Sigurd to sit near him again. "My steward says you are a hard worker—what do you hope to gain from this?" Hakon asked.

Sigurd felt a flash of irritation at Hakon, always looking for hidden motives. "I needed something to do," he said. "The winter here will be dull and hungry. And I was hoping that you would let me and some of the families from our ship stay in the hall over the winter."

"And you want me to feed them too, I suppose," said Hakon.

"Many will have to survive the winter on gifts and hospitality," said Sigurd. "And you have some stores here."

"I would never let anyone starve," said Hakon. "And I did not need your labor to do this. I am the ruler of this place. None will starve while I have the means to feed them."

"You are generous," said Sigurd, the words bringing with them memories of Sogn farmers coming to praise Ragnvald at year-turning feasts. Instead of brushing it off quickly, as Ragnvald always did at such praise, though, Hakon looked pleased.

"I thought you were trying to prove yourself so you could join my ships. I offer that freely. We have tarried longer than we should have here. It lacks only two months until Yule."

"Why not stay out the winter here?" Sigurd asked. He would feel safer if Hakon remained on these strange islands at the end of the world. Without that anchor, it seemed that the winter storms might wash them all away into the sea.

"I would go mad, I think," said Hakon. "There is even less to pass the time here than in a hall in Norway. You will see, if you stay."

When Sigurd told Egil about Hakon's offer, he said, "We must go. We can continue on to Iceland from Dublin easily enough. In the spring many ships will be making that journey."

"In the spring, Dyri may be willing to go," said Sigurd. "Perhaps we should stay."

"Or he may not," said Egil. "I do not want to wait. Hakon is your great friend now—ask him if I may go with you."

Sigurd did, as Hakon reviewed the ships making ready to leave. Fulmars circled in the air above the shore, diving toward the ship from the cliffs that ringed the bay and crying out when they saw no food to scavenge. Sigurd had packed his belongings, though he had still not made up his mind to go with Hakon.

"Egil Hrolfsson wants to join me?" Hakon asked. He laughed, for no reason Sigurd could see. "He is Harald's sworn man, is he not?"

"Yes," said Sigurd, "though Harald has never called upon that oath."

"I value loyalty as highly as Harald does, and I will expect it from you and your friend. But I do not ask for oaths that might conflict. Only know that if you betray me, you will die."

"What of Egil?"

"I would be pleased to have him with me," said Hakon.

19

EITHER BECAUSE OF HARALD'S LUCK, OR HIS MOTHER'S MAGIC, the wind carried his warriors swiftly from Nidaros to Geiranger Fjord. Heming captained his own ship, since he and Harald could not share the same space peaceably. Harald had not worked out the guardianship of Sogn with Ragnvald, but Atli refused to go to sea against Solvi or anyone else, so the matter could be delayed for a time.

"Did your sister tell you anything that could be helpful?" Harald asked as the pilot began to weave between the islands that guarded the entrance to Geiranger Fjord.

"Just that we will meet Solvi and his three ships, not only Ulfarr. He has allies, but Svanhild did not think they had left Iceland yet," Ragnvald related. She had not been sure, though; memories of Solvi's plans were mixed up with her memories of her son's death. Ragnvald let his words stand. Harald did not do well with uncertainty.

"Yes, you told me already," said Harald impatiently. "That is why we are attacking with eight ships and every man willing to quit a warm hall in this weather."

"That is all she told me. She has been grieving." She had changed greatly in their six years apart. Her features, which Ragnvald had never been able to picture without her smile upon them, now looked fey and haunted, with shadows around her eyes and under her cheekbones. The image Ragnvald had carried of her had been erased by this new, shattered woman.

"How long do you think she will be grieving?" Harald asked. "I offered to marry her once, and I would still like to. She is a woman of spirit. I have married the sisters of men I value far less than you. And she is still a beauty, or will be, when she learns to smile again."

Ragnvald had always hoped that Svanhild would return to him and he could marry her to Harald, cementing them as kin. Svanhild's sons should be as close to Ragnvald as his own, his second heirs, and if they were Harald's also, then he and Harald could never be parted, not by Guthorm or Hakon's plotting, or by any of Ragnvald's missteps. But he did not know what Svanhild's answer would be, and could not bear to cause her any unhappiness, especially not now.

"You honor both of us with this offer. I will speak to her about it," he said cautiously. "She may need time, though." Harald looked at him, uncomprehending. No woman save Gyda had ever even hesitated to join with him. He would do well to think of Svanhild as another Gyda, rather than like any of his other women. "Svanhild follows her own mind. More than any man or woman I have ever met. She'll be a better wife to you if she thinks the marriage is her idea—think of her as a better-looking, more charming Hakon. That's the way to manage him as well."

Harald gave Ragnvald a bemused smile. He probably did not understand that way of handling either a king or a woman—he had only to ask for a thing to see it fall into his hand. "Whatever you think is wise," said Harald. "But I would have it done sooner than not. This match brings nothing but advantage."

✣   ✣   ✣

FOG CHOKED GEIRANGER Fjord when Harald's force passed the last barrier islands and entered the narrowing waterway. It hid the ridges that flanked the fjord, and blurred the points of land that Ragnvald remembered passing by in Solvi's ship. He squinted, wishing his vision could pierce it. At least if Solvi's sentries patrolled the cliffs, they would be as blind as Harald's force down in the ravine.

Still, sentries could hear. This many ships were not silent, especially in the quiet of the fog. The oars made a slapping sound when they hit the water, the oar master called out the rhythm, and the ships creaked and groaned. Best assume that Solvi had news of their coming and would be prepared. Heming said that Ulfarr had two ships, lightly crewed, and Solvi brought with him another three, while Harald had brought eight, stuffed with warriors, as many as he could spare while leaving enough at Nidaros to defend against any who might try those defenses. Solvi might be planning to attack Nidaros, after luring Harald to Tafjord. Ragnvald flagged down a passing fisherman, hoping to see the face of his old friend Agi, who had saved him from the fjord, but encountered strangers instead, who told him only of ships sailing east and inland, and none coming out.

"The cliffs are growing steep," Ragnvald said to Harald, who stood murmuring with Guthorm at the prow, staying well out of the way of the rowers. "From here on, there is nowhere to dock until we reach Tafjord, and I don't believe Solvi will let us get that far."

"You think we should go no farther," said Harald. "Tell me what we should do instead." Guthorm nodded at Ragnvald and made room for him at the stern. It seemed Guthorm planned to keep himself out of this decision so he could criticize it later. Harald looked expectantly at Ragnvald. When Harald turned all of that regard upon a man, he felt as though he was the most valued person in the world. Ragnvald had never ceased to be dazzled by it.

"I think we should investigate more," said Ragnvald. "Send men over the hills."

"Murder a few sentries?" Harald asked with an arched eyebrow. "We will not sneak up on them. We have enough men to take Tafjord even if Solvi has gathered allies. Cheer up—this is an adventure."

"You do not value me for my cheer," said Ragnvald, still peering up at the cliff tops.

"No, you are my raven of ill omen," said Harald affectionately. "Half-drowned, with wet feathers." The byname had ceased to bother Ragnvald very much, but here in the fog he shivered. In this fjord, not far from where they now drifted, Solvi had sent him into the water. Beneath these ripples lay the drowned palace where he had seen his vision of Harald, the golden wolf.

"If I were Solvi, I would have stashed some ships up one of the tributaries, and trap us in between," said Ragnvald.

"If I were Solvi, I would bet on you thinking that, and coax you to divide your force by sending ships into the tributaries," Harald returned. "Trust in our luck. Trust in our numbers."

Harald did call for the oars to be muffled from here on. The convoy drifted while the oarsmen stuffed batting into the oarlocks. Voices quieted too, so the only thing Ragnvald could hear was the creak of rigging and the lap of water against the boards. The men rowed at half pace, long pulls all in unison, and then a longer rest in silence, letting the ships' momentum carry them forward, as the cliffs rose higher with every stroke.

Solvi's force emerged from the layer of fog before them. The leading ship cut through like a sword, mist falling away on each side as it glided forward, and then the rest formed out of the gray. Eight ships with shields arrayed along their sides, and men behind those shields who broke into battle yells when they sighted Harald's ships.

Eight of Solvi's ships to eight of Harald's. The ships were far away, and too obscured by fog for Ragnvald to see individual faces, but he recognized the way the foremost ship moved. It came about quickly, like a water-skater on a pond, like no ship could move, unless it was piloted by the ablest man ever to steer a ship, aided by perfectly trained oarsmen, who had fought more sea battles than any other living men—Solvi's ship.

Solvi had three more ships than he should, meaning his allies had come. "We need to retreat," said Ragnvald.

"I don't retreat," said Harald. "They do not outnumber us."

"They are moving better," said Ragnvald. "They can surround us, and our numbers will be our downfall. We need to get into better position." He met Harald's eyes for a long moment as Solvi's ships approached, and finally Harald nodded, and raised his horn to his lips where he blew the signal for the ships to reverse direction.

The oarsmen swiftly stood and turned so they faced the other direction, then began pulling on the oars with all their might. The padding that had been used to silence the oars shifted and fell out into the water, leaving a wake of white batting behind each ship. The space between Harald's ships and Solvi's began to open, slowly, then more quickly. Ragnvald felt a breeze on his face, and for a moment his worry lifted, for the moving air made it feel as though the ships had picked up even more speed. The sail flapped and clattered, pressed back against the mast.

Then the breeze began to grow stronger, pushing them back toward Tafjord. The gap between the two forces remained the same for a few strokes of the oars, and then started to close again. The rowers pulled harder, accelerating their pace, but the distance still shrank until, a handful of breaths later, the first of Solvi's ships collided with Harald's.

Solvi's men threw grappling hooks across so they could lash the ships together for easier fighting, one shaking the boards under Ragnvald's feet as it landed next to him. He pulled his ax from his back and cut through the line, scoring deeply into the deck of the ship. Another landed farther away, and pulled their ship closer to Solvi's before Harald's man there could cut it away.

"No retreat now," said Harald with a tight grin at Ragnvald. He stumbled as the stern of Solvi's ship swung around to crash into theirs. Then Solvi's men were upon them, leaping over gunwales, landing with swords bared and axes swinging. Ragnvald was trapped behind a line of rowers who had stood to defend themselves, next to Harald, who had his sword drawn, looking for a gap in the crowd he could get through to the front of the battle.

"We must cut them away," said Ragnvald. "We can still avoid being trapped, and use our numbers."

"You worry too much," said Harald, this time with less affection in his voice. "I never lose."

One of Harald's warriors fell, and his attacker moved to face Ragnvald. Ragnvald pressed him back, forcing him to turn and jump over to his own ship. He did not pursue, instead using his ax in his left hand to cut away a line connecting the two ships. The wind usually blew away from Tafjord, Ragnvald remembered. It made Tafjord hard to attack. If they survived long enough, it would turn for them.

Without the stern rope connecting the two ships, Ragnvald's began to pivot from the forces of wind and current on it. He looked up and saw where a short fork of the fjord joined the main body. Fog had hidden its shores before. Now Ragnvald saw another line of ships strung across its width, all bearing down on Harald's. Solvi had gathered many allies for an out-of-season sea battle. Harald's men, and his dreams of a united future for Norway, would die today with so many against them.

"This is too many," cried Ragnvald. "We must flee—better a retreat than a rout." Fear flashed in Harald's eyes. He nodded, and then had to turn all his focus toward the man attacking him.

"Nidaros men," Ragnvald called out. "Do not board their ships. Make the sails ready!"

Harald repeated the command, and Ragnvald heard it picked up by other ships. The breeze eddied, and the fog swirled.

The moment the water began to ripple in the other direction, Ragnvald yelled, "Make sail, make sail," and the creaking of the lines filled the air as each of Harald's eight ships lifted their huge sails. The fabric bellied out as it filled with wind. Ragnvald's ship began to move last, stretching the remaining ties between it and Solvi's ship. Ragnvald scrambled to cut them.

Solvi's force had been too busy attacking to make ready for the wind to shift, so they lagged behind. The gap widened until they shrank to toys in the distance, but they had made a barrier in the fjord that Harald's ships could not pass.

"We won't get by them. We must make truce," said Ragnvald. "Perhaps they can be bought off."

"I will never make truce with Solvi Klofe or his allies," said Harald. "Since we cannot avoid them, we must fight and trust to luck."

Ragnvald should have foreseen this better—Solvi would not have sent his men to reclaim Tafjord without a plan for keeping it. This was the same trap he had sprung on Solvi in Vestfold, and now it closed in on Harald. "We have time to reach the shore—you can depart over land," said Ragnvald. "We can still save many men."

Harald shook his head. "No, this is my battle. If I flee, no man will ever follow me again."

Ragnvald searched desperately for a way to save Harald. He could not win this battle at sea, but on land his warriors could claim the high ground. Leave some ships out in the fjord as bait to divide Solvi's forces, crewed by men destined to die, and lure the other attackers into the woods. That might serve. Solvi's numbers would be against him as his men tried to tie up on the narrow stretch of shoreline wide enough for only a few ships.

He spoke his idea to Harald, who resisted only briefly before commanding his ships to the shore. As soon as the lead ships were pulled up on the sloping grass, Harald asked for volunteers to crew the decoy ships. "I will ransom you for a jarl's wergild, and when that is done I will pay you or your family a jarl's wergild. If I fall, my uncle will make sure this is done," Harald promised.

That drew men to the task, and Ragnvald stepped forward as well. "I will lead the ships," he said. He was a better sailor than those who had volunteered already.

"Ragnvald, do not," said Harald. "Others can go."

"The day of my death is already chosen, and if it is not today, I will claim my reward, I promise," said Ragnvald.

"I'm with you as well," said another man—Aldi, the son of Atli. A quieter and more agreeable man than his father. And braver too.

Ragnvald nodded his thanks. "Leave a few men to defend the ships on the shore," he said to Harald. "Keep watch and see if, by some chance, it is better for you to come to our aid. But draw them into the woods." He seized a pot of flammable pitch, usually used for sealing the ship's seams, and passed it to Oddi. "If the battle is going against us, use fire arrows to burn the ships. You will destroy at least half of Solvi's fleet."

"Ragnvald, don't," said Oddi.

Ragnvald turned away from him. There was no more time. He climbed over the shifting maze of planking that the tied-up ships had formed, while looking out at the fjord, where Solvi's two forces drew closer to each other. Harald gave him a pleading look, and twisted a strand of his beard between his fingers, a nervous motion. His wide eyes made him look like a boy again. Ragnvald shook his head slightly. This was the only plan that had a chance of keeping Harald alive.

Harald hesitated for another breath, and then inclined his head. Ragnvald nodded in return and set his ship loose. He was a fair pilot, but without oarsmen, and with the strange, shifting air currents in the fjord, the sail could not be depended upon to give him speed. The decoy ships could only drift about and confuse their attackers, then surrender and hope for ransom. It would buy Harald more time though.

While Ragnvald waited for battle to be joined again, he stripped the gold from his belt, and put on a battered, old steel helmet rather than his usual polished and decorated one. In the confusion, he might have an opportunity to disguise himself as one of the enemy soldiers. Even if this disguise lessened his honor, he could not know which path might lead him away from death. Ronhild's prophecy said that he would not die until Harald had united all of Norway. Ragnvald calmed his fear with that thought.

The force from Tafjord reached the decoy ships first while the other ships hovered in the distance. "Your allies wait for your success," Ragnvald yelled across the gap. "They are cowards." He received no response as Solvi's ship came crashing into his. Ragnvald recognized the bulk of Ulfarr in the prow, waiting for his chance to leap.

"These ships are empty," he heard Ulfarr say.

"They're probably hiding beneath the rowing benches," said someone else. Usually the rustle of hundreds of men ready to fight, no matter how still they tried to be, drowned out the voices of the enemy. The quiet made the coming battle seem unreal.

"I don't think so," said Ulfarr. "It's some other kind of trap."

Ragnvald adjusted the steering oar with his foot, to better catch the small breeze. He would take every moment he could to give Harald time to arrange his men in the woods.

"It *is* a trap," said Solvi. Ragnvald recognized his voice immediately, the clear, resonant tone that seemed too loud and deep for Solvi's stature, a voice for shouting between ships in a gale.

Ragnvald only expected his shifting of the steering oar to keep the ships apart for another few breaths before Solvi's rowers brought them together. He felt the clear detachment, the freedom from emotions, that battle often granted him, and a sharpening of all his senses. A small gust gave him another moment to steel himself before grappling hooks landed on the ship—too many to repel—and pulled the ships together with a crunch of wood.

"They mean to entangle us in those near-empty ships and then attack from the shore," said Solvi. "These poor wights on board must want a quicker death than we will give their friends."

One of the volunteers on board Ragnvald's ship called out, "King Harald will ransom us for a jarl's wergild."

"I'll pay more than that for their heads," said Solvi to his men.

Ragnvald stood so Solvi could see his face above where the gunwale rose in the stern. "Harald will pay even more for me," he said.

Solvi looked shaken to see him. His fierce battle-grin faded. "Yes, take the surrendering coward alive," he said of Ragnvald. "Just that one—kill the rest."

He moved as easily between the shifting ships as a squirrel climbing among high branches. The man next to Ragnvald was not ready for Solvi, who slashed him across the throat with his short sword, not even watching as he fell. Bjorn was his name, Ragnvald remembered; he had been orphaned at a young age and raised by his older sister, who would now wait forever for his homecoming.

Solvi advanced toward Ragnvald. Ragnvald held his ax in his left hand but had not drawn his sword. In the close quarters of a ship battle, his ax would be more useful.

"I promised my wife that I would not kill you if it was in my power to do so," said Solvi. "Now I can keep my promise, and trade you for her."

"She doesn't want you," said Ragnvald. "And since you are outlawed, it is as if she was never your wife."

"I do not accept your Harald's laws, laws that make every man a slave," said Solvi. He commanded Ulfarr to tie Ragnvald up and take his sword. Ragnvald flexed his wrists while Ulfarr bound them to give himself as much room to free them as possible. If battle started to go against Solvi, he did not know if he would be killed or traded. The latter was likely only if he kept close to Solvi.

Solvi sent half his ships to trap Harald's against the shore, as Ragnvald had hoped he would. His men would follow Harald's into the woods and die on the steep slopes. Ulfarr threw Ragnvald to the floor of his ship, and brought a few men across to work the lines and steering oar. This ship was a fine prize for Ulfarr, built by Harald's master-builders of the straightest, strongest wood that Norway's forests had to offer, and worth as much as a star-steel sword made by the finest Frankish smith.

From where Ragnvald lay, he could only hear the fighting. He could tell from the cries of dismay when Solvi's men discovered Harald had hidden his men in the woods. He twisted himself onto his stomach, and then to his knees, awkward on the ship's curving floor, with his hands tied behind his back. He saw that the ships of Solvi's allies had come no farther, and felt the reason why: the wind from Tafjord, a sodden wind, blowing out toward the sea. The ships' oars beat the water, trying to draw them nearer, and failing. The sky grew darker.

Ronhild's magic, or the gods' favor, it mattered not. Ragnvald struggled to standing and called with all his might across the water. "We are more than them. Harald, do not hold back."

He did not know if Harald heard him, through battle and over the water. Someone hit Ragnvald's head hard and sent him sprawling over the deck. His teeth slammed together when his chin hit, and he tasted blood. He lay there for a moment gathering his wits, but when no other blow came, Ragnvald pulled himself to his knees again. One of his lower teeth felt loose. Ragnvald clenched his jaw to press it back into place.

Harald's men poured out of the woods, killing Solvi's men where they stood. Soon they regained their ships and began to fight back against Solvi's men. Bodies splashed into the water at the shore. Ulfarr maneuvered Ragnvald's ship closer to the fighting. Good, he would have a better opportunity to escape. He worked at freeing his hands, and by the time his ship crashed into the next, he had made enough slack to force his fingers through the binding. His captors no longer paid attention to him, too busy fending off Harald's warriors, who leaped from ship to ship. Ragnvald crawled over the oar benches behind the fighting, until he reached his sword. He belted it on again, drew it, and fought his way forward, killing another of Solvi's men before he reached Ulfarr.

"Ulfarr Torvisson, Solvi's dog, fight me," said Ragnvald. In these very waters, Ulfarr had been the one to hold back Egil from helping

Ragnvald when Solvi had tried to kill him. He had been a mighty warrior then, and he was still bigger than Ragnvald, with a longer reach.

Ragnvald was not sure he could best Ulfarr in a fair fight, but he was fresh, having spent most of the battle tied up, while Ulfarr was tired. Ragnvald pressed Ulfarr back a few paces until he backed into Oddi, who had fought his way to Ragnvald's ship.

"Do you want him?" Oddi asked Ragnvald.

"Coward," Ulfarr spat. "Solvi should have killed you in Ireland."

"Solvi was never better than a murderer for hire," said Ragnvald. "You follow a coward."

That made Ulfarr angry, as Ragnvald had meant it to, and Ulfarr rushed toward him. He tripped over one of the rowing benches, and Ragnvald thrust his sword up into Ulfarr's belly, his hand growing hot from the spilling of Ulfarr's blood upon it. The force of Ulfarr's falling body embedded his sword so deeply in his stomach that Ragnvald had to push Ulfarr onto his back to free it. Ulfarr did not struggle, knowing his wound was mortal.

"Do you want to die slowly of this wound, or quickly?" Ragnvald asked him. The few duels that remained on the ship were quickly coming to a finish. This ship was Harald's again.

Ulfarr held his hands to his bloody waist. Blood soaked into the ship's boards beneath him. Ulfarr might bleed out rather than die of the rot and fever Ragnvald wanted for his end. He felt at his belt for his dagger. Ulfarr could still be dangerous. "I do not want to die by your hand," he said.

"Good," said Ragnvald, and slashed Ulfarr across the throat. Ulfarr retched and choked on his death even before he could move his hands from his stomach to his neck. Ragnvald reached down to free a clasp of silver and lapis from his breast, while blood covered the white linen of Ulfarr's shirt, and his eyes, staring up at the sky, began to collect rain.

In the distance, sheets of rain hid the rest of Solvi's allies. Dead bodies littered the deck of his ship, and Harald's soldiers stood panting, swords and axes gripped limply in exhausted fingers. Most of the ships were still lashed together, but Ragnvald saw that one, Solvi's, with its dragon head that Ragnvald remembered so well, had freed it-self from the morass and now rowed out into the middle of the fjord, where it caught the storm gust and was carried away. Solvi had es-caped them again.

He looked down at Ulfarr's bloody corpse. "Strip him and throw him into the water," he said to Aldi, who stood near to him. "You can keep his armor. You fought well today."

Ragnvald guided his ship to where Harald stood on the shore. "Luck was with us," he said to Harald. "Your luck."

"Too modest," said Harald. His hands were red to the elbow with blood, his face spattered with it. He sounded as though he still wanted to kill. "You won this battle—with your hands tied behind your back. You, and not me. Hornklofe!" He called for his favorite skald, who accompanied him to all battles to make his songs. Ragnvald liked Hornklofe too, for he was a warrior as well as a poet. Hornklofe had wet his sword today, and was wiping it off on the trousers of one of the fallen. "Hornklofe, I want you to put in your song that Ragnvald won this battle with his hands tied behind his back."

"Some will think the trick cowardly," said Ragnvald mildly. "It was weather that won this for us. Without the storm, your only choice would have been escape."

"Don't put that in your song," said Harald. "If Solvi's allies had not hesitated, they could have outrun the storm and been upon us. I will thank you for your bravery, my mother for the storm, the gods for my luck, and drink so much I can't see straight tonight. We make for Tafjord!"

20

AS SOLVI SAILED AWAY FROM THE BATTLE, HE SAW TRYGGULF'S ship making its escape as well. Solvi was the more daring sailor, but Tryggulf had taught him everything he knew. Solvi's and Gudbrand's other six ships fell into the hands of Harald's forces. Now he had Solvi's men to torture for information or ransom for treasure.

Solvi had watched Ragnvald cut Ulfarr's throat. Ulfarr, dead. Ulfarr, who had carried Solvi on his back when Solvi was a boy and his legs had been too injured for him to walk. Ulfarr, who taught Solvi to ride, and had fought every battle by his side. Svanhild had hated him, but Svanhild had not known Ulfarr as Solvi had. If a warrior like Ulfarr, strong in battle, cruel in victory, who had never known defeat, followed Solvi, then any man could be proud of doing the same.

"Should I kill this Jarl Rane or should you?" Ketil Flatnose asked, coming to stand next to Solvi. His voice was grim. The wind that had prevented Rane's ships from reaching the battle brought Solvi's and Tryggulf's ships up next to them within a few breaths.

"His inaction cost me a son, you a friend, and all of Norway a great victory," said Gudbrand.

Solvi took strength from his allies' anger. Gudbrand would always back him, and defer to him, because Solvi had shown more bravery at Vestfold, and now Solvi would have a hold over Rane that would make him into a tool as well, one who could question Solvi even less than Gudbrand did.

"Neither," said Solvi. "We need him."

"Any kind of sailor, or man, would have found a way to come to us," said Gudbrand. Solvi could not argue that. He had not seen the oars extended until near the end of the battle, when it was already far too late. "I cannot let him live."

"You must," said Solvi. "If he ever ceases to be useful, though, I will hold him while you cut him however you like—butcher him like swine. You have my word."

Rane stood on one of the ships with Tova by his side. Tova's neck was taut with fear. Rane's eyes shifted when he saw Solvi, and his grip tightened on Tova's waist.

"You coward," said Solvi. Rane's hand went to his sword. "You fucker of goats, you *nithing*. That battle should have been impossible to lose." These were insults that a man must kill over, yet Rane still merely rested his fingers on his sword's hilt without drawing it. He knew the justice of them.

"The weather turned against us," said Rane. "Your men had all the advantage of the wind, while mine were fighting it."

"Have your captains never learned to tack against the wind? Or command their rowers?"

"I did not want them to be too weary from rowing to fight," said Rane. "I thought the wind would blow the battle onto us."

"Not with ships lashed together and sails lowered," said Solvi.

"I am not versed in sea battles," said Rane.

"Is that how you justify this?" Solvi gestured at the sparse crews of his two remaining ships, the blood that spattered his armor. "You cost me my best warrior, who has been a friend to me since I was a boy. We could have defeated Harald today, but at least you are 'well rested.'"

"You are a small man to say such things," Rane retorted. Now he did draw his sword.

"And you are a large man to be such a coward," said Solvi. "If this is the best the men of Norway can muster, we deserve to be ruled by that overgrown boy-king Harald. I am done with all of this."

"Now, Solvi," said Gudbrand, though he seemed uncertain what part Solvi wanted him to play, and turned to Rane. "Because of you, I have lost my namesake Gudmar, one of my two remaining sons."

Solvi's anger burned hot enough that he almost added that it was no great loss to lose one of Gudbrand's thickheaded sons, not compared with the loss of Ulfarr. "I do not think much of your king either, if you are all he sends," he said to Rane. "He may as well resign himself to King Harald as a neighbor now, and come to terms with Harald's ambitions, for he means to rule the whole Norse peninsula, even the parts that Sweden claims now."

"You need to stop insulting us," said Rane. "These are my men, and they will stand by me."

"Will they?" Solvi asked. Rane's men exchanged glances. "Or, next time, will they support a man who has a chance of winning a sea battle?"

"This is your fault," said Rane, thrusting his chin forward. "Your strategy failed."

"Let us see what your men think," Solvi called out. "Would they rather follow me in their next sea battle, or you—come on, raise your hands if you would rather follow me into a sea battle? If you would rather win than be 'well rested'?"

The men in Rane's own ship were slow to raise their hands, but from the other ships came cries, and raised hands, cries that resolved into a chant, "Win, win! Solvi! Solvi Klofe! Solvi Klofe!"

Solvi smiled a calculated, hungry grin, and turned so that all of Rane's men could see his face. "I will give you a victory. I will give you a victory that men will sing of a thousand years hence."

"How will you do that?" Rane asked.

"I am going to Uppsala, to the Swedish court, with our forces," he said. Rane's men were his now, and Rane knew it. "You will tell him what happened here, how you left me to fight Harald alone, and how the only way to settle the debt is to defeat Harald so thoroughly that none will ever count him a champion again. And if I hear the words 'well rested' again I will laugh in your face."

"If you continue insulting me . . . ," said Rane.

"I will say what I want," said Solvi. "The only way to redeem your name is to defeat Harald with me. Don't worry, next time your ships will be captained by men trained by me, and they will follow my orders. I am not going to die as the man that Harald defeated twice."

✢ ✢ ✢

THE STORM KEPT Harald's forces from reaching Tafjord that night. They spent the remaining daylight beating against the wind and then made camp shipboard, tied up under narrow rock overhangs. Harald gathered his leaders, among them Ragnvald, Guthorm, Oddi, and Heming, in one of the ships. Another was full of prisoners from the battle, those who had surrendered rather than fighting on to the death, a mixture of Solvi's and Heming's men.

"Your mother overdoes it with the storm, I think," said Ragnvald.

"Are you going to tell her that?" Harald asked, without the humor Ragnvald expected. "You are the bravest man I know, but no man is that brave." He held a torch, which made his face look like a strange wooden mask. "I have been thinking of Tafjord's betrayal. We have taken prisoners who must be punished. Once we arrive, my men will cut the left foot and right hand off all who fought against us. Those who survive this will be sold as slaves. You will make sure this is carried out."

The words drew a vivid picture in Ragnvald's mind: of men screaming, bleeding, and dying, of piles of hands and feet, like skalds described in the most terrible of underworlds. He was tired of death. "Is this a king's work?" he asked. Surely Harald must be tired of death as well. "Those were Heming's men. He should choose how to punish them."

"They should not have fought me," said Harald.

"If they had not, Solvi's men would have killed them," Ragnvald replied. They stood close together on the crowded ship, and they all stank of battle, of sweat and gore, of the contents of voided bowels and bladders that lay on the decking. Now Harald wanted to add to the carnage. "Why do you order this?"

"There is rebellion on my shores—Maer was conquered and it should have stayed conquered. This is how I punish rebellion, and now all will know it," said Harald.

"If you mean to push districts to ally with Solvi, this will do it," said Ragnvald. "And make very poor slaves."

"Do not question me again," said Harald. "It is you who told me that I must win every battle, and if I lose a single one, I will fail. And you know how close we came to losing today."

"Harald, my boy," Guthorm began, "Ragnvald is right."

A drip of water from the cliff above fell into Harald's torch, sending up a puff of steam, and another splashed onto his face. He rubbed it away angrily. "Do not argue with me, uncle. Ragnvald, today, has earned that right—you have done nothing useful for me lately, except sow discord among my allies."

"I stand in agreement with Ragnvald," said Heming quietly. "These were my men, some of them."

"As do I," said Oddi.

"You never do other than agree with Ragnvald, Oddi," Harald snapped, then added more quietly, "I will think on it tonight. That is why I spoke with you. I value your advice."

✝ ✝ ✝

WHEN HARALD'S FORCES reached Tafjord the next day, Vemund's traitors, Grai and Illugi, gathered all the captured enemy fighters in an empty stable. Ragnvald heard the screams, and knew that they were carrying out Harald's original orders. He went to find Harald at the shore, where his men were unloading Solvi's ships, laying out the axes and pieces of armor on the shore so he could distribute them as rewards to his warriors.

"You must stop them," he said to Harald.

"I did not give the order," said Harald. "They must have wanted vengeance."

"You expect me to believe that?" Ragnvald cried. Harald shrugged. "None will believe it, not unless you punish these men—kill them yourself, before witnesses. Even then, many will think you ordered it. Harald—"

"I did not order it," said Harald. "You do not trust my word?"

Ragnvald could not answer, so he turned away from Harald, and flinched as another scream rent the air. "I will stop this, then," he said, taking off at a run.

"It is too late," Harald called after him. "Come back, Ragnvald."

Ragnvald ignored him. Grai and Illugi had gathered like-minded

warriors to them, wolf-souled men who enjoyed cruelty for its own
sake. There was no place for them in Harald's shining plans for Norway. When he entered the building he saw slim Illugi holding a man
down. He stared at the man's face, contorted in fear and pain, for a
moment before recognizing Dagvith, a warrior he had known from
Hakon's *hird*, back when Ragnvald had first joined with Hakon at Yr-
jar. Before Ragnvald could stop him, Grai brought down his ax upon
Dagvith's ankle, shattering bone. Dagvith screamed again.

"By order of Harald, King of Norway, you will stop this immediately," Ragnvald commanded.

Illugi looked up. "He wants this to happen," he said. "You know it,
and I know it. You only wish he didn't. It is almost done. Go outside,
and your maidenly eyes will not have to see it."

"I should kill you for that insult," said Ragnvald.

"I withdraw it," said Illugi. Dagvith whimpered, and Grai slapped
him across the face. "Now go outside."

"Ragnvald," called out Dagvith in a broken voice. "Kill me, please.
Kill me like a man before I die like a slave."

He could do that at least. "Stand aside," he ordered Grai and
Illugi. Illugi shrugged and moved away. Bile rose in Ragnvald's
throat. Dagvith was fading as blood poured out of him. His eyelids
fluttered. Ragnvald drew his sword and put it in Dagvith's remaining hand, then used his dagger to cut Dagvith's throat. He had died
with a weapon in his hand, at least, and so his spirit would reach
Valhalla.

"Are you here to kill all of them?" Illugi asked, with what sounded
like real curiosity.

"I am no butcher," said Ragnvald. "Not like you."

"Then you had best leave us to our work."

"Your work is done now," said Ragnvald.

He took a step toward Illugi, who retreated with insolent slowness.
"Very well, my lord," said Illugi finally, after Ragnvald backed him up
against the wall.

He took one last glance at Grai and Illugi's moaning victims before leaving the shed, and again tasted the sourness of bile. He stumbled outside and retched until he had made a mess on the ground.

Behind him, Illugi was laughing. He remembered what Harald's mother, Ronhild, had promised him: "You will give everything you have to give to Harald, and when you have nothing left, you will give your life." He fell on his knees.

Oddi rushed to his side to help him up, and said, "'There is cruelty all over the land, full of broken shields. An ax age comes, and then a wolf age, before the doom of the gods'"—a saying from an old poem in which a seer spoke about the end of the world. Ragnvald felt he would collapse in his filth if Oddi said another word. Harald was his king, his choice, his fate, his golden wolf. Ragnvald should have seen this in him, that when Harald refused to cut his hair, he had allied himself with wolves, with wildness, with cruelty. He had sworn to be a wolf until he had conquered all of Norway.

✝   ✝   ✝

SINCE GRAI AND Illugi had turned over the responsibility for their victims to Ragnvald, every morning he had the grim task of pulling bodies from the outbuilding, and burning them, for more died of their maiming than survived it. When he completed that task, he avoided Harald and instead worked himself into exhaustion with Heming and Oddi to clear signs of Solvi's habitation from Tafjord.

"I want my king to be harsh to his enemies," said Heming, on the second day of Ragnvald's silence. "Better that than weakness." Ragnvald remembered Hakon torturing men after a battle, and did not respond. At least those men had information to give.

Finally, the night before they were going to leave, Oddi found Ragnvald, and handed him a heavy fur blanket and a jug of spirits. The night was clear, the stars like chips of ice in the sky. "I cannot stand to see you like this," Oddi said, his voice near to breaking. "Say something dark and humorless to me, to take away my sleep—I know that is what comforts you, even if it is horrible to me."

"You have been able to sleep?" Ragnvald asked. He took the jug of spirits from Oddi and took a long swig. It burned his throat like the coldest winter air, which he welcomed, though the warmth it lent his stomach made him queasy. He did not want to feel warm, or better in any way.

"Yes, but Harald's cruelty did not surprise me. You thought better of him, did you not?"

Ragnvald thought of his own hand holding the torch to Vemund's hall—at Harald's order. "I thought better of me," he said. "I was wrong."

"You thought well enough of him to spend your life like cheap brass at the battle against Solvi," said Oddi, ignoring Ragnvald's last words.

"The day of my death is already determined," said Ragnvald. "And it was not that day."

"Don't do it again," said Oddi dryly. "Next time I'll have to go with you, and I am not god-blessed." Beneath his self-mockery, Ragnvald heard the depth of his concern.

"I should have known about Solvi's alliances. I should have questioned Svanhild properly . . ."

"You should have known?" Oddi asked. "Is there nothing you are not responsible for? You advised Harald to avoid battle more than once, and then risked your own life when Harald refused your suggestions."

Oddi did not understand. "Harald could not flee," said Ragnvald. "He has to win every battle."

"Win every battle, not fight every battle," said Oddi.

"I still should have known that Solvi would bring allies," Ragnvald insisted.

"If anyone should have known, it is Guthorm—he has his spies. What did Svanhild tell you? How do you know she did not come to Nidaros to lure you into this?"

Ragnvald went cold. "No," he said. "I should have asked her for more information. I thought that Solvi's allies would not join him until the spring, and I never asked her . . ." Svanhild had come to him with her spirit bruised, her face hollowed by grief for her son. Ragnvald had not looked further than that. But he remembered that she had lured him into a sort of trap many years before in Vestfold to allow Solvi's escape. Harald's actions—Grai's and Illugi's—had shown Ragnvald how soft and trusting he still was, no matter how hard he tried not to be. "I will ask her." He put his head in his hands. "Either way, I am at fault for every death here."

"You are not," said Oddi. "But she may be at fault for some of them."

✝ ✝ ✝

HARALD'S FORCES DEPARTED a few days later. Harald sailed in the
lead ship, the fastest and smoothest sailing ship in this convoy. Ragnvald left him to it and joined Heming's ship. He felt warmer toward
Heming since he had argued against the torture of his men. Heming would not make him pretend contentment, and, unlike Oddi, he
would not try to cheer Ragnvald either. Whenever Ragnvald closed
his eyes, he saw again Grai raising his ax, the terror on Dagvith's face,
the blood and filth. He could not turn his mind from it, no matter
how he tried. It followed him from dreams into daylight, and wherever he turned his eyes was overlaid with a smear of gore.

He spent the short days looking out over the cold, pure sea, thinking of what he could say to Svanhild. He had lost his trust in Harald—
must he lose his trust in Svanhild as well? He rehearsed conversations
with her in his head, imagining a soft approach and then a harsher
one, though he could imagine a satisfying end to none of them. These
thoughts kept his gruesome memories at bay for a time but gave him
no more peace, and the memories always came back. He had more
sympathy for Atli now; the waves that had taken his nerve for sailing
must feel like this, a wave of fear and horror that Ragnvald could not
control.

21

WHILE HARALD'S WARRIORS WERE AWAY, THE GUARDS OF NI-
daros kept watch for them along the fjord, all the way out to the barrier islands. The weeks passed slowly for Svanhild. She used the excuse
of her grief to stay out of the way of Hilda and Vigdis, though lethargy
no longer kept her in bed. She felt as though the same day repeated
itself over and over again. She woke next to Hilda, helped her bring
the boys to breakfast, and then begged off when Hilda invited her to
the women's room. It reminded Svanhild far too much of what she had
escaped at Ardal, down to Vigdis's honeyed barbs.

She was happier bundling herself up against the cold and walking
around the town, or climbing up the hill that overlooked Nidaros so
she could see the layout of buildings, and compare it to the vast cities
of the south that she had visited with Solvi. She would likely never feel
the heat of Constantinople again, though whenever she sweat herself
clean in the bath, she imagined herself there.

Harald's forces returned to Nidaros a little more than a month before Yule, sailing just ahead of a late fall storm that bore winter on its
back. His men looked half-frozen as they stumbled into the hall, jostling for places before the long fire. Their voices shattered the quiet of
the previous weeks as they called for ale, for help with frozen boots, for
healers and food, for all the things that cold, hungry warriors needed.
They were so covered with frost and cloaks that Svanhild could not
pick out Ragnvald from among them. Only Harald stood out, his head

above all the rest, his shoulders the broadest. Svanhild drew herself up straighter on seeing him, and she remembered her glimpse of him at the bath, a memory that made her suddenly hot, even with the cold that the men's cloaks gave off.

Then she saw Ragnvald, who had been hidden by the bulk of Harald's frame, and relief overcame her. He crouched down and held his hands, bone-white with cold, toward the fire. Other men gave him the space due his rank, enough that Svanhild could squeeze herself between them and embrace him.

"You're alive," she said. She had not doubted it, but every battle, every sea voyage, was a chance to die, and he had neither Harald's luck nor Solvi's cunning.

"Yes," said Ragnvald dully. "And your husband is still alive as well." Svanhild tried to keep her relief from showing, but she had never been good at hiding her feelings. Ragnvald's face seemed to close in upon itself. The white scar that split his dark beard pulled tight. "Do you want me to send you back to him?" he asked. "I had rather you be there than here, sending Harald's men to their deaths."

"Most of you have returned," she said, feeling stupid. She had missed Ragnvald's warmth these past weeks, his pleasure at her company, and now it seemed he had left those things behind in the fighting.

"Some did not," said Ragnvald. "Some will never come home."

"That is battle," said Svanhild. "Should you not say instead that it was their time?"

"I do not want to speak to you further," said Ragnvald. "You should put yourself on the next ship bound for Iceland and return to your true loyalties." He rose from his place at the fire, wincing as he clenched his frozen fingers into fists.

"I don't understand," said Svanhild. "Who has been poisoning you against me?"

"Solvi's allies—they came in such great numbers we are lucky to have escaped." He turned away from her.

"Brother," she called after him. She pushed between bodies of men that closed ranks behind him, only to find Oddi's hand on her elbow. She shook his grasp off. He had no right to keep her from

Ragnvald. Oddi caught her by the waist with a strong arm, and held her until she stopped trying to push him away. "Let me go! I need to speak with him."

"He does not want to see you," said Oddi.

"Why is he angry with me?" she asked him. She struggled against his arm as he held on to her until she realized she could not get away, and instead felt for his fingers on her hip, sliding hers over them in a way he might think was flirtatious. She grabbed his forefinger and bent it back until she felt resistance. "Let me go and I won't break your finger," she said.

"Ragnvald thinks you came here to betray Harald for your husband," said Oddi coolly, though he loosened his hold.

"And you think so too," said Svanhild, finally understanding. She let Oddi's finger slide out of her grasp.

"You came here, while Solvi went off to Tafjord. You said nothing of his plans when Ragnvald asked. What else could he think?"

"I did not—" said Svanhild indignantly, then brought herself up short. "I did not come here with that intent. I was too overcome with grief to tell Ragnvald much of anything." She looked up at Oddi's face, set in a stern expression that did not sit naturally on his broad, friendly features. Ragnvald had hardly asked her anything about Solvi. She could blame herself for many things, especially for Eystein's illness and death, but not that. "I do not need to defend myself to you." Only to the dead.

"You will need to defend yourself to someone," said Oddi. "Come, tell me, and I will convince Ragnvald."

"Is this how you have worked, these past five years?" Svanhild asked. "People come to you because you are less frightening to approach than my brother?"

Oddi shrugged. "Perhaps so. Shall I fetch you a glass of wine? We can find somewhere more comfortable to sit."

Svanhild nodded gratefully. Oddi cleared off a bit of bench near a fireplace, and sat down close to her. He smelled of blood and leather, scents that made Svanhild think of Solvi with a wave of almost pleasurable sadness, rather than the sharp stabs of loss that she had flinched from in the previous weeks. She sipped the wine, a sweet apple, and smiled at its honey.

"Nidaros has fine apple groves in the summer," he said. "You should stay and see them."

"Ragnvald wants to send me back to Solvi," she said. Part of her wanted to let him. She could persuade him to take her back, no matter how angry he had been.

"Tell me what you knew," said Oddi. "I don't think Ragnvald should send you back."

"I did not know much—Solvi made alliances with Rane of Vermaland, and Gudbrand of Hordaland. We left Iceland without them, when my—we were to winter in Iceland, and I to stay there, and that is where we met Rane. He was a jarl that Harald ousted from Vestfold in the early years after the death of Halfdan, Harald's father. Harald was a mighty king even at ten, they say."

"I think that was Guthorm—his uncle," said Oddi. "But the outcome was the same."

Svanhild hardly heard him, lost in her memories of leaving Iceland. "At first it did not seem as though Solvi wanted an alliance with Rane and the Swedish king. But then . . . I don't know." She told Oddi about the arrival of Geirny and her father, Nokkve, how Svanhild threatened her with a knife, and how that had cemented the alliance. "On the trip back to Norway, all I cared about was Eys—was my son. He was dying. He died on the northern strand of Trondheim Fjord. Solvi said he would get better when he was on Norse soil and he did not. He said we were going to Tafjord, that Ulfarr had taken it for us."

She could see the pattern now. "I used to help him," she continued. "He talked to me about strategy and we planned together, but he did not let me know his true purpose. I didn't care about getting Tafjord for our son. I just wanted to be safe. Safe and free, as we were together. He wanted more, and I ignored it. I was blind all those years. I told my brother what I knew, I swear it." Svanhild had raised her voice and a few of the other men and women in the hall turned their heads. Oddi put his hand over hers and stroked it gently, as if quieting an anxious horse.

"Solvi is a fine liar," said Oddi. "It is what I have heard of him. One of the best. He did not tell you what you did not want to know. It was not your fault."

"And you will say that to my brother? Like you said it was my fault in the first place?" Svanhild asked. Oddi dropped her hand and stood abruptly. She smiled up at him, a smile she had learned from Solvi, all edge and no warmth.

"I only guessed," she said. "Sit down, and tell me why." Oddi looked around the hall, as though one of the other men would save him. At benches all over the hall, men now told parts of the battle to each other, forming it into stories that they would retell for the rest of their lives, forgetting their cowardice and remembering their bravery—until at the end every man would think himself a hero.

She looked at Oddi until he returned his gaze to her, and sat, putting his head in his hands. "I blamed you because he blamed himself for not knowing more about Solvi's plans," said Oddi. "I did not want to—perhaps you deserved better, but so did he."

Svanhild had floated above grief and every other feeling for the past few weeks, but Oddi's words threatened to break through the film of ice and anger that protected her now.

"What happened?" she asked. "What blame is there?" He hesitated for a long moment, then told her a tale she would hear repeated in a skald's alliterative poetry at the feast that night, though the prose of Oddi's telling had more truth than that would. "Why did my brother bare his throat for Solvi's blade?" she asked when he was done. "Why should he be the sacrifice?"

Oddi had been sitting close to her so she could feel the heat of his body, and now he leaned back. "Your brother never has one reason for doing anything. He thought your—he thought Solvi was more likely to let him live than any other. He still does not believe Harald truly values him, and so he was trying to win what has already been won." Oddi gave a short laugh. "And he told me that it was not his *wyrd* to die that day."

"And it was not," said Svanhild.

✛   ✛   ✛

RAGNVALD LOOKED LIKE a thundercloud at the feast that night. His seat at the high table was far away from Harald, with Oddi, as well as Hakon's son Geirbjorn, interposed between them. Halfway through the skald Hornklofe's telling of the battle against Solvi, Ragnvald rose and left the hall. He might only be going for a piss, for this late into a feast, many bladders strained. Still, it was rude not to remain for his own praise. Svanhild waited through another verse of the song, and when Ragnvald did not return, she followed him out into the night.

Curtains of white light swept across the sky, pulsating as if to the heartbeat of some strange beast. Ragnvald whirled when he heard her approach and put his hand on his sword. His shoulders slumped when he saw who it was.

"Oddi says I was harsh to you," he said gravely, ducking his head so she could see only his profile, silhouetted against the dim lights in the sky. His expression was hidden; all she could make out was the shape of his face as it would look carved into stone.

"Oddi is a good friend to you," said Svanhild.

"Oddi's head is easily turned by a beautiful woman," said Ragnvald. "But I do not accuse you of that. I have not wanted to know why you came here, because I was glad that you came. I should have asked more, and then I could have spared Harald—"

"Spared him what, an astonishing victory? He is well pleased, I am sure. Too well pleased."

"I should have known what to expect," said Ragnvald.

"But you knew that Solvi had allies," said Svanhild.

"What?"

"You did. I have already heard the song. 'None but Ragnvald the Wise could see what lay beyond the bend.' You knew. So I must have told you. Or you figured it out. Why come here blaming me for your victory?"

"I left before the song was over," said Ragnvald thickly. "Did it say what happened after the battle, what Norway's protector did then?"

"It said he punished the traitors."

"He did," said Ragnvald. "Did it say how?" She shook her head, and so Ragnvald told her of the screams, and the dreadful deaths that followed. "He will lose followers for this."

"It sounds as though he has already lost you," said Svanhild. "Why does this trouble you so? Traitors should be punished. My—Solvi would have done the same thing. Or gotten Ulfarr to do it."

"That is not a recommendation," said Ragnvald. And, as an after-thought, "I killed Ulfarr."

"Good," said Svanhild. "I hated him."

"You hated him, and yet Harald did what Ulfarr would have done."

Svanhild wondered if anyone lived who was wise and patient enough to follow all the threads of Ragnvald's self-blame and anger, and lay them out straight. As long as Ragnvald did not blame her any-more, she could hope for nothing else. "How else is he to make men frightened to betray him in the future? If the choice is loyalty and an easy death in battle or betrayal and maiming, he has made it more tempting to choose loyalty."

"Or outright rebellion."

"What concerns you more, that he has hurt these men or hurt his chances to unite Norway?" Svanhild asked. Or hurt Ragnvald's shining image of him, the golden king, the law bringer, the bringer of peace.

"I will trouble you with this no further," said Ragnvald. "It seems not to trouble any of Harald's other followers."

"Was your vision of him not as a golden wolf that sometimes de-stroyed what it touched?" Svanhild asked. Ragnvald turned toward her, his features picked out by the lamplight shining from within the hall. She gave him an ironic smile. "That one is sung as far as Dublin, at least. Is your vision betrayed? Should I take you as my prize back to Solvi?"

"No, of course not," said Ragnvald.

"Then you must forgive Harald for being a man and not a legend."

"I never thought I would hear that from you. Did you not think that we should both be legends if we could? Did you not want to be another Gunnhilda, and murder our stepfather for what he did?"

Svanhild flushed. "Everyone grows up eventually. And you got there first." He turned over her hand, and touched the fading calluses from ships' lines and her dagger grip. He gave it a squeeze, and her a rueful smile.

"You are cold," he said. "Let us go back inside."

"What will you do?" Svanhild asked. She understood Ragnvald's hurt in some way, but she could never be shocked by what men did, even men considered wise and just. Could it be that her travels at Solvi's side had taught her more of the world than all of Ragnvald's battles?

"I want to speak to my king," said Ragnvald. "I have a new bargain to make with him."

22

RAGNVALD FOLLOWED SVANHILD BACK INTO THE FEASTING hall. She, Oddi, even Harald—none of them cared about Ragnvald's missteps in the Solskel battle, or seemed concerned about the cruel punishment of Heming's men. Even Heming had accepted it. So these misgivings were Ragnvald's alone, like his dreams, his vision, and his black moods after a battle. And, like those, he must accept these misgivings as a part of himself, without expecting anyone else to join him in them. On the return trip from Tafjord, he had been short with his king, hoping to make Harald feel his disapproval. But Harald refused to admit he had done anything wrong.

For a long time Ragnvald had reproached himself for not having Harald's ease and charisma, his magical luck. Those lacks might be a blessing, though; he did not need to conquer all of Norway, only hold on to what he had. Though the tethers that bound him to Harald, formed of *wyrd* and oaths and companionship, could only be broken by the gods, Ragnvald could put some distance between them and return to be king of Sogn. He had been too eager to fulfill Ronhild's prophecy, but if it were a true prophecy, it would be fulfilled without his striving. Of the many things Svanhild had said to Ragnvald, one was certainly true: Harald was a man, not a god.

Whether Harald's punishment had been a king's necessary cruelty, as Svanhild would have it, or not, it had tainted Ragnvald's victory and made him reluctant to continue fighting at Harald's side. Harald wanted to marry Svanhild—very well, Ragnvald would put that question to Svanhild, and tell Harald her answer, whatever it was. He no longer feared her decision. A man, even a prophesied king, must hear a refusal sometimes.

He rejoined Harald at the high table, sitting in the empty seat that had been occupied by one of Harald's women. The skald reprised the high points of the battle and Ragnvald's sacrifices. As he finished, the hall filled with cries of "King Harald Tanglehair! Ragnvald the Mighty!" When he was a boy, Ragnvald had told himself that one day a hall of warriors would shout his name, and he tried to imagine how that boy would feel now, to enjoy this moment without bitterness.

"What is his reward?" someone called out.

Harald rose so all could hear him. "I promised those nine men on the boats a jarl's wergild as reward, and they shall have it. But Ragnvald is already more than a jarl—my friend, what will be your reward?"

Ragnvald stood as well. He had dressed to be admired tonight, in a deep red tunic of costly silk, with a gold arm ring that Harald had given him clasped around his bicep. Later, he would exchange it for livestock to help his Sogn farmers, but tonight he could wear it, and look the part of Ragnvald the Mighty.

"What is more precious than gold?" Ragnvald asked. "That is what I will ask for."

"What is more precious than gold?" Harald repeated. "All of my daughters are too young for marriage yet!" The crowd laughed, and Ragnvald waited for them to quiet before he spoke again.

"Time," said Ragnvald. "Time is more precious than gold. Give me leave to defend my home from rebels like Solvi, and time to raise my sons into your loyal subjects. That is my request."

Harald looked hurt for a moment, and then covered it quickly. "What happened to Ragnvald's never-ending reticence?" he asked the hall. "I expected to have to press a reward upon you. But this is not right—what you ask is not enough reward for your service." He pulled a gold ring from one of his arms and handed it to Ragnvald. "Your arms should match."

Ragnvald molded the soft, pure gold around his unadorned arm as men cheered. Harald leaned over to say in his ear, "You are too valuable a captain for me to lose. No one else could have won that battle."

"I cannot be everywhere," said Ragnvald. "Let us talk tomorrow."

✣ ✣ ✣

ON THE HILL above Harald's main living and entertaining halls stood a smaller building, a little hall built for only one man. Harald slept there, with his favorite woman of the moment, and servants who could wait upon him at any time of day or night.

Within the single room, before a backdrop of woven hangings heavy with gold, Harald sat with his uncle Guthorm. A bottle of wine and fine pewter goblets stood on the table, with a plate of bread and cheese, but no servant hovered, ready to pour for them: true privacy. Harald must fear spies.

"What you said last night was close to rebellion," said Guthorm, before Ragnvald could sit down. Ragnvald felt a punch of panic in his stomach—what Guthorm intended for him to feel—and swallowed it. Guthorm wanted to put him on the defensive. Ragnvald had used that trick himself from time to time.

"No, uncle," said Harald. "Ragnvald is my loyal captain. I have never before had reason to doubt him."

A softer approach from Harald, but still an implication of blame. Ragnvald gave them an amused half smile. He took his seat before them, poured himself a glass of the wine, and then tugged the food toward himself and cut off a hunk of the hard-aged cheese. He took his time collecting the flavorful crumbles onto a slice of bread.

"Thank you for the cheese," he said, pretending he had not been paying attention to either of their words. "Your housekeeper at Nidaros knows her business. Is this Asa Hakonsdatter's handiwork?"

"Yes," said Harald. "She is not my comeliest wife, but she gives me sons and her cheese is—"

"Did you come here to discuss cheese?" asked Guthorm testily.

Ragnvald glanced at Harald, who shrugged. "I came at your invitation," said Ragnvald.

"You want to leave King Harald's service," said Guthorm. "As I said, it is close to rebellion."

Ragnvald pushed the plate of cheese back toward him, and poured his glass and Harald's full. "We should toast before we conduct any business. May the gods grant we all make wise decisions."

Harald and Guthorm returned the toast, Harald with a smile for Ragnvald that excluded Guthorm, who met Ragnvald's eyes with a scowl.

"My king," said Ragnvald. "You have won notable victories, but without men to hold those lands, the victories are meaningless. The northwest coast was your earliest conquest, and will remain yours only if you can keep it. Your subject kings, among them Hakon's sons and myself, can hold the land, so you are free to attack farther south, and root out the pockets of dissent. And Sogn needs me to fulfill the promises I have made as king. I have been trying to return Sogn to prosperity so it can add to your wealth, but when I am gone during the whole of the growing season—"

"You're no farmer, Ragnvald," said Harald. "You're a warrior."

"I was raised to farm and defend my land, like my forefathers," said Ragnvald. "Do you mean to conquer, or do you mean to rule?" His anger at Harald's treatment of Heming's men made his voice harsher than he intended. He wished Guthorm absent. Without him, Ragnvald thought he could at least have persuaded Harald to punish Grai and Illugi for violating his later order of mercy. Harald should make a show of justice, even if he did not mean it.

"I will conquer until I rule," said Harald. He twisted his matted beard.

"Until you do, you need rulers," said Ragnvald. "You call me king, so let me rule. You do not need me at every battle."

"But I would not have won that battle without you," said Harald.

"You would not have had to fight it had Maer been fully defended," Ragnvald returned.

Guthorm frowned. "Ragnvald the Wise has an answer for everything," he said.

"A man cannot be everywhere," said Ragnvald.

"I don't understand why you no longer want to be by my side," said Harald, and then glanced away as though he had not meant to speak so plainly.

Ragnvald looked at Harald until Harald met his gaze again. He could not entirely hide his disappointment with Harald, and the anger he still felt. Though he would not sustain that anger in the face of Harald's need for him—that was a headier draught than the wine Guthorm had given him. He forced himself to remember the maimed men at Tafjord. Harald would disappoint him again, even in victory. In his own land, Ragnvald could protect those who fought for him.

"Ragnvald is right," said Guthorm, with sudden good cheer, turning toward Harald. "But what good does it do to send a man of his ability to Sogn, which has never been under threat? It has no rebel king who wants it back. Before you took battle to Solvi, you agreed that Atli the Slender should watch over Sogn, while Ragnvald makes Maer into a strong district that will never fall again."

Harald still looked troubled. "Is that why you want to leave?" he asked Ragnvald. "I will expel Atli from Sogn at once, if it keeps you by my side. You have been with me at so many battles. For me to lose you would be as if you—as if you lost Oddi."

Ragnvald had occasionally imagined Oddi leaving him, going to fight for one of his brothers, or for his father. He wanted to test his feelings, to see if he could survive the loss, but he could never even imagine it without a wrench in his gut. And he never allowed himself to picture Oddi's death. Harald could not possibly see Ragnvald the same way, as a loyal companion, a brother warrior. He was a god-blessed king. With this new bargain Harald offered him everything; Ragnvald could choose to keep Sogn and Harald, or lose both.

"Atli is an ally," said Guthorm, interrupting Ragnvald's thoughts. Ragnvald looked away from Harald, and turned toward Guthorm: an image of Harald aged, grown cold to anything but victory.

"I have yet to see that do us any good," said Ragnvald softly. Atli was a wedge Guthorm had tried to drive between him and Harald.

"He has freed you to protect Maer and greater Norway," said Guthorm. "For that good alone I will praise him."

"You sent Atli to Sogn, told him the seat stood empty," said Ragnvald. "Were you sending him to kill me, or me to kill him?" Guthorm stood and reached for his sword. Harald put a hand on his arm and made him sit again.

"Your love for this man blinds you," said Guthorm to Harald, speaking more bluntly than Ragnvald had ever heard before. "He doubts you at every turn and makes you doubt yourself." To Ragnvald he said, "You are still angry at Harald, are you not, even when he rescinded his order against the traitors?" He did not wait for Ragnvald to answer. "And, nephew, you took back your order, and made yourself look weak when your men carried it out anyway. Let Ragnvald stay home if he's no more stomach for battle."

"I cannot lose when you are with me," said Harald to Ragnvald.

"You will never lose," said Guthorm. "Your mother dreamed you as a tree whose branches spread over all of Norway."

"Ragnvald?" said Harald.

"Your uncle is right," said Ragnvald. He looked at Harald's beard rather than into his eyes, and then at his hands, big and sword-callused. "Let me defend your lands for a time. I will return to you if you need me, I swear it."

"I will give you South Maer all for yourself, to add to Sogn, if you protect it and help Heming protect North Maer," said Harald.

"Hakon and Heming will not like that," said Guthorm.

"Heming can protect North Maer better with Ragnvald's help," said Harald. "Ragnvald should be compensated with something for quitting his home."

"Sogn is still mine," said Ragnvald. "I will agree to this if Atli swears never to claim kingship. The leading men of Sogn will come to the *ting* every year and renew their oaths to me. Everything he does for Sogn must be in my name."

"That is well," said Guthorm. "You will make your oaths at Yule, and move your household to Naustdal in South Maer in the spring." He had agreed quickly enough that Ragnvald wondered if this was the direction Guthorm wanted to steer him from the beginning.

✛ ✛ ✛

HILDA STARED AT Ragnvald with the blank expression she always wore when she was unhappy. She had been sorting through the children's clothes when Ragnvald told her of his conversation with Harald and their decision, and now finished folding a tunic, smoothing it out with an elegant motion of her long fingers. At times when he looked at her, her straight, tapered back, and saw her profile over the side of her shoulder, he saw a woman's mystery, a loveliness that he wanted to touch and possess. Now he thought that what he had believed to be strength of character and a rebellious spirit when they were young was only stubbornness, and a willful dullness, a refusal to see anything beyond petty concerns about her comfort and her household.

Then he thought of how she had defended his sons when Atli came, and decided she was more like a female bear who did little violence unless her cubs were at risk. On hearing of her bravery against Atli he had admired her more than at any moment since the Sogn *ting*, when she had defied her father and claimed Ragnvald as her betrothed. He should not blame her for not being more like Svanhild, or Vigdis.

"I do not like it either," said Ragnvald. "But he is my king. Your king too. Would you rather I spend another five years fighting, always away from home?"

"That is what warriors do," said Hilda. "No, I didn't mean that. Of course I want you home—I mean, isn't Heming warrior enough to protect his land?"

"None of us can protect our land when we are weeks' travel away," said Ragnvald bitterly.

"Then Harald should do it," said Hilda. She picked up the comb and found a tangle to attack, frowning when she pulled her own hair.

"He is. He is sending me," said Ragnvald. The longer he had to defend Harald's decision, the more he agreed with it. He could muster five hundred from Sogn, at least, and more from Maer, where word of his deeds had spread. He could choose captains to defend both districts from the water—let Atli help defend Sogn from land, since he was useless at sea.

"I do not want to leave Sogn. That is our hall. We built it."

"Harald's builders made it for us," Ragnvald reminded her.

"It is ours."

"Would you like to stay in Sogn?" he asked bitterly. "I am sure Atli would welcome you as housekeeper. Perhaps he might even welcome you into his bed—he seemed to like you well enough. But my sons are coming with me to Naustdal, and someone will need to care for them."

"That was ill said." Hilda's mouth tightened. "I do not deserve that of you. I want you to protect your land, not someone else's. Do you think Atli will continue your projects? Do you think he will make Sogn what it was when your grandfather was king?"

"He will swear to it," said Ragnvald wearily. He knew that a man swearing an oath and fulfilling it were different things. Sigurd had also sworn to protect Sogn, but when Atli came it made no difference. "You are my wife. We must move to Naustdal." Ragnvald put his arms around her, trying to take away her stiffness. "Or dress me in one of your shirts and ask for a divorce." An old joke between them— Ragnvald had often said that because of Hilda's height, he must be very careful not to put on her clothing and give her an excuse for divorce, for a man dressing as a woman was often used as justification for divorce when nothing else could be found.

"Do you think now is the best time for that jest?" Hilda's voice was thick, with tears or anger, Ragnvald could not tell. "I want to be with you, and our sons. If this is—I will try to give you more sons if I must. I know you may divorce me over that." When Ragnvald did not answer, she added, "Even if the next child kills me."

Ragnvald let go of her waist. "I did not come here to fight about this."

"No, you've spent all your time with Svanhild since you returned from battle—I had to hear it in a song that you nearly threw your life away in Tafjord—"

"At least Svanhild listens to me," said Ragnvald. "You did not even ask what it was like in Tafjord."

"Svanhild! Why not marry her, then, if she is a better wife to you?"

"You seem determined to fight with me," said Ragnvald. "I have told you what you need to know." He turned to leave.

"And your sister will not argue, I suppose. Did she ask of your troubles, or did you simply pour out your woes to her, a woman who has lost her son and her husband?"

Ragnvald had no reply to that, except to feel ashamed. Svanhild had come to him with her hurts when they were children, but no

longer. Her son was dead and her marriage broken. He did not know
how to mourn for a boy he had never met, except to feel that a promise, the promise that he would meet and know his nephew, had been
broken. The sons of a man's sister were said to be the sons of his heart.

"Did she not come to you with her troubles?" Ragnvald asked.
"They are a woman's troubles."

"I don't think your sister is much used to going to women for comfort," said Hilda.

"We will leave Nidaros after Yule," said Ragnvald. "You will have
another winter in Sogn, and spring as well, for it will take time to
build a living hall for us in South Maer."

"I have heard that you burned a hall there," said Hilda. "Again
from a song and not from you." Her words filled Ragnvald with anger
that choked off his speech. As he walked toward the door, she called
after him, "I have been trying to find you a suitable concubine."

That stopped him short. Hilda had hated Vigdis, and she would
surely hate any other woman he brought. She would be jealous, as
was natural, and only accept it because she wanted to bear no more
children herself.

"She should be beautiful," said Hilda in a strained voice. "She
should have some useful skill I do not. She should not be high-born,
so her sons will not compete with ours, unless they prove themselves
worthy. That is what I have heard makes a good concubine."

"Hilda," said Ragnvald, bemused.

"I am your wife," said Hilda. "I was not born to be the wife of a
king, but I am one now. Our sons will be worthy sons for a king, and
I am their mother. I fear this move to Maer, because I fear that Atli
will take Sogn from us forever. But if it is what must be, then . . ." She
spread out her hands, a conciliatory gesture. "You are a man of honor.
You would not humiliate me by divorcing me."

"No," said Ragnvald. "I—it was a jest. A poorly timed jest." He
took her hands. "You are a better wife than I deserve. Do not compare yourself with—with anyone. As for the rest"—he shrugged—
"these are choppy waters. But I will ask your advice next time about
how I should steer."

✢   ✢   ✢

OUTSIDE WAS COLD, with a biting wind that drove frigid rain against Ragnvald's cheeks. Above, the sky rippled with clouds as turbulent as a stormy sea. He tightened his cloak around him. This weather suited his mood. He needed to talk with Svanhild, relay Harald's proposal, and see what she wanted to do. He needed to tell his sons—Einar and Ivar were old enough, at least, to understand the practicalities of moving. Ragnvald had been an inconstant presence in his sons' lives until now, away for half the year fighting, and often away with Harald at Yule as well. He should tell Oddi too, and see if Oddi wanted to follow him to Naustdal in South Maer, though the opportunities for battle spoils there would be fewer.

He had seen his sons only briefly on returning from Tafjord. Einar had a newly bruised eye, bright red and swollen shut—likely from one of Harald's sons. Ragnvald found a group of children hiding and chasing one another among the curtains outside the women's room. Nearby, Ivar played knucklebones against a girl child close to him in age. Mafa, one of Hilda's servants, rolled an inflated pig's bladder to Thorir, who rolled it back to her as hard as he could. A young thrall came out of the women's chamber, holding a baby on her shoulder. She walked with a soothing, rolling step, and the baby snored wetly.

"King Ragnvald," she said. "Do you seek your sons? Do you want to hold little Rolli?"

"No," said Ragnvald. "Do not wake him." He asked Ivar, "Where is your brother Einar?"

Ivar looked up, and seeing his father, smiled broadly, though his face grew quickly troubled. "He is in the women's chamber. With the lady Vig—Vig—"

"Vigdis," Ragnvald finished for him. It was ill-luck for a man to enter the women's chamber, especially uninvited. He sent the thrall to fetch Einar. Instead Vigdis emerged, brushing white wool fibers off her clothing. She dressed simply today, in a brown homespun that would make most women look plain, but made her look warm and inviting.

"I am looking for my sons," said Ragnvald.

"Einar rests," said Vigdis. "He tells me he has hardly slept in Nidaros, too worried about protecting his brother from Harald's boys.

But I hear you have broken with Harald, and he will need to fear them no longer. I hear that we all depart for Sogn after Yule. That gladdens me, for the child needs true rest." Ragnvald had not thought about Vigdis's presence in Sogn, which would certainly spoil his new peace with Hilda. "Perhaps you will leave him with me in Sogn sometimes," she added. "We will be neighbors. It will not be hard to arrange."

"I will ask him," said Ragnvald, absently. Vigdis's pleasant expression faltered. "Would he not desire to be with his mother?"

"You know that he would not agree to leave Ivar unless his father told him to," said Vigdis.

"Then you have your answer," Ragnvald replied. He wondered if he should order Vigdis to fetch Einar out. But if he slept, Ragnvald would not disturb him. He envied that sleep, surrounded by the voices of women, and clouds of wool that smelled like a new-washed spring day.

"I could visit you in South Maer," said Vigdis. "Atli trusts me, and lets me do as I wish. And I know you would like to see me again."

"Atli is foolish to trust you," said Ragnvald.

"I miss you," she said, looking at the rush-covered floor. "I didn't think I would, but Atli does not understand me as you did." Her golden hair brushed over her face and would be soft as a caress if Ragnvald touched it.

"I wish I did not," said Ragnvald.

She moved close to him, and whispered in his ear. "Meet me. The bathhouse is empty after dinner. It is cold, but we will warm each other."

Ragnvald's whole body heated, but this would break his fragile peace with Hilda. He stepped back from Vigdis.

"Is Svanhild within?" he asked her.

"No," said Vigdis softly, still standing close to him. "Will you be there?"

He shook his head. "That time is past," he said. "If Atli manages Sogn well for me, then you will see your son from time to time."

23

HARALD BEGAN HIS YULE CELEBRATION WITH A GREAT SACRIFICE to placate the gods in the darkest part of the year, ensure the return of light and sun, and begin the greatest of the year-turning feasts. All of his guests and the residents of Nidaros made a procession to the temple grove in the depths of the darkest night. Harald and men he wished to honor, including Ragnvald and Oddi, presided over the sacrifice of two of every type of farm animal, including horses, and let the blood flow into a vast cauldron that had been set into a pit. Ragnvald's arms grew tired from holding the ax before he was done, and the smell of blood reminded him too much of Grai and Illugi's bloody hut at Tafjord.

Every person in attendance, from the oldest down to the youngest child, dipped his hands in the blood, and blessed the carvings of the gods that lined the grove. Einar dipped his on his own, while Hilda had to coax Ivar to wet the palms of his hands and then wipe them clean on dry leaves. The sacrifice meat would cook in the grove for three days and be served on the final night of feasting. Until then, they would eat cheese, fish, and grains, making the first meat of the new year taste all the richer. Before men grew too drunk from feasting, they made oaths they intended to keep for the rest of their lives, for the gods watched closely at Yule.

Harald called Ragnvald to swear an oath to protect South Maer and Sogn in his name, and then he called up Atli. Atli swore, on pain of death, that neither he nor his sons would seek to inherit Sogn, that he would never speak ill of Ragnvald, and that he would continue to improve the fortunes of the people of Sogn, according to Ragnvald's plans. Ragnvald required that Atli agree to remain in Nidaros until he and his family had quit Sogn. Heming Hakonsson swore to follow Ragnvald's advice in protecting North Maer, and to uphold Harald's laws. He met Ragnvald's gaze and gave him a slight smile and a nod when he swore, as if he welcomed Ragnvald's presence.

Harald called Hakon's sons Geirbjorn and Herlaug next. Ragnvald had not seen Herlaug since his wounding, and looked on his face with a thrill of horror. The flickering torches that lit the sacrifice grove made it look even more ghoulish than it would in bright daylight. Ragnvald had heard that his wound had healed poorly, and Harald's mother, Ronhild, though she was the best healer in the Norse lands, had been forced to cut away infected flesh to preserve his life. The result was a scar so tight and angry that he could barely open his mouth, and it tugged down the flesh under his eye so he could not fully close it.

"I have decided a price for your wounding," said Harald. "Your father swore on your behalf, but you are men who must swear for yourselves. Arnfast is outlawed from all districts controlled by King Hakon and his sons. I further impose a fine of four measures of gold, paid to Herlaug for the injury, if you swear to agree to it. You will swear not to visit other punishment on Arnfast, or try to drive him from his home into land where you can kill him."

"Both of us?" Geirbjorn asked.

"All of Hakon's sons will swear," said Harald. "Heming, Oddbjorn Hakonsson, do you both swear to this?"

"I will swear," said Heming. "I swear that I will take no revenge against Arnfast."

"I do swear as well," said Oddi.

"Traitors," Herlaug hissed.

"You're getting paid very well for a mistake," said Oddi. "Swear."

"What if I don't?" Herlaug asked. His scar distorted his words.

"Then you will be outlawed," said Harald.

"A fine thing," said Geirbjorn, "that my brother should be outlawed for his own wounding."

"Your brother will be compensated like a king," said Harald. "And both of you given kingdoms after you spend some seasons defending Vestfold."

"You think you're giving us kingdoms?" asked Geirbjorn with a sneer. "The sons of Hakon are not given such things—we take."

Harald should separate these two, Ragnvald thought. No good could come of Geirbjorn stoking his brother's anger.

"So you will not swear?" Harald asked. "You would rather be outlawed? Very well, you have until the Yule feast is over to quit Norway."

"We will swear," said Herlaug thickly. "Won't we, brother? Our father agreed to this. I swear not to punish Arnfast for this wounding."

"I likewise swear," Geirbjorn repeated. Then, under his breath, he added, "A coward like that will give us some other excuse to punish him."

Others had oaths to swear, though none that needed Harald's witness, and so he led the procession back to the drinking hall for the feasting. Svanhild fell into step next to Ragnvald, as the procession swelled around them in the crowd's eagerness for food, drink, and warmth.

"That looked worrisome," said Svanhild as she reached Ragnvald's elbow.

"Harald sends them to Vestfold," said Ragnvald. "That will keep them out of trouble." Oddi just shrugged.

"I am sorry," said Svanhild. "They are your brothers."

"And I hope Vestfold is far enough," Oddi replied. "Do not worry—feast and be merry tonight. Tell me you are to sit by me, fair maid."

"Fair matron." Svanhild laughed, returning Oddi's flirtation. Ragnvald had found reasons over the past few days to avoid asking Svanhild if she wished to marry Harald. But Harald had given him enough significant looks tonight, tilting his head toward Svanhild, that Ragnvald could delay no longer. He feared her refusal, and he feared her acceptance. What more would he owe Harald if he did Svanhild this honor?

Ragnvald handed Oddi his torch and guided Svanhild out of the crowd, trying not to mar her festival clothes with his bloody hands. "Harald has offered for you," he said abruptly, as soon as it seemed they might not be overheard. "Do you want him?"

She laughed incredulously. "I'm pregnant with Solvi's child. Did you tell him that?"

Ragnvald's face grew cold. Svanhild brought betrayal with her in her very body if she bore Solvi's son. He moved away from her without meaning to, putting space between himself and women's mysteries. "No, because I did not know. What do you mean to do with the child?"

"Raise her as my own," said Svanhild. "Will you help me?"

A daughter, that would be better—and women sometimes had such magic that they knew these things. Ragnvald need fear Solvi's daughter far less than his son.

"Do you think Harald would accept me anyway?" Svanhild asked.

"Do you want him to?" Ragnvald asked. "I swore I would not try to influence your decision."

"Who did you swear to, brother? Harald?"

"Myself," said Ragnvald.

She laughed again, a broken sound. "Then you can break that oath and advise me."

"I cannot," said Ragnvald. "I do not know what is the right thing for you, or for me."

"I thought you knew everything, Ragnvald the Wise." Svanhild slipped her arm through his. "Must I decide immediately?"

"No," said Ragnvald. "I will tell him that you want to wait to bear this child if you like." He turned her to face him. "I swear I will care for your child, if you swear that you will not send the child to Solvi, whether it is a boy or a girl. If it is a son, I will make him one of my heirs. If it is a daughter, I will dower her." Svanhild hesitated. Ragnvald could see that a part of her wanted to bring a son back to Solvi to replace the one they had lost. "Promise me, Svanhild."

"It will be a daughter." Svanhild hugged her arms around herself. "But I swear. This child will not go to Solvi. He will not kill another of my children."

✛ ✛ ✛

SVANHILD WALKED WITH Ragnvald until they reached the hall, and then followed the other women into the kitchen. So, Harald wished to marry her. She hoped she was not mistaken when she told Ragnvald of her pregnancy. She had passed another month without her courses, and suffered occasional bouts of sickness. Her stomach had a curve to it that it had not when she had left Solvi. Now that she had spoken it, she must admit the truth to herself: Solvi's child had taken firm root. And she had told Ragnvald. Soon Harald would know; soon everyone would know.

Every woman in Nidaros was needed to help with the Yule feast, and work would prevent her from worrying for a time. Harald's wife Asa Hakonsdatter had set the menu for the feast, and directed the kitchen staff, while his famous betrothed, Gyda Eiriksdatter, was in charge of serving and entertainment. Asa sent Svanhild out to the feasting hall with a jug of ale, and instructed her to pour a glass of ale for each guest who entered, which she did, returning to the kitchen many times over to refill her jug. The feast would last for three days of eating and drinking, with entertainment and fresh food in Harald's drinking hall day and night. Guests had arrived early and would stay late, and must have food at all times. Even the lowly must have their chance to celebrate.

So many torches lined the hall that it seemed as bright as a dragon's cave, with golden light spilling into every corner. At the high table Harald sat with Asa on one side and Gyda on the other. Asa wore a fresh scarf around her hair, and a new overdress rather than one covered with kitchen stains. Gyda had been well named the most beautiful woman in Norway. She looked as skalds described the light elves, with high cheekbones, gently curling, red-gold hair, and eyes as blue as the depths of a glacier. She seemed to be carved of ice and fire, not the wood and earth that made up most people. Svanhild tried to imagine herself as another of Harald's wives, small and dark-haired next to these two golden beauties, and failed.

Harald gave a toast, invoking Yules past, and calling down blessings for a rich new year. Svanhild remembered dipping Eystein's hands in the blood at other Yule celebrations on other shores, and telling him about the wolves that chased the sun and the moon, and, on the darkest night of the year, caught and devoured them. The wolves then, given the right sacrifices, vomited them back up so the year could begin anew. She had clasped bloody hands with Solvi, shared a kiss that tasted of the sacrifice ale, and felt herself well blessed.

Harald finished his blessing, and then the sound of spoons in platters and people eating and calling for more drowned out the musicians except the high piping of the flute. Harald met Svanhild's eyes and raised his glass to her. She returned the gesture, taking a moment to admire him: his brilliant hair, his shoulders that stretched his tunic tight. She would not mind a night or two in his bed, but she did not want marriage with him, not yet.

"You stare intently at the high table," said Oddi to her in an undertone. "We are lucky to be seated here, away from the power games."

"Not far enough," said Svanhild.

Atli called out across the table to Ragnvald, "Perhaps when they are grown, you will marry a daughter of mine to one of your sons, if you are pleased with my work."

"We shall see," said Ragnvald after a pause. "Have you any daughters?"

"Not yet, but I still have time." Atli nodded, smiled—grossly, Svanhild thought, his wet lips pulling back over long teeth—and raised his glass in thanks. She could not imagine how Vigdis could stomach taking him to bed.

"You mean to stay with my brother?" Svanhild asked Oddi. "Not follow Harald in his conquests so more songs can be made of your deeds?"

"A man who stands by Ragnvald the Mighty will always have songs made about him," said Oddi lightly. "Hornklofe means to send one of his apprentice skalds with him to Naustdal, in case anything heroic should happen."

"That is flattering," said Svanhild.

"Yes," said Oddi. "They are Harald's spies, though they make a song or two when they have nothing else to do." Svanhild did not reply. She felt terribly naive. "Their memories are well trained. Horn-

klofe, it is said, can repeat any conversation he has ever heard perfectly. He goes into a trance to do it."

"I don't believe it," said Svanhild. "Does it come out with allitera-
tions and meter? Does he remember to call a sword a sword, or does
he have it an arm-eel eagle-feeder?"

Oddi laughed, as she intended him to, at the excesses of bad poetry. "He is a better poet than that," said Oddi.

"True," said Svanhild. Hornklofe's songs had the force of magic to
bend minds and memory. He made the words that defined Harald's
reign and evoked his vision for Norway. Solvi should have had a skald
by him, to sing of how Harald would betray the freedom of their fathers. She tried to put him from her mind. She need no longer think
of his ambitions.

"You grow quiet," said Oddi.

"I am thinking of the work I must do tonight. A feast does not
serve itself. Or clean up after itself."

"We men have skalds to sing of our work, but who sings of the
work of women?" Oddi asked. "Except your adventures. We have all
heard of those."

"Yes," said Svanhild. "Now I must go and do some of that unsung
work. If you find a skald who wants to make a song of it, bid him find
me in the kitchen so he can follow and record my great deeds."

Svanhild returned a while later, after overseeing the food to be
stored in the cold pantry for tomorrow. When she returned to the
drinking hall, the feast had progressed into more quiet drunkenness.
Harald had pulled Gyda into his lap. Her cheeks wore a blush of pink,
and her eyes a sparkle that made them more human, though she still
sat upright, holding herself somewhat away from him.

Ragnvald and Hilda had both departed the hall. During a celebration that lasted this long, guests might come and go, or sleep where
they fell and wake to celebrate in the morning. Oddi had a woman
in his lap whom Svanhild recognized as Mafa, Hilda's servant and
nursemaid. Nearby, on the floor, Ragnvald's son Einar tried to free
the tail of his shirt from a small black dog that had taken hold of it,
while Ivar giggled with the sort of hectic laughter that Svanhild had
heard from her own son sometimes that could easily turn to tears of

exhaustion. Eystein would have liked his cousins: thoughtful, serious Einar, and sweet Ivar.

Svanhild walked over to the chair that Oddi and Mafa shared and stood in front of them until the girl looked up at her. "Don't you think you should put them to bed?" She put her hands on her hips, and tilted her head toward the boys.

Mafa shrugged, and moved with irritating slowness away from Oddi, arranging her clothes as she did. She had a rounded body that Svanhild thought would grow stout as a barn when she grew older, though now she looked like an inviting armful, no chance of encountering a hard hip bone when throwing a leg over her.

Oddi did not seem annoyed to have his companion ordered away from him. "Sit with me," said Oddi, patting the narrow space next to him on his chair.

"I'm sure Mafa will come back," she said. All around her, the sounds of sleep and copulation carried to Svanhild's ears. Even the crackling of the fire sounded satisfied with itself, the soft rustles and plinks of logs breaking apart into glowing embers.

"I don't think she will," said Oddi. "She thinks that you are jealous of her, and she does not want to compete with a king's sister."

"Ha," said Svanhild. "And what do you think?"

"I think I could never aim so high," said Oddi, with mock deference. He must have no difficulty talking women of all ranks into his bed.

Svanhild did want him, she realized. He was not handsome, but his expression, and the way he held his arms open to her, as easy and lazy as a cat in the sun, appealed to her. Why should she sleep alone when couples all around her enjoyed each other? Her husband was leagues away, and would be no longer her husband as soon as a year passed or Harald pronounced a divorce. She would not marry Harald until this child was born. She was free for now.

"What are you thinking?" Oddi asked. She had been looking at him for a long while, she realized.

"I was making up my mind," said Svanhild.

"To do what?"

She bent down so she might whisper in his ear. "To take you to bed," she said. "What else is there to do tonight?" She enjoyed the look of surprise on his face.

He recovered quickly, and put an arm around her so she fell down into his lap. "Happy to help you pass the time."

"I won't be pawed out in the open," said Svanhild. She pushed herself up off him so she could stand again.

He reached out his hand, and Svanhild took it. "As long as you don't try to break my finger again," he said.

"As long as you remember that I can." She led him by the hand, out to one of the barns she knew had been newly cleaned, and was only half-full of sheep. It was so dark within she could hardly see Oddi except where he blocked the faint blue light that came from between the gaps in the barn's wall. The dark and privacy made her bold. She stripped off her overdress and underdress, leaving them aside until she stood, cooling and naked in the hay-sweet air.

"Warm me up," she commanded. He obeyed quickly, stripping off his tunic and laying it down on the straw, and gave her pleasure before taking his own. A rush of tears stung her eyes when he was in her, for until now she had known no man but Solvi. She did not regret this, though, and when the tears passed, she knew she would crave him again.

"You are a very direct woman," said Oddi, when he held her afterward. She pressed back against him, enjoying the full, naked length of his body wrapped around her from head to toe so all parts of her were warmed. Solvi had not been tall enough to offer that. "Don't you believe in flirting?"

"Sometimes," said Svanhild. "I thought it would take too long."

"Have you always been this way, asking for what you want?"

"Yes," said Svanhild. She did not care, but she asked anyway: "Do you mind?"

"Of course not," said Oddi. "I should not be surprised—I have heard the songs of your deeds. I only fear you will not want me again."

"We will see," said Svanhild. "Do you seek to hold me beyond Yule?"

"I will hold you as long as you let me," he said, tightening his arms around her. She suspected he had said that to many women before her.

"Yule is a time of license," she said. "I do not promise more."

"As you like," said Oddi. He kissed her shoulder. She felt him stirring against her and moved so he might press into her again, and move slowly, now that the initial urgency was over. She drifted in pleasure, half in and out of a doze until he thrust more forcefully and finished. Now he fell away and asleep, his breathing gone heavy almost as soon as he finished.

She wanted to sleep, wrapped up by him, but she did not want to be discovered here in the morning. She wriggled out of Oddi's embrace and pulled her dress on. When she opened the door, a shaft of moonlight illuminated his face, slack in sleep. She waited to feel ashamed of her forwardness, to feel some grief that she had betrayed Solvi, but all she could feel was the satisfaction in her body. In her spirit too, proud that she had taken what she wanted. If she were a more foolish woman, this feeling could make her want to marry Oddi—her brother's best friend, a choice that would mean she need never part from Ragnvald again. Part of her joy in this night came from her free choosing of it, though, and knowing that she could choose differently tomorrow.

+ + +

AT THE GAMES the next day, Svanhild felt Oddi's presence among the competitors like a current pulling at her, though she found as much pleasure in resisting it as giving in to it. She could take Oddi back to bed, or not, as the mood struck her, and it seemed pleasant simply to dwell in the longing, the waiting that would lend savor to their next joining. Her memory of Oddi's embrace made it easier to ignore Harald's looks as well. Harald wanted another wife for his collection, and an unbreakable connection to Ragnvald, considerations far more important to him than Svanhild herself. And she enjoyed the knowledge that Oddi's dark eyes followed her everywhere. After six years of marriage with Solvi, he had often taken her for granted, except when he first came home from a trip away. It was the way of anything that ceased to be new, the question at night no longer whether she would let him into her bed, but if she had enough energy to enjoy it, or only to satisfy him so she could get her sleep.

That would happen in time if she married Oddi or Harald or anyone else.

She had no time to seek out Oddi's company until late that night. He had won a knife-throwing contest, and Svanhild cheered him with an enthusiasm she had not felt for anything so simple in a long time. She met him in the same barn as the night before, where he touched her as if he craved her skin against his, and then afterward as though she were something precious. A woman could fall in love with this feeling. She fell asleep next to him this time, and woke at the sound of servants stirring in the early morning before crawling back into bed with Mafa and Hilda.

She spent much of the day tending the meat cooking in the sacrifice grove, now stewed to perfect tenderness for the final night of feasting, and then at the bathhouse, washing off the grease and ash. Ragnvald met her as she left in the late afternoon, as the sky grew dark.

"Do you mean to insult Harald?" Ragnvald asked, without even greeting her first.

She considered angry denial, or feigning bafflement, but his words only made her feel weary. She had been gone for six years and returned to exactly what she had left behind in Vestfold. A brother who loved her, but less than he loved his own honor, his king, and his pride.

"This has nothing to do with him," she said. "Or with you."

"My sister and my best friend—and after I told you of Harald's offer," said Ragnvald.

"Every man I know is tied to you in some way, by duty, by friendship, by enmity," Svanhild answered. "I thought you wanted to put distance between you and Harald."

"If he hears of this, it will be far more distance than is safe for me." Ragnvald spoke in a low, urgent voice. "I told him that you want to wait to make sure you are not pregnant by Solvi before coming to his bed. Not that you preferred Hakon's base-born son."

"And you think that he will blame you? I was Solvi's wife, raider, and sea queen, and he still thinks that you can control me?" Svanhild laughed. Ragnvald's worries seemed so small compared to all that she had endured. "He values and loves you, Ragnvald. It will take more than my choice of men to break the two of you apart."

"When you are delivered, you should marry Harald. His wives are well treated. They live with their families if they like. They are wealthy."

"You sound like Vigdis when she told me the joys of widowhood," said Svanhild.

"When was that?" Ragnvald asked suspiciously.

Svanhild waved the question away. "A long time ago. Tell me more of how wonderful it is to be one of Harald's wives. They don't have lovers, do they?"

"No," said Ragnvald in a choked voice, "but Princess Gyda commands upland armies."

"I do not wish to command armies," said Svanhild, and immediately knew it for a lie. If she could trade fates with any woman living it would be with Gyda, not for her betrothal to Harald, but for her power, and the way nothing seemed to touch her. Svanhild did not have the knowledge to command armies, but she might command a sea battle, if it came to that—she had been in enough of them.

"What do you wish?" Ragnvald asked.

"For now?" Svanhild's anger turned to grief and she faced him with tears in her eyes. "To mourn my child and my marriage. To care for my brother and his sons. To see if this child of Solvi's I carry draws breath, or if I must mourn her too. Would you add something else to that list, brother, or may I live my own life?"

"Oddi would marry you, even if you bear Solvi's child. He would acknowledge it, I am certain."

Svanhild shook her head. "I will not marry him, and I do not think he wishes to marry me, although he would do it gladly to please you."

"What are you doing then, Svanhild?" Ragnvald asked more kindly.

"Pleasing myself, taking a lover, nothing less than you did with our stepmother." Svanhild smiled wryly at him.

"It is different for you," Ragnvald replied.

"Today it is not," said Svanhild.

"I will forbid Oddi."

"If you must. It was not meant to last very long between us."

"Did Solvi make you like this?" His voice carried a grief that made Svanhild's eyes burn again.

"Perhaps," she said. "I have learned to take what I want when I can, for I may not keep it long. Is that such a terrible lesson to learn?"

Ragnvald stopped his swift walking and faced her. "What was he like, Svanhild?" he asked. "This boy that I will never meet?"

"Please, brother," she said, turning away. "I can survive anything but your kindness. See, I have put it behind me—I have already taken a lover."

"If I make you mourn him, will you then leave Oddi be?" Ragnvald asked, his voice soft, making it a gentle jest. Their walking had carried them down to the harbor. In the still air, the water hardly moved. Ragnvald sat on a wooden bench and waited for Svanhild to sit next to him. "You named your son after our father. Was he like him?"

She gave a short laugh with tears in it. "Nothing like. I don't remember our father very well, but you told me he was reckless, joyous. I thought he might like . . . Solvi, even if you did not."

"I did like him once," said Ragnvald. He hesitated. "I am sure our father would have liked him."

"Eystein was nothing like our father. He was quiet. Long limbed. He reminded me of you a little. Too much dignity for his own good." Ragnvald laughed ruefully at that. "But he was himself, and I have never known anyone like him. He was not bold." Her tears flowed more freely now, easing the pain in her throat that she had felt whenever she cried before. "He loved Iceland. He loved the land. He told me he was not in pain when he was dying. Only tired, he said. Do you think it was true?"

"Do you think he would lie to you about something like that?" Ragnvald asked.

Svanhild hesitated, then nodded. "Perhaps. He hid his coughing from me until it was too late."

"No one recovers when they have been coughing blood for long," said Ragnvald. "I have never seen it. You can ask Ronhild. She is a notable healer. And you say he was not strong."

"He was strong," she said, sitting up. "It was not the sort of strength that . . ." Then she fell back against Ragnvald's side. "I thought he might grow up to be a strong and just farmer, whose stock always increased because he knew it so well. I wanted to find a place for him. Solvi would not . . ." She could not continue, though, to share what had been wrong between her and Solvi with Ragnvald, to give him that triumph.

"You can tell me about Solvi if you want," said Ragnvald. "I forgive you for that."

She sat up angrily. "You forgive me, do you? Keep your forgiveness, brother, I do not want it."

"Fine, then. I do not forgive you. But I love you."

She smiled a bit. "We never fought like this when we were children."

"Perhaps now we can make up the time," said Ragnvald. "We can fight in Sogn and then in Naustdal."

"I would like that," said Svanhild. "Very much."

24

THE SOUND OF HILDA AND SVANHILD ARGUING IN THE KITCHEN woke Ragnvald from his dream. He could not hear the words, only the cadences and tones—this fight was just beginning, polite, with an edge of tension in Svanhild's higher-pitched voice, and resignation in Hilda's. Soon, Svanhild's would become shrill, and Hilda's more plodding, then something would fall or be thrown, and someone would storm out of the kitchen in disgust. Since the birth of Svanhild's daughter and a long recovery that kept her confined to her bed for most of the summer, she had found fault with everything Hilda did.

Ragnvald rolled over next to Alfrith and kissed her shoulder, glad every morning that she had come with him from Smola. His traveling party had stopped on the island on the way back to Sogn after Yule. Alfrith met Ragnvald and his family as they walked from the ships to the main hall, as if her magic had told her he would be coming. She had worn dark homespun, woven finely enough that it molded over her breasts and her long waist. She carried herself as upright as a queen. A streak of white made the rest of her hair look as dark and glossy as a raven's wing.

"Ragnvald the Mighty," she said. "We hear of you always and wonder when you will return."

"I am here," he said. "And this is my wife, Hilda, and my sister, Svanhild."

Alfrith bowed again. "Would they like to see the grounds where you became a saga-hero? It was on this very plain that you fought the *draugr.*"

Ragnvald thought he heard a touch of mocking in her voice, and did not mind, for it meant that Alfrith saw him clearly. "Hilda and Svanhild both know the truth of that," he said. "That the creature I fought was only your brother, wounded and near death."

"King Hakon has passed by this way again," Alfrith had told him. "He seemed less pleased with you than last time."

Ragnvald shrugged and Hilda stepped forward. "I have come to meet you," she said to Alfrith. "My husband has spoken well of you." Ragnvald was caught between embarrassment at Hilda involving herself in something so personal, and pride at her calm and dignity. She and Alfrith walked aside and spoke while Rafni, the new master of Smola, made Ragnvald and his family welcome.

Alfrith joined him later, after dinner, sitting down next to him before the long fire. "I have a husband now," she told him, "but your wife thinks I should leave him and go with you."

"I think you should too," Ragnvald said. She sat forward, her hands under her thighs, her hair swept over one shoulder so he could see the tan skin of her neck, marked with small brown dots from the sun. He had come to Smola for her and no other reason, and if she refused him, he would sail away and never return. That, combined with Hilda's approval, made him bold. He put his hand on her shoulder. He had not touched her before, when he had known her for the sister of his *draugr* and she had known him for a scared young man, not a hero. When his fingers brushed her skin, all of his memories of her, his imagining her as a creature as supernatural as her brother had seemed, solidified into a living woman with warm skin. "Is your husband a king?" he asked, in a low voice.

"No, he is a farmer and a horse breeder," she said.

"Is he kind to you?" Ragnvald asked.

"Not particularly," she answered.

"Tell me you will come with me."

"You could have me and go away again," she said, leaning back against him.

"Would he not mind that?"

She shrugged. "You are a king. He will understand. You will get bored with me. You only want the excitement of a new woman."

"I have many faults, but fickleness is not among them," said Ragnvald. He thought of Vigdis. He would have kept her in his household if Hilda had not insisted on her going, even if he no longer shared her bed. He owed her that much for his killing of Olaf.

Alfrith did not have Vigdis's melting allure, or Hilda's solidness, or the otherworldliness of Gyda. Instead she reminded him of driftwood washed up on a shore, whorls and curves and complications, a purely natural thing shaped by wind and waves. She did not need him, and so if she chose him, it would be for himself, not for her ambition.

"I have thought of you often," said Ragnvald.

"I am flattered that you remember me from your short time here, when so much has succeeded it," she said.

"Do you hate me for ending your brother's . . . walking?" He did not say life, for the man had been nearer to death than life when he fell upon Ragnvald's sword.

"No," she said. Some tension went out of her body where her back pressed against his flank. "He was already dead."

"What did you and Hilda talk about?" Ragnvald asked.

"She said she did not want to bear any more children. I told her I could give her magic and herbs to prevent that, but she wants you to have children if you want them. She said you are hard to please but worth the effort."

Ragnvald put his arm around Alfrith's waist, moved by a wave of affection not only for her but also for Hilda, who loved him more than he deserved, and for Svanhild, who loved him also. If Alfrith consented to be his, he would consider himself more blessed in his womenfolk even than Harald. "Come with me," he said. "If you bear me sons, they will be wealthy warriors. Do you have any children already?"

"A son," said Alfrith. Ragnvald immediately felt a mixture of jealousy and pride—she had borne a son to another man and could soon produce sons for him. "I will leave him with his father, I think. They are of one spirit."

"I can elevate him, if you like," said Ragnvald. "He could train with Harald's sons and become a wealthy warrior." He spoke in her ear now, close enough to smell her hair, which had been washed with something sharp and herbal.

"He has brothers and friends. He will train the horses of Smola and fish its waters. I am happy to leave a part of myself here." She tilted her head in invitation. "I will be happier still to be gone."

"You can send for him anytime you like," said Ragnvald. "He will always be welcome with me." The following day they departed Smola, Ragnvald's ship heavier by another woman and a pair of foals he had bought from Alfrith's husband, paying many times their worth to soften the blow of her going.

On this chilly morning in Naustdal, as he looked at her in the dimness of his room, he saw only a curve of pale shoulder and a spill of dark hair, and the voices of the other women receded into meaningless noise. Alfrith woke at his touch, and welcomed him into her arms.

"I dreamed," he said.

"Tell me," she replied. She had shared his bed for more than half a year now, and every morning, he told her his dreams, when he remembered them. Often they contained scenes of battles he had fought, though in these he fared far worse than in his memories: he could not fight his way past his opponent, while in the distance men he loved fought and failed without his help. These she called only fears and dismissed. Others she listened to with more concern.

"I dreamed of Vemund's hall again," he said. The dream fell away as he tried to grasp it, breaking apart like threads of rotten fabric. "I was inside. It seemed that King Hakon held the torch." He could remember no more than that, it seemed, though some details lingered just out of reach. "If only I could see more . . . I think this is an important dream."

"It may be. Or it may only be that burning alive is a terrible way to die and it haunts you still," she said.

"And King Hakon?" Ragnvald asked.

Alfrith placed her hand on his cheek, her thumb tracing the path of the scar on his cheek. He had seen her scars too, one made by an errant coal from a cook fire, another from a man's knife. "You fear he moves against Harald," she said. "And you."

"But does he?"

"It was your dream. Did it feel like prophecy, or fear?"

"I have always feared burning," said Ragnvald. "That is cowardly, perhaps."

"All men have fears," said Alfrith. "And all women too."

Svanhild's voice became loud enough Ragnvald could hear her words clearly: "If we run out of cheese this winter, the fault will be your stubbornness." A thud sounded as something fell to the floor— nothing breakable this time, at least.

"It wasn't this bad before Svanhild came," said Ragnvald.

"And that was when I came too," said Alfrith. She always spoke truth, quietly and firmly, though not as loudly as Svanhild. Sometimes only Svanhild was willing to give voice to the annoyance that Ragnvald felt, and he found it satisfying to hear someone tell Hilda that she fixed her mind, at times, on unimportant problems, and ignored those that mattered. Svanhild was the one who told Hilda that she needed to pay more attention to Thorir, that she should stop nursing young Rolli, and that no amount of ill temper would cause them to move back to Sogn until Norway was at peace.

☩   ☩   ☩

A LATE FALL snowstorm beat against the walls of the new hall at Naustdal for three days and nights, even as daylight grew shorter, so it seemed that the snow brought the darkness with it. Most of the hall's residents still went outside during the short days, to see the sun and escape from the stink of a hall full of people and farm animals, and a floor covered with hay that never seemed to be changed often enough. With the luxury of more than enough wood to last the winter, and plenty of servants to wait on him, Ragnvald bathed at least once every seven days. Alfrith's patience seemed preternatural, but even she snapped at a thrall who dropped a bundle of her precious medicinal herbs onto the floor and then walked over them.

"It will be better when the weather clears," Ragnvald said to Alfrith when they lay in his bed that night. "We can take out the sledge." He had asked Harald's builders to make one when they came to raise the hall and outbuildings. One of the apprentices had used the project to prove his abilities. A small, elegant contraption, it fit two adults and some baggage. Carved knotwork that dissolved into faces and beasts covered every surface. The apprentice had sanded it to a smooth gloss and rubbed it with bear fat so it glowed in lantern light. When the snowstorm stopped, Ragnvald could hitch two fjord ponies to it and take Alfrith away from the hall for a night or two.

The weather did clear a few days later, but before Ragnvald could make arrangements for his and Alfrith's journey, a messenger came to the hall, skiing on top of the waist-high drifts. Arnfast's howl of anguish at his news was audible through the wood and clay-daubed walls of the long hall. Ragnvald rushed out into the narrow, shoveled path between the hall and one of the outbuildings. Arnfast's younger brother stood where Arnfast knelt in the snow. The boy's face glistened with a sheen of sweat that turned to mist in the cold air. With his skis suspending him on the surface of the snow, he looked like a spirit come out of the woods.

"What has happened?" Ragnvald asked. He walked swiftly to Arnfast's side.

Arnfast recovered himself enough to look up and say, "This is my king, Ragnvald of Maer."

Arnfast's brother bowed. "I am Tofi—Thorfast, my lord. I came to tell my brother"—his face contorted in pain—"a young lord came to our house and attacked us. He killed our father, and cut up our mother's face. I got away into the deep snow and they could not catch me. Their sledge did not fit between the trees."

"One young lord or two?" Ragnvald asked grimly. It could only be Hakon's son Herlaug, in defiance of Harald's justice.

"Two," said Tofi. "One did the . . . cutting, while the other kept off our—he killed anyone who tried to stop it."

"This is more than revenge," said Ragnvald. "I must be sure—tell me what you remember of them."

"One had a fearsome scar," said Tofi. "He—"

"What of the other?" Ragnvald asked. It is likely that Geirbjorn accompanied his brother, especially after the Yule oaths, but if Heming had involved himself in this, nothing could stop the coming war.

"I don't . . . very like the other, but without the scar."

Ragnvald questioned him further, and learned enough to satisfy himself that it was Geirbjorn who accompanied his brother on this bloody errand.

Tofi swayed on his feet, exhausted. He was built to be as fine a runner as his brother, and had been named for it. Eagle-fast and his brother thunder-fast.

"You skied here?" Ragnvald asked. Arnfast's farm was high on the ridge that marked the border between Sogn and South Maer. He had said the property was wide and beautiful in the summer.

"Yes," said Tofi. He struggled to hold himself upright. "I sheltered with—some of the neighbors were kind."

"One of them was not," said Ragnvald. "These young men would have needed someplace to stay, or they would have been caught in the blizzard."

"Who would say no to a king's son?" asked Arnfast, miserably. "Blame Hakon's sons, not my father's friends." Ragnvald went over to him and helped him up to his feet.

"Come inside, my lord," Alfrith said from the open kitchen door. She had ventured outside in only her indoor dress, and the wind blew her hair out like a banner. She looked as though she had stepped out of a different season, too fine and pleasing for this wet and cold. Ragnvald would wrap her in furs before he took her far from the hall.

"Yes," said Ragnvald. "You need rest and warmth, Tofi."

The hall's heat made Tofi sway as soon as he stepped inside. He would have crumpled to his knees had not Ragnvald and Alfrith held him up. Alfrith settled Tofi on a bench near the fire, tucked a blanket around him, and gave him a bowl of porridge to warm him from within as well.

Arnfast sat down next to him and put his head in his hands. "This is my fault," he said. "If I had not cut Herlaug's face—"

"That was an accident," said Ragnvald. "And I paid the wergild." With Harald's help. Hakon and his sons must know Ragnvald did not have the gold to pay himself. They probably took it as another insult that Arnfast and his family had not had to pay a wergild that would beggar them.

"They must know Harald will outlaw them," said Oddi. He stood behind Arnfast, half in the shadows. He looked as grim as a grave-cairn. Songs told of feuds that began like this, and then stretched over generations, destroying families and districts. The most peaceful reso-lution might prove to be death for all of Arnfast's family so none could carry on the cycle of revenge. The only other outcome Ragnvald could see was war between Hakon and Harald. Harald might want that, but Guthorm would advise against it. Such a war would tear apart all the work Harald had done making Norway into a kingdom.

"What of . . . ?" Arnfast asked. Ragnvald wondered if he saw the same outcome. Arnfast looked over to where his brother Tofi had dozed off. "I did not even ask about my older brother. My sisters. I must—" He rose to his feet and stumbled toward Tofi.

"Let him rest," said Alfrith. "He would have said something."

"Your older brother is with Harald," said Ragnvald. "Tofi would have said something if your sisters had been harmed."

"He might not," said Arnfast. He sat and put his head in his hands again.

"You wanted to take me away," said Alfrith to Ragnvald. "This is where we must go—to Arnfast's family, to care for them."

Ragnvald gave her a look he hoped would silence her. He had not yet decided how to involve himself in this. He was already tangled in the affairs of Arnfast's family from paying the wergild, and did not wish to be drawn into an outright feud with Hakon's sons. Af-ter keeping Heming from death at Harald's hands, and now helping him set up Maer's defenses, Ragnvald could count Heming a friend these days. Oddi might remain neutral, but Heming? Hakon always used his sons, their inheritance, and their quarrels as excuses to do his own will. He might be behind this, exploiting the opportunity of Herlaug's wounding to drive a wedge between Ragnvald and Harald.

"A woman is injured and alone," said Alfrith. "You said you would take me somewhere—that is where I would go."

Hardly the pleasurable trip that Ragnvald had pictured. Alfrith could ride in the sledge, but Ragnvald would need to bring warriors to protect Arnfast's family, and that meant a few days of hard skiing through deep snow, late in a bitterly cold fall, when a blizzard could strike at any time.

"We will make some plans," said Ragnvald. "Now Tofi needs to rest."

✝ ✝ ✝

TOFI WOKE IN early evening, when the smells of cooking food filled the hall. The growling of his stomach spoke for him before he opened his mouth. Ragnvald asked Svanhild to bring him a cup of ale and a bowl of stew. Arnfast went to sit by his side before the fire as soon as he sat up.

"What of our sisters?" he asked his brother as Tofi rubbed sleep from his eyes. Arnfast had not stirred from his seat since hearing the news, and Ragnvald had not asked him to, though he would need Arnfast's help in planning their journey to his farm. Travel at this time of year could be dangerous. Tofi could easily have died of exposure, lost in the woods, during his journey to Naustdal, if a snowstorm kept him from finding shelter. Winter was an army that could never be outflanked. Still, Arnfast was Ragnvald's man, owed the protection of his king.

"Our sisters were visiting a neighbor," said Tofi. "I sent one of the servants to bid them remain. And you know as much of our older brother as I do."

"He will want vengeance," said Arnfast.

"Or Herlaug will kill him too," said Tofi. Arnfast glared at him.

"There is nothing to be done in winter," said Ragnvald, trying to regain his authority.

"Except go to help this woman—what is your mother's name?" Alfrith asked.

"Jorunn," said Tofi. He began to cry. Alfrith went to stand next to him. He could not be older than fifteen. He only topped Alfrith by a finger's breadth, and she was not a tall woman.

Ragnvald would have to go, and bring Alfrith. If he had received Tofi more formally from the beginning, questioned the boy from his high seat, flanked by pillars carved by Harald's artisans, he would have found it easier to delay until spring.

"Very well," he said. "Alfrith is a notable healer. We will go and make sure your mother is cared for, and your household is protected for the rest of the winter." As for Herlaug, he could wait until summer and Harald's justice, though Ragnvald could not imagine Hakon accepting outlawry for any of his sons. Maybe Hakon would get the lung sickness and die over the winter, Ragnvald thought spitefully. His sons would make much less trouble without their father to protect them.

"I want to go too," said Svanhild. She had been lingering on the edges of all of the conversations this afternoon. "The sledge has room for two."

"You're just recovered from your daughter's birth," said Ragnvald.

"And I'm as tired of being trapped inside as anyone," said Svanhild. Ragnvald wanted to allow it—he wished he could have given her the pleasant summer that her difficult labor had denied her, but he needed her at home to keep Oddi from doing anything foolish.

Alfrith spoke softly, in the voice Ragnvald seldom heard from her except the rare times when she tried to make peace between Svanhild and Hilda. "There is some danger. It would be better for the lady Svanhild to remain here."

Oddi had kept himself away from Arnfast and Tofi all day, and after dinner asked to speak with Ragnvald in the pantry area just off the kitchen—usually a place for servants' trysts, since it was both warm and private between the walls of ale barrels. "I should go and see what my brothers did," he said as soon as Ragnvald joined him. His voice had the flat tone that Ragnvald had heard from men who had witnessed destruction they could not yet believe.

"No," said Ragnvald. "I want to keep you out of this."

"I've been hiding too long from—"

"What good can come of it?" Ragnvald asked. "There are too many involved already. This is a whirlpool that will pull down anyone who touches it. I would not go but . . ."

Oddi gave Ragnvald one of his grins, though it looked forced. "You are besotted, and your lady will give you no peace."

"Yes," said Ragnvald. And he would have to face it eventually.

"What will you do?" Oddi asked. "This is more than a whirlpool—it is a storm that touches every shore. It could destroy every-thing."

"Would you come with me to make sure that none of Arnfast's family survives?" Ragnvald asked, deliberately harsh.

Oddi gave Ragnvald a horrified look. "Is that why you're going?"

"No," said Ragnvald. Oddi had the right to know this. "Arnfast gave me his loyalty, and he is in the right. By Harald's law and decree, your brothers are already outlawed. You stayed by my side to avoid your brothers' battles. Avoid this one too." He hesitated. "I don't want to fight you." He would, though, if he had to. His oaths, his vision, meant he could not choose Oddi over Harald.

"I would never," said Oddi. "I have sworn it."

"We will both be happier if we are not so tested," said Ragnvald. "Stay here, guard my family." He gave Oddi a wry smile. "Guard my sister."

Oddi flushed. "I would marry her if she would let me," he said. "I would be a father to Solvi's child."

"She does as she pleases," said Ragnvald. He shrugged. "I can speak to her if you like."

Oddi waved that aside. "As you say, she will do as she pleases."

        ⁘   ⁘   ⁘

OVER THE NEXT day of preparation, Ragnvald hoped in vain for another snowstorm. The weather remained clear, though, and a day of strong wind scoured off some of the deeper snow. The morning of departure dawned bright and sunny. Alfrith rode in the sledge with food and supplies. Two fjord ponies pulled it, seeming not to mind the snow that sometimes drifted up to their withers. They too had been penned up inside too long. Ragnvald had convinced Svanhild to remain at home and, as much as she could, keep Oddi occupied and not brooding on his family. She cared for Oddi, though they were no longer lovers, and would not want to see him drawn into this feud.

A guard of ten young warriors jogged along behind the sledge, joking that they wished they could pull it to make it go faster. They played and raced one another on side jaunts that left them grinning and panting when they returned. Even Tofi and Arnfast seemed happier to be moving, leaving Ragnvald alone in his dread. They crowded into the house of one of Ragnvald's tenant farmers for a night, covering every inch of the floor, sleeping wedged up against pigs and chickens, and left in the blue light before the dawn of the following morning. Ragnvald was amused to note that his men had less energy now, while he had more, having not exhausted himself the day before. Alfrith skied beside him for some of the time when she grew cold sitting in the sledge. Tofi rode there instead, and dozed. He had been escaping into sleep often.

They reached the farm of Arnfast's family near evening on the third day. Lower down in the foothills, the breeze had been pleasant, cooling the sweat that bloomed on Ragnvald's skin from skiing through deep snow. Up here it bit hard, driving ice crystals against his face. The land had a uniform look, all differences blended together under windswept snow. Even the stone fences were hardly more than ridges in that blinding whiteness.

As soon as the noise of their approach could be heard above the sound of the wind, one of Arnfast's sisters put her head out the door. She ran out to meet the sledge. Her face hardly lightened when she saw Arnfast and Tofi, though she gave a tight wave.

"Come, please. She is worse. I don't know how much longer—" She broke off with a sob.

Alfrith jumped out of the sledge before it stopped moving, and ran toward the girl, half stumbling over the deep snow. She disappeared into the black maw of the open door. Ragnvald took his time unhitching the ponies, drying them in the barn that Tofi pointed out to him.

"What they did to her," he began. "He said he would cut off her face. He cut . . ." Tofi shuddered.

"You got away. That is good," said Ragnvald, his words as meaningless to Tofi as those said to a panicked horse.

"I should have protected her," said Tofi. "They were many, though, the lords and their men. My father told me to run."

"You would have been mutilated or killed if you hadn't escaped," said Ragnvald. "You have done more for your family than if you had stayed."

When Ragnvald spoke the word *mutilated*, Tofi blanched. Ragnvald put his hand on Tofi's shoulder, feeling the bone through his cloak, shaken by his trembling.

"We must go in and see your mother," said Ragnvald.

Tofi lowered his head. "Yes," he mumbled. He followed Ragnvald into the house.

25

RAGNVALD WAS GRATEFUL THAT HIS EYES TOOK SOME TIME to adjust to the dimness inside the living hall, so he could steel himself for the sight of Arnfast's mother, Jorunn. The hall had high beams and comfortable proportions, as befitted a successful farming household. A crowd of women collected on one side, hiding Jorunn's pallet from Ragnvald's view. Arnfast sat at a long table with his head flung down on his forearms.

Ragnvald crossed the room and sat down next to him. On this journey Arnfast had alternated between high energy, when he vibrated like a bow about to loose its arrow, and deep mourning. Now Ragnvald thought Arnfast would take more strength from toughness than sympathy.

"Your mother needs you strong," he said. "Do your weeping later, where she cannot see you. Alfrith is tending to her." Arnfast picked his head up. His eyes were dry, though red. Ragnvald had seen an expression like his on a berserker, crazed by battle, a man who had emerged from gore and certain death to find that he lived after all, but in a world forever changed by what he had seen and done.

"I will do this to him, tenfold. I will do this to his own mother," Arnfast said, the clarity of his voice at odds with the wildness of his expression.

"I cannot support this feud," said Ragnvald. "Hakon's sons will be outlawed, and your family will be paid." He wondered if he should simply let Arnfast carry his feud to Herlaug and Geirbjorn. Arnfast would certainly die, as would his brothers, if they tried to avenge him, and that would be an end of it. But if Ragnvald allowed that, it would endanger his kingship, and possibly Harald's as well. A king's protection and his justice must be as strong as steel, or none would follow him.

"Gold," Arnfast spat. "What good is gold?"

"No good," said Ragnvald. "But neither is the torture of women. This is the work of a coward, a *nithing*. Would you make yourself another Herlaug, and face the cold hell of oath breakers and criminals after your death? No. You will have justice, but if you hurt any of Herlaug's women over this, I will kill you myself."

"It's what she wants," said Arnfast, indicating the back of the room with a nod. Ragnvald heard wails and whimpers from that corner, nothing as coherent as a call for revenge.

"If so, it is because she is crazed with pain," said Ragnvald.

"He must die," said Arnfast. In this state, it seemed that he hardly heard Ragnvald.

"I do not make threats lightly," said Ragnvald. "You will be killed or outlawed if you pursue a private feud. Think on it." He spoke quickly: "And if you will not think of your life, think of your brothers' lives, your sisters'. Your mother is not the only one who can be hurt. Think."

"I don't care—" Arnfast began.

Ragnvald quelled him with a glare. "Think," he commanded.

"Look at my mother's face, then come back and tell me if you would still do nothing," Arnfast spat. He was too blinded by anger to see how this would end: war with Hakon. But he was Ragnvald's sworn man, and if he did not do what Ragnvald ordered, he would be an oath breaker. He would see that.

Ragnvald had to witness what was done to Jorunn, though, or his imagination would show him a hundred pictures far worse than the reality to haunt his dreams. He walked over to the circle of women, servants in dark homespun. Two held down Jorunn's shoulders. Alfrith bent over her, wearing fine dark wool, her sleeves rolled up, her hands red with blood. She blocked Ragnvald's view of Jorunn until she turned to ask a servant for a pair of scissors, and then he saw a mess of flesh that hardly looked like a face anymore. Most of one cheek had been torn away entirely, exposing her teeth back to the molars. The other side of her face was a seamed and puckered mass where Alfrith had sewn it together and begun the work of cauterizing the wounds to keep them from growing infected. Could such devastation heal? Ragnvald's stomach heaved. He cast his eyes down, so he would not be seen to be turning away. He barely escaped vomiting on the floor, swallowing down the remnants of his last meal, which rose, bathed in acid, to his mouth.

"It is very bad," he said to Arnfast when he rejoined him. "To do this to any woman is a crime even the gods would have trouble punishing harshly enough."

"I did not cut him in malice," said Arnfast. "I would have offered my life to spare her this. Now I can offer my death in the service of revenge."

"You have heard my decision," said Ragnvald. "Promise me at least you will not do anything until Alfrith tells us what healing she can bring."

Arnfast stared up at him, and then, finally nodded.

"Come," Ragnvald continued. "I am sure that chores have been left undone since this happened. See, there is hardly any wood in the fireplace. Let us fetch some, and bring in some snow to melt for water."

They found wood, and many other chores to fill their time. Out on the woodpile, the corpse of Arnfast's father lay frozen among the pieces of timber, awaiting spring for his burial. Wind had torn his shroud from him, and Ragnvald met the dead, staring eyes, before quickly covering him again, hoping Arnfast had not seen.

✢   ✢   ✢

BY DAWN, JORUNN had retreated into fever and delirium. Alfrith dosed her with jealously hoarded opium brought with her from Smola, purchased at great expense from southern merchants. She mixed up a tincture and dripped it into the woman's mouth, rubbing her throat to make sure she swallowed it. It kept Jorunn quiescent except one horrible moment at dinnertime when she stood up and lurched around the hall, and Ragnvald barked at the servants to put her back to bed and tie her there if need be.

Neither he nor anyone else in the house could eat after that. Ragnvald lay next to Alfrith that night with his stomach roiling still, and the thin, keening noise from Jorunn's pallet keeping him from sleep.

"Will she live?" Ragnvald asked.

"She is fevered now," said Alfrith. She had worn the same grim look all day that Odin's Valkyries must wear when they walked among the dead on a batttlefield. It made him both fear her and love her all the more, for facing what he dreaded. "If it passes, she may live, though horribly scarred. She will always be prone to fevers in the wound, and more of the flesh may die."

Alfrith spoke, Ragnvald noticed, as impersonally as possible about the injury. He nodded, and resigned himself to a long, sleepless night. Jorunn's face haunted him whether he closed his eyes or left them open.

"When will you know?" he asked.

"I will know when the fever passes or she dies," Alfrith snapped. She sighed. "Forgive me."

"No, you have more right than I. You may be as ill-tempered as you wish." He needed whatever goodwill she could spare for the question he meant to ask her tomorrow.

In the morning, Alfrith packed cloths full of snow around Jorunn's face to draw down the fever and the pain. When Jorunn slept, she walked with Ragnvald outside, her rigid calm melting into exhaustion.

"I do not have much opium left," she said. "Her pain and fever will make her mad if they have not already."

The wind that greeted their arrival had calmed and the sun shone bright. If Herlaug had not made this farm a charnel house, he and Alfrith might be sledging this day, riding down the hills fast enough to blow Alfrith's hair back.

"I will make sure we trade for more in the spring," said Ragnvald. "That is a problem, though. How many days longer can you dose her?"

"Every day she needs more," said Alfrith. "At this rate, three or four more days, perhaps."

"Are there other potions you can use?"

"I have some mushrooms that induce a stupor, but I have only used those . . ."

"What?"

"I have used those to help those who cannot live to die peacefully," she said. "I do not like to do it. But I begged my mother to use those mushrooms on my brother. You would not have had to kill him then."

"It was his *wyrd*," said Ragnvald. He had been frightened that night, but so much had come from that moment of fear, including Alfrith by his side now. "And yours and mine as well."

"They are superstitious on Smola and would have killed me for an evil sorceress if they knew I exercised this power," she said, still half to herself. "But I saw many on the edge of death who asked for my help so they might not see another pain-filled morning. Can you love Hel's handmaiden?"

"I can love you," he said. "Could you not help Jorunn to die? What kind of life will she have as she is?"

Alfrith shuddered and touched her own cheek, the first instinctive reaction he had seen from her in all this time. Herlaug's knife had cut through all of them, and all who would see Jorunn in the future. "She asked me," said Alfrith. "When I first came. I could hardly understand her words."

"Why did you not do it then?" Ragnvald asked.

"She is not old, and she is fevered. I do not deal in death to all who are in pain. Only if they cannot live."

"I fear it would be better if she died," said Ragnvald. "If Arnfast takes his vengeance successfully, there will be war between Hakon and me. Harald will lose honor if he does not outlaw Herlaug and Geirbjorn, but he will lose Hakon as an ally if he does."

"And you think if Jorunn dies . . . ?"

"Then at least Arnfast will not think he can ease her pain by killing Herlaug," said Ragnvald. He could feel how thin the argument was as he spoke it.

"He will still desire revenge," said Alfrith, her voice rising in anger. "I will not kill for your convenience. Or because you cannot look on such a wound without blanching. Have you not been in battle?"

"Men die of wounds like that in battle," said Ragnvald. "They die screaming and delirious with fever. Their wounds stink and fester and they breed plague." And they died in tents, under the care of Ronhild and other healers, hidden from view. "If you do not do this, I may have to kill her sons, or watch feud tear apart Harald's Norway." He saw Alfrith start to waver and pressed his case. "You are the only one who can do this thing. If I cause this woman's death, her sons will hate me too. If you do it, you will give her mercy. Do not answer me now. Tend her and think upon it. Think upon her suffering. Think upon her living like that."

Alfrith gave him a look of such fury Ragnvald worried he had lost her forever. "You are as cold as one already dead, Ragnvald Half-Drowned," she said. "I cannot tell if you ask this for your own comfort, or if it truly will save more lives. I will not decide today. Now leave me be."

✛ ✛ ✛

RAGNVALD WANTED TO hate Alfrith for what she had said, but he had never learned the trick of hating those who told him an unpleasant truth. Half-Drowned, Alfrith called him. More people called him Ragnvald the Wise, or Ragnvald the Mighty now, but Half-Drowned felt truer. Half cold, a creature of shadows and chilly water, only half a feeling man.

He kept out of doors as much as he could and was not the only one. Both Arnfast and his brother found excuses to be outside, chopping kindling for fires that did not need to be made. If Ragnvald went inside he might have to look at Jorunn. Alfrith made it as chilly inside as out in the cold wind, though Ragnvald did not think that Arnfast or Tofi noticed. They were too lost in their own misery.

The next day, when Ragnvald went to tend the ponies, he found Arnfast there already, opening the feed shed. "What are we waiting for?" he asked Ragnvald.

"I am waiting for Alfrith to be willing to leave her patient. Your mother is still fevered."

"She will not heal," said Arnfast. "I tell you, she begged me to let her die, and then to avenge her."

"Alfrith can ease her passage," said Ragnvald. "You must speak with her if you think that is what your mother wants." She had lain next to him like a block of wood the night before.

It was a bad day for Jorunn. Her fever made her see things, and she tore at the bandages on her face so that her sons had to restrain her arms, though not before she bared her wound again, and the gleam of her white teeth through her missing cheek made the scar on Ragnvald's own cheek ache in horrible sympathy. He had been lucky with Solvi's cut. Lucky that Solvi meant to kill, not mutilate. He carried his scar to the Sogn *ting* trials, calling it an insult wound. He had not known what such a thing was.

Jorunn was quiet during dinner, dragged down into an unnatural sleep by the last of Alfrith's opium. Alfrith looked worn out, the lines of her face severe in the firelight. Her beauty was the type that would grow greater with age, and be called handsome even until her death. She was only a woman, though, not a healing goddess, and Jorunn's wound tested her sorely.

"We must speak privately, my lord," she said to Ragnvald after their silent meal. Ragnvald walked with her out into the night. No moon shone, and the stars made a cloudy ribbon across the arc of the sky. The aurora hung in sheets above, pure white curtains, like the fairest of maiden's hair, or like the silver streak in Alfrith's.

"When you came before, my brother lost his life and became a *draugr*. Now this woman has become like a *draugr* as well. What fate do you bring me, Ragnvald Half-Drowned?" she asked.

Ragnvald shuddered to hear the name spoken again in the darkness. He had brought men and a few women terrible fates with his own hands, and the hands of his men, starting fires that burned families to death, bringing armies that killed and plundered. His foster-brother, Einar, had died on Ragnvald's sword, his blood poured out on the ground of Ardal.

"She has asked me to die," said Alfrith. "Her son has asked me to let her die. You have asked me to let her die. She is crazed by pain, though, and she may want to live once she heals. I have seen it."

"Would you want to live like that?" Ragnvald asked. "Your beauty gone?"

"Time takes beauty from all of us," said Alfrith, quoting the proverb. "I would live. If I still had my wits, and could collect herbs and bring healing. Jorunn can live to hold her grandchildren in her arms, to know her mutilation is avenged at least with the outlawry of Hakon's sons."

"Her grandchildren will fear her," said Ragnvald.

"Children are kinder than you," said Alfrith.

Ragnvald thought of his sons Einar and Ivar, the bond between them stronger than the ties that bound some grown men. "I will do as you bid," he said.

She took a deep breath. "I may yet do this, but only if Jorunn and her children—Tofi, Arnfast, and her daughters too—all agree. I will not do this in secret or let any turn their face from the decision. I do not care about what this feud means for Norway or for your precious king."

"If you want to prevent bloodshed—"

"Do not lay that burden on me," she snapped. "I came for Jorunn. I cared for her when her servants could hardly look upon her. I will not carry the lives and decisions of every foolish man who can pick up a sword."

✝ ✝ ✝

ALFRITH KEPT VIGIL by Jorunn's side that night, lit by one candle. Near morning, Jorunn stirred and opened her eyes. Alfrith gripped her hands. "The opium will wear off soon, and you will be in pain again," she told Jorunn. "You have told your sons that you want to die. You have told me that you want to die. Is it because of the pain?"

Jorunn's eyes, still beautiful, a rich, warm blue, like a summer midnight sky, washed with tears and she shook her head no.

"Is it because of your face? Because you will be troubling to look upon? Because eating will be difficult for the rest of your life?"

Jorunn nodded.

"If you die, you will never see the women that your sons choose as wives. You will never hold their grandchildren in your arms. You will never be able to advise them. If you choose to live, you choose pain and difficulty. But if you choose death, you choose this as your last moment, and you will never move beyond it. I will deliver your choice to you, but you must choose it freely. I want you to decide now, before the pain returns. Because it will, and the help I have left for it will not work as well."

"I don't know," said Jorunn.

These words Ragnvald could make out. He sighed.

"What . . . you think?" Jorunn asked.

"I think you should live," said Alfrith.

Arnfast choked out a sob and turned away.

"I promise you vengeance on Hakon's sons," said Ragnvald. He had the glimmerings of an idea now, indistinct as lightning on the horizon that augured a storm. "You must leave it to me, though. It will take some time, and it will fall on Hakon and his sons as though decreed by the gods."

"Yes," said Jorunn. "I will live to see that."

"I will give you willow bark to ease the pain," said Alfrith. "Remember though, when you feel the pain, it is because you are alive and your body is trying to heal itself."

Alfrith patiently dripped the medicine down Jorunn's throat. She took Tofi by the hand and taught him how to tend to his mother, and make sure she drank enough water, so she would not be parched by her fever.

"She will live to see my revenge," said Arnfast. "I suppose that is good."

"No," said Ragnvald. "I command you to remain here to tend her. I command you to leave revenge to me, as your sworn lord."

"It is my duty—mine and my brothers'," said Arnfast.

"Your mother made a hard choice," said Ragnvald. "It would have been easier for her to choose death and to end her pain, but she was brave. Far braver than you are being now. It is easy to pursue Herlaug, perhaps even kill his mother or his brothers. Leaving to do vengeance is the easy choice. Staying here to protect her, showing her that her sons still love her even with her beauty gone—that is the hard choice. Your mother made the hard choice—honor her by doing the same."

"But—"

"You may come back to Naustdal in the spring and tell me how she fares. At that time I will be able to tell you more of my own plans. Be sure, Hakon's sons will be punished for this. But they will be punished by the laws that they have broken. That is the vengeance that I owe them."

"Law," said Arnfast scornfully. "Law was meant to protect my family—you paid wergild, and I am outlawed from half of Norway for three years."

"When the god Loki killed Alfather Odin's son Baldur, do you recall the vengeance Odin visited upon him?" Ragnvald asked. Arnfast nodded, but Ragnvald continued anyway, for Arnfast must understand and trust him. "He turned one of Loki's sons into a wolf, who tore out the guts of the other. Your enemies are too powerful for you alone. They must be made to turn on each other. Do you understand me?"

"No," said Arnfast. "But you are called the Wise, and I will trust you. Still, if I can hold the blade that kills Herlaug, I will never ask for anything again."

Over the next few days, Alfrith taught Jorunn's children all that they must do to care for their mother and her wounds. Jorunn stood and went outside for the first time to bid farewell to her husband's corpse. Ragnvald spoke the words of blessing for him, those that could be said without laying him in a proper barrow.

"The wound is knitting as well as it can," said Alfrith after she laid Jorunn back in her bed. "Now that she has decided to live. What changed your mind, my lord?"

"You did," said Ragnvald. "You gave me the words that I think will keep her sons here over the winter. And then I will see what is to be done."

"I wanted to hate you for asking that of me," she said.

"Do you not?"

"No. Fear makes all of us less than ourselves."

"Not you," said Ragnvald.

"I do not feel fear at the side of the wounded," said Alfrith. "My mother feared life without my brother too much, and she kept him alive when she should not. I have never lost someone I feared that much to live without."

Ragnvald shivered. She had called him cold, yet Ragnvald would willingly kill or die for Svanhild, for his sons, especially Ivar. If either of them had been served as Jorunn had—he did not know what he might do. His anger would blind him to any but the bloodiest revenge.

✛ ✛ ✛

SVANHILD STOOD AT a loom in the women's chamber, stringing the warp for sail wool. The new hall at Naustdal was always damp. Some of the moisture came from the wet weather that forced water droplets inside even the best-daubed hall, and some from the beams of wood and the turf, still fresh from its construction this summer. The wool's dampness made it hard to weave, and some flax had started to mold. It would have to be boiled to kill that growth, and even so, anything made from it would turn out mottled and musty.

"It only snowed a little last night," said Hilda. She sat down on her favorite stool, arranged her skirts over it, and took up her spindle.

"Yes," said Svanhild. "I think we may get a thaw before true winter." She glanced at her mother, Ascrida, who sat dozing in a darkened corner. The lamp overhead swung a little, enough to make Svanhild feel slightly dazed. She wore a short tunic and skirt under her overdress these days, to make it easy to nurse her daughter, Freydis.

Thora, Freydis's wet nurse, who had given birth at the same time as Svanhild, carried Svanhild's daughter into the chamber, bouncing her as she walked, to soothe Freydis's hungry cries. Svanhild still shared feeding duties with Thora—Freydis would accept a wet nurse, but not as well as Svanhild's own breast. She undid the large bronze brooch that held up her overdress on the right side, and pulled up her tunic to bare her breast. She beckoned Thora to bring her daughter to her. Freydis stopped crying as soon as she came close to Svanhild, her perfect rosebud mouth curved as though it anticipated this feeding. She had been a fussy feeder at first. Now, as she neared her fourth month of life, she had become an easy child, and seemed to grow bigger each day.

Freydis began to fret again, and Svanhild loosened her grip and transferred her to her other breast. She was stronger than Eystein had been, even at this age. This child would likely have survived all of Solvi's voyages, and Svanhild would never cease to blame herself that she had not protected Eystein better. Sometime earlier in the fall, while Svanhild lay abed, recovering from the weakness of Freydis's hard childbirth, she realized that a year had passed since she saw Solvi last. Legally, their marriage was no more.

At least when Freydis nursed, Svanhild did not have to spin or do any of the other women's tasks. She saw that Hilda plied some black sheep's wool, a color that would never be used in a ship's sail, and wondered at the purpose. She would not ask, though. Hilda ran Naustdal, not in the way that Svanhild would have, but well enough, and resented any of Svanhild's questions.

She watched every day for Ragnvald and Alfrith's coming. She had not been able to fulfill Ragnvald's request that she keep Oddi distracted. He needed someone to soothe and calm him, but their conversations went in circles. He said he hoped that Arnfast's brother was mistaken and the wound was not that bad—then he swore he would kill Herlaug himself. He hardly seemed to hear Svanhild when she flirted with him and offered him the distractions of games, conversations, or walks in the snow.

When Ragnvald finally returned, he looked as though he had aged years. He sat staring into the fire, holding a cup of ale long after most of the household already slept. Even Oddi, to whom Ragnvald would say little of what had passed, had gone to his bed. Svanhild sat down next to him.

"Oddi is . . ." Svanhild spread her hands. "I do not know what he will decide. I suppose it depends on what happens, and what has happened."

Ragnvald looked down at the cup in his hands. "I don't know," he said. "Harald will hear of this and punish Hakon's sons. Hakon will go to war over it, and these wars will never end until Harald's dream is dead."

"I thought you had lost hope in his dream," said Svanhild. "That is why you are in Naustdal now and not by his side."

"We are in Naustdal because Harald asked me to protect Maer," said Ragnvald. "If Harald does not punish Hakon's sons, then Hakon

will be the true king of Norway, and all will know it. Harald un-
derstands this. He will punish Hakon's sons." It sounded like he was
trying to convince himself.

"Would it truly be so bad if he didn't?" Svanhild asked.

"Yes and no. It will come to war sooner or later. You think Harald
will choose the easy path here but . . . I know him better." Svanhild's
skepticism must have shown on her face, and Ragnvald's lips curved
slightly. "Say what you think, Svanhild."

"I think he will take the easy path, and stay on it as long as he
can," she said. "Unless you force him off it."

"How?"

"Push Hakon into open rebellion. Go with Arnfast, take an army,
and punish Hakon's sons. Hakon will come after you, and Harald
will come to your aid."

"Or he may say I am in rebellion, taking his justice for my own."

"He values you more than that," said Svanhild.

"His poorest ally, who will owe him taxes for generations? Who
could not defeat Vemund without treachery?" Ragnvald asked. He
asked it with his usual irony, but Svanhild saw a wound that went
deep.

"His friend," said Svanhild. She touched Ragnvald's arm, wishing
she could push her conviction, her knowledge, through her fingers
and into him. Every man in Norway save Ragnvald himself knew
how much Harald valued him. "His friend who did defeat Vemund,
who won an impossible battle at Solskel. His friend who he would
grant any favor because he knows you would do the same for him.
His friend he values so much he is willing to suffer without your
company for a few years because you asked it."

Ragnvald did not seem to hear her. "No," he said, softly rejecting
all that she had tried to give him. "But you are right, Hakon is close
to rebellion. He hardly needs a push—he only needs to fall where he
will do himself the most harm."

26

SIGURD'S JOURNEY TO DUBLIN IN HAKON'S SHIP WAS MARKED
by cold and darkness. They sailed in dim light, shadowed by clouds,
while Hakon's pilot navigated the dangerous currents around the Shetland and Orkney islands, and then through the protected channels of
the Hebrides, steering by the black silhouettes of land and the stars
overhead as often as by the sun. On a whim, Sigurd had asked Hakon to put Egil in a different ship from him and enjoyed being among
strangers. He found calm in working himself to exhaustion every day.
He shared a sleeping bag with a man who knew nothing of him but his
name, and that his brother was a mighty king. They slept soundly and
warmly together at night, and passed the days rowing, for the pilot
needed the oars out to help keep the ship close enough to shore that he
could navigate by it, and far enough away to avoid death on the rocks.

The waves grew smaller when the ships reached the more sheltered sea between England and Ireland, and near Yule they finally
reached Dublin. Its river and natural harbor welcomed them in, and
King Imar allowed all of Hakon's men to sleep on benches in his long,
high-ceilinged hall.

Sigurd had never seen such richness mixed with so much squalor
as he did in Dublin. Smaller buildings housing Norse-Irish artisans
packed around King Imar's hall, the space between filled with half-
frozen human and animal refuse that stuck to his feet. The town jut-
ted out on a bend in the river called the Black Pool, and was easy to

defend for that reason, but always muddy and, in the winter, choked with fog that smelled of shit.

The Norse kings of Dublin had been fighting with the Irish for a generation now, and each battle enriched their hall with treasures, among them hangings that depicted strange beasts, decorated with gold thread and glass beads. Sigurd sat by Egil at the Yule feast, and drank heavily, falling asleep during a tale told by a visiting Spanish merchant, dark of skin and heavily accented, before the toasts for the new year were finished. When he slept, he dreamed of endless seas, endless wakefulness, endless responsibilities that he had never desired.

✜   ✜   ✜

SPRING ARRIVED IN Ireland with softer rain and milder wind. Small buds appeared on brown trees. And, on a blustery day when the sun glinted occasionally through rents in the clouds, King Imar said that the spring attacks would begin soon. "Every winter the Irish sit inside their turf barrows, getting drunk and planning revenge," he added to King Hakon as they sat playing *tafl*.

"Sounds like us," said Egil to Sigurd.

King Imar's warriors arranged a raid of their own against some Irish in the hills. With Egil by his side, Sigurd killed a man, and took a copper brooch from him. He was giddy from his success that night at the feasting to celebrate their victory, and grew drunk quickly. He toasted King Imar so loud and long that the king, who usually loved flattery, told him to sit down and be silent. As Sigurd rose one last time to escape his embarrassment in sleep, King Hakon caught his eye and beckoned him over.

"I have heard you did well on this raid. Come, show me what you won," said Hakon.

Sigurd's face heated as he held out his prize to Hakon. "Thank you, my lord," he said. "My king."

"Did Ragnvald train you in battle?" Hakon asked.

"Some," said Sigurd. He had trained with Sogn warriors, and sometimes with Ragnvald himself, though he never fought well when he faced his stepbrother.

"I have wondered if Ragnvald allowed you to learn anything from him, or whether he preferred to keep you weak."

Sigurd saw the room spinning around him. He had not learned enough wisdom from Ragnvald to frame a response to that. "He—he—I—thank you. Yes. He—"

Hakon held up a hand to stop him speaking, and Sigurd closed his mouth gratefully. "Come and sit and tell us what you did learn from him. You did well in this raid, I hear, and I like a man who will praise a king." Sigurd ducked his head, ashamed even through his drunkenness. "I think you should rise higher than a simple warrior," said Hakon, "and I want to see if you are ready for the task."

When Sigurd sat down with him, Hakon raised a hand to call over a serving woman, who filled their cups with ale again. Sigurd drained his immediately, while Hakon ran his thumbnail over the bubbled glass. The man sitting on the other side of Hakon turned toward them, startling Sigurd. He was so massive that Sigurd had thought at first that the broad stretch of chest behind Hakon was a wall hanging, not a man.

"If this young man is half as crafty as his brother, he will be useful," said the giant. "I am Jarl Rane of Vermaland. Well met, Sigurd Olafsson."

"Don't blame craft when you should blame poor weather and poor sailing," said Hakon. Rane huffed and took a swig of his ale. "I am more interested in what Sigurd knows about Ragnvald's plans and loyalties," Hakon continued. "Come, Sigurd, tell us—who among Harald's allies does he trust, and who does he fear? Who does he think he can betray to gain his next district?"

"I don't know any of that," said Sigurd. It startled him to hear Hakon talk of Ragnvald as planning betrayal. And this Rane whom he treated as a friend—this man had fought his stepbrother.

"And if you were given the opportunity to take revenge against him, would you not take it?" Rane asked.

Hakon laughed. "Sigurd's loyalty is exemplary. Still, I wager he would do his duty to his father, if things fell out that way."

Sigurd wondered which of his loyalties Hakon meant, to Ragnvald, Harald, or himself. Or his father, years dead on Ragnvald's blade. Sigurd had killed a man last night, and found it easier than he had feared.

"Come, you must know something," said the giant Rane. "Tell us of your brother. Everything you know."

Hakon and Rane gave Sigurd more ale to quench his thirst, for he had much to say about Ragnvald, words that he did not remember when he woke the next day with an aching head. Hakon and Rane had pestered him with many questions that he did not know how to answer, and tried to trap him into saying that Ragnvald meant to betray someone: Harald, Hakon, or another, Sigurd could not tell. Finally, when they had reduced Sigurd to repeating, "I don't know. He is my stepbrother. He is wiser than me," they sent him to his rest.

✢   ✢   ✢

AFTER THAT FIRST, uncomfortable night, Sigurd grew to like Jarl Rane of Vermaland. He asked no more questions of Sigurd. Sigurd heard that he had fought on Solvi's side against Ragnvald and Harald, but the Dublin court often hosted enemies. Hospitality right protected all of them.

Rane seemed an incarnation of Thor set down to walk among mortals, a Thor in his later years, with a wind-chapped face and a broadness so vast it could be confused for fatness until he sprang into action. Rane's preferred weapon was an ax most men would wield with two hands, but his massive forearms, protected by firm leather wrist guards, supported it in either hand alone.

On a misty, muddy morning, he gave a demonstration of lifting stones and bested every man in Dublin, then lifted up a stone that two of Imar's strongest warriors had strained to lift together, carried it up a hill, and rolled it down the other side, knocking down a stone fence. Curious chickens came scurrying to see what had happened.

"Are you big because you lift stones, or do you lift stones because you're big?" Sigurd asked, chasing after him as he returned to King Imar's hall.

"Both, I think," said Rane. "My father's father trained him this way, and my father was even bigger than me." He looked at Sigurd. "You did well today." Sigurd had picked up a large and heavy stone and lost it by slipping in the mud rather than his strength failing. "Next time you'll lift it higher if you push your hips through like you're trying to make a woman pregnant with one thrust."

Sigurd laughed and said he would.

That night Rane told the tale of how Harald's father, Halfdan, had taken his land from him and exiled him, and how now, with the backing of the Swedish king, he planned to take it back. King Imar hosted many of Harald's enemies as guests, so the cheer that rang up did not surprise Sigurd. What did was Hakon's announcement that he and his forces would accompany Rane to Vestfold.

"My younger sons are in Vestfold," Hakon said. "We will go together and see how they fare."

The next day, Hakon set his men to provisioning his ships for the crossing to Norway. Sigurd made sure he worked at Egil's side, carrying endless loads up the planks into the ships. In Imar's storehouse, he tipped a barrel of ale on its side, and then pulled it up onto his thighs, remembering what Rane had said about using his hips.

"Do you think Rane and Hakon mean to betray King Harald?" he asked Egil as he waddled up to him with his load. Egil stumbled, his foot caught in the mud, and nearly dropped the sack of grain he carried onto the ground.

"Rane is not Harald's subject, so he cannot betray him," Egil replied.

"King Hakon is," said Sigurd. "And you swore an oath to Harald directly. Remember, you swore when Ragnvald married your sister?"

"I remember," said Egil, guarded.

"Hakon means to bring his ships and men to Vestfold," said Sigurd. "With this Rane. What else could it be?"

"Many things," said Egil. "He might only wish to keep Rane's friendship until he knows his plans. And if Hakon is planning a war against Harald, what would you do about it?"

Sigurd had left Sogn; Hakon and Egil would say that he owed his brother no more loyalty, even though he had sworn an oath to Harald and had vowed to take no revenge for his father. Hakon would see Sigurd dead if he thought he would take news of Hakon's betrayal back to Ragnvald. He could stay in Dublin when Hakon left—King Imar always needed more warriors. He could keep silent, follow his original plan, and avoid being called oath breaker, especially if he went on to settle in Iceland.

Sigurd continued walking with his keg of ale, and when he came to a ship, set it on the ramp that led up to the gunwale. Or he could try to make his way back to Sogn and Ragnvald, and honor his oath with more than simply silence. Ragnvald would want to know what happened here, the company that King Hakon kept. If he did not go with Hakon, he would have to wait in Dublin for a ship traveling to Norway, and try to convince an unknown captain to take him on. He could as easily sail with Hakon until open sea no longer separated him from his kin.

"You're in my way," said Egil, wheezing from the weight of his grain sack. Sigurd rolled the keg up and into the ship.

"We could find other passage to Iceland," he said, after Egil joined him at the top of the ramp.

"I've a mind to see where Hakon takes me," Egil replied. "I have heard there are not many women in Iceland. Perhaps I will find one in Vestfold, and earn some treasure in Hakon's service before settling down."

"You would break your oath to Harald," said Sigurd.

"I will see where the wind carries me," Egil replied. He leaped down from the ship, and began walking away from Sigurd.

"That's what you did to my brother at the *ting* trial and look what happened," Sigurd muttered.

"Stepbrother," said Egil, turning to correct him. "One day you'll realize he's only a man, not a god, and I hope you take his head off for it."

"He is—" Sigurd began.

"Why ask me about Hakon," said Egil, "when you can simply ask yourself what would Ragnvald do? I had hoped to get away from him, and now I find you have carried him with you."

"Wait and watch, I suppose," said Sigurd.

"What?"

"That's what Ragnvald would do. You asked."

Egil nodded. "And that's what I am doing also. See, he is not so clever."

"Neither are you," Sigurd muttered again, and this time Egil ignored him. Egil was right about one thing: in his place, Ragnvald would go along until he learned something of value to him. Hakon's plans were no clearer to Sigurd at this moment than the mud of the river that curled around Dublin, and would carry his ships to the sea.

✦ ✦ ✦

THE STRONG, WARM winds of late spring afforded an easy crossing from Dublin to Vestfold. Sigurd hardly had time to grow weary of attempting to sleep shipboard, sharing a sleeping bag with Egil this time, before the coast of Norway appeared in the distance, and then broke into the collection of islands that guarded the mouth of Stavanger Fjord. Seabirds tracked the convoy, scavenging bits of food that washed out of sailors' slop pots. Sigurd became friendly with a gull, a great, black-eyed creature with a cry more plaintive than its fellows, who avoided the snares of the sailors who tried to catch it. It ate crumbs once from Sigurd's hand, and Egil chided him for not wringing its neck, for everyone would have liked fresh meat, but Sigurd was glad he had not. On their voyage to the Faroes, Dyri had told Sigurd that the killing of some birds was unlucky, and Sigurd needed luck traveling with a man as crafty as Hakon.

He could not read the currents as Ragnvald, or even Egil could, but it seemed to him that Rane and Hakon sailed to Vestfold to take it from Harald. It was plain that Rane believed Harald had taken Vestfold from him, and that Rane had an alliance with the Swedish king.

As the ships passed south along the coast of Rogaland, Hakon pointed out a narrow channel opening. "That's Kvernevik—it leads into Haversfjord. You could hide a hundred ships in there and none would ever know."

"It looks like it ends right there," said Sigurd.

"Most people think so," said Hakon. "But King Gudbrand—he was against Harald at Vestfold—his father fought a mighty battle there, and secured Stavanger Fjord for his son, so he could charge a toll of anyone who wanted to pass. Of course, Gudbrand was defeated, but only because he allowed himself to be drawn to battle on Harald's terms. If he'd stayed, Harald could never have pried him out."

"I have heard that Harald has a god's own luck," said Sigurd.

"Luck, yes," said Hakon.

✤   ✤   ✤

IN VESTFOLD'S HARBOR, the sails that hung slackly over the empty ships were in Hakon's own colors of blue and white. "See, my sons are already here. I told you—Harald has given them defense of Vestfold to prove their worth." He said it slyly, Sigurd thought. But Egil had told him that Hakon and Harald were always at each other's throats. That there was a difference between betrayal and searching for advantage. A very small difference, probably, in Hakon's case.

Rane took a few hundred men into the hills to regain his ancestral land, the woods and pastures of Vermaland. This was the site of Harald's first conquest, Sigurd knew, and Hakon did nothing to prevent it. Still, Hakon might think that Rane might make a good guardian for it, with Harald in Nidaros. Sigurd thought of finding passage on a ship back to Naustdal, but he had little of worth to bring Ragnvald, even now. He must wait for news that Hakon could not explain away.

He spent the summer patrolling and drilling with Hakon's other warriors, and helping with the local farmers' harvest when the hay ripened in the field. Hakon kept Vestfold at peace, and Rane's conquest, if it had even been a conquest, had passed with hardly a ripple, no refugees fleeing his battle or tales of bloodshed reached the hall at Vestfold. If Sigurd told Ragnvald what he knew, his brother might dismiss it as troublemaking and rumor.

Herlaug and Geirbjorn departed after the harvest and did not return until after the first winter storm had wrapped Vestfold in snow and fog. Sigurd found himself seated near Hakon's sons at the feast that welcomed them home, for his status as Ragnvald's brother, if only through marriage ties, elevated him. Hakon had many scarred men among his company, a complement of destroyed ears, missing fingers, and ragged scars cording necks, but none that gave Sigurd the unpleasant thrill that the stretched, red flesh of Herlaug's face always did.

"I've often wondered, why did you come to Vestfold?" Geirbjorn asked Sigurd during the night's feasting.

Sigurd told him the tale of leaving Sogn for Iceland, and how their feckless captain had stopped in the Faroes. "It was my *wyrd* to meet up with your father in the islands, I suppose." Then, with some slyness of his own added, "It did not seem right to continue fighting at the side of my father's killer." Hakon and Rane insisted he must want revenge; let all believe that as long as he traveled with men who hated his stepbrother.

"Well enough," said Geirbjorn. "I would help you get revenge myself, as soon as my father gives me leave. You should rule Sogn, since Ragnvald's line could not hold it." Atli—that was Sigurd's fault.

Geirbjorn darted a look at his father. Sigurd had noted some constraint between Hakon and his sons since their return, though he could not tell the source of it. Surely Hakon should be pleased to see them, but his face was harsh and closed off.

"Brother," called out Geirbjorn. "You should tell the tale. Our father's men have not yet heard."

"How she screamed," Herlaug said, the side of his mouth that could move twisting into a smile. His eyes were flat, as unreadable as an overcast sky. "You tell it." He looked at Geirbjorn until he nodded and continued the story. Sigurd listened with horror as Geirbjorn related a tale of cruelty far out of proportion to Herlaug's wound. This was why Hakon's face was so still and hard.

"Yes," said Geirbjorn. "I held her down while he"—he jerked his chin at Herlaug—"carved up her face." Herlaug nodded, his hands tightening on his dagger and spoon and he leaned slightly forward. Geirbjorn continued, warming to the tale. "Her serving girls screamed as though we were cutting them instead. I had two of them when we were done and Herlaug had another. Not a woman in that house we didn't make scream before we left."

Some laughed at that, though Sigurd thought it sounded hollow. His own laughter stuck in his throat. He looked at the faces of the men nearby. Most refused to meet his eyes, or each other's. Geirbjorn seemed to sense the uneasiness his tale had engendered. "We had to take our revenge," he said, not laughing now. "We could not let this go unanswered."

"Harald has done worse," said one of Hakon's old warriors. "He killed those men in Tafjord—Heming's men, who were forced to fight for Solvi."

"They should not have fought for Solvi," said Geirbjorn.

"He didn't have to kill them like slaves," said the old warrior.

Hakon cleared his throat. "Revenge is necessary," he said with an air of finality. "Otherwise men would kill and injure each other with impunity. They have to know their actions will be punished—and if not them, then their families."

27

RAGNVALD STILL ATTENDED THE SOGN *TING* THE SUMMER AFTER moving his household to Maer. Maer had not hosted a *ting*—at least not one blessed by its king—in generations, not since before Solvi's grandfather ruled. Ragnvald had let it be known that any Maer men who wanted justice from a jury rather than their king were welcome to join him in Sogn. Several families gathered at his hall at Naustdal in the weeks before and traveled with him to the *ting* grounds.

Ragnvald set up in Olaf's old booth, which had been his father Eystein's before Olaf's usurpation. He had reinforced and expanded the area over the years, so it could host the full *ting* feast after the midsummer sacrifices. The glacier still watched over the *ting* grounds, a frozen river of white and blue dividing the mountains, though the ice cave Ragnvald remembered exploring with Oddi had collapsed. As usual, the plain was colder than the surrounding woods as the wind from the ice field swept across it.

Ragnvald hosted a welcome feast with Atli and Heming the night before the midsummer sacrifices. He had Alfrith by his side; Hilda remained at Naustdal with all of the children, who were suffering from a mild pox. Alfrith had said when they left that all of the boys were past danger, and Ragnvald had never known her to be wrong about illness or injury. He wished he could have brought Ivar, though, who always enjoyed the races and the games, and would benefit from the midsummer blessing.

Alfrith was now far enough into her pregnancy that it showed in the rounding of her belly, softened the stern lines of her face. She shared hostess duties with Atli's wife, Bertha, while Vigdis sat among the lesser women at the *ting*. Ragnvald gave the welcome toasts he had given in years past, and invited Heming to make his own.

"If I am king of North Maer, I should host a *ting* there," said Heming after finishing a brief blessing for all of the attendees from Maer. "I remember attending the Halogaland and Trondelag *tings* sometimes with my father, but that land is so vast that few can usually make the journey."

"You are king of North Maer," said Ragnvald. "You should do it."

"You do not think Harald will take it from me when he hears what my brothers have done?" Heming asked. He had never fully recovered his confidence from his capture at the battle at Vestfold seven years earlier, and losing Tafjord to Solvi, however briefly, the previous year, had made him even more skittish. Ragnvald preferred this cautious Heming to the one he had met on these very grounds, years previous. But if he ever wanted to be allowed to return to Sogn as its king, Heming had to be king of North Maer in truth, and prove himself able to defend South Maer as well.

"No, I do not," said Ragnvald. "Harald keeps his promises to those who remain loyal to him."

"Yes," Atli agreed, "even when he would rather not." He gave Ragnvald a knowing smile, and Ragnvald presumed that he meant giving Sogn to Atli.

"You hold Sogn in trust for me," said Ragnvald. "Do not forget your oath. One promise Harald always keeps is to punish oath breakers."

Atli tipped his head forward in an obsequious bow. "I would never do such a thing. I hold Sogn for Ragnvald the Wise, Ragnvald the Mighty, while he performs more important tasks elsewhere."

Ragnvald took a deep breath and reminded himself that Atli had never sworn an oath not to irritate him, and if that was all he did, Ragnvald should be well pleased. The Sogn farmers that Ragnvald had spoken with at the *ting* all had fine reports of Atli and his sons. They settled disputes fairly, ran off raiders, and still called Ragnvald king.

He had nothing he could complain about to Harald, and no proof that Atli had paid off the farmers at the *ting* to speak well of him.

"What do you think Harald will do about Herlaug and Geirbjorn?" Heming asked. Ragnvald searched his narrow, handsome face for calculation or anger, but found no emotion beyond worry that furrowed his brow.

"Outlaw them," said Ragnvald. "They could still seek lands in Iceland, or your father's other holdings overseas."

"Do you think they would leave?" Heming asked.

"They are your brothers," said Ragnvald. "What do you think?"

"They will do what my father says they should," said Heming, sounding dispirited.

✛　✛　✛

TO SHOW HIS unity with Heming and Atli, Ragnvald shared sacrifice duties with them on midsummer night. The day after the sacrifices, the trials began. The weather had turned chilly, with clouds ringing the *ting* plain, though overhead the sun shone down and warmed Ragnvald in his wool cloak.

Hrolf acted as law speaker. With Egil gone to Iceland, perhaps Einar should become law speaker after Hrolf, since he could never inherit Sogn. Hrolf would be pleased to foster one of Ragnvald's sons. He listened to Hrolf recite the laws—the cycle had come around twice since his trial against Solvi, and Hrolf repeated the same laws again, betrothal and kin laws: to which kin marriage was permitted, to which forbidden. Marrying a stepparent was not allowed unless the parent had been married less than a year before divorce or death. Ragnvald made sure that his eyes did not find Vigdis's.

Hrolf continued; marriage between brother and sister, half-sister and half-brother: forbidden. Marriage between aunt and nephew, uncle and niece: only allowed when no other spouses of appropriate rank could be found. Marriage between cousins: allowed unless the parents of either had also been cousins. The laws had a repetitive quality, and Ragnvald found himself nodding along almost as to a song. He thought Einar might not have the patience to memorize long passages of law unless he saw a benefit for himself. He was a quick boy, for whom deed followed thought so immediately that he often appeared not to have considered his actions at all, though he always had a good reason for them when questioned afterward.

When Hrolf finished reciting the laws, he called forth accusers for the most serious crimes. Ragnvald tensed when saw Arnfast and Tofi step forward, accompanied by Jorunn, whose head was covered with a linen shroud. A braid of many colors, from bright gold to deepest brown, hung down from beneath the shroud, long enough to reach past her waist. She must have been a beauty before her wounding.

"King Ragnvald, it is you they want justice from," said Hrolf, a voice that carried across the plain to where Ragnvald walked around the outside of the spectators.

Ragnvald crossed the open field, forcing himself to walk slowly, not to let the weight of eyes upon him hurry him along. He should have known Arnfast's patience would run out eventually. He had wanted more time to see how the news of Herlaug's revenge spread, and Harald's reaction. Harald would probably avoid taking action unless forced into it, as Ragnvald would be forced today. He glared at Arnfast and his family; he had a plan, and it did not involve their bringing suit today. With Heming and Oddi present, he would have to be careful. For his plan to work, it must appear that Hakon had taken the first step into rebellion against Harald.

"Against whom do you bring suit?" Ragnvald asked.

"It is against Herlaug and Geirbjorn, King Hakon's sons," said Arnfast.

"They are not here. What justice can I dispense?"

"You promised vengeance for my family. Where is it?" Arnfast asked. Dark shadows ringed his eyes, which he would not raise to meet Ragnvald's.

"I promised justice," said Ragnvald. "By their actions, Herlaug and Geirbjorn are outlawed from all Norway, and I now declare them outlawed from Sogn and South Maer so all may hear it. They are outlawed for life for the double crime of disobeying their king and breaking a sworn oath." Arnfast could hope for nothing other than that to be done at the *ting* assembly.

"This was already known," said Arnfast. Now he met Ragnvald's gaze, his hand drifting near his sword. "Outlawry is not enough. They must be killed."

"They will be, if they are found on Norse soil. Anyone who gives them aid will be punished. Any man who sees them is honor bound to kill them on sight," said Ragnvald. "Harald has given justice, and it will find these outlaws."

"Is that all you can do for my mother's pain?" Arnfast asked. "Forgive me if I doubt this justice when Heming and Oddbjorn Hakonsson stand by your side? I expect more from my king."

Ragnvald grew angry. His duty was to protect Arnfast and his family, but Arnfast called his kingship into question before the men of two districts. If Heming and Oddi had murdered Arnfast's family to end the feud before it began, the men of Norway would recognize it as the gods' bloody will, necessary to prevent a larger war, and no one would be punished. Arnfast did his family no good today.

Hrolf stepped forward, putting the bulk of his body half between Ragnvald and Arnfast. He laid a heavy hand on Arnfast's shoulder. "If King Heming of North Maer, or Oddbjorn Hakonsson failed to see their brothers, or found their swords too heavy to lift, others would do the deed for them," he said. "King Ragnvald's friendships do not make his justice any less binding."

Ragnvald gave him a nod of thanks.

"I do not accept this," said Arnfast.

"What more do you want that can be demanded at a *ting*?" Hrolf asked.

"Revenge," said Jorunn, the word indistinct, so Arnfast repeated it louder for the crowd.

"She wants revenge for what was done to her. Everyone knows that Hakon's sons do Harald's bidding in Vestfold. That is no true outlawry," said Arnfast.

"You asked for my justice, and I have given what I can," said Ragnvald. "If you are dissatisfied, go to Harald, or to Hakon himself." Under his breath, to Arnfast, he added: "We will speak later. You will be on the wrong side of my justice if you disobey Harald's laws against feud."

"Your justice—" Arnfast began, but stopped when his mother put her hand on his arm. He flushed, bowed his head, and let her lead him away.

Other trials followed, disputes over land and promises of marriage that had not been fulfilled. Ragnvald gave judgments when he was called on, and invited Atli to give his when the case was clear, or Ragnvald did not have a stake in the outcome.

After Hrolf dismissed the trials for the day, Ragnvald returned to his tent. Oddi, looking grim, came to sit by his side. "I have heard myself spoken about more than I have been spoken to today," he said to Ragnvald, "and no word from you to defend me. Do you doubt my loyalty to you?"

"No, I trust you," said Ragnvald quickly.

"You trust me, but you will not tell Arnfast's family that I will uphold your laws. You trust me, but you will not trust me with your justice, your vengeance, or your plans. You trust me, but you do not trust me with your sister."

"I trust you," said Ragnvald. "I trust you to believe me when I say there are things you want no part of—and Arnfast's family is one of those." Svanhild was probably another, but Oddi did not need to hear that. "I am trying to keep you from being drawn into this."

"But—"

"Do you want to choose between me and your father?" Ragnvald asked. "I am trying to prevent you from having to make that choice."

"By keeping me ignorant?" Oddi asked.

"You know all there is to know," said Ragnvald.

"Except your plans."

"Even I barely know those," said Ragnvald with a rueful smile that he hoped would keep Oddi from asking more questions. There was no benefit to Oddi knowing that Ragnvald hoped to lure Hakon into a rebellion that would turn every king loyal to Harald against him. If it succeeded, then he wanted Oddi to feel certain that standing by Ragnvald's side and Harald's was the honorable course.

In the distance, Ragnvald saw Arnfast, Tofi, and Jorunn approaching, two tall, narrow silhouettes flanking her small form. "Now you must go," he said to Oddi. "And trust me."

Oddi gave a short, mirthless laugh, drained his cup in one draught, and retreated to his own tent. Ragnvald arranged his features sternly, taking up the mantle of kingship again. As Arnfast's family approached, he heard snippets of argument. Tofi spoke first. "King Ragnvald, we should not have come like this—my brother grows anxious." He glanced at Arnfast, who looked like a storm about to break.

"Your brother feels guilty and wants to purge his guilt," said Ragnvald.

"I do not," Arnfast protested.

"You do," said Ragnvald. "But the guilt belongs to your *wyrd* or the gods for placing your first sword-stroke. Or to Vemund, who lured us into a trap, he whose bones are now ash."

"I should have understood the trap better," said Arnfast.

"Or I should have," said Ragnvald. "One thing the gods cannot do is turn back time so we may make different choices. The true guilt is upon Herlaug and his cruelty. But you cannot stand against me and Hakon's sons both. You should not have come today."

"You are so mighty now that you will not help my family?" Arnfast cried.

Ragnvald had been considering different plans since returning from Arnfast's home. He could not sanction Arnfast or Tofi bringing vengeance to Herlaug. He could advise Harald that he should no longer keep Hakon as an ally; but, save for this transgression, Hakon was still more help than hindrance to Harald. He controlled vast swaths of Norway's coast, with his fleets and his warriors, his army of sons. His control extended from the northern wastes of Halogaland to Vestfold's coast, and across the ocean to the Faroe Islands. No, Hakon must be pushed to rebel. Ragnvald did not think it would take much, but he must seem to do it on his own.

"I want you to live, live and be my lieutenant again," said Ragnvald slowly. "I promised your mother grandchildren, and I want you to give them to her. Herlaug is your enemy, and he will die for what he did, in time. For now storytellers will carry the tale of your mother's wounding everywhere a ship can reach. Herlaug will be shamed and scorned."

"Not enough," said Jorunn. "When—revenge?"

Ragnvald was willing to force Arnfast to do his bidding, but not his mother, this emissary from the lands of death. "Soon," he said.

"Swear it," said Arnfast. "Or I will unleash such bloody vengeance on Herlaug that people will cringe from hearing about it."

"Like he did your mother?" Ragnvald looked at Jorunn. "Should another woman suffer this too? Should your sons die for your vengeance, and your family be erased? What do you want, my lady?" Only her eyes were visible through the leather mask, a dark blue that glowed in the low sun.

"*Your* vengeance," she said. "Better . . . worse than ours." Her voice made Ragnvald think of something out of a dark tale, a woman who could straddle the worlds of the living and the dead, and carry messages between them. "Tell us. I decide."

Ragnvald had planned only to use Tofi in his plans, and tell him as little as possible, so even under torture he could not reveal Ragnvald's part in this. If Ragnvald loosed an arrow at Hakon and failed, he would forfeit his life and his kingdom. Hakon would demand no less.

"Tofi must travel to Vestfold with a message for Harald: Atli Kolbrandsson, lately of Sogn, plans to ally with Hakon's son Heming to attack King Ragnvald at Naustdal, kill him and his sons, and claim Sogn for himself." Ragnvald turned toward Tofi. "But you will not find Harald—I think he is in Nidaros now. Instead you will fall into Hakon's hands, and with some reluctance, give him the message."

"That is all?" Arnfast asked.

"That is all," said Ragnvald. "Tofi must do exactly as I say, and Hakon and his sons will suffer for it."

"He . . . tortured?" Jorunn asked.

Ragnvald wanted to look away from her but forced himself to meet her gaze. "Perhaps," he admitted.

"No." Jorunn shook her head violently. "No—revenge."

"Mother, I promised you," said Tofi. "I can do this."

"My son—not worth it. Kings kill," Jorunn said to Tofi. She then turned toward Ragnvald. "Tell me. I think yes, then he goes."

It took Ragnvald a moment to understand: Jorunn wanted to

know more about his plan before she agreed to it. "Let me talk to her alone," said Ragnvald. Tofi and Arnfast removed themselves some way into the woods.

"What is plan?" Jorunn asked.

"You cannot repeat it to your sons," said Ragnvald.

"Can hardly talk," said Jorunn, though she was still able to communicate scorn with her garbled voice.

Ragnvald spoke quickly, hoping Jorunn could understand the years of maneuvering among Harald's allies that led Ragnvald to this point. "If Hakon is as close to open war against Harald as I suspect, he will jump at this chance—he will send men to help Atli, and likely to support his son Heming as well. They will think that they can defeat me between them. But Atli is doing nothing of the sort, and so Hakon will reveal himself without putting me in danger. And Harald will never stand for such disobedience."

"What if . . . ?" Jorunn asked.

"If Atli agrees to help Hakon, then I will know that Atli is a traitor as well." And Ragnvald would have a more difficult battle on his hands. He would need to gather Sogn's warriors to him before Hakon could come with his forces.

"No matter—you win," said Jorunn, still scornful.

"You win too—this will destroy Hakon and his family," Ragnvald replied. "His sons will no longer have his protection, and Harald will be able to hunt them down without fearing the larger consequences. You will have brought down the mightiest ruling family in Norway."

"What if Hakon—not traitor?"

"Then he will come and kill Atli for me and I will know that he needs a stronger push. If that happens, I will help Arnfast pursue his vengeance. Hakon will take this bait, though, I am sure of it. He has been waiting for this. If he does not come himself, he will send someone, and no matter what, Harald will punish him."

"I go, not son," said Jorunn.

Again Ragnvald had to pause to work out what she meant: that she should put this false intelligence into Hakon's hands, not her son. He shook his head. "Hakon would never believe that I would send you as a messenger."

"I go to King Harald for justice. I go," she said fiercely. Ragnvald thought it through. Yes, that made more sense. After Arnfast's performance today, everyone would believe it: Jorunn going to Harald for better justice for her injury than Ragnvald could give. Then she could still fall into Hakon's hands and give the false message. If her speech made it hard to understand, Ragnvald could even more easily deny that the message had come from him.

"Not alone," said Ragnvald. "Tofi would go with you."

"Go with. I—captured. He—escape."

"You will die," said Ragnvald.

She pulled off her mask, showing a patchwork of flesh, some healed, some that looked as though it was decaying away. Ragnvald could hardly make sense of all he saw and resolve it into a living face. His eyes pricked with tears.

"I will send Alfrith to you again," he said quickly, turning away. "She may be able to help. You will still hold your grandchildren."

She reached toward him, grasped his chin with fingers that felt like bare bone, and turned him to face her again.

"I *die*," she said. "Then they all die."

28

A SUMMER STORM SWEPT RAGNVALD BACK TO NAUSTDAL FROM the Sogn *ting*, the rain soaking the fields, and making Svanhild feel trapped and restless. She wished she had gone to the *ting* with Ragnvald, but Alfrith had said that Freydis was in some danger from the pox that all the Naustdal children had contracted. Svanhild could not bear the thought of losing another child, so she stayed, though Freydis had a mild case and recovered quickly. She was a strong girl, already beginning to crawl away from Svanhild whenever she turned her back for a moment. Her world was opening up, while Svanhild felt buried here.

She nursed Freydis in the women's room, listening to Hilda and Naustdal's other women talk over the gossip that Alfrith had brought back from the *ting*. Alfrith and Hilda had an odd relationship, and rarely spoke to each other, but they also did not argue. The two women moved like dancers who could predict each other's steps, or perhaps like Solvi's best sailors, who knew how and when to pull on the lines, to turn the sail, to place the whisker-pole, so they need never exchange so much as a glance to move in concert. This morning Alfrith sat tying herbs into bundles with different colors of string, placing them in various baskets.

"What does that one do?" Svanhild asked at random, when the silence began to feel oppressive. She wanted a distraction from the sensation of Freydis's nursing.

"This—it's only thistle, my lady," said Alfrith. "Good for soothing sore stomachs when men have drunk too much."

"Women too?" Svanhild asked.

"Yes, my lady," said Alfrith. She would answer any of Svanhild's questions, but volunteer nothing. Svanhild might have warmed to her, but Alfrith's consciousness of her status in the household, higher than servant, but lower than wife, that or Alfrith's natural coolness, kept most of their interactions awkward. She switched Freydis to her other breast.

"You're still nursing her?" Hilda asked.

Svanhild bit down a tart reply. The ache when Freydis latched on went deeper than her breast, a stab of pain that always brought tears to her eyes. Sometimes when she had nursed Eystein, Solvi came and sat next to her, saying nothing, only warming her body with his, as sustenance flowed to their son. Freydis and Svanhild's life with Ragnvald at Naustdal kept her distracted from her grief except in these moments. She wondered if Solvi considered them divorced now, if he had a new woman. Soon it would be two years since their parting, and he would not have remained celibate.

"I will nurse her at least until she grows a few more teeth," said Svanhild. "I've no desire to be bitten. Let Thora put up with that." Hilda gave her a nod and a slight smile. "You nursed your Rolli for a long time."

"He could not bear to be apart from me," said Hilda, smiling more fully. Svanhild could not fault her feeding the child for so long, for she had never seen a stronger boy, strong in body and will. "I expect he'll come in here soon."

He did, toddling on sturdy legs, wrapped up in the furs Hilda liked to put him in, which made him look like a little bear. He behaved like a bear cub too: curious, destructive, and impossible to dislike. He played in mounds of wool, mixing carded fleece with raw, undoing days of work, and Hilda never scolded him for it.

"What are you going to do when she is weaned?" Hilda asked. This was the first time she had asked outright, though she had alluded to the question before.

"You mean when will I leave?" Svanhild asked, with some heat.

Her mother, Ascrida, still dozed in the corner. Svanhild wished she would wake and say something either foolish or wise to distract all of them.

"Ragnvald will find you a husband," said Hilda mildly.

"Is that what I should want?" Svanhild stood abruptly, jostling Freydis, who began to cry.

"How should I know? He will give you whatever you wish," said Hilda, and her voice became bitter. She plucked a tuft of wool from her yarn to remove an uneven spot.

"I suppose it's too much to ask that I raise my daughter, and spin some wool, and live in peace," said Svanhild.

"You can't spin," said Ascrida, looking up.

Svanhild rolled her eyes. "Of course, now you have something to say," she said. Ascrida blinked slowly in response. "I'm going outside."

"As you wish," said Hilda. "We will be here."

Svanhild carried Freydis out through the kitchen, and out into the misty morning. Droplets of water coated the tiny flowers at her feet. Hilda only voiced the question Svanhild had been asking herself since she recovered from Freydis's birth.

"Do not grow your teeth too quickly, little one," said Svanhild to the top of Freydis's head. Her hair was red gold, soft as silk. It was hard to nurse her standing, and made Svanhild's shoulder grow weary. She settled on one of the damp benches. She would go inside soon. She could stay here in Naustdal for the rest of her life, if all she cared for was marking time until her death.

⁜　⁜　⁜

A FEW WEEKS later Svanhild was nursing Freydis outside again when she saw a line of warriors marching up the hill toward the hall, and quickly adjusted her blanket to cover her bared breast. Ragnvald's scouts had reported sightings of friendly ships yesterday. A flutter of birds announced Harald's coming, followed by the heavy tread of footsteps, and then he appeared, clothed in crimson and gold, his tangled hair falling over his shoulders.

Freydis stirred as Svanhild straightened her back, and began fretting when she lost her latch. Svanhild stroked her cheek until she took hold again, bracing herself for that tug. She waved gingerly to Harald when he was close enough to recognize her, then ducked into the kitchen, sweating as soon as the warmth hit her.

"Harald is here," she said to Alfrith, who tended some bitter-smelling potion over the fire.

"Along with a hundred men, I presume," Alfrith replied without looking up. "It will deplete the stores, and the king"—by this she meant Ragnvald—"will fall further behind with South Maer's taxes." She sighed. "But Hilda has it all in hand, my lady, do not worry." Again, that wordless communication between her and Hilda, and nothing for Svanhild to do. Neither woman saw Svanhild as a permanent part of the household, or a desired one, and saw no need to bring her into their planning.

Svanhild gave Freydis to a nursemaid, and went to the feasting hall to see if Hilda needed any help. She looked frazzled, her hair escaping from a dirty wrap. Perhaps she and Alfrith were not as well coordinated as Svanhild thought.

"Please," said Hilda. "Welcome Harald, get the servants to bring him and his men some ale, and for Frigga's sake, keep them out of here until dinner."

Svanhild marshaled servants and Ragnvald's younger guards to the task. She emerged at the head of a column of servants that mirrored Harald's own, though shorter and less richly attired. Harald and Ragnvald greeted each other, embracing and backslapping fondly. Ragnvald grasped arms gravely with Guthorm. Harald turned and bowed when he saw Svanhild, and gave her a broad smile and an appraising look that swept her from head to feet. She flushed, pleased that he should see her again, grown round and lush now that she had recovered from Freydis's birth.

"Your welcome will be the poorer when you marry off this lady," he said to Ragnvald, accepting a cup of ale from Svanhild's hands. "No disrespect meant to your wife, but with the lady Svanhild here, yours is the only district in Norway that can boast such a storied heroine as its mistress."

"I'm hardly its mistress," said Svanhild.

"Hostess, then," said Harald. His fingers lingered on Svanhild's.

She had hoped to gauge Harald's interest in her, and found her own interest rising as though she had never slaked it with Oddi, then left it banked under the ashes of childbirth.

"Yes," said Ragnvald, giving Svanhild a significant look. Then, with some grandeur, he announced: "We will feast you tonight. Now bathe and be welcome. You will have my chamber, of course, and your men may sleep indoors, if some of them do not mind sharing space with horses."

"Of course not. You have already provided the welcome of a king and a queen. No more is needed," Harald replied, and led his men where Ragnvald bade.

✢ ✢ ✢

RAGNVALD WANTED TO give Harald a proper welcome feast for his first visit to Naustdal, but it was too early in the summer to slaughter any of the livestock, still scrawny from the deprivations of winter. Hilda convinced him that pork preserved in salt and fat, and then stewed with the last of the previous summer's dried fruit, fresh rye bread, and thick slices of cheese and butter, would be rich enough even for the king of all Norway. It tasted good to him, the sweetness and tang of fruit a welcome change from the winter's salt-fish. He watched to see if Harald would enjoy it as well.

Harald had spent the previous summer fighting minor kings in Rogaland. Every time he rooted one out, he said, one of their brothers or sons, or an old rival came to claim the position. Harald accepted oaths from new kings only to find them killed and replaced when he returned. As Harald told him of the past summer of battles, Ragnvald noticed the strain in Harald's expression.

"And there have been rumors that Solvi Hunthiofsson"—Harald glanced at Svanhild—"is mounting an even bigger force against me. They say he is in Sweden advising King Eirik, that the old king does nothing without his advice." Ragnvald looked at Svanhild also. She sat upright, an expression of bemused pride on her face. "My lady, do you know where he would attack?"

Svanhild pressed her lips together before answering. "He wanted to make a base at Tafjord last time—it is easy to defend and hard to

attack. But that failed. And there were many arguments between him
and all of his allies. Rane wanted his land in Vestfold back. He thought
that would be a better place to attack from, closer to Sweden and Eirik's forces."

"Do you have any news from Vestfold?" Ragnvald asked.

"Hakon's younger sons, Herlaug and Geirbjorn, have been there, as
I commanded. And Hakon too—he has sent me a messenger to tell me
that all is well there."

"Even after Hakon's sons disobeyed your law and took cruel vengeance upon Arnfast's mother?" Svanhild asked.

Harald looked uncomfortable. "I have heard that, my lady," he said.
"I had hoped it was only a rumor."

Ragnvald gave Svanhild a quelling look. Better this come from
him. "I have seen the ruin he made of her face," he said quietly. "It was
ill done, and against your justice."

"Then I have a double need to go to Vestfold," said Harald. "My
justice will be upheld, even should it punish my allies."

Guthorm had been sitting quietly, scowling over his meat as he put
fatty bits to the side. Now he glared at Svanhild. "You will need Hakon
as an ally more than ever if the rumors of Solvi Hunthiofsson are true.
Now is not the time to anger Hakon."

Ragnvald felt a moment's panic. Guthorm was right, but Ragnvald's
arrow was already loosed, Tofi and Jorunn flying toward Hakon. "I
have outlawed Herlaug and Geirbjorn from Sogn and South Maer,"
said Ragnvald. "I thought I would not be your true king if I did not
uphold your justice." He glanced at Guthorm, then back at Harald. "If
I acted in error, tell me so."

"Hakon is a king," said Harald uncertainly. "He will understand the
necessity of justice."

Guthorm barked out a short, disbelieving laugh. "So many lies
spoken here tonight. Ragnvald, you cannot possibly believe you have
acted in error, and Harald, you know how little Hakon cares for justice." He glanced at Oddi, smiling thinly. "Do you fear that Hakon's
bastard will report back to him? Is that why both of you dissemble?"

Oddi's face grew troubled. "I have sworn oaths of brotherhood with my friend Ragnvald, and loyalty to my king Harald. Do not doubt me."

"King Hakon will not forgive you outlawing his sons," said Guthorm to Ragnvald, and then turned to Harald, "and you cannot have him as an enemy. Justice must bow to that."

"Who is king of Norway then?" Harald asked his uncle. "Is it me or Hakon? I should have killed Heming when he murdered my friend Thorbrand."

"That is past and done with," said Guthorm. "Heming is the least of your problems now."

In that, at least, Ragnvald could agree. And he agreed that Hakon was still Harald's most powerful ally—powerful enough to make Harald into the puppet he feared to be. If Hakon were gone, Harald could install Heming as king of Halogaland—a weaker king, who would happily put all of his forces at Harald's disposal. He prayed to Odin that Jorunn would find her mark.

"What should I do, then?" Harald asked Guthorm angrily.

"Outlaw Herlaug and Geirbjorn Hakonsson. Justice requires it. But let them leave peaceably, and tell Hakon they may return in time," said Guthorm.

"Ragnvald?" Harald asked.

Ragnvald met Guthorm's eyes briefly. Harald had never put his counsel up against Guthorm's quite so nakedly, and Ragnvald thought it evidence of his desperation. "Your uncle is right," he said.

"What of this Arnfast?" Harald asked. "How far will he go for his revenge?"

"I can delay him," said Ragnvald. He met Harald's eyes, and hoped Harald read a little of what he meant but could not say before Oddi: Arnfast was welcome to Herlaug and Geirbjorn as soon as Harald no longer needed Hakon as an ally, which would be possible as soon as Solvi was defeated.

"Very well," said Harald. "Tell me of Naustdal. Have you had any trouble?"

Ragnvald told him of a peaceful year—save for Herlaug's revenge—and of how he arranged his defenses. Harald gave rapt attention to

Ragnvald's description of guard placements, the use of small boats, signal fires, and smoke signals. He had never held a district against raiders—his experience was in conquest. "The scouts work in pairs," said Ragnvald. "They rotate among positions. Heming, Oddi, and I, and some of the other captains, take regular watches so the men know we are willing to share in the boredom and danger. None are chosen from farms that cannot spare a man or two."

"And it works well?" Harald asked as he chewed a mouthful of meat.

"I set Oddi to test it," Ragnvald told him. "With no warning. Heming's forces were alerted and sailed down Geiranger Fjord to confront him."

"Heming boarded my ship and would have killed me if Ragnvald hadn't been there to tell him it was only a drill," said Oddi dryly. It had not been as bad as that, but Oddi took every opportunity to distance himself from his brothers, especially since Herlaug and Geirbjorn's crime.

"Heming has shared defense of Maer admirably," said Ragnvald. "I worried, but he has—he is better out from under his father's shadow, as usual."

"That is good to know," said Harald. "I came here to ask you to join me in battle this summer. This confrontation with Solvi is inevitable, and I want you by my side."

"Let us speak on it later," said Ragnvald. "Where does your progress take you next? Will you visit my friend Atli Mjove in Sogn?"

"Do you want me to check up on him for you?" Harald asked. "I say he is too lazy to make the kind of trouble you fear, but I will make certain."

Lazy was not the word Ragnvald would have chosen, though he supposed Atli's trickster nature was a way of getting others to do what he wanted, to spare himself the trouble. "Do not depart too quickly," he said. "You should see Naustdal. All the clearings where we fought two summers ago are peaceful now."

"And Vemund's hall?" Harald asked. "Do I sit now where he sat once?" Ragnvald had been uneasy returning to that burned patch of land, where white grubs in the soil could easily be mistaken for shards of bone.

"It is a garden now," said Svanhild, filling Ragnvald's silence. "It grows healing herbs." Alfrith had done some magic to put any lingering spirits to rest, and planted the garden. Tonight she waited upon tables with the servants, and would continue until the guests had eaten their fill.

"Do you know healing magic?" Harald asked Svanhild warmly. "My mother is a great healer."

"So I have heard," said Svanhild. "Her skills are renowned. I can sew up a cut and set a bone, but little beyond that." She smiled back at Harald.

"Perhaps you can learn from her someday," said Harald. His concerns seemed to prevent him continuing his flirtation with her further that night. He guided the conversation back to Ragnvald's defensive tactics at Maer, and again listed kings and jarls from whom he had extracted oaths over the past year. He commanded the loyalty of leaders over the full stretch of Norway's coast, though near the mountains, some upland kings and jarls still thought themselves independent. The drinking did not continue very late into the night, for Harald's demeanor forbade celebration. Before he left the table to sleep for the night, he asked Ragnvald to assure him they would have time to speak in private the next day.

✝ ✝ ✝

THE FOLLOWING MORNING, Ragnvald found Harald already awake and eating his breakfast porridge outside, alone except for a few guards standing well back. The dew was strung like jewels along the grass in the shade, though already dry where the sun had touched. When Ragnvald sat next to him, he pushed away his bowl and spoon, and sat upon his hands, looking more like a boy than a king.

"Ragnvald, my friend, I need you by my side again." Harald looked off into the woods rising behind the hall, where pale green buds shadowed the bare underbrush. "Marry your sister to me, leave Oddi in charge of South Maer, and come with me to Vestfold."

Ragnvald could not help but laugh at the list of demands; Harald spoke his desires like a child who had never been denied.

"What?" Harald asked. "Why do you laugh? I am your king and your friend—why won't you join me?"

"Let us talk of them one at a time," said Ragnvald. "Beginning with the easiest: I think Svanhild would agree to marriage. She has not been happy in my household."

"Why not?" Harald asked.

"She likes adventure—compared to sailing with Solvi, sitting in the women's chamber is poor entertainment."

"Don't you miss adventure as well?" Harald asked.

"Not as much as she," said Ragnvald.

"But a little," said Harald, pouncing on the opening. "Solvi will attack this summer, I am sure of it. I need you with me."

"We don't know where he will attack." Ragnvald had only a year here in Naustdal, free from battles, taking time to raise his sons and make Alfrith pregnant. Even that had been marred by Herlaug's vengeance upon Arnfast's family.

"I need you, Ragnvald. I hear rumors of Solvi gathering allies in Sweden and Iceland. Even my uncle won't admit how easily all this can fall back into fighting and chaos." He gestured at the wooded hill that rose before them, and Ragnvald imagined the gold of his touch spreading, like sunlight on water, to encompass all of Norway.

"That is why someone must guard Maer for you," said Ragnvald.

"Heming and Oddi Hakonsson can do it," Harald countered.

"With Oddi in Naustdal and Atli in Sogn, you would leave me king of nothing at all," said Ragnvald. He spoke more bitterly than he meant to.

"You are still king of Sogn," said Harald.

"In name only," said Ragnvald.

"I thought you were my friend." Harald sounded truly confused. "If I am king of all Norway, there is nothing I cannot give you. If I am not, I can do nothing for you at all."

Ragnvald wanted to protest that Sogn was his by right, by vote, by blood, but Harald could easily respond that none of that would have come without him by Ragnvald's side, and they would both be correct.

"When have I served you ill?" Harald asked, seeing some advantage in Ragnvald's hesitation. "Do you doubt my generosity? I need you. I will reward you, of course." With some other land, on which

Ragnvald would need to build yet another hall, and win over a new set of subjects.

"I asked for time," said Ragnvald. "And now I tell you that we do not know where Solvi will attack. It is better to keep guard where we can—you in Vestfold, I here. I promise you this: I will come to your side if you have need of me. Can you truly tell me it would be better for me to abandon Maer and Sogn if Solvi comes this way?"

"My uncle said you were still angry with me over those men in Tafjord," said Harald. Ragnvald sighed. His anger over those deaths was like banked coals, not hot like his anger at Herlaug's more recent crime. Those men had not been his subjects. "I thought that was ill done. I still do. But that is not the question now—your question should be where I can do your kingdom the most good, and the answer is here. You should ask your uncle about that as well."

"You are wise," said Harald. He gave Ragnvald a tired grin. "At least I will be able to carry your sister away from here."

"Take her to Sogn first," said Ragnvald. "Remind Atli who is king there."

Harald nodded. "And then I will bring Svanhild to my new town of Tonsberg—it is well protected, only a day's sail from my Vestfold halls. From there I will see what happens in my old district—if as many mass against me as I fear, I think my fighting will be from there for the next few years."

"I will come when you need me," Ragnvald promised again.

Harald smiled and clasped his forearm, then pulled Ragnvald in for an embrace. "This gives me great joy. I have not liked warring without you this past year. Together, we will defeat all of our enemies."

29

SVANHILD WAS STILL RUBBING SLEEP FROM HER EYES WHEN Ragnvald and Harald came into the kitchen. They both greeted her, exchanged a look, and then Harald left Ragnvald alone with her. He drew Svanhild outdoors, and away from the men who slept outside, in case they should overhear.

"Harald still wants to marry you," he said. "Do you want to?"

Svanhild sat down abruptly on the bench. She had expected this, of course, at some point in the future. In her vague imaginings, it came after she had heard of Solvi's death, or his taking another woman. And she had wished, foolishly, for Harald to be the one to ask her, not to send the question through Ragnvald, even though that was the proper way to do things.

"Do you want me to?" she asked. "I wondered. After the battle at Solskel, it seemed you and Harald were not as close."

"I did not want to fight his battles at the expense of my own family," said Ragnvald stiffly.

"And you were angry with him for how he treated those men of Heming's," Svanhild added. He had come to her looking as though his insides had been scooped out. "Now you would marry me to a man like that?"

"You have practice being married to a man like that," said Ragnvald.

He had never thrown Solvi at her in that way before. Svanhild rose to her feet in anger. She would never apologize for choosing Solvi.

Even with all the pain, she would do it again. Harald was not so different from Solvi—that is what Ragnvald seemed to be saying. The violence that Solvi and his followers visited upon their enemies and the targets of their raids had rarely troubled Svanhild. A sea king brought death and cruelty in his ship and traded them for treasure won. Ragnvald's words made her feel soiled, though, as if her role was to absorb the ugliness that he had turned away from.

"Sit, Svanhild," said Ragnvald. "I should not have said that. Harald is a good match. He is king of all Norway. Who would not want a marriage alliance with a man like that?"

"So I should do with my body what you will not?" Svanhild asked. She paced away from him. "You want me to spread my legs for him and risk my life in childbirth because you will no longer bloody your sword for him?"

"I'm asking you what you want," said Ragnvald. "You seem unhappy here."

"You want me gone too," said Svanhild angrily. "Just like Hilda." She felt as though she could see Solvi here, like a ghost strong enough to appear in sunlight, as she made this decision.

"You plague her," said Ragnvald. "I do not wish you gone—but Harald's wives are spared much of the pain of other women. I would be pleased if you were among them."

"The dowry will be expensive," she said with a small, helpless laugh. She looked down at him. His face had settled into forbidding lines from years of rarely smiling. He was bound to Harald by his dreams, his *wyrd*, his oaths, and he wanted Svanhild to share that burden. She gave him a half smile, and hit him on the arm. "Oddi would have been cheaper."

"If you are Harald's wife, you cannot take a lover," said Ragnvald. "You cannot. If you wish to be married to Oddi, that can be made to happen. I think you know that. And I know you do not dislike each other."

And Oddi would let her take a lover—but he deserved better than that. "Oddi and I have run out of things to say. If there was ever much. Like you and Hilda, perhaps."

"Hilda and I speak little because we understand each other. Anyway,

I had not thought speaking to be the main part of it," said Ragnvald, voice teasing. "As long as you like the look of Harald . . ."

"And who could not?" Svanhild answered recklessly. Solvi was not here to stop her. "I will go, if that is your wish. I wonder, though, if my marrying Harald will give you more trouble than it avoids."

"I don't know," said Ragnvald. "It may be trading one kind of worry for another. But I would like to see you settled with a husband I will never do battle against."

"I will go with him to Sogn for you," said Svanhild. "I will see if I like him still, and if he likes me." Her, her past, and her daughter. He must accommodate all three, or she would not give up her place in Ragnvald's household. Harald's wives were the first women of Norway, with near infinite wealth and freedom, especially after Harald tired of them or made them pregnant. She could be useful to Ragnvald and please herself. "You may tell him that—I will consider marriage but I must decide."

✛　✛　✛

HARALD REMAINED IN Naustdal for a few more weeks, and then sent one of his captains to Tafjord to see how Heming ruled his portion of Maer. Harald would find no fault; Heming had followed Ragnvald's direction, both in defense and organizing North Maer's tax collection. It might fall apart when Ragnvald returned to Sogn, or if Maer had a bad harvest, but for now, Heming and Ragnvald had imposed order on Maer that had been missing since before Solvi's father, Hunthiof, was king.

Harald made no move to speak with Svanhild alone while he remained at Naustdal, only complimented her extravagantly in public, and gave her some looks that heated her blood, and made it easier to brush aside thoughts of Solvi.

When she departed with Harald's convoy Svanhild left her daughter at Naustdal. She would take Thora's milk if Svanhild was not there, and she was strong and could be weaned early if necessary. Svanhild's breasts ached after a day without nursing, but she knew that would pass, and otherwise, she craved this distance. She did not feel bound to Freydis as she had to Eystein, when it seemed his fragile body was an extension of her own, and his every hurt pained her. Ragnvald's household could take in her daughter as a sister to all of his sons. Alfrith would bear him another son—she had the magic to assure it—and Ragnvald would need foster-daughters to make alliances.

The sound of the sail fluttering and then catching the wind filled Svanhild with her old, familiar longing for motion, for shore slipping by, for days consumed by the tasks of travel. Whenever she and Solvi spent too long in one court or another, this craving welled up in her—the desire to return to the freedom of the sea.

She looked up to where Harald stood in the prow of the ship, talking with one of his captains. He looked as tall and strong as he had last year coming from the bathhouse in Nidaros; his beauty took her breath away and made her face flush when she looked at him. Sometimes she felt she could only steal glances at him—looking too long was like looking into a sun that would not burn her eyes, but set her face aflame and make her foolish. Foolish enough to travel with him now, knowing that she would end the journey in his bed, tied to him by marriage. He wanted it, and Ragnvald wanted it. If she went to his bed but did not consent to be his wife, she would insult them both.

"I heard your brother could not be beaten in an oar race," he called out to Svanhild. "Do you think I could run the oars?"

Svanhild weighed her answer, and opted for honesty. "You are too broad in the shoulder, my king. I do not think my brother could do it now either. He was much slighter then." If Harald replied as befit a man, rather than a boy, she might marry him. If he let his pride dictate his response, she would not. Solvi could always laugh at himself.

"I'm sure you're right," said Harald. "I was not born for shipboard tricks of agility. But I can climb the mast, as any man aboard must."

"Any woman too," said Svanhild, giving him a smile. His answer had pleased her.

"Can you?" Harald asked with an incredulous grin.

"With a stout leather thong, and the right shoes," said Svanhild. She had not done it in more than a year. Solvi had taught her—it was more a trick of balance and timing than strength, letting the leather and the weight of her body hold her.

"Bring me the climbing strap," Harald commanded. "I would see this."

"Nephew, is this seemly?" asked Guthorm. "She is your ally's sister, not a traveling acrobat."

"The lady Svanhild must do what she pleases," said Harald. "I will think no less of her if she does not wish to display herself." His eyes looked a challenge at her that belied his words. He would think less of her, and she would think less of herself.

"It has been a while," she said. "And I was wearing britches when I did it before."

"Do you need britches this time?" Harald asked, still holding her gaze.

"Yes," said Svanhild. "If one of your men can loan me a pair—and a tunic, I will climb."

These were found, and pressed upon her—and did not even smell too foul. She changed in her small tent at the base of the mast, and found the trousers fit well enough also, though she had to roll them up a few times at the ankle. The man whom they belonged to must be a slender fellow. His shirt fit her less well, pulling under her arms, and falling far enough over her thighs that she might as well have put on a dress again. She made a hole with her knife and ripped off the extra fabric. If the man minded, he could ask his king for another.

She flung open her tent and strode out onto the deck. The wind filled the sail, though not tightly, and the ship cut through the waves as smoothly as a man might walk on land. She could not hope for a better time to make this climb.

Harald handed her the leather thong she would use to climb the mast. She inspected it; the soft, flexible leather had just enough give, and little slip. She had already roughed the soles of her shoes against a piece of rope and laced them tightly, for she did not have the calluses to go barefoot anymore.

She walked over to the mast and realized the wood was newly sanded, with none of the roughness, the catches and splinters, that might help a climber when it grew older and weathered. Nothing to be done, though; her pride required success, and she thought it an-

other test for Harald. If he could accept her when she had done this—
for she did not plan to fail—she might accept him as her husband.

Her heart beat quickly and her palms sweat. She wiped them off on
her trousers, put the strap around the mast, and put her hands through
the loops at the ends. She set one foot against the mast and leaned back
against the leather. She then set another, so she was suspended a few
feet off the ground. The position stretched the muscles in her back
pleasantly. She had spent too long hunched forward over her mending
in Naustdal.

The next part was the hardest: giving herself a little slack and
throwing the thong a hand's breadth or two up the mast, then stepping a bit higher. When she made the first step, a smattering of applause greeted her, growing louder when she fell into a rhythm,
throw, step, step, lean back. Her wrists ached where the loops of
leather dug into them. With each throw, she gained a moment of release from the tension, and her hands flooded with sensation, which
the bite of the leather cut off again. She concentrated only on the
climb, not on the applause that quieted as she gained more height.
Farther up, the sway of the mast grew more pronounced, until she
had to time each throw to the apex of the motion. Only when she
reached the yard did she glance down at the figures on the deck,
made small by her height. She was even with the fjord's cliff walls
now. A bird flew by below her. Ahead, a cloud bank hid the open sea
and barrier islands from view.

"Come down, Svanhild," she heard Harald say from below, finally.
The sky had grown darker as she tarried here. She took one last glance
around, held the leather in her fists to spare her wrists for a moment,
and then leaned back against it. From here she could slide, and she did,
in great swoops, letting herself fall and then catching herself again,
until, in no time at all, she stood on the deck again, giddy with excitement. The first time she had climbed the mast all the way to the top
had been after several false starts, propelled by her growing anger at
Solvi—that he could do it, boys of ten could do it, and she could not.
Afterward, she threw her arms around him and kissed him all over his
face while his men looked on and laughed, and Tryggulf jested that if

he knew teaching a woman to climb a mast was the way under her skirt, he would have tried it long ago.

Svanhild looked around at her audience, meeting Guthorm's disapproving gaze before she saw Harald's broad grin.

"I believe you're faster than me," he said happily.

"It helps to be small," said Svanhild.

"Give this woman some ale, for she must be thirsty from her work," Harald called out. "And cheer her again, for she has a man's strength and skill. Svanhild Sea Queen."

Svanhild's grin faded—Solvi had called her his sea queen too. She recovered in time to smile at Harald when he brought her a leather cup of ale, and she drank it greedily.

"I want you to tell me how you learned that," said Harald.

"I have spent several years shipboard," said Svanhild lightly. "There is little I can't do here."

"Sea Queen indeed. Should I give you a ship and a crew so you can fight my sea battles for me?"

His tone was light and jesting, but Svanhild answered him seriously. "Yes," she said, "I think you should."

+ + +

THE SHIPS CONTINUED on to the south through blustery weather: short, violent squalls that ended as quickly as they began. Svanhild sat wrapped in an oiled blanket near the steering oar, where Harald's pilot kept his heading. He was a young man named Falki, so called because his eyesight was keen as a falcon's. Svanhild did not think much of his steering, though, for he had lost a few good winds and had almost allowed the ship to turn to its beam end when a freak gust hit it.

The next time he grew restless, and asked for another sailor to hold the oar so he could stretch his legs, Svanhild offered to do it. The weather had calmed in the late afternoon, so Falki allowed it, giving her an indulgent smile. When he left, she ordered some adjustments made to the sail and her heading, and opened up a wide gap between Harald's leading ship and the ones following.

"I think I made it go too fast," she said with a self-deprecating smile when Falki returned. "How do you keep it from getting too far ahead of the others?"

Perhaps she had not kept the irony from her question, for Falki looked at her for a moment, then laughed. "Don't treat me like a fool, my lady. How did you do it?"

She told him, and pointed out the shadow on the water, which meant the breeze would shift again soon, and what she would do to adjust for it. Falki looked around the ship. No one else paid them any mind, except the men whom Svanhild had asked to move the sail. They waited to see if Falki would scold them for following her suggestions.

"My father was a fisherman," he said. "I know how to sail."

"A dragon ship is different. It has more sail than a fishing boat, and it's longer, so it turns less easily, though it also flexes more over the waves," said Svanhild. She shrugged slightly. "At least a fishing boat will have taught you to come about quickly."

"Yes." Falki gave her a small smile. "It may be better training than a merchant *knarr*."

"I think so." Svanhild rewarded him with a more genuine smile of her own. "Can I show you more?"

Falki nodded, and Svanhild sat down by him. She put enough distance between them so no one could accuse her of flirting, she hoped, and talked with him about wind and weather, and how the ship moved across the water.

That night Harald's convoy beached on a low barrier island, covered with green grass that took on a bluish tinge as the sun lowered. After Harald and his men had eaten their fill of stewed dried fish, he beckoned Svanhild to sit by his side at the fire. She had watched him with his men these past days, seeing him differently now that she had emerged from the cloud of sadness that hung over her in Nidaros. Then, grief had been a just-healed wound, painful when she put pressure on it, and she could not seem to keep from testing it with thoughts of Eystein and Solvi. She could find that pain now if she wanted, but she had to dig deeper.

Harald was more pleasant to think of. He seemed as though he had been born a king. He commanded everyone around him with no thought that an order might ever be ignored. But he also watched and listened, took advice and weighed it against his own desires, almost as Solvi had with his crew. Harald was a better king than Ragnvald believed. He saw Harald as a symbol, a rallying point, god-blessed even, with luck that outshone his brilliance. Svanhild had thought even worse of Harald when she was at Solvi's side: a pawn for his uncle, a greedy conqueror who cloaked his greed in ideals of safety and kingship. Now she saw that Harald might be young and impulsive, but he took care as a king, approached his work with cleverness and joy. She could see a man worth marrying here, even if she had to be one of many wives. Marriage to Solvi had consumed her, body and spirit, and torn her in two when it ended, but she could remain herself in a marriage with Harald.

Sitting close to him, his size dwarfed hers. She felt like a little fjord pony next to one of the elegant Moorish horses she had seen caparisoned for war in Spain. That thought brought a wave of longing for Solvi so intense that her throat ached, followed, as always, by anger. She put him from her mind yet again and looked up at Harald. His eyes shone down at her, as though he beheld something precious.

"You and I are the same age," he said. "And we have both lived lives worthy of songs. I know your brother told you that I wished to marry you—that I wanted it before I had even met you, when I heard of your deeds and your beauty. I have waited a long time for you. Do not make me wait longer. Let us marry in Sogn. I will send a messenger to your brother, so all your family can meet us there."

"You are asking me?" Svanhild asked, teasing him. "Should you not make this arrangement with Ragnvald?"

"He has given his blessing, as you well know," said Harald, laughing. "Ragnvald has discussed every eventuality and negotiated your dowry down to the smallest sliver of gold. Did you think he would do any less? He said that I should ask you, and I am. If you do not wish it, I will not ask again. But what could be better? Your daughter will have every advantage, as though she were my own, and your sons will be kings in Norway. As my wife, you may travel with me, or you may return to Naustdal and live with Ragnvald and his family. Many of my wives remain with their families, and I visit them."

Any woman should want that, as Ragnvald had said: all the benefits of marriage and none of the inconveniences. She need only walk the path set out for her.

"That was impressive," he added, filling the silence she left. "When you climbed the mast. And now you give my pilot lessons." Svanhild looked up at him surprised—she did not think he had noticed, absorbed in talk of his summer battles with his uncle. He raised his eyebrows. "You must frighten other men."

Svanhild shrugged. "I have not worried enough about the opinions of other men to care," she said. In truth, she had been protected by the reach of Solvi's power since she emerged from girlhood.

"Whose opinions do you care about?" Harald asked.

"My brother's," said Svanhild. "And I know what he would say."

"Is there no one else's? Your mother's?"

"Her mind is gone," said Svanhild. An image of Vigdis flashed into Svanhild's mind. Svanhild did not want her congratulations on snaring Harald, nor her sneers about Solvi. She would likely face both in Sogn.

"Whose do you value?" Svanhild asked.

"Your brother's," said Harald promptly. "And my uncle's, for it is he who raised me, who set me on this path." He bent his head down to her. "Though I am growing beyond him," he added quietly. "The men who I command—I care about their opinions, and still more that of kings and jarls who will or will not swear to me. And I care about the gods' opinions—I know they see what I do."

He was very close to her now, his breath warming her cheek, his beard tugging at the loose hairs at her temple. He smelled like earth and leather, and fresh sweat.

"From my childhood, I had no one I could depend upon save Ragnvald," she said. "So I learned to depend on no one else." A lie, for she had depended on Solvi too much. "I fear dependence, but it is a woman's lot."

"Do not fear it," said Harald. "You can stand on your own, as well as any man—but no woman was meant to be alone. What can I say to convince you, Svanhild?"

Should she ask, then, to be the first of his wives, to exact concessions for her hand? Should she ask for ships and warriors so she might fight his battles for him? She could read wind and waves, but she could not wield a sword. The thought of making demands made her uneasy; she did not want to measure the exact depth of his interest in her.

"I will give you an answer in the morning," she said.

"I will not sleep then."

"Neither will I," said Svanhild. She turned her face to his and touched their lips together. He held back. She put her hand on his thigh, hard and ridged with muscle. "Convince me tonight that I would be pleased in your bed."

"Is this how I prove my worth?" Harald asked.

"You have proven it in many ways," said Svanhild. "Tonight is . . ." She bit his lip instead of finishing, and he picked her up as easily as she might pick up a sack of wool, light and springy. She knew, as he must when he carried her from the circle of light and to his fur-lined tent, that she had already accepted him, already made her answer known to his men, his skald, to the whole of Norway. One day soon word would reach Solvi that she had done this.

For now, though, she narrowed her focus to the golden skin under her fingers. When they entered his tent, and he laid her down upon his furs, he showed his willingness to please her. She had things to teach him too, which seemed to surprise him, tricks she had learned from the whisperings of courtesans in a dozen kingdoms, and tried in Solvi's bed. She liked Harald, and he liked her—marriages had been made on far worse.

In the end they did sleep, Svanhild nestled in the circle of his arms. He woke before her, and tickled her awake with his beard in her ear. One of the long matted locks of his hair lay over her shoulder like the tail of a cat.

"So will you be my wife?" Harald asked.

"Should I not be the one to worry about that, having taken you to bed with no promises?" Svanhild asked, snuggling into his warmth. The sound of the ocean lapping on rocks had lulled her to sleep. Now it pushed memories upon her that she did not want to face.

"Do not toy with me, Svanhild," said Harald.

Solvi had said the same thing to her when Svanhild could not make up her mind whether to be a true wife to him or not. She had power over Solvi then, though not enough, and she had even less now over Harald.

"Yes," she said. "Send a messenger to my brother and bid him meet us at Sogn for the betrothal and marriage. I will be your bride."

He kissed her neck and ran his fingers up her thigh, softly bringing her pleasure through her soreness, until she wanted him again. It was pleasant, to be desired by this beautiful giant, and when they tired of each other, she would have wealth, and every freedom except taking another man to her bed.

30

HARALD SENT A SHIP BACK TO NAUSTDAL BEFORE THE CONVOY
entered Sogn Fjord, bidding the messenger send word to Tafjord as
well: all free men and women should come to Sogn and see him marry
Svanhild. When they reached Sogn, Svanhild thought the halls and
outbuildings looked far more permanent and settled than the brand-
new hall at Naustdal. They stood on the sacred ground where her father's hall burned when she was a girl. She had grazed sheep where a
high-roofed drinking hall now stood, its crossbeams decorated with
carved wolves' heads.

Vigdis was part of Atli's formal welcome to Sogn, standing behind
two slim young men who wore Atli's features, and his wife. Atli conducted them to outdoor tables where servants brought cool ale and
bread. Atli sat at the table with his wife and sons, and made room for
Harald, Guthorm, and Svanhild herself, while Vigdis retreated, leaving Svanhild on edge. She had hoped to get their confrontation over
and done with.

The farm certainly looked well cared for. Fat sheep grazed upon
the hills. The only cows she saw were a mother and its calf born out
of season, perhaps too fragile to be risked up at the shieling. Svanhild
resolved to ask Atli to take her there if there was time. She had passed
many summer nights in the mountain field above Ardal, tending the
cows and overseeing the cheese making. At times it had been a refuge
from her mother and Vigdis's fighting at home.

"You know this land well, do you not?" Atli's wife asked. Her name was Bertha, and she had the fiery red hair that Svanhild had seen on those of mixed Irish and Norse birth in Dublin, salted with strands of silver.

"Yes," said Svanhild. "I grew up at Ardal. I hope to visit my old home while I am here."

"A Thorkell manages Ardal now, I think," said Bertha.

Svanhild experienced a chill on hearing his name that was almost pleasurable. Yes, Thorkell. He would see that she had married Harald and know that he had been foolish to aim as high as she. He could not hurt her now.

"I remember him," she said. She glanced at Harald. "He tried to marry me."

"He shall not do that now," said Harald. "Atli, the feast you have planned for us will be a betrothal feast, for I am to wed Svanhild, Ragnvald's sister, as soon as he and his family arrive." All gave their congratulations, while Atli's sons gave Svanhild an appraising look, measuring the woman who could capture a king. She did not like the dismissive glance from the elder one. She had more value to Harald than simply being Ragnvald's sister.

✢ ✢ ✢

"YOU HAVE NO words for me besides a greeting?" Svanhild asked Vigdis the next morning. Vigdis had brought her spindle outside, and sat with some of the women servants, spinning fine singles from oatmeal-colored wool.

"Should I have?" Vigdis asked.

"Yes," said Svanhild. "You are still my stepmother." And best situated to tell Svanhild what was happening at Sogn, so she could report back to Ragnvald. It seemed to Svanhild as though Atli did obey his oath—he had welcomed Harald in Ragnvald's name, never called himself king—but Ragnvald could not have enough reassurance on that point.

"And mother to your nephew, and concubine to your husband's steward. Yet you will be wife to the high king, and next to that I am lowly indeed," said Vigdis.

"Very well," said Svanhild. "If you wish to hide behind our difference in rank, so be it." Alfrith had done the same, and Svanhild did not have the power to demand more of her. "Should I tell my husband-to-be how you served me when last we were in Sogn together, how you bid Olaf to tie me up so I could not ruin your plans against my brother? I am not sure what parts of the story he knows, but he would surely find them interesting. He likes me well."

"He does—now," said Vigdis. "He has many wives."

"Here he only has me," said Svanhild, knowing she should not show that she felt the sting from Vigdis's words even a little.

"Many wives, but no queen," Vigdis replied. "I cannot imagine that the girl who played at battles with the boys does not dream of ruling by his side." Her smile turned malicious.

"You do not think I could make myself his queen?" Svanhild asked. She should not rise to the bait, but Vigdis set her hooks well.

"I think you should try," said Vigdis. "Though I'm not sure you ever were good enough at the womanly arts—perhaps you have learned better in Solvi's bed. A queen must always know her king's secrets, and others besides." Vigdis could not have known how close those words cut to the bone, far worse than her comments about Harald.

"You would be better at it than I," Svanhild said, her voice quavering. "What harm did I ever do you, Vigdis? I needed a mother. If you feel I have taken your place—"

"What place is that?" Vigdis asked. She leaned in close. "Is it your place in Harald's bed or in Ragnvald's that I should envy? The rumors from Maer have said that you are uncommonly close, and that he loves you better than his wife."

Svanhild slapped Vigdis hard across the face. "You are the one who took your own stepson to your bed," she said so all could hear. "Well, as you said, I am above you in rank. You have not even the protection of a marriage for when you lose your beauty. I should not stoop to argue with you."

Vigdis held her hand to her reddening cheek. Svanhild had a firm slap that she had learned from Solvi's man Snorri, who showed her how to make every blow count.

Svanhild sighed. "I did not come here to fight you," she said, now ashamed. When Atli tired of Vigdis, she would have no support except a family she seemed not to like, who lived high in the Keel Mountains. She looked at the servants who had been watching the exchange. They now bent back to their spinning, suddenly unable to perform so practiced a motion without giving it their full concentration. "You were as much a mother to me as my own, I suppose. And if you were sometimes more cruel, you were also less indifferent. If you ever need my help, wherever I am, I will grant it."

Vigdis gave her an ironic bow. "Your nobility shines through, my lady," she said.

Svanhild thought of Vigdis's words later that night as she tried to sleep. This bond with Harald felt fragile, and not in the way her early marriage with Solvi had. Vigdis was right to say she needed to push Harald to give her some power, something to make her important to him even after the initial blush of attraction had worn off.

✤ ✤ ✤

THE NEXT DAY Bertha showed Svanhild the stores of fabric that she could offer for her wedding dress. Svanhild had spent the night next to her, for she felt less comfortable sharing Harald's bed this close to her childhood home, and with Vigdis's knowing gaze to meet the next morning. Vigdis walked toward them as Bertha laid out the bright bolts of cloth on the grass so Svanhild could see them in the sunlight.

"You are not needed here," said Bertha to Vigdis when she took a tentative step toward Svanhild. "I am sure one of the servants needs your help." Vigdis shrank away, her face blank, except for a small pinching of her lips.

At dinner that night, when Vigdis passed by, carrying food to the servants' tables, Svanhild called out, "Come, stepmother." Vigdis flinched at the title, and Svanhild pressed quickly on. "I would like your company. Sit by me."

Vigdis sat down and one of Harald's captains made a crude joke about the two women, but Svanhild ignored him. "I taste your work in the meat tonight—sweet with spring onions. You always knew where to find them growing wild. Do you ever go back to Ardal?"

Vigdis nodded. She looked discomfited by Svanhild's kindness. "Yes. Your brother set Thorkell up to run Ardal after Harald built him this new hall."

"Has he been a good neighbor?" Svanhild asked. "I remember he had a penchant for stealing cows."

Vigdis gave a low laugh. "I do not know what Ragnvald threatened him with, but I know he gave an oath that he would never raid again."

"His manhood, probably," said Harald, laughing.

Atli held up a rough glass bottle full of clear liquid. "I brought this spirit from Dublin. The Irish make it there—they call it *uisge-beatha*."

Svanhild accepted a small amount. She knew its potency enough to take very small sips. She had seen men die from drinking it like ale. Even watered, it could make a big man roaring drunk in a single glass.

"Do you like it?" Svanhild asked Vigdis. While even unhappiness could not take Vigdis's beauty from her, nor the smugness that seemed carved into the very bones of her face, she was clearly tired and unhappy tonight.

"I have liked it in the past," said Vigdis. "It removes all cares and fears. Sometimes, though, I fear I will get lost in it. You know the proverb: a drunken woman is a shame to herself and her family."

Svanhild took a small sip and let it burn away her own cares and fears. She knew the danger, and she was bold enough without the *uisge* that tasted of earth and fire. "I've seen it kill a man," said Svanhild. "They grow insensible, and do not wake, yet small Irish men can drink it in volumes our tall warriors cannot."

Vigdis took another, a more reckless, mouthful, then wiped her bottom lip with an elegant finger.

"What would you have me do for you, if I had the power?" Svanhild asked her quietly. "If I asked, Harald would marry you to a rich jarl—as his first wife."

"Would Harald force my lord Atli to divorce his wife and marry me instead?" Vigdis asked.

Svanhild looked at Bertha, the wife of Atli's youth, a handsome woman past her childbearing years, whose face had settled into kind lines. Atli was telling a story, and Bertha laughed, looking at him with love. "I would not ask that," said Svanhild. "I could press him to marry you as well, though. Then you and your children by him would inherit."

"I have had enough of being a second wife," said Vigdis.

"Is it not better than being a concubine?" Svanhild asked.

"No," said Vigdis firmly. She took another drink of the whiskey. "At least my position is known. She outranks me. If I were another wife, there would be endless fighting for position. I do not want that. Usually she ignores me." She spoke without calculation, the drink having loosened her tongue. "I think she was only cruel today because"—she glanced at Svanhild—"she had reason to think you would appreciate that."

Svanhild felt as though she should apologize, but Vigdis had needled her, baited her, and made her doubt her decision to accept Harald. "You sought to dissuade me from becoming another of Harald's wives. Did Atli ask you to do that?"

Vigdis sighed. "It will probably be different with Harald. I spent ten years fighting your mother over ground that neither of us wanted, only because it was there."

"Olaf didn't care about my mother," said Svanhild.

"He did at first," said Vigdis. "You only remember what Ascrida became, but she was charming and lovely, and she loved your father, Eystein. Olaf loved him too."

"Olaf killed him," Svanhild protested.

"You can kill what you love," said Vigdis. "You can hurt what you love. You can hate what you love, even." Solvi's face sprung to Svanhild's mind again; he was a wight that haunted her. No one had ever hurt her so much, and she loved him still, as much as she hated him.

Vigdis stared into the long fire that divided the hall. "I was very young when Olaf married me and brought me to Ardal," she said. "Only fifteen. I was closer to your brother's age than to Olaf's." She felt something for Ragnvald still, Svanhild realized; her words of love and hate had been about him as much as Olaf. "I was young, and I knew nothing about running a household. I learned all of that from your mother, and then I turned Olaf against her." She drained the glass. "I will accept your offer."

"What offer?" Svanhild asked. Vigdis's words were slurred. She put her arm around Vigdis to support her.

"That you will care for me if Atli puts me out. I like him—he is a good match for me. He is not a bad sort, only he can't help himself from stirring trouble. If you tell Ragnvald that he is doing badly by Sogn, Ragnvald will make Harald give it back to him. He is not, though. Atli is caring for the farmers as Ragnvald wanted. If you would do more for me, let Atli stay in Sogn."

"So many requests," said Svanhild. Vigdis was heavy against her shoulder, in the circle of Svanhild's arm. "I will," she agreed, "if you will be my eyes and ears here. I don't trust Atli."

"You mean be Ragnvald's eyes and ears," said Vigdis.

"They are the same, these days," said Svanhild. "Do you want to see your son? Ragnvald might send him here."

Vigdis laughed, soft and hopeless. "He told me he would not. You see, he wants to hurt me as badly as I want to hurt him."

"He does not want that, I don't think," said Svanhild.

"I thought he would be my escape from Olaf, and he was, but he sent me away. Do not trust him. You can only trust yourself." Vigdis's voice sounded as though she was on the verge of tears.

"Do you want me to ask for Einar to come here?" Svanhild asked. She could do nothing else for Vigdis's other hurt, even if she wanted to.

"Best not," said Vigdis. "I am not a very good mother. I was relieved to leave Hallbjorn with my family, and to leave Einar with his father. You will think ill of me for it. As if you do not already."

Svanhild did not know what to make of that. She ached for Eystein still, and yet she had left Freydis with hardly a pang. "I think you are yourself," said Svanhild. "And I think you are tired and drunk. Shall we retire?"

The men were wagering on a dice game, and cheered a good throw as Svanhild stood and helped Vigdis out of her seat, and to her bed behind a curtain. The room spun when she lay down next to her. Vigdis snored softly. The smell of rushes, of Sogn air, of Vigdis herself, whom Svanhild had slept next to often enough at Ardal, gave her an odd sense of being a girl again, with only the future before her. Perhaps it was, with Harald.

✛ ✛ ✛

RAGNVALD ARRIVED A few days later. "I still thought you might be contrary and say no," he said, smiling and pulling her into a one-armed embrace that nestled her against his side.

"I do things for my own reasons," said Svanhild. "Just as any man must."

"Yes, well," said Ragnvald. He gave her another squeeze. "You must admit I had reason to be fearful."

"Doesn't your wife feed you well enough?" Svanhild asked. She could feel his hip bone and ribs pressed against her.

He shrugged. "I think the fault is with my eating, not with her and her cooking," he said.

"Perhaps the food of two women disagrees in your stomach?" Svanhild asked. He gave her an exasperated look, and she shrugged. "Don't answer that. I am glad to see you here. Have you brought either of your women?"

"Alfrith," said Ragnvald. "Hilda said she must stay home with the children."

"And you did not fight her," said Svanhild.

"I think there is one here she did not wish to see," said Ragnvald. "Enough about her. I want to witness this day, when my king weds my sister, bringing all my worries to an end."

"All?" Svanhild asked. "I have heard that the Swedish king might send forces against southern Norway. Harald said that he wants you to raise an army from Maer and Sogn. He said that all of Norway must rise against the Swedish forces, and those as yet unsworn will have to do so soon, or be outlawed."

"You are well informed," said Ragnvald.

"Yes," said Svanhild. "But he will succeed. I have no fear for either of my kings." For Solvi was no longer among them. "Harald sings your praises daily," she added.

"Harald's kingcraft consists in knowing his audience," said Ragnvald dryly. "Did you learn anything I should hear in Sogn?"

Only that Vigdis's anger at him burned bright. He did not need to know that. "I think Atli serves you better than you feared."

"I still don't trust him," said Ragnvald. "But I do trust you." He kissed her forehead. "Now go make ready."

✛ ✛ ✛

SVANHILD ASKED VIGDIS to dress her for the wedding ceremony, even knowing that it would anger Bertha, who deserved better. Still, she and Vigdis were as near family as two women could be without sharing blood.

"I had no one to dress me at my last wedding," said Svanhild. Vigdis combed Svanhild's hair with efficient strokes, unsnarling tangles with neither pain nor gentleness. "My hair was still wet from the bath."

She remembered the shame and lust, disgust and fear that marked that night. She had woven those emotions into the fabric of her marriage to Solvi, and turned that rough beginning into part of what bound them together. She shook her head, trying to push the memories away into the past, and pulled her hair out of Vigdis's hands. Vigdis put a hand on the crown of her head, positioning it.

"Don't move," she commanded. Then more gently: "Your hair is still as fine as when you were a little girl. It hardly wants to stay in these plaits." She had divided Svanhild's hair into three braids close to her scalp then joined them into a single braid which she looped in a knot at the nape of Svanhild's neck.

"Harald will pull it free soon enough." Svanhild smiled at the thought.

"He looks like he'd be a young bull in bed, crashing everywhere," said Vigdis. "A king has no need for skill."

"He is very pleasing," said Svanhild primly. "And not just to the eye. He has been taught by mistresses who valued their enjoyment." She threw a mischievous glance at Vigdis over her shoulder. "And I made pleasing me a condition of my agreeing to marry with him."

"Ha," said Vigdis. "That is a good trick. If you dower me well enough that I can choose, perhaps I will try that."

"Is that what you want?" Svanhild asked.

"No," said Vigdis. "I am happy enough with Atli, I promise you. And you know what they say: 'Ask a man drunk'—or a woman, I suppose—'and ask a man sober, and if the answer is the same' . . ."

"Yes," said Svanhild. Vigdis patted her hair and held up a silver mirror before her. Her face, cloudy and wavering, looked back. Her eyebrows arched over eyes small and smiling, already wrinkled at the edges from many years of peering at the horizon over a sunlit sea.

She held the mirror up to see the precise, even braids Vigdis had made for her. "Beautiful work," she said. "Thank you."

"Now your veil." Vigdis placed it on her head, a fine piece of silk from traders beyond the middle sea, given to her by Atli's wife.

"Who did this for you when you wed Olaf?" Svanhild asked.

"My mother," said Vigdis, her voice taking on a hollow tone. "My veil was wool, so thick I could not see through it. My father was a poor trapper with too many sons. Olaf and your father came to our door the winter before your father died. Olaf said that he would come back and buy me as his wife for an armband of silver. My father consented immediately."

"And you leave your son Hallbjorn with him?" Svanhild asked.

"He gave me to Olaf—he can raise Olaf's son," she said. "And Ragn—your brother has promised him a place when he is grown."

When Ragnvald arrived, he and Vigdis had exchanged a glance that Svanhild could not read. "Whatever wrongs are between you—leave him be," said Svanhild.

"You cannot know," said Vigdis. "He owes me."

"What does he owe you?" Svanhild asked. "He no longer thinks of you."

Vigdis pulled Svanhild over to adjust her hair and stabbed a pin into her scalp. "I think you are even more cruel than him, sometimes," Vigdis said.

Svanhild ducked her head out of the way. She and Vigdis would always rasp against each other, like a rough skin against fine silk.

"I pray you have no reason to regret your marriage to Harald as I did Olaf," said Vigdis. "I pray your stepchildren are kind to you. I pray he does not tire of you before you tire of him."

"Your prayers sound like curses," said Svanhild. "Keep them for yourself. They are not for me."

✝   ✝   ✝

RAGNVALD HAD BEEN only a year away from Sogn, and it was strange to come as a visitor rather than as its king. He had built this hall believing he would live there for his life's span, and his sons after him. The longer Atli and his sons had possession, the more Sogn would seem like theirs.

The sun shone for the wedding, splitting through the high banks of clouds. In the distance, a curtain of rain drew across Sogn Fjord, and Ragnvald saw a rainbow emerging from the gray. Svanhild deserved no less for her wedding day. Harald stood resplendent, hair like golden wheat. Svanhild looked like a tiny jewel next to him, draped in gold and silk of deepest red. Ragnvald glanced at Oddi during the ceremony—he looked peaceful enough. He and Svanhild had not shared a bed for some time, and if Oddi felt any hurt at this, he hid it well.

After she had made her promises, Harald said, "My sea queen, Svanhild Eysteinsdatter, sister of my beloved friend, I promise to make a good husband, to provide for our children together and make them equal in inheritance with all my others." He looked up at Ragnvald. "Because of the love I bear your brother, I will provide your dowry myself, in hopes that Ragnvald will again consent to fight by my side."

Ragnvald smiled at Harald, trying to cover his displeasure. "I have already promised to come to your side when you need me," he said.

"Heming guards Maer well, and can continue to do so with his brother Oddi. Atli Mjove has continued to enhance Sogn's prosperity. I miss my favorite captain. I will winter in Vestfold. Defend Maer for the summer and then come to me in Vestfold in the fall."

In front of so many witnesses, Ragnvald could not do anything other than agree. "My king does me too much honor," he said. "Of course, I will fight at your side."

Harald looked delighted, Svanhild less so, whether because Harald's request left Ragnvald king of nothing again, or because Harald had taken attention from her at this moment, Ragnvald did not know. Ragnvald pronounced the words that sealed their union before the gods and the laws of the land. At least now she could not return to Solvi.

And Harald was bound to him further. Now when Ragnvald's push sent Hakon tumbling from his high seat, Harald would have as much reason to stand with Ragnvald as with Hakon. Even better if Svanhild gave Harald a son, and quickly—Hakon's daughter had already given him three sons—but at least Ragnvald's claim to Harald's loyalty was as strong now.

31

SOLVI CELEBRATED ANOTHER MIDSUMMER AT THE SWEDISH court in Uppsala in a grim humor. Many of his allies and followers who had scattered over the previous year came for the celebrations, and to see if it was time to bring war to Harald. Rain marked the day, turning into a sticky mist in the evening. Through the mannered court ceremonies, performed in an alien dialect, Solvi's thoughts lingered on past years, celebrated on beaches with Svanhild, when they welcomed the summer together smelling of sea and sweat, when his men who did not have slaves found pleasure with each other, for his ships were a world in themselves, and needed nothing from beyond them. The memories would not leave him be, not when he had drunk his fill of sweet summer mead and watched the touches between the men and women of King Eirik's court grow bolder.

He took Tova to bed in a curtained corner, wishing for complete darkness, so she could not see him, nor him her, that he could drown himself in sensations and memories, and wake blank and cleansed. He succeeded in losing himself in long and drunken sleep, and woke with a sore head, next to a woman he did not want and kept only because she said she did not like being without a protector in Eirik's court. She must have some master or another, and she stayed by him to remind him that he still owed her—a rich husband, or riches in her own right.

When Solvi's headache subsided enough that he could stand, he splashed some water on his face and found Thorstein hanging about the kitchen door, flirting with one of the maids. Thorstein had gone to Rane in Vermaland, and returned when the Vermaland folk accepted Rane as jarl there, though if Eirik did not decide to send more forces soon, Rane would lose it as easily as he had won it.

Solvi pried him away from the girl, and took out a small skiff with him into the fjord. Thorstein would make a good captain one day soon, for he had the confidence and bravery required to lead a ship, and the ability to make even his mistakes seem well chosen. Solvi blindfolded him, steered the ship to a point among the islands that surrounded the approach to Uppsala, and then set him the challenge of navigating back. The town lay within a warren of narrow passages that made it maddening to find for anyone who did not already know the route.

Thorstein made a turn that took the boat around an island they had already passed, and he cursed. Solvi looked up from where he lay sprawled across the boat's benches, cushioned by the cloak that he had put off in the warm weather. It did not matter to him if Thorstein brought them home tonight. His drinking left him with little appetite, and a hungry night would give Thorstein more incentive to find Uppsala again.

Through half-closed eyes he saw a long dragon ship pass over Thorstein's shoulder, as if sailing out of a dream of better days. He sat up and rubbed sleep from his eyes. The dragon ship's figurehead was stowed, and its oars out—it came in peace. Another followed behind it, and another still, all with sails striped in blue and white, the colors of King Hakon Grjotgardsson. If he came to offer alliance with Eirik on Harald's behalf, Eirik would have a reason to let yet another summer pass through indecision. Solvi thought sometimes that he never meant to do anything at all.

If Hakon came with his ships, Solvi would take up his own cause with more energy, and leave off drinking and pitying himself. It had been Hakon who made Solvi and his father, Hunthiof, into Harald's enemies. Solvi could not let Hakon turn Eirik into Harald's ally.

"You could follow them," said Solvi to Thorstein. "They look like they know where they're going." Rumors had reached Uppsala that

one or more of Hakon's sons stood at odds with Harald. Solvi had
not heard the whole story, but it was known that Harald had tried
to have Heming killed at one time, and now threatened to outlaw
two of Hakon's other sons. These ships might bear those young men,
in rebellion against their father. No matter if they brought warriors,
Solvi still might refuse to ally with them. Even Eirik, who wanted
to tear Norway apart more than he wanted his allies to regain their
lands, must see that a man who betrayed his father in anger could
easily return to him when that anger cooled.

The last ship in the convoy flew different banners, and Solvi recognized it as Rane's, from when it had failed to turn the tide of the
Solskel battle in his favor. When Solvi arrived with Rane just before
Yule of the previous year, he found a warm welcome from King Eirik,
who had ruled all the coastal lands of southern Sweden for near on
fifty years. Eirik was old now, and felt it, surrounding himself with
young warriors and adventurers, spurning the friends of his youth
whose wrinkled faces reminded him that death comes even for kings.
Rane had done his duty, painting Solvi as the best general of sea battles living or dead and taking responsibility for his own mistakes at
the battle of Solskel. Solvi, grudgingly, allowed that the weather had
been difficult for a novice sailor. Eirik had sent Rane out to retake
Vermaland, and not return without good news or more allies, ideally
both. Rane had been gone for more than a year.

All through the winter, Solvi had felt as though his spirit were
made of stone. He had made a place for himself in Eirik's court as
an adventurer, an explorer, quick to tell a tale so wild it might not
be true. He spoke of cities that stretched as far as the eye could see,
where a man could grow as lost as a child in a forest. He spoke of the
vast sands of Northern Africa, where no plants grew. He spoke of
men with skin as black as night who, among them, had warriors as
fierce and explorers as brave as any in the Norse lands.

He had passed other winters this way, as a pleasing guest for
wealthy men, buying food and shelter with his wit, but never before
without Svanhild. Each night he drank deeply of Eirik's ale, trying to
reach the numbed state where he would not miss her so much. When
he had told his stories before, he always rested his gaze upon her.

Sometimes she listened to him, and then it was as if he relived their adventures together. Sometimes she was busy talking with other women, and then he made the stories as outrageous as he dared, waiting for her to turn and give him a look of fond exasperation. She even stood from time to time and said something like, "My lord husband is seeing what foolishness he can sell you. I promise, the world serpent only has one head, not two."

Now he altered all of his stories so she played a smaller role. If he must mention her, he only called her "my woman." He grinned at the ladies in his audience, inviting them to see themselves adventuring by his side.

The heeling of the little skiff brought Solvi back to the present. Thorstein, never one to discard an advantage, had drafted in the wake of the larger ships, and then pulled the boat into the harbor at Uppsala just after the last ship docked.

"What did you think of their approach?" Solvi asked Thorstein.

"They sailed before the wind," Thorstein answered promptly. "It takes no great skill. Some of the ships were not laden well"—he pointed to one of the trailing ships still rocking in its berth—"that one needs more ballast. And that one has more weight on the port side than the starboard."

"Good, that's right," said Solvi.

An older man disembarked first from the ship and led his warriors toward Uppsala's receiving hall. He was stout in the stomach, and by his rich dress, could only be King Hakon himself, followed by the giant Rane. Could Rane have made peace with Harald? Solvi did not think it any more likely than Hakon breaking with Harald. Without Hakon, Harald might not have exiled so many kings and jarls from Norway, since Hakon had demanded kingdoms for his true-born adult sons—Heming, Herlaug, and Geirbjorn, with more coming into manhood soon.

Solvi had learned all the hidden ways into the complex at Uppsala, so while Hakon and his party made their entrance through the hall's great doors, Solvi reached Eirik's side before he had fully assembled his court. He placed himself among the group of Eirik's advisers who flanked his outdoor throne in the courtyard where he received visitors on fine days. Hakon's herald announced him, "King Hakon Grjotgardsson, King of Halogaland and North Trondelag."

Hakon and his entourage bowed to Eirik. Solvi recognized Hakon's younger sons, though he had only seen them at a distance since their boyhood. One had the same arrangement of features as Hakon, his youth giving him a raw-boned look that Hakon's age had softened, and the other bore a disfiguring scar that distorted his right cheek so it seemed he could hardly move his jaw. Near the back of Hakon's entourage stood Egil Hrolfsson, still struggling to grow a beard, and by his side a tall, blond man who looked familiar to Solvi, though he could not call to mind a name.

Hakon made eye contact with Solvi and gave him an ironic nod. He did not seem surprised to see him, so Rane must have told him who he joined. Hakon had come anyway.

Rane spoke next. "King Eirik of Sweden, I have brought a powerful ally. King Hakon of—"

"We heard the titles already, thank you, Rane," said Eirik. "You have brought Harald's most important ally into our court, to learn everything he can." He spoke mildly, his voice quavering with age. Eirik was not given to rages or strong emotions, and men often underestimated him until the moment he ordered their exile or punishments. Solvi heard the danger in his voice, though, and by Rane's expression, he did too.

"I have brought King Hakon to be our ally—he will rebel against Harald of Vestfold, and end Harald's quest to be king of all Norway," said Rane.

Hakon stepped forward, and made another bow. "Jarl Rane of Vermaland speaks truly. I can follow Harald no longer."

"We have heard that he raised you up far higher than you could rise on your own," said Eirik. "Why would you rebel against him?"

Hakon narrowed his eyes at the insult. "Harald does not apply his laws fairly. He makes different laws for his friends and enemies, and uses them to keep me down," he said. "He sets the sons of peasants above the sons of kings." He then told of how each of his three eldest sons had been threatened by Harald's justice. When he saw that this did not convince Eirik, he went on to tell of Harald choosing which existing kings to honor, and which to deprive of their land on no more than a whim, no matter the desires of their people, or even their willingness to swear allegiance to Harald.

"Because of you!" Solvi burst out. "Harald would not have required my father to give up North Maer and Tafjord if you had not insisted that you wanted one of your sons installed in my seat."

"Is this so?" Eirik asked.

Hakon shrugged, making the rings decorating his neck clink together. "Harald has not made good on his promises."

"Does your son Heming not sit in my Tafjord hall even now?" Solvi asked. "Why is this oath breaker here? Tell me it is for justice, and then you can pronounce his sentence and take his head. That would leave much of Norway leaderless."

"Hospitality forbids it," said Eirik, with a wry quirk of his lips. "Still, I have come to know Solvi Hunthiofsson by his words and deeds, and it seems to me his questions have value."

"I did swear to Harald," said Hakon. "I thought it the quickest means to secure districts for all of my sons."

"And now the bargain doesn't look so good?" Solvi asked.

Hakon shrugged. "Do you know how many armies I can bring to your side? Send me away, and you have no chance. Agree to my terms, and Norway will split apart, for all of us to take the pieces." He looked to Gudbrand, who sat with his remaining son. He had come from Frisia for the midsummer feast and to learn if Eirik might finally make a decision. "You know this is true—without me, you have no hope against Harald."

Eirik shifted in his seat. "You discount my ships and armies."

"I had heard they were busy fighting the Danish," said Hakon.

Eirik had a truce with a young Danish king, though it could not last, not when they both wanted control of the entrance to the Baltic Sea. "I do not lack forces to send against Harald. Still, you are powerful, King Hakon. If you have abandoned Harald's cause, that does help us."

"He is an oath breaker." Solvi felt the tide turning against him. He could see the sense in Hakon's words and Eirik's, but it went against his every instinct to throw in with Hakon. He would trust Hakon only as long as he had Hakon in full view, with Hakon's hands empty and his mouth shut—and not very far even then.

"Many of us are oath breakers here," said Hakon. "Did you not swear in front of the Sogn *ting* that you injured Ragnvald Eysteinsson of your own will and no one else's?"

Solvi flushed with anger. He had broken other promises, many of them, but never before the gods so blatantly, and never since. At times he wondered if every bit of bad luck he suffered since then was punishment for that moment.

"I make no excuses," said Hakon. "We are all men of action. My alliance with Harald has never served me as well as I'd like, and now it has ceased to be useful at all. I offer my armies and my ships, and I expect to be greatly rewarded for putting them in the service of this alliance."

"And you will share the west coast with me?" Solvi asked. "Me, Solvi Hunthiofsson, whose father you warred with your entire youth? You will support me, my rule of Tafjord and Maer?"

Hakon gave him a thin smile. "Marry one of my daughters. If she gives you a son, let him inherit. Then it will be both of our blood on the throne of Maer, and I will be well satisfied." Solvi looked at him for a long moment, and Hakon met his gaze. How could anyone believe Hakon's word now? He had revealed, finally, what sort of man he was: a man who abandoned even the pretense of honor if it served his ambitions. Did he feel any loyalty except to himself and his monstrous sons?

"I do not know how you can trust this man," Solvi said to Eirik. "I can think of no circumstances where I would trust him. You should put him in irons and hold him hostage against the good behavior of his followers. Send a messenger to King Harald, say that you have his oath-breaking ally here, and offer him in exchange for an alliance that favors you. Perhaps he will even give you Vestfold as a reward."

"And will he give you Tafjord?" Hakon asked.

"Probably not," said Solvi. "But how can—?"

Eirik beckoned Solvi over so they stood close enough for private conversation. "You are usually craftier than this," Eirik said, in a low voice. "You must truly hate this man."

"I do not respect him," said Solvi, loudly enough that Hakon would hear.

"And I respect the opinion of Solvi Hunthiofsson," said Eirik to his court. "I do not know this Hakon."

Solvi watched Hakon, looking for a sign of anger in his expression. Hakon's face looked calm and impassive; he could have been a wooden statue but for the flint in his eyes when they met Solvi's. The guest-right that protected Hakon also protected Solvi, and he was glad of it.

☩ ☩ ☩

SOLVI WRESTLED ALL night with the thought of allying with Hakon, whom he hated far more than Harald. Harald was like a storm—inevitable. Kings would always want more land, and they would see the Frankish emperors, the high kings in Sweden and Denmark, and want the same in the Norse peninsula. Others had come before him, and failed. Solvi might have come to an accommodation with Harald eventually, as long as his taxes were not too high. It was Hakon who had set in motion the events that took Solvi from Tafjord, and killed his father before his time. If his father had lived to pass on Tafjord to him, a home for Svanhild and his son, they might still be a family.

So many lived in the complex at Uppsala that the women served breakfast at long tables outside in the summer: a line of surly, squinting warriors spooning rye porridge into their mouths. Little conversation occurred until men were fed and watered in the morning.

Egil's tall friend sat near Solvi at breakfast the next morning. Solvi called out to him, "You there, why do I know you?"

"I am Sigurd Olafsson," the man replied. "Br—stepbrother of Ragnvald Eysteinsson and Svanhild Eysteinsdatter." He gave Solvi a puzzled look and seemed to want to say more, but eventually chose not to. Solvi remembered him now, an awkward boy at the side of the sour Olaf, who had visited Tafjord at Yule sometimes.

"Do you think King Eirik should ally with your Hakon?" Solvi asked.

Sigurd shrugged. "It seems the only way any of you can win," he said.

"And what about you?" Solvi asked. Sigurd suddenly seemed very interested in his breakfast. There was some mystery here, a secret that this Sigurd hid, and seeing hints of it made Solvi weary. He did not want to care what happened to Olaf's son.

"You divorced my sister," said Sigurd suddenly. "Should I take offense?"

"Stepsister, I thought," said Solvi. Was that the rumor, that he had divorced her? He supposed that was some salve to his pride.

"It freed her to marry Harald, though, so I suppose it is better for her now," Sigurd continued. "She is a fine girl, though. Did you think you could do better?"

It took a moment for the words to make sense to Solvi, and then he had to exert all of his will not to leap from his seat and strike Sigurd, pound his face until it was a battered ruin. He knew it showed on his face, and he hoped Sigurd would think his expression came only from the reminder, not from learning this news for the first time. The only thing that kept him seated was knowing it was better to hear it now, from this guileless young man, than from Hakon in full view of the court.

Harald: boy, king, god. Not a man, a golden legend. A hero in battle, skill and luck buttressed by the cunning of Ragnvald Eysteinsson. This marriage had Ragnvald's mark on it, securing his position by marrying his sister to his king. Every king in Norway had done the same. Svanhild, though—Svanhild liked her tales and songs, and now she had married one, flawless, tall, and golden. Solvi had loved that about her, a touch of innocence that she clung to, refusing to let it be sullied even when she came to know the gore that made those shining tales. Now he despised her for it. He would kill Harald and make Svanhild beg him to take her back. He could do it; he knew his own cruelty. He had already made her hate him. He smiled at Sigurd, biting his teeth together as if on the flesh of his enemy.

✛ ✛ ✛

KING EIRIK SENT for Solvi after breakfast. With Uppsala already full of midsummer guests, King Eirik could not house all of Hakon's warriors, but he offered clean tents and hay for mattresses, which now spread out over the Uppsala grounds. Solvi walked between them to reach Eirik's outdoor court, now mostly empty. When Solvi arrived, Eirik stood and paced around the muddy ground near his high seat.

"Is there truly no circumstance under which you will ally with Hakon?" Eirik asked. "Gudbrand and his son, Nokkve, Rorik of Dorestad, perhaps even Imar of Dublin, other displaced kings in Iceland and the Orkney Islands—all of them would follow you over any other."

"Yes, I suppose that's true," said Solvi. They would still fight without him, probably under Hakon's leadership, but they would trust Solvi more. The weight of their expectations, or simply the fact that he was the pebble that could start the rock fall, always made him feel rebellious. "I did not ask for this." Nor for his son to die, nor for Svanhild to marry Harald.

"I think that is why they trust you. No one believes that you want to be high king, only to guarantee freedom for yourself and your brother kings."

"It's true," said Solvi. "You may rule this flat and easy Swedish coast entirely, but the Norse peninsula is different." Eirik gave him a sardonic look, and Solvi shrugged. "If I thought your ambitions stretched beyond Vestfold, I would sail away from here tomorrow."

"Then I would have to ally with Hakon," said Eirik. "Though I mistrust him. Harald will never give me Vestfold—it is the land of his first conquests."

"Might you ally with him to put pressure on the Danes together? Control the entrance to the Baltic Sea?" Solvi suggested brusquely. He cared little for Eirik's ambitions if they did not help him. Let Hakon and Harald play endless *tafl* games with ships and men. Their blessings meant they no longer counted the cost. "I want my home back." He had last said those words to Svanhild, hoping to give her a kingdom and hall to rule. Eirik peered at him, and Solvi wondered how much he had revealed. He usually hid his feelings better than this. "Hakon sounded willing to give you Tafjord," Eirik said.

"He will 'give' me nothing," said Solvi. "Not unless forced." Hakon had risked everything by coming here, though. Harald would certainly hear of his visit and what he had offered Eirik.

"You look like you did just before you steered my boat to victory in the Yule races," said Eirik, after a long pause from Solvi. "What are you thinking?"

"Harald must be defeated in one battle, and so decisively that none will ever believe him blessed by the gods again," he said. "I have raided his lands, and it only makes him stronger, for he can raise more warriors from among angry farmers. No, we need to lure Harald into a battle without his allies—a sea battle—then destroy his ships and kill him." Then Svanhild would have no choice but to return to him. "Harald's luck is so good that we must have double his forces, at least. And that is what you and Hakon can provide."

"How, if Hakon can't be trusted?" Eirik asked.

"He thinks himself so untouchable that he brought hostages to us: his sons," said Solvi. "They are the only people he truly cares about. Give one of his sons to me, and keep another here in Uppsala. Then he may behave."

"Do you think he will agree to that?" Eirik asked.

"I do not know," Solvi answered. "But even if he does, then I would give no more than even odds of his betraying you. If he does not agree, send your messengers to Harald. Better to make an alliance now when he needs you than be forced to make it later."

A servant announced Hakon, and he arrived, followed by many of his warriors, including Sigurd and Egil. Eirik returned again to his outdoor throne to receive Hakon, the sun behind him, shining in Hakon's face.

Hakon bowed only slightly, and then said, "You need me. You know it."

"I don't think that's true," said Solvi.

"You need us," Eirik countered. "In coming here you have made a choice that you cannot undo. Whether I agree to ally with you or not, Harald will know you plot against him. I might agree with my counselor Solvi Hunthiofsson, and think it better to tell Harald of your plans and make my alliance with him."

Hakon looked at Solvi and tilted his head. His eyes watered from the sun in them, though he tried not to squint. "I am puzzled that Solvi of Maer, sea king, would rather ally with the boy who killed his father and married his wife than with one who comes in friendship," said Hakon. He said it with some triumph. So he had been hoping to ambush Solvi with this news. If Sigurd had not prepared him, Solvi would never have been able to smile back in Hakon's face. Even now it was difficult.

"Let that be the measure of my distaste for allying with you," said Solvi, his voice rough and harsh. He had anger enough for Harald and Hakon both. "You have your sons here, and they are the only thing you have ever shown regard for other than your own advancement. The scarred one will be my hostage, while the elder remains in Uppsala, as a surety for King Eirik. If you or they betray us, all of your lives will be forfeit. Otherwise, you can go back to Harald and wait for rumors of your betrayal to reach him."

Solvi pictured it: Norway splintered by war between three factions, broken apart. Eirik, secure in Uppsala, would benefit the most by it. He must be salivating to imagine how easily he could control Norway's southern coast with every Norse king at one another's throats. He would have access to Norway's bounty of furs and take tax from the best farmland on the peninsula. At this moment, Solvi did not care. Let Eirik have what he wanted—as long as it meant Solvi could wet his sword in the blood of those he hated.

"What if you betray King Eirik?" said Hakon to Solvi. "Your reputation is no more clean than mine."

"It was you who came here boasting of how easily you can betray your king," said Eirik. "That was your choice alone."

Solvi watched Hakon's face grow angry, a cold anger that he could only envy, as the heat of his own made him shake and burn. "You drive a hard bargain," said Hakon. "I will think on this."

32

SVANHILD WOKE WITH AN ACHE IN HER BACK FROM THE COT
she shared with Harald. Wind-driven waves beat a steady tempo on
the beach, scraping its pebbles against one another. She hoped today
would bring challenging sailing, with more opportunities to put her
hand to the steering oar. Harald still slept, curled on his side, looking
smaller in sleep than he did waking. A hank of snarled hair fell down
over his cheek. The open neck of his tunic showed his white-gold skin,
soft with youth, hard with muscle, that she itched to touch even now.
She sat up carefully, wishing not to wake him. He was a light sleeper;
in this and the self-protective ball he made in sleep, he reminded her
of Solvi. And on waking, they both put on a new face. Harald, though,
did not seem to know it was a new face, or that there was any difference between his sleeping and waking self. As she watched, he opened
his eyes and uncurled, growing from boy to man in the space of a few
breaths.

"You're rounder than you were in Nidaros," he said. He put his arm
around her and pulled her back to bed. She had grown plumper in
Sogn, and then in Maer. Hilda, for all her faults, fed her household
well.

"I'm happier," said Svanhild. Hard to be otherwise; she had never
felt worse than those early days in Nidaros, having lost the family she
had built over six years of hardships and joy. Better now to be ship-

board with her new king. She need never worry about a farm again, or about anything except her own comfort and happiness.

That day, the ships' route down Sogn Fjord would pass Kaupanger, and Svanhild asked Harald if they could stop there.

"Indeed, yes," said Harald. "Their council owes me their taxes. They swore loyalty to me last summer, finally. I should have been harsher with them, but I did not want to kill so many of Norway's finest artisans."

Harald's casual suggestion of killing off the entire town—for that is what he would have done if they had not agreed—troubled her more than Solvi's raiding ever had. Perhaps because of the scope of Harald's ambition: he would remake everything he touched into what he desired. It seemed outside the natural order of things, a second creation that usurped the power of the gods.

Kaupanger stank as Svanhild remembered, the shore lined with rotting seaweed and a layer of flies feeding on it so dense that in places the ground itself seemed to writhe and pulse. Harald called his servants to put down boards for them to walk over.

"You will not like the town, if you dislike this," said Svanhild, amused to see Harald's fastidiousness. Nidaros was far cleaner, with animals penned far away from the artisans' workshops. Nidaros artisans were nearly as pampered as the harem women Svanhild had met in Spain, while Kaupanger artisans had to keep their own households, including livestock.

Svanhild walked with Harald through the town, holding her skirts high above the mud. She did not remember the layout of the town very well, but it seemed to her that it had changed, become dirtier, with more houses falling into disrepair. She asked a few vendors where she could find Gerta the ribbon maker, who had helped her when she came to Kaupanger before, and received blank stares until Harald gestured at his servants, who fanned out to get the information they needed, then returned to Harald and showed them the way. Gerta's home, when Svanhild saw it again, was just as she remembered: a simple one-room house with a wide-open window out of which she sold her ribbons and veils.

Harald's servants announced them, and Gerta returned the greeting with a slight nod. "The king is here again," she said, with a mocking edge to her voice. "And the king's woman. Will you pay for my
ribbons, or only take what you want?"

Gerta had grown fatter since Svanhild saw her last, and completed
the journey from middle-aged to old. She had been handsome when
Svanhild met her before, her face retaining hints of what she must
have looked like as a young woman. Flesh and crumpled skin buried
her youth, and her brusqueness, which had seemed like strength, was
now no more than ill temper.

"I am Svanhild Eysteinsdatter," she said. "You helped me, a long
time ago."

Gerta squinted at her. Years of fine weaving must have made her
nearsighted. "The girl with the brother—running away from a marriage."

"She is my wife now," said Harald proudly.

"I suppose you can't turn down a king," said Gerta. "Well, perhaps
you can persuade him not to tax us so harshly."

"Harshly!" Harald scoffed. "It is no more than I tax Nidaros and
Tonsberg artisans."

"Yes," said Gerta. "And now all the merchants flock to Nidaros
instead because they know the king will buy from them. You cannot
milk a starving cow."

"I remember you," said Harald. His good humor seemed to be
wearing thin. "You voted against me when I came before. You said
that if my uncle and I went away, we would not come back. You were
wrong."

"Victory over an old ribbon-weaver must count among your finest
accomplishments," said Gerta.

Svanhild could not see why Harald would stoop to argue with
Gerta—he must see that she would argue with anyone. She put her
hand on his arm, as she would have touched Solvi when he grew ag-
gressive. She would have felt Solvi's skin soften under her touch, his
body turn toward hers, the two of them aligned like slivers of iron.
Harald seemed not to feel her touch at all.

"I would like to visit with my old friend," said Svanhild to Harald.

"She helped me when no one else would. I owe her a great debt. I am sure you have other business here."

After a moment, Harald nodded, and one of his servants gave her a pouch of hacksilver, enough to buy whatever she wished from Gerta. Once the noise of Harald's footsteps receded into the distance, she said to Gerta, "I see you are as you ever were. Do you really remember me?"

"I do," said Gerta. "Not many women come to me alone. Here is the other—Signy!" A woman came in from the back door, the hem of her dress trailing mud along the floor-planking until Gerta scolded her for it.

"This is Signy," said Gerta. "She came fleeing a bad marriage. She's not as clever or pretty as you, but she can weave." Signy was a bit moon faced, plain and pale, though self-possessed enough that Gerta's words did not seem to bother her.

"I shall have the shop when Gerta is dead," said Signy, as if in explanation for why she put up with Gerta's insults. Svanhild heard a kind of wry affection in the words and felt a twinge of jealousy. "And she has taught me many things," Signy added.

"King Harald and I are going to Tonsberg," said Svanhild. "He says it is a great market town, with far more trade than Kaupanger. You could come with us, both of you." Gerta scowled, and Svanhild added, "In another ship, of course. I would not want you and my husband sharing close quarters for long."

"And will I get a vote in the town's business, or does he settle all of that as well according to his whim?" Gerta asked. "Signy may do as she wishes, and see what her skill can gain her there. I am not tempted." She looked at Svanhild, daring her to argue.

Svanhild was not sure what she had expected from this visit, perhaps that Gerta would share some Kaupanger gossip with her, and then compliment her on making a good marriage. But Gerta did not like Harald. Svanhild felt foolish in coming here.

"You are welcome if you like, Signy," said Svanhild. "But do not tarry, for I do not think we will spend the night here." Harald would not want his fine tents set up on Kaupanger's reeking beaches. Svanhild hesitated, wondering if she should offer to intervene on Kaupanger's behalf with Harald, ask him to give them privileged tax status. She might, if Gerta had asked, but she only stared rudely at Svanhild, until Svanhild bought some ribbons in red and blue and left.

Harald's ships departed in the afternoon, without Signy, and sailed through until evening before finding a good campsite: a flat patch of ground on the top of a fjord-side cliff. Harald's men climbed the steep path, carrying the heavy tents, to make camp for them.

"Did you get your taxes?" Svanhild asked Harald, after their brief lovemaking. She heard some of Gerta's tone in her own voice, though she had meant to inquire for information, without judgment. Harald unwrapped his sweaty arms from her and lay on his back. The breeze drying her skin made her shiver.

"Some," he said. "They are cheats, like all merchants. I will send my agents back for more later in the summer, and show them a force they will understand."

"Good," said Svanhild. "They deserve no special treatment."

✢ ✢ ✢

SVANHILD HAD SEEN every kind of weather in her years at sea with Solvi, from blizzards to sandstorms. This summer reminded her more of the Mediterranean than any previous Norse summers, especially after an early, cold winter that had begun with Herlaug's bloody revenge. Relentless sunlight, rarely tempered by clouds, made the breezes slack and fitful. Constantinople had been like this in the autumn when she and Solvi traveled there, though there at least the nights had been cool.

On some nights a fog boiled up out of the sea and locked Harald's ships into their campsite until it cleared in the afternoon. On clear days, his ships had to sail outside the barrier islands to catch any breeze at all, and the sun at noon felt like a smith's fire. Svanhild grew faint with thirst during the day, and drank so much water when they beached at night that she was up half the night emptying her bladder.

It did not help her temper that Harald wanted her every night regardless of the heat and the exhaustion of the long days. She continued to hope for her courses to come, so he would spare her a week, but when they did not, she thought it likely she was pregnant again. Scarcely a year after the birth of Freydis, not long enough for her to forget the blood and pain of childbirth, and the exhaustion of early motherhood. If she fell pregnant now, her freedom with Harald would be over as soon as it began. He would not allow her to accompany him on his journey and risk his growing son.

He was no less kind to her than he had been before he had her marriage promises, though, as she predicted, he exerted his charm less often now. And she found she liked his lovemaking less than Oddi's—or perhaps Oddi had never given up his eagerness to please her. Harald had to treat her well, but he did not need to keep winning her. Even Harald's beauty stirred her less as she grew used to it, except at odd moments when she saw him as a stranger again.

Finally the ships reached the mouth of Oslo Fjord and the town of Tonsberg, a smear of brown upon a green shoreline. In the distance, Svanhild saw sails, flashes of white and colors that were easy to confuse among the reflections of sun on water. These were dragon ships, their narrow lines unmistakable, even with figureheads too small to see. Shields arrayed upon their gunwales meant that these ships came for plunder, not trade. She squinted to see if she recognized anything that would mark these vessels as Solvi's. These moved wrong, she thought, and the colors were not his.

She was so caught up in watching that she did not realize Harald's men had not yet noticed these were other than merchant ships. The quiet around her felt strange and heavy compared with the noise and confusion that must be occurring onshore. Quickly she crossed the ship to Harald. "Look there, are those ships attacking Tonsberg?" she said to him. He seemed ready to brush her off, then squinted at the horizon. She continued, "Those are dragon ships, and some still have their shields out—the rest are already onshore."

"Bring us there quickly," Harald commanded his pilot, who, in response, ordered men to their rowing posts, and the command signaled to Harald's four other ships. Svanhild stood in the middle of the ship, craning her neck to look at the shore. From this far out, it looked peaceful, but she knew that within the town, panic would be mounting. Men and women would pick up whatever weapons were available to them, or they might try to buy off the raiders. At least a town like this could provide enough treasure that the raiders might not take slaves as well, though they could do both, and sell a skilled slave in any market in Europe.

All was chaos in Harald's ship as the men clambered to their oar stations. They had not kept the ship as neat as Svanhild was used to, and it seemed to take a long time before the first pull on the oars set them moving toward the shore, adding speed to the small push from the wind. By the time they drew close to Tonsberg, some of the thatched roofs, dried out by the hot days, were burning, and a white, choking smoke obscured the shore. Harald's ship docked first, followed by the others with a precision Svanhild could admire. Here Falki's fishing background served him well.

"This is my town," said Harald. "Fan out and find all of them. Bring them alive if you can, for I will want to question them." Harald's men began leaping out of the ships, swords drawn.

"Remain here," he said to Svanhild, and then gave her a kiss that left her giddy and smiling at her warrior king, until she gave a moment's thought to his command.

"Wait," she said. "Some of your men should take the raiders' ships so they cannot escape."

Harald gave her a grin. "They will not. We will kill them all."

"Why chance it?" Svanhild asked.

"Stay here, wife," he said. "Now is not the time to play warrior." He ran toward his men, and then overtook them, for he would allow none to be braver than him.

Svanhild strained to hear the sounds of battle above the roar of the burning buildings. Some women ran toward the shore carrying buckets, and filled them before running back to the town. Svanhild had seen a settlement like this burn before—the only thing to stop it was a firebreak, or rain. Harald had told her to stay, but these women did not seem to know what to do to save the town, and their menfolk would be busy fighting. She tugged on the trousers she had commandeered from one of Harald's men on the earlier voyage, and shrugged off her overdress. She kept her shift on and bundled up around her waist.

"Come with me, help me fight the fire," she said to the servants left behind. Fear had paralyzed the women and they clung to one another, knuckles white, eyes wide and blank. Svanhild could not wait or cajole them. She clambered toward the front of the ship and jumped out where the distance to the ground was the least, flexing her knees so she could land easily without hurting her ankles. The seaweed cushioned her drop. She started toward the town, then broke into a run while a group of armed men sprinted past her and into both of the enemy ships.

"Not enough men," she heard one of them yell. "Better to lose one than both."

Men from the farther ship quickly climbed into the closer one, and pushed off from the shore. They rowed the ship out into the harbor, where they caught a wind that pushed them so swiftly, they would disappear from view around a point of land in a few moments. Fine raiders— perhaps trained by Solvi, even if he was not here to guide them. Harald's men could not have moved so swiftly, for most of them were farmers or sons of farmers, and fought their battles on land, using ships only for transport. In the town, some men had begun to help the women pull down houses that had just begun to burn. They did not need Svanhild after all. She followed the sounds of fighting up to the hall, passing fallen bodies and the wounded, bleeding out their last moments of life.

In a clearing overlooking the town, she found Harald and his men standing in a circle. Below in the town, the flames were growing less intense. The fire had consumed only four houses in total, and damaged a dozen others. Svanhild pushed past some of Harald's warriors, threading her shoulder between them, until she saw what lay within the circle. They had captured some of the raiders, bound them hand and foot. A large man named Illugi wrenched back a raider's head, holding him by the hair, while his partner Grai held a knife to the man's throat. These were Harald's murderers and torturers, skilled not in battle, but in doing things that other men shrank from, as Ulfarr had done for Solvi.

"They all say the same," said Grai. "They say they are men of Jarl Rane of Vestfold, and this raid was to punish the villagers of Tonsberg who refused to pay taxes to them."

"Jarl Rane?" said Harald. He laughed incredulously. "My father used to tell me how easy he was to defeat—he was Jarl of Vermaland—it borders Vestfold—when my father was in the north. My father took his land long ago. I thought he was dead."

"He lives," said one of the men, and spat at Harald's feet. "He is the true ruler of Vermaland." Harald backhanded the man with a gesture that looked casual, but sent the man sprawling onto his back.

Svanhild walked around to stand next to Harald. He did not see her until she was quite close, nor did he look pleased at her presence. She let her shift fall back around her ankles, but she knew she still looked slatternly and poorly dressed for the wife of a king.

"Their fellows escaped on one of their ships," said Svanhild, in a low voice to Harald, though Grai heard it too. Immediately he dug his knife into the throat of another raider, whose eyes were already nearly swollen shut from earlier blows. He whimpered slightly. Grai and Illugi had found the weakest-spirited of the men, and quickly. A useful, if distasteful, skill.

"Where did they go?" he asked.

"Back to Vermaland of course," the man sobbed. "Where do you think?" Illugi smashed the already swollen edge of his eye socket with the handle of his dagger and sent the man crumbling to the ground, keening in pain and clutching his ruined cheek.

"We still have the other ship," said Harald.

"We could have had both, and all of his men," said Svanhild.

Harald looked as though he would like to hit her too. Svanhild would never have questioned Solvi like that, before all of his men, and she looked down at Harald's feet, feeling both ashamed and rebellious. Solvi would never have left an escape route unguarded either. Did Guthorm and Ragnvald do all of Harald's thinking for him?

"A woman," said Illugi, scornfully. "Pay her no mind, my king."

Svanhild's shame kept her quiet until she and Harald were alone in bed that night, in a private room in a hall that Harald had built when he first took possession of the town. The boards of the hall still leaked sap, a sharp scent that took Svanhild back to the forest near Ardal when she closed her eyes. When she opened them, Harald was looking down at her. His victory had made him lustful, and he held her arms over her head as he entered her.

"Why did you not leave a guard behind?" Svanhild asked when he finished. "You would be richer by another ship now."

He sprang away from her. "Why do you question me when I have never lost a battle?"

"You value my brother's advice," said Svanhild, pulling her knees up to her chest and tugging her shift over them. Her skin stuck to itself. It was hot inside tonight. Buildings meant to stay warm in the winter were stifling in this weather.

"He is a man, and a warrior, and he has proven himself," said Harald.

"Your betrothed Gyda commands the armies of Hordaland," said Svanhild. "You would take her advice."

"And I suppose now you would like an army," said Harald. He laughed mirthlessly. "Jewels would be easier."

Svanhild smiled, and tugged at a strand of his hair where it fell over his naked shoulder. "You said a ship—or perhaps a fleet," she said. "I am a good sailor."

"You are a woman, and will be mother to my fiercest sons, the next generation of Norse kings," said Harald. "Why else did you think I married you?"

"Because songs have been sung of me," said Svanhild.

"Of your beauty," he said. He touched her cheek. "Wait until you are pregnant—then you will be happier."

"I am pregnant," she said, curling away from him. He put his arms around her and pulled her close. She did enjoy this, his warm and supple skin on hers, even in the heat. "I fear it will cage me."

"I have heard of that too," said Harald. "Women are often restless when they are with child. I will bring my mother to us in Vestfold when we spend the winter there. I think you will understand each other. You are both strong-willed."

"And I have heard that if more women were skalds, the songs of battles between wives and their mothers-in-law would make men tremble," said Svanhild lightly. It was impossible to stay angry with Harald, and now that she had told him of her pregnancy, he would treasure her again. "I admire her, though, and I would learn healing craft from her. Yes, please bring her."

33

AFTER A FEW DAYS' CONSIDERATION, HAKON AGREED TO KING
Eirik's terms and joined forces with him and Solvi, against Harald.
Rane had returned to Vermaland. Sigurd had seen his growing bore-
dom and discomfort at the constant bickering in Eirik's court.

Now Sigurd had learned enough to return to Ragnvald with useful information. Ragnvald would reward and respect him, not simply
because of the bonds of family, but because he had done something
worthwhile: bloodied his sword in Ireland and brought back news of
betrayal.

Ragnvald would not yet know of Hakon and his Swedish alliance.
With every day that passed, Sigurd grew more anxious to be away
from him. Surely he, so experienced in betrayal, could see Sigurd's on
the horizon. Hakon and Solvi's plan began with an attack on Harald's
town of Tonsberg. Sigurd did not understand the whole of it, only that
Harald must be lured into a trap, and raids on his favorite towns and
settlements would help steer him where Solvi and Hakon wanted him.

Hakon and Solvi gathered their men and departed ten days later. As
Uppsala grew smaller, Sigurd watched Solvi's line of ships pull even
with and then pass Hakon's, cutting through the water with hardly
more space than a man could leap between them, every oar moving
in unison. A demonstration, Sigurd thought, of Solvi's mastery here.

He hoped this meant Hakon's pilot would ask them to row as well.
He wanted the activity, and the peace of exhaustion, so he would not

have to think about his deceit. Now that Svanhild had married Harald, Sigurd had even more reason to become a warrior in his army. He had missed Svanhild when she left Ardal, though at first only because he missed being able to bully her. She pushed back sometimes, and could be vicious, but at least she felt his equal, another overlooked child. When Olaf was still alive and Ragnvald believed dead, Sigurd had wondered if he should marry her—then his father's betrayal of Eystein and his son could be redeemed, for Eystein's line would still sit at Ardal. Now her marriage to Harald meant even more opportunities for Ragnvald's kin.

+ + +

RANE AND HIS forces were at the Vestfold settlement at the end of Oslo Fjord when Hakon's and Solvi's arrived. He greeted Hakon with a perfunctory embrace outside the main living hall. His bright red face gleamed with sweat from the heat. He wiped it with a rag and said, "Harald came and ran us off from Tonsberg just as we were attacking. How can one man be so lucky?"

"We have heard that he wed and sailed south," said Hakon. "And you set off from Uppsala when the weather broke and you finally had a wind, did you not?"

"Yes," said Rane.

"Harald's forces would have covered the most ground on that day as well. This is only weather, not luck," said Hakon.

Rane grinned. "We have had some luck too. It is mostly a loss, but we did capture a woman who was traveling south with her son to ask for Harald's justice."

"What do I care for this?" Hakon asked.

"Your son knows her." Rane's grin faded quickly. "She says she is the mother of one named Arnfast. She came from the Sogn *ting*, and said that Ragnvald would not give her justice. He would not alienate his allies."

A touch of breeze cooled the sweat on Sigurd's neck, making him shiver. He glanced at Herlaug, who stood next to his father. Herlaug had been almost entirely silent since leaving Uppsala, without his brother to speak for him. His face was pale and his jaw worked. He looked as tense as a trapped animal, torn between flight and immobility.

"That is interesting," said Hakon.

"My men took her, thinking her a comely woman who might make a good slave." Rane shuddered. "She wears a mask and they saw her from behind."

Hakon smirked. "All cats are gray in the dark," he said.

"You will not say that after you see her," said Rane.

"What became of her son?"

"Her son got away. He did not even try to save her."

"Let us see her now," said Hakon gravely. Herlaug tried to turn and leave, but Hakon grabbed him by the arm and spun him back so his feet stumbled on the uneven ground. "You must see her," he said, his voice hard. Sigurd started to back away. "Sigurd, come with us. I want you as a witness. This woman should not be living."

Rane's guards had bound the woman's hands and left her in a tent. When Hakon's guard pushed the flap open, Sigurd saw her kneeling on a bed of straw with her head bent forward. She raised her head, recognized Herlaug, and launched herself at him, before Herlaug flung her onto the ground.

Her veil came off in the struggle, as did her leather mask. She looked up at Hakon, freezing him in place as his guards pulled his son off her. Sigurd's stomach roiled at the sight and he looked away, though the image seemed burned onto his eyes. He stole another glance, in a vain hope that he had been mistaken in what he saw. For a moment, her face looked more false than the mask that covered it, a creation of fabric and paint, meant for scaring children. Then Sigurd resolved it into tatters of skin, with teeth and gums visible through a wound that could never heal. Hakon was correct: this woman should not be living. This was the face of one dead in battle, left to decay, the face of a shade—a vision of what Herlaug might look like in the afterlife, his crimes carved even more deeply on his flesh.

"She tried to kill me," said Herlaug. "That means I can kill her." Sigurd looked at Hakon, trying to read what he thought of his sons' revenge, now that he saw the wounds in person. "She should have died," Herlaug added.

"I am dead," said the woman. "I am your death."

Hakon blanched. "How did you come here, woman?" he asked.

"Let me kill her, Father," said Herlaug. Hakon ignored him.

"I come," she said. "Vengeance. King Ragnvald, King Harald, you—deny my justice?"

"Get her out of my sight," Hakon commanded, his voice rising in panic. His guards hesitated, hardly able to look at her.

"Where should we put her, my lord?" one of them finally asked.

"I mean—tie her up. Securely. She is a menace."

Hakon walked out of the tent as the guards bent to their work. As soon as Sigurd and Herlaug followed him outside, he turned toward his son. "This? This is what you did? Killing her would have been bad enough. But this? Valkyries weave battle tales on a loom of entrails, and you have given them another sister. Her vengeance will pursue you into death and after."

Herlaug's eyes widened, but he summoned up the courage to say, in a mocking tone, "You are prophesying, Father? Leave that to sorceresses."

"I do not know how to wipe out this crime," said Hakon, shoulders bowed down. "Yes, she will be killed. She cannot be allowed to live like this. But you—"

"I told you what I had done, Father!" said Herlaug. "You said it was fair revenge."

"If the gods agreed, she would have died, and I never would have seen her face," said Hakon. "Don't come into my presence until I call you. And do not kill her yet. We need to know what she knows, and who has seen her."

+ + +

SIGURD EXPECTED THAT his dreams would be troubled by the face of Herlaug's victim. Instead he woke from a dream of certainty: she pursued Herlaug, and Sigurd was only in danger from her if he remained at Herlaug's side. The fates beckoned him to Ragnvald, but first he needed to find out what Hakon would learn from the woman. He must make sure to be present at her questioning, no matter how unpleasant.

Hakon had planned to speak with her again this morning. Sigurd found him stalking between the tents, his face reflecting thoughts that passed over it like the clouds moving overhead—a storm that would reach them soon. The lines that age had made in Hakon's face, vertical slashes through his cheeks, were deep furrows this morning. For a moment, Sigurd saw them as true wounds, as bloody and raw as those in the woman's face. Herlaug had made those slashes in his father's cheeks just as surely as in the woman's.

As Hakon walked toward the woman's tent, Sigurd ran to catch up with him. "Arnfast comes from Sogn," said Sigurd to Hakon. "So does his mother."

"What?" said Hakon. "I have no time for you this morning."

"Do you think that she came here without Ragnvald's knowledge?" Sigurd asked.

"What do you want?" Hakon asked.

"I know Arnfast," said Sigurd. "We guarded Sogn together for many years. I might—I want to learn what my brother is up to. And she might know." Hakon nodded—he seemed to like Sigurd best when he spoke of revenge on Ragnvald, or perhaps he did not want to be in this woman's presence without the support of other men.

Arnfast's mother had been left to sleep on her pallet of straw with no blanket to protect her from the night's chill, though at least she wore her mask again. It made her look, lying on her side, as though she were carved of wood, a ship's broken figurehead.

"I can offer you an easy death, or a hard one," said Hakon without preamble. "How did you come to be here?"

"Fool. I come for vengeance. I kill your son. Your family. Cursed." She reached up with her bound hands to take the mask from her face.

"Don't." Hakon's voice went high with fear. "Don't, or I will torture you worse."

She made a hideous sound, which it took Sigurd a moment to identify as laughter. "Worse? Than this?" She pulled the mask off. One of Hakon's guards kicked her in the stomach, a movement more of panic than defense. She was still laughing as she struggled to her feet with her hands tied before her, her face clear for all to see.

"Tell me," said Hakon.

"No secret. Son bring to Harald—king. He see. I kill your son, he kills son? Don't care." From the tension in her shoulders, Sigurd could see that every word pained her, and that was why she spoke so few.

"Your son is going to Harald. You will kill my son or he will kill my son?" Hakon said, trying to make sense of her garbled words.

Her face moved, approximating a smile on the less wounded side. She raised her hands in a motion that looked beseeching until she drew a finger across her throat. "Yes. He dies."

"You came from Sogn? Which son brought you here?"

"Younger. To tell Harald: Atli—attacked Ragnvald. Wants Harald help." She could hardly say the names, especially Ragnvald's, which sounded, when she spoke it, as though she had swallowed something that choked her. Hakon questioned her further, probing for details of Atli's attack, and growing frustrated with her short, difficult answers. When Hakon was finally satisfied that he had enough information from her, Sigurd's feet had become tired from standing.

She brought strange news: Ragnvald fought with Hakon's son Heming in Maer, while fending off attacks from Atli in Sogn, and Harald delayed sending aid. If this were true, Harald was a poor king indeed—he had just married Svanhild, and still would not send aid to her brother.

"This is good," Hakon said, his face briefly lighter as he glanced at Sigurd, then darkening when he looked down at the woman on the floor again. "You will have your revenge on Ragnvald sooner than I thought. We will go to Maer to help my son Heming and this Atli. If Ragnvald is dead, I can give Tafjord to Solvi, and then he will give me my son back."

Sigurd tried not to look shocked at the news the woman had brought, but he feared he did not make a good show. Hakon gave him a grim smile. "I know, you had not intended for your vengeance to come so quickly. Do not worry, I will make sure you live to enjoy it. Now you can do something for me." He glanced at the woman, who sat on her heels, with her head bowed down, her hood mostly covering her face. "Kill her."

"No," said Sigurd, surprised into speaking before he could think. "I do not want her curse."

"Do you believe my family cursed by her?"

"I do not know, my lord," said Sigurd. "But I will not kill her. I am no killer of women. Your son wanted to do it—let him finish it."

"I should give the knife to her and let her get her vengeance before she dies or her shade will haunt us forever," Hakon muttered, then gave Sigurd a look of such cold rage Sigurd knew if he repeated what Hakon said, he would die by his hand. Hakon shook his head, as if to dispel the thought. "You're right. She is cursed, and she has cursed my son. He should do it."

Sigurd did not hear when it was done, but later that night, a pyre burned in a clearing in the woods, carrying the sparks and ashes of the woman's beautiful figure and ruined face up into the sky. Sigurd swore to himself that he would help her get her vengeance. Herlaug would not be allowed to live long with this crime to his name.

✛ ✛ ✛

SIGURD HEARD HAKON and Solvi arguing about Hakon's new plan that night. They had been discussing it all day, and neither would veer from his course.

"We only have time for one battle before the fall and your men have to leave for their farms," said Solvi to Hakon. Solvi said the word *farms* with some sarcasm—his men, his raiders, did not have farms to go home to. Sigurd had wondered at first, when meeting Solvi with King Eirik in Sweden, how Solvi had impressed the king of a great and powerful country so deeply, why he followed the advice of a landless raider. Solvi was as fine a sailor as the songs claimed, but what Sigurd found more impressive was how every time he spoke, even when his head was hidden behind the shoulders of taller men, everyone listened. His face was as clear and bright and attractive as Harald's, though formed along a different pattern, with knife-sharp features. He was firm in his judgments, and uncompromising in the standards he held himself and other men to. But unlike Hakon, Solvi seemed to bring joy to his every task. Perhaps that was the source of his power, joy that burnished his confidence and certainty. Hakon could not help but picking at everyone, even his sons, until they bled.

"Harald is here in the south, as are all of our forces," Solvi repeated.

"Now is the time to lure him into a sea battle and defeat him. I have seen him fight—and he is not as lucky or as agile by ship as he is on land."

"And let all his northern allies come to his aid again, as they did in Vestfold?" asked Hakon. He gave Solvi a piercing look, hoping, Sigurd thought, to see some shame at losing that battle. He would be disappointed, for Solvi's face showed nothing but mild skepticism.

"If Ragnvald is fighting Atli Kolbrandsson on one side and your son on the other, then we need not fear him sailing to Harald's rescue," said Solvi. "Now seems an ideal time."

"I will not risk it," Hakon replied. "I do not like to leave Ragnvald Eysteinsson alive. He has a way of spoiling my victories. Yours too. Who do you think it is that married your wife to Harald?"

Sigurd watched carefully, to see if Hakon could finally wring an angry reaction out of Solvi. His face did grow stern, but he showed little other change.

"This is foolishness," said Solvi. "This is about your pride. You hate Ragnvald for leaving your service for Harald's, when it was you who chased him away."

"Do you bait me, Solvi Hunthiofsson? I do not need your permission."

Solvi gave a pointed look at Herlaug, who sat by his father. Sigurd had avoided looking at him since the death of Arnfast's mother; now he tried to see if that murder had made any impression on the young man. His twisted face was hard to read, and his eyes as well, flat and hard, though he flinched and looked away when Solvi turned his gaze on him.

"My son is hostage against betrayal," said Hakon. "He does not make me into a slave, nor say I should substitute your judgment for my own."

"Perhaps he should," said Solvi scornfully, "if you continue on this course."

"Then kill Herlaug if you must—he is my least useful son, and I must aid my best," said Hakon, disgustedly. Sigurd looked again at Herlaug, who now wore an expression Sigurd had only ever seen before on a man who had been stabbed in the stomach and was about to vomit blood onto the ground. Herlaug sprang from his seat and ran out into the night. Solvi jerked his chin at one of his men, Snorri, who followed him with a few other guards.

Solvi smiled, not pleasantly. "That was cruel," he said. "I wonder when you will find that boy's dagger in your back. Or perhaps he will carve up your face too. He does keep his blade sharp."

Those words seemed to shake Hakon, and he replied in a low, urgent tone, "Ragnvald and Atli are fighting. If they receive word that I have joined with you and King Eirik, they will stop their fighting and come to Harald's aid. Ragnvald may not have your silver tongue, but he can be persuasive when he wishes—he may even persuade my son Heming to help Harald. He has done it before. Then the trap we spring on Harald becomes a trap we are caught in, as at Vestfold. Come with me, and take back Tafjord for yourself."

That made Solvi hesitate for a moment. "No, if I am sitting in Tafjord, I will only be a lure for Harald." Solvi crossed his arms. "I will not sanction this. But you are right. Your son is hostage against betrayal, not stupidity. If you do not perish by this foolishness, come to me and we can see if it is not too late to make Harald's death."

"And if I succeed?" Hakon asked.

"If you succeed, you can have one of your sons back."

✝ ✝ ✝

EVEN AS HAKON sailed north, the summer continued hot, baking Sigurd's pale skin a bright red that cracked and scabbed. He took to wrapping a cloth around his head like a woman's veil, and hiding in the shade of the ship's walls whenever he was not needed to help row.

On every beach where they camped at night, Hakon asked the local farmers and fishermen for news of Ragnvald, Heming, and Atli, and every night heard nothing. Peace, they said, held in the western districts. The hot summer meant the farmers had to work hard to keep the fields from growing parched, but those who had enough labor to keep irrigation trenches flowing could count on good harvests. The high pastures gave better grass this year than ever before. No one had time for raiding.

"Do you not think we should have heard of the fighting?" Egil asked Sigurd when they sighted the entrance to Sogn Fjord.

"I don't know," said Sigurd truthfully. If the fighting had been quick and one of the leaders was dead, that news would have spread, and if it dragged on, news of a war would have reached them. Perhaps the farmers and fisherfolk they met did not care for much beyond their own horizons. They would repeat any songs made of this summer's battles in the same way they did the battles of centuries earlier, making little difference between them and their local gossip. Sigurd could not mistrust the words of the woman who had died under Herlaug's knife. A god-sent, half-spirit woman like that must speak truth.

They made the turn into Sogn Fjord on a strange day, bright sun overhead, and a sea mist on the water. All of Hakon's men in his four ships sweat and cursed, and squinted at the fog. The air hardly moved, and they had to row. In the blank sameness of the swirling gray, it seemed as though they made no progress at all. It took three days' rowing, through that same strange weather, before the ships reached the end of the fjord. Shrouded in fog at the top of the hill lay the hall that Harald had built for Ragnvald, the hall Sigurd had guarded, poorly, the hall that Atli held for Ragnvald now. All was quiet.

"What is the best way to approach?" Hakon asked Sigurd. "You know this land."

"I thought you came to join with Atli against Ragnvald," said Sigurd.

"We do not know what we will find," Hakon replied. "I would be ready."

"There is no way but this," said Sigurd. "The hall is up the hill. The fog will hide us at least."

"This is sorceress weather," said Hakon. "I do not like it."

Sigurd shrugged, trying to seem unconcerned. It did not matter what Hakon liked—this was his home ground. He would see Ragnvald soon.

"Lead the way," Hakon invited him. The fog seemed to rise with them, keeping them hidden as they made their way up toward the hall. Atli's guard stopped them halfway up the hill, a guard like the one Sigurd should have set to prevent Atli's coming in the first place. The man tried to yell out a warning when he saw so many advancing on him. Hakon had two hundred following in his wake. The sound caught in his throat, choked off, Sigurd imagined, by the sudden dryness that he felt himself.

"You may live if you remain silent," said Hakon. "Is your master here?"

"Atli Kolbrandsson is at home," said the man in a whisper.

"Good," said Hakon. Then to Sigurd, "Tie him up."

Sigurd took two lengths of rope from one of Hakon's guards and tied the man hand and foot, and after a moment, ripped a strip of fabric from his shirt to bind his mouth.

"We will come and free you if all goes well," said Hakon. "If not . . ." His smile made Sigurd's sweat feel clammy.

The next set of guards that met them sent up an alarm before Hakon could silence them, and he held back his men's swords. Atli emerged from the hall, still drawing his sword as they reached it.

"Atli Kolbrandsson," Hakon called out. "I am King Hakon Grjotgardsson, ruler of Halogaland and Trondelag." He glanced at Sigurd. "Soon to be king of all Norway. I have heard that you fight my enemy Ragnvald of Maer, and I have come to offer you aid."

"Ragnvald of Sogn, you mean," said Atli.

"I thought it was Atli of Sogn," said Hakon. "It can be, if you join with me."

Atli had looked incredulous at Hakon's words, though he recovered himself very quickly. "I have heard rumors, and here they are in truth: you have betrayed Harald Tanglehair, prophesied king of all Norway. You claim that title for yourself. I suppose now you shall tell me of your sorceress mother, who predicted your rise as well?"

"No sorceress," said Hakon, "only right of arms and allies. All of Norway's dispossessed kings fight for me now, as does King Eirik of Sweden. With Harald, you are a steward for this Ragnvald, Ragnvald Half-Drowned, a boastful boy with no family. With me, you will be king in your own right."

"You do not know what I will be," said Atli. "I know that you have delivered yourself to me for justice. You will make me a hero in my king's eyes—in thanks for such a gift, I think I should not kill you, but I must."

"Kill me?" Hakon asked. "I am offering you a kingdom."

"You are offering me the cold hell of oath breakers," said Atli. "That is not for me. These men you lead deserve better than you. Fight me in single combat, and whoever lives will have Sogn for as long as he can keep it. Swear to spare their lives, and if I die, my men will stand down."

"You don't have enough men to fight me," said Hakon.

"Do I not?" Atli asked. "Do you think that King Ragnvald would leave me so poorly defended? You do not think well of him, but you must know him better than that." As he spoke, more and more men gathered around them, emerging out of the mist—not as many as Hakon had brought, but they surrounded Hakon's forces. If they fought well, on ground they knew, against Hakon's men who had been exhausted by three days of rowing, they would win.

"You have one more," said Sigurd to Atli, loudly, so all could hear. "I came to deliver news of this oath breaker to my brother." He spoke in a rush, relief coming over him that he could finally speak honestly. "I don't think I am the only one of Hakon's men who has grown ill at the idea of following him. Who is with me?"

"Silence," said Hakon, before any man could speak and add his voice to Sigurd's. "Atli Kolbrandsson, I will fight you in single combat, as you say."

Men formed a circle and made room for them. Atli called his son as his second, a slender man like him, though favored with more pleasing features. Hakon commanded his closest guard to stand second for him, to hand him shields, and fight in his place if he fell to an unfair blow. With no judge to call a start or finish, Atli and Hakon touched shield bosses and leaped at each other immediately.

Sigurd could tell from the first step that Hakon would lose. He remembered seeing Atli fight briefly when he took over Sogn—he had never seen a man move like that before, sinew and speed, flashing like water in a mountain river, moving too gracefully for a man to notice his deadliness until it brought his death.

Atli forced Hakon to stumble once. Hakon escaped by blocking a downward stroke with his left forearm, a blow that drove him to his knees and made that hand useless. Blood flowed steadily over it onto the ground. Atli must have nearly severed the bone, for it took him a moment to pull his sword free—a moment that Hakon used to thrust his sword up into Atli's belly so it came out high on his back.

Atli, trapped on Hakon's blade, swung his sword around and crashed it down on Hakon's neck, severing the artery so the blood burst forth over both of them as they fell together. Hakon died immediately, his blood soaking the earth.

Atli's son rushed to his father's side, and eased him to the ground. He drew the sword from Atli's body. Blood foamed around Atli's lips. His sons laid him down on an outdoor table, and Vigdis came to tend his wounds. His narrow chest, now bare for Vigdis's work, grew pale as life began to leave him, making him look so small that Sigurd regretted ever having feared him.

Atli spoke to Vigdis and to his sons while Sigurd lingered nearby, wondering what should be done. Hakon's men showed no will to fight. Some of them sat down where they had stood during the duel. Atli's wife worked quickly, and brought ale to all of the men so they might drink together and claim hospitality rather than fighting. Atli's son Aldi announced a funeral and funeral feast the following day.

"For who?" called out Egil.

"For both of them," said Vigdis. "Atli will not last until morning."

In the middle of the night, Vigdis shook Sigurd's shoulder to wake him. He had been dozing outside against the wall of a shed, wrapped in his cloak. He had not wanted to leave Hakon's warriors for long enough to retrieve his sleeping bag from the ship.

"My lord Atli would speak with you," she said.

"About what?"

"Ask him," she said impatiently. "Heed him well. He is a man worth listening to, even when he is not dying." Her voice broke, and Sigurd put an arm around her shoulder, grateful that he was not a stranger to her.

Atli's lips were blue in the dimness. "Sigurd, thank you for coming. Please, tell your brother I kept my oath," he said. He seemed more peaceful now than he had in the afternoon, when Vigdis still labored to save him.

"What should I do?" Sigurd asked.

"My sons will take my men to Ragnvald at Naustdal. You should lead Hakon's there as well. They will follow you." He took a labored breath. "Tell your brother I kept my oath," he said again.

"He will know," said Sigurd. "The gods will know, and Harald's skalds will know. You will be sung of."

"My sons—my eldest, Aldi. He would make a good steward for Sogn. Tell your brother that."

"I will," Sigurd promised.

"I'm sorry I embarrassed you when I came here. You are a good man. You will be a brave man, I see it." They said that those on the edge of death could see between the worlds, and Sigurd hoped it was true. "Now send my sons back to my side," said Atli. "My wife. And my Vigdis."

Sigurd did as he was bid. Atli died as the sun rose. That day Atli's sons buried him, while Sigurd spoke prayers for Hakon and marshaled some of his men to bury him as well. As an oath breaker, perhaps Hakon should be burned instead, but Vigdis said she knew the spells that would keep his corpse from walking. She spoke a few words as she tied his toes together, and they buried him facedown.

Sigurd gathered Hakon's men to him the following day. At the funeral, he had seen uncertainty and hopelessness on their faces, and Atli's dying words had given him the courage to speak to them. He stood on a slope, with Hakon's men ranged below him. Those who owned armor had put it on this morning, Sigurd saw, to make themselves ready for anything that might come.

"I respected and honored Hakon as a great king and warrior," Sigurd said. "But he betrayed his oaths, and in so doing, made all of you into oath breakers as well." He remembered seeing Ragnvald speak, and how he put pauses into his speeches to allow men time to absorb his words, and to see how they reacted. Hakon's men murmured to one another. "My brother, Ragnvald, is a few days' journey away in Naustdal," Sigurd continued. "He fights for Harald. Hakon's son Heming guards North Maer and is also Harald's man." No one at Sogn could give Sigurd any reason to believe Jorunn's testimony that Heming attacked Ragnvald. "Come with me, and redeem yourselves."

Sigurd saw eyes brightening, along with skepticism and resignation on the grizzled faces. "You betrayed him," called out one man.

Sigurd's face grew hot. He must not grow defensive now. Atli had told him he could lead these men. He must show no doubt. "I followed him until he betrayed Harald," he said. "Then I followed my hope of bringing Harald the news of his betrayal." The faces before him still looked skeptical. "Harald is the prophesied king of all Norway. Many of you have won gold fighting in his battles. How much gold did you win fighting against him? Would you rather fight for a Swedish king, who would keep Harald weak? Fight for Solvi Hunthiofsson, another oath breaker, another betrayer? Fight for Herlaug, outlawed, criminal?"

"We need to get home to our farms," said one of them.

"No, we don't," said another.

As an argument threatened to erupt, Sigurd raised a hand and tried not to show his surprise when the voices quieted. "You are Trondelag men? Halogaland men?" Agreement sounded. "Those districts lie to the north. Come north with me to Naustdal, and we will decide what to do from there. Who is with me?"

He heard shouts of assent that were louder than the grumbles so he repeated, "Who is with me? Let us pack up the ships—I promise you those same ships will take home any man who is needed on his farm, and take the rest of you to blood and gold and glory."

They looked at him expectantly, so Sigurd took up his pack and his cloak and began running down the hill toward the ships, his heart pounding with joy when Hakon's men surged after him.

34

LATE IN THE SUMMER, WHEN MAER'S HAY WAS DRYING IN THE fields, a scout arrived with a message for Ragnvald, telling him that four ships were approaching Naustdal, and would reach them by midafternoon. Naustdal lay on the coast near a short, narrow fjord that led to open sea through a gap in the barrier islands. After his years of living at Sogn, with a network of scouts to keep him informed of ships coming and going, Ragnvald found the swift arrival of visitors to Naustdal disconcerting. He had raised taxes on South Maer to make sure that he could support a larger number of warriors than King Vemund had in the past, and he had also asked Harald to send a shipbuilder from Tonsberg to turn Maer trees into more power to protect his coastline. Vemund had feared attack by land, and his men, who could melt into the forest and scavenge for months if necessary, had defended it well. Ragnvald's enemies would come from the sea.

The narrow fjord leading to his hall permitted the passing of only one ship at a time, easy targets for fire arrows. These visitors did not have their shields out, and they let the afternoon's fitful breezes push them along rather than using oars. Harald's ships, Ragnvald assumed, though it would be strange for Harald to go south, intending to pass the winter in Tonsberg and Vestfold, and then return so quickly.

Still, Ragnvald met the ships with all of his warriors behind him, their swords and axes drawn. Heming had been visiting with some of his men, and these Ragnvald commanded to guard the hall itself, in case attack came from more than one direction. Ragnvald was surprised to see Sigurd leap down from the lead ship and run toward Ragnvald, unarmed, looking as happy as a hunting dog greeting its master. Ragnvald kept his sword out, though Sigurd did not look like a threat. He stopped only a hand's breadth before reaching the tip of Ragnvald's sword.

"Brother, I mean you no harm," he said, "and neither do these men. But I have much to tell you." Sigurd had never been good at hiding his emotions. From the look on his face, turning from joy to hurt, Ragnvald thought he could trust him. But perhaps he had learned to lie over the two years he had been gone.

"Tell me then," said Ragnvald warily.

"These are some of Hakon's men and also Atli's—his eldest son is with me. Hakon and Atli are dead. Harald is in danger." Sigurd threw up his hands. "So much has happened, I do not know where to begin."

Before Ragnvald could react to so much information, Einar and Ivar came running down the hill behind him, and Sigurd immediately scooped them up, one under each arm. "Oof, you're growing heavy," he exclaimed, spinning them around while Ivar shrieked and wriggled, and Einar waited patiently for Sigurd to tire of his game and put him down so he could collect his offended dignity. Sigurd looked taller and broader than when he left, his golden beard had filled in, and he held himself more like a man, though an overgrown puppy of a man, still thirsty for praise.

Oddi had been a few paces behind Ragnvald, and now came to stand shoulder to shoulder with him. "What has happened to my father?" he asked, his hand on the hilt of his sword.

"These are Hakon's and Atli's men?" Ragnvald asked. "And they are to be trusted?" Sigurd had brought more men than Ragnvald had ready to fight at Naustdal, though he could muster more with a few days' warning. Behind Sigurd, men climbed down from their ships and, seeing the drawn swords of all of Ragnvald's followers, unsheathed their own weapons. Even if Sigurd spoke the truth, the smallest misstep would lead to bloodshed.

"Command them to return to their ships and wait for my wel-come," said Ragnvald. "Once I am satisfied that they mean no harm, they may come ashore."

Sigurd looked troubled but nonetheless he ducked his head, and turned to address the gathered men, some still climbing down.

"My friends," he said in a loud voice that filled the beach, "my brother, King Ragnvald, is rightly worried that so many armed men have come to his shore. He will give us hospitality once he learns the whole tale, I am sure of it. For now, return to your ships and wait there for my word." As the warriors sheathed their swords and walked back toward the beach, Ragnvald felt a sudden burn of tears in his eyes. He could not name all that he was feeling, but a part of it was fierce happiness that Sigurd had come back to him, and pride that he had returned more of a man than he had left.

Ragnvald sheathed his sword as he saw Aldi Atlisson climb up from the shore to stand next to Sigurd. "I lead my father's men here," Aldi said. "I should hear whatever is said." Ragnvald nodded. Aldi had been at the battle at Solskel, where he had been one of the few men brave enough to join Ragnvald in the decoy ships. He bore the marks of grief upon his narrow face: shadowed eyes and a sickly pallor.

"Very well," said Ragnvald. "Sigurd, my brother, tell me what has passed."

Sigurd related a long tale that took him across the North Sea, and into Sweden. He told of Hakon's betrayal, Solvi and Eirik's alliance, and a trap for Harald on the southwest coast. "It did not become clear until we reached Uppsala that Hakon meant betrayal. I let him think that I wanted my revenge upon . . . upon you, my brother, but only so he would trust me. An oath breaker is more likely to trust another oath breaker." He raised his eyes to Ragnvald's. "It was a lie, I swear it."

Ragnvald put his hand on Sigurd's shoulder. "I believe you," he said.

Sigurd told then of the coming of Jorunn, her message, and how Solvi and Hakon had been divided over her message.

"Did you believe it?" Oddi asked.

Sigurd shrugged. "I wasn't sure, but I knew that I must return to

Ragnvald and tell him what I learned. I'm sorry, Oddi, I know he was your father, but I could not follow an oath breaker like King Hakon."

"But you say Atli killed him?" Oddi asked. Ragnvald shot him a quelling look.

Sigurd continued, "Hakon asked Atli to join him in his betrayal by attacking you. Atli said he would not and they killed each other. It was a marvel."

Ragnvald stumbled half a step back. He had hardly dared hope his plans would lead to this: his enemies each finding their end on the other's blade. Jorunn had been an arrow shot blindfolded on a winter's night, and she had found her mark.

"My father was honorable," Aldi added, his voice low and troubled. "He fought for you, King Ragnvald. Though you never trusted him, he would not betray his oath, even to save his life."

Sigurd nodded. "Atli proposed single combat to spare his men, and Hakon agreed. They died upon each other's swords."

"How did—tell me the rest," said Ragnvald.

"Let me," said Aldi. "A man's finest deeds are better told by other tongues. King Ragnvald, your brother invited Hakon's men here to erase the stain of his betrayal, and turned enemies into allies in an instant. They deserve your hospitality tonight, whoever they decide to follow tomorrow, and your stepbrother deserves your praise."

"And they shall have it," said Ragnvald. "Sigurd, brother, as I welcome and bless you, please welcome them on my behalf." To Aldi he said, "You have the honor of a jarl. Your father avenged his death in the moment of its making. Odin will welcome him in Valhalla. For you, I will pour out my generosity. I had promised your father marriage between our families, now I say that your daughter shall marry my eldest son, rejoining our families. I will have other gifts of gratitude as well. Your father was a truer man than I could have hoped."

Aldi clasped his arms and thanked him. Ragnvald sent Oddi to ask Hilda to make ready whatever feast could be managed this quickly. Happily, the cows had given bountiful milk this summer, and so the warriors were fed well with *skyr* and rye, stewed apples, and ale. Not a feast worthy of Harald's table, but plain food that a man might miss after a long time shipboard. Ragnvald remembered that Sigurd loved honey cakes—he had never lost his taste for sweets as he grew into manhood—and asked Hilda to bake as many as she could.

When all had eaten their fill, Ragnvald proposed a toast. "King Harald's vision is of a Norway of peace and concord, and you men have brought that vision ever closer tonight. Out of betrayal, you have made companionship. Out of death, you have made friendship. Tonight we feast; tomorrow we sail to Harald's aid, for Solvi Hunthiofsson, enemy to us all, masses his allies to threaten Harald's peace." Some pockets of discontent greeted his toast, though most raised their glasses and drank.

After the noise from the toast quieted, and Ragnvald sat again, Oddi leaned forward and said to Sigurd, "There is much I still don't understand about my father's death. What word did this woman Jorunn bring?"

"She spoke of war," said Sigurd. "She seemed as an emissary from the land of the dead, so all thought she must speak truth. Only Solvi doubted her. And it was strange, when I sailed north with the oath breaker, we heard no talk of war."

Ragnvald glanced at Heming, who was frowning and looking at his hands, clasped around his dagger and his spoon. It was a measure of how he had changed that he did not immediately leap to challenge Sigurd for naming his father an oath breaker, no matter how true it was. Oddi looked no happier.

"Yet I find you are all well, and friends," Sigurd added. "And Atli died defending Sogn for you. Oddi, I know no more than that."

Aldi leaned forward so he could speak in Ragnvald's ear. "My father was brave, and fought as he swore he would. He was loyal to you. I do not know that King Hakon's other sons can say the same. This must be decided, if not tonight, then tomorrow. Some things cannot go unsaid."

"I agree," said Ragnvald, quickly, measuring hostilities. He felt sure of Oddi, but was less so of Heming. The men who had followed Sigurd here were still more Hakon's men than his. Loyalties needed to be declared soon, before they joined any battles together. Ragnvald would not punish anyone for following Hakon in the past and never, as Harald had, with slavery and maiming. Any who did not want to be part of Harald's army should be sent home to Halogaland where they could wait out the coming battles.

Ragnvald rose again, and spoke to the men in his hall, who he could now see had divided themselves into groups, Hakon's and Atli's, turning away from one another. "Much has occurred, and much needs to be thought over. You are all welcome here in Naustdal, and while you are on my lands, you will behave as friends. I am sure that there are many different thoughts and desires in this room, loyalties that may conflict. These are murky waters." He waited until he heard murmured agreement, and continued. "We are lucky to have so many wise heads here to chart our course: Hakon's elder sons, Atli's son, my brother Sigurd." Sigurd smiled, flushed with drink.

Ragnvald sent up a prayer that they would all remain on Harald's side. He did not know who else stood against Harald, except Solvi, and some Swedish allies, which he had known before. He must question Sigurd further, but matters could not be discussed before so many armed men who owed allegiance to different kings.

"Sigurd has brought important news for King Harald, to whom I owe my loyalty," he continued. "I do not know what made Hakon abandon Harald, but his sons Heming and Oddi have always been Harald's faithful allies. This is what binds us now. Feast, sleep, and repair your tack. If some of you want to go hunting before you eat up all my stores and have to dine on the benches"—some laughter sounded at this—"that would be useful." Ragnvald looked around the room, trying to read the faces. He saw weariness and confusion on some of the warriors, while others appeared tensed for a fight.

"For now," he said, raising his glass, "another toast, this one to Sigurd Olafsson, scout, warrior, and brother—brave, loyal, and true!" All stood and raised their glasses. In this, at least, they were united. Ragnvald glanced at Heming, who wore a bemused expression, as though he did not know how to feel—natural enough, with the news of his father's death and dishonor still fresh. He must watch Heming for when that brew might boil over. Oddi sat staring into his goblet. It took him even longer to come to his feet than it did Heming. Finally, he raised his hand in a toast as well, his expression dark, and only then did Ragnvald take a drink.

✤ ✤ ✤

AFTER THE FEAST was over, Ragnvald left the drinking hall to go
to his bed where Alfrith waited for him. He was happy almost to
the point of giddiness that his plan had worked so well, and even
brought Sigurd back to him, though he must keep a close guard over
his emotions to avoid offending Heming and Oddi. He would have
to go to war, but Solvi was weakened, and might finally be defeated.
The gods smiled upon him. Alfrith would welcome him eagerly into
her bed tonight, at this point in her pregnancy, though her sickness
had prevented it earlier.

Oddi walked toward him in the dark between the buildings, his
face blue in the twilight, shadowed by his dark hair. He grabbed
Ragnvald's arm tightly, almost as if he might fall down without support, though when Ragnvald went to steady him, Oddi shrugged
him off with a violent shudder. He had never, in Ragnvald's memory, laid hands on Ragnvald like that, not even when they had been
equals—or at least when the distance between their stations had been
impossible to determine: base-born son of a king and true-born son of
a dead jarl. As soon as Ragnvald was named king of Sogn at the *ting*,
with Harald by his side, Oddi had deferred to him, and Ragnvald had
blessed him for it, for where Oddi went, other men followed. It had
come to seem natural to Ragnvald that he should walk before Oddi,
and Oddi should serve his interests, for Ragnvald looked out for him
better than his father or brothers ever had.

"That was a strange story Sigurd told," Oddi said, his voice rough.
Ragnvald stared at Oddi's hand on his bicep until Oddi let go.

"Are you drunk?" Ragnvald asked. His women had served only ale
tonight, but Oddi had a knack for charming servants, and they would
certainly have brought him stronger stuff if he asked.

"No." Oddi shook his head. "I say: it was an odd tale, especially the
part about Arnfast's mother, Jorunn, showing up in Vestfold. That is
very strange."

Ragnvald wanted to take a step back, to put more space between
them. His fingers itched to feel the weight of a sword in them. This
was Oddi, though, not a threat. "Sigurd said Herlaug was in Vestfold,"

said Ragnvald. "It was not so strange that she would want revenge." Oddi met Ragnvald's eyes, finally. He looked wary but hopeful, as though he wanted to be talked out of his suspicions. "When Alfrith and I went to her, she did not want to live with her face so mutilated. Only the prospect of revenge changed her mind."

"And now she has it, but on her attacker's father, not on Herlaug, is that what you mean?" Oddi asked, his voice still low and dangerous. "My father came here because he had been told my brother Heming and Atli both stood against you. Why would she say that?"

"People say all kinds of things under torture," said Ragnvald. "I've always thought it better to lie under torture than remain silent. I am sure your father was not gentle with her. Do you think he was?"

"I'll never get to ask him, will I?" said Oddi. He still met Ragnvald's eyes, though he had lost his pleading look. "Unless you walk past his body and it begins to bleed again." As a body was said to do when its murderer passed by.

"I?" Ragnvald asked. He had comforted himself that if Hakon took the bait Jorunn offered, he would deserve his fate. He did not think he could explain his lie to Oddi, though, not in this mood.

"You, Ragnvald the Wise." Oddi said the byname bitterly, the name that he had given Ragnvald originally, and meant as gentle mocking between friends, before Harald took it up in earnest. "Here is what I think: you sent the woman to my father with that message, knowing he could not resist coming to the side of his true-born son. His favorite son, I think."

"Your father betrayed Harald," said Ragnvald, knowing it sounded like an excuse. "He made an alliance with Solvi—Solvi Hunthiofsson, the son of his old enemy. And Eirik of Sweden. His life would have been forfeit, no matter where he went."

"But you couldn't leave it be, could you?" Oddi asked. It seemed as though he hardly heard Ragnvald. "Ragnvald the Wise, acting alone, tying everything up in a neat bundle—let your enemies destroy one another, and anyone else who gets in the way, as long as you come out on top. You killed my father, and Aldi's, as much as if you held the blade. Did Atli Mjove deserve that of you? He died defending your land."

"Land he stole with Guthorm's help," said Ragnvald.

"You have an answer for everything," said Oddi. "But you will not tell me I am mistaken? That you had no hand in this, that this woman and her family acted alone?"

"If they did, will you take your brother's feud to them? Should all of their faces be sliced open to satisfy your family's vengeance?" asked Ragnvald, his anger building. He and Oddi would come to blows soon if he did not defuse this.

"It does not matter," said Oddi in a high voice. "You did this. You."

"Your father was an oath breaker," said Ragnvald. He tried to speak deliberately, in the same measured tone he used for dispensing justice as king. "Herlaug and Geirbjorn defied Harald's justice, and your father supported them in that." Hakon's betrayal had been as inevitable as winter.

"Tell me though," said Oddi, tears in his voice. "Tell me you did this."

Ragnvald sighed. "I did this. I will never lie to you, my friend, though it pains me to tell you. I did not know the arrow would find its mark, but I am not unhappy that it did, except if it loses me your friendship."

"Tell me truly then—would you have done differently, if you knew it would?" Oddi asked.

"What would you have done, if I told you what I planned?" Ragnvald asked. "I thought you wanted to stay out of your father's struggles, and your brothers'."

"I have been a coward," said Oddi. "But no longer. You are my sworn brother, and I will not be forsworn, but I cannot fight at your side anymore. I will see what my brother Heming thinks, and my father's men. Be warned, Heming has a hotter temper than I."

"Let us do it now," said Ragnvald. He could not believe that he had lost Oddi's friendship. At this moment, Heming had not yet decided what to think about his father's death, but Oddi, in his anger, could push him toward rebellion.

Ragnvald asked one of Heming's men where to find him, and learned that he kept vigil for his father, sitting by Naustdal's burial mounds. Before Oddi could speak, Ragnvald began: "Heming, I am sorry for your father's death. It is only fair to tell you of the part I played in it." He explained that he feared that the only other choice was letting Herlaug destroy Arnfast's family down to the root, and see the feud cause a rift between Harald and Hakon that would destroy Norway. "And I thought to put your father to a test—a test that he failed, for he had already betrayed Harald and allied with Solvi Klofe. Your brother Oddi hates me for this. Do you?" His stepfather, Olaf, had taught Ragnvald that an unanswered killing was like an invisible wound that brought pain to all who knew of it. Sometimes gold could heal it, sometimes only blood.

Heming had hardly looked at Ragnvald as he spoke, and only on Ragnvald's question did he turn his eyes up. He laughed brokenly. "You cannot give me time to mourn my father before I decide whether to kill you?" he asked. "When you tell me this, I know I should feel anger. But when I learned my father was dead, and had avenged himself in the moment of his death, I felt nothing except relief."

"Relief?" cried Oddi. "He"—Oddi shoved Ragnvald hard enough to make him stumble—"tricked our father, he killed him!" Ragnvald put his hand to his sword.

"Yes, relief," said Heming, with a shaky laugh. "Now he will never mock me again. I do not think I will kill you, Ragnvald. I am not wise as you, but I see that my father's path would have led him onto your blade or Harald's for his betrayal. My father cannot include me in his betrayal now. Your path will lead to peace."

"Peace?" Oddi asked Heming. "What do you care for peace?"

"Since I have ruled Maer from Tafjord," said Heming. "Are you not tired of blood, brother?"

"It does not matter what I am tired of. Ragnvald did not ask me—"

"And that is why you are angry," said Heming. "Not over our father. He was an oath breaker, and a fool who thought himself wise. He is my father and I will mourn him, and he was my enemy and I am glad he is dead. Make your peace with Ragnvald. He has been better to you than our father ever was."

"Never," said Oddi. "You are, both of you, fools and cowards." He walked away across the grass until he was lost in the shadows.

Ragnvald did not want to leave Heming like this. "I want to keep vigil with you," he said. "I too will mourn."

They sat in silence for a while, watching the horizon turn from orange to deep blue. At midnight, a few more stars pressed through the fabric of the sky, faintly winking overhead. Ragnvald usually loved this part of summer, the long days, the heat that made him feel relaxed and easy, though he mistrusted it too for the same reason. War and death came out of that heat: breezes brought convoys of ships, sudden rainstorms brought crop-killing hail.

"He was a great man," said Heming.

"Yes, he was," said Ragnvald. No one could deny that. Hakon had shaped the western coast, won countless battles, and opened up the far north for trade. It must have been hard for him to see a man like Harald, younger than his sons, win effortlessly what it had taken him a lifetime to bring within his reach. Hakon had been the first to notice Ragnvald's abilities, to encourage him rather than try to crush him, as Olaf had. Even after Ragnvald broke with Hakon, he never forgot Hakon's early praise, so precious after a boyhood marked by Olaf's constant doubt. "He will be remembered forever," he said to Heming.

"For his betrayal," said Heming.

"Perhaps not," Ragnvald answered. "Perhaps he went to Atli because of a misunderstanding, and they killed each other for it."

"You know that is not what happened," said Heming.

"Harald's skalds may hear it another way," said Ragnvald. He could be generous now; Hakon could no longer harm him.

Heming threw him a skeptical glance. "I do not think that is likely."

"Harald will not want everyone to know of Hakon's betrayal either," said Ragnvald. "He is the prophesied king, and the strength of his claim rests on everyone believing in that prophecy. If your father did not . . ."

Heming laughed shortly. "So your generosity is for Harald after all."

"I prefer when everyone can win," said Ragnvald.

"Or all of your enemies can lose," said Heming. Ragnvald shifted uneasily, until Heming sighed and bowed his head. "Don't worry, I am not going to duel you. My father killed Atli and is thus avenged. Oddi won't either. Sometimes it is hard, though, to feel as though you are a chess piece, with Ragnvald the Wise moving you about the board."

Ragnvald's throat tightened. "Oddi is my sworn brother."

"He feels guilty that he did not do more for our father," said Heming. "Do you know why our father bought him from his family? My father went to visit Oddi's mother, but she had died, and he sees this boy with an ax who is the right size to be his son. He asks the family, and they say yes, he is. And my father takes him home, and makes him demonstrate chopping wood, killing a pig, all with his ax. He said to me and my brothers, 'See this boy, this is my son, you should be more like him. Be as strong as him. Stronger than him.' Remember the jarl I killed at the Sogn *ting*?"

Ragnvald made a noise of assent. He would never forget that duel, which he had watched when Heming had seemed as golden and distant as a god. The jarl he had killed, Runolf, had been dark-haired, like Ragnvald.

"My father compared me to Runolf until I could not stand it, until I thought I was less than a man if I allowed him to live. I sent one of my men to trap him into insulting me and demanded the duel. I thought it would make my father respect me, but of course, then he chose you."

"His endless quest to provide you with good examples, I suppose," said Ragnvald sardonically. That was what Ragnvald had seen of Hakon. He had been a great king, and a disastrous father. He hoped to raise his own sons better. Even Olaf had done better than that. He had taught Ragnvald to be strong and self-sufficient, to prefer deeds to words, to watch and listen more than he spoke. Olaf had been as much his father as Eystein, giving him a double legacy, lessons from two men that Ragnvald did not know how to balance or discard.

"I've never heard you boast before," said Heming, and Ragnvald grimaced. He wished he could see Heming's expression. "Once he realized that Oddi was not going to play his game, that he would not compete for my father's attention, or rise to his baiting, my father ignored him. Used him as an example of what not to be—until Oddi distinguished himself again at your side. Oddi made a fair show of pretending it didn't bother him but . . ."

Ragnvald could fill in the rest. Oddi had shaped himself to avoid notice, to please and charm everyone, to need nothing. Svanhild had used and discarded him much as his father had. He must feel that Ragnvald had done the same. "I suppose your father wanted the best for you," said Ragnvald.

"I'm not sure of that," said Heming. "He killed his uncle, warred with his own father, and banished any skald who sang his father's praise songs. I think he feared one of us would do the same to him." Heming began crying, suddenly, sobs that embarrassed Ragnvald, even as tears prickled in his own eyes and he envied Heming's release.

When Heming quieted, Ragnvald called for a servant to bring him and Heming some bread and watered ale. In the morning when the rooster crowed, Heming went to his bed, and Ragnvald to his morning tasks. He did not think he could sleep, not until Oddi returned, or at least until he knew that the hundreds of armed men staying in and around the hall at Naustdal would not kill each other. Heming woke in the afternoon and brought Sigurd to join Ragnvald where he labored out in a field, repairing one of the stone walls.

"We must plan," said Heming. "A force masses against Harald."

Ragnvald turned to Sigurd. "You said that Solvi means to attack this summer?"

"He means to gather a great force in one place," said Sigurd, "and trap Harald with it. He said that little raids were not enough—only a great battle would defeat Harald. He will not do it unless victory is certain."

"Where does he plan to fight this great battle?" Heming asked.

"I do not know," said Sigurd. "Solvi would not reveal it to any but Hakon and his captains. But I know he means to do it soon."

Ragnvald heaved up a stone, then dropped it when one of Hakon's men got in his way. "Let us have a council. Has Oddi returned?" He had not, so Ragnvald gathered with Heming, Sigurd, and Aldi in Naustdal's sacrifice grove, a shaded clearing by a small brook, lush with grass that grew tall in soil fertilized by blood. "Heming, what do you think we should do?"

"Stop them," said Heming. "Drive Solvi Hunthiofsson and his allies out of Norway once and for all."

"Not kill Solvi?" Sigurd asked.

"I've heard that he made a pact with Loki and he cannot be killed," said Heming.

"And," Ragnvald added, "I have sworn to Svanhild I will not kill him unless I have no choice."

"I have sworn nothing," said Aldi, "so if he needs killing, I will do it. King Ragnvald, what do you think we should do?"

Ragnvald fell silent for a moment. A breeze came up the cliff and stirred his hair. Out in the fjord, a small fishing boat passed by. "We do not know how many allies Solvi has, nor how many men the king of Sweden will send. We have here ten ships in all, lightly crewed. Aldi, can you muster the men of Sogn? Heming, Maer is for you. I will take my brother Sigurd, for he is the witness to all of this. We will go to Harald in Tonsberg and let him know how things lie. I will send a messenger to tell you where the battle will be."

"How will you know?" Aldi asked.

"Someone will have to lure Harald there," said Ragnvald. "That will teach us where the ambush will be, if nothing else does. Come south, keeping to the innermost passage, and that is where my messengers will find you. If Solvi wants a great battle, he will have all the kings of Norway to meet him."

"What of my father's lands?" Heming asked.

"I will send a messenger," said Ragnvald, "or Heming can, that would be better—so Halogaland can send warriors as well."

Oddi stepped into the clearing. Ragnvald had not told the guards to alert him if Oddi came. He could not begin to think of Oddi as an enemy.

"I will go," said Oddi. "It is what I should do for him."

Ragnvald felt a loosening in his chest. Oddi could not give up being his friend so easily, though he still refused to meet Ragnvald's eyes.

"Very well," said Ragnvald. "Are all satisfied?"

"Satisfied that you will get the glory," Heming grumbled, but with a fond look for Ragnvald.

"As always," said Oddi, with a good deal less warmth.

"I can stay and muster men from Maer," said Ragnvald, with a shrug. He did not want Heming and Oddi to take him up on it. Harald would only believe this news from Ragnvald's lips, especially after Hakon's betrayal.

"No," said Heming. "Harald will trust your words more than any of ours. You go."

✛ ✛ ✛

RAGNVALD SPENT THE next few days arguing with Heming and Aldi about how many men should accompany him and how many should remain behind in the western districts to recruit their fellows. Finally Heming and Oddi, using Ragnvald's guilt to wear him down, made him agree to depart with only two ships, a hundred men in total. Ragnvald went only to deliver a message and to plan for war.

Oddi avoided Ragnvald whenever Ragnvald tried to find him for a private talk. The day Ragnvald was to leave, he found Oddi playing with Einar and Ivar, chasing them around a tree, and tickling them when he caught them. It caught Ragnvald off guard to see Einar laughing and joyful. He stopped as soon as he saw Ragnvald.

Oddi grew solemn as well when he saw Ragnvald approach. He looked so much like an overgrown boy, standing with Ragnvald's sons with his dark hair flopping down over his eyes, that Ragnvald wished he had been able to hide his manipulations from him forever.

"Boys, it's time to do your chores," said Ragnvald. He sent them off to water and feed the chickens and gather pails of milk. "I am sorry," he said, before Oddi could speak. "I tried to protect you from your family's troubles, and I see that was the wrong thing to do." This was what Oddi wanted to hear, so Ragnvald would say it.

Oddi looked at Ragnvald, searching his face, evaluating him. Ragnvald clenched his fists, willing Oddi to forgive, forget, become his friend and brother again.

"You said you would not lie to me, but this is a lie," said Oddi finally. "You would do it again without hesitation. I know you. You trust no one, and you think you know what is best for everyone, especially if it is what is best for you and your beloved Harald. You know he is only a man, whatever . . . vision you claim to have had. And I think Harald is weak—what is the difference between him ordering the mutilation of all those men in Tafjord and what my brother Herlaug did?"

"My vision . . . ," said Ragnvald. He had clung to it when Harald disappointed him, used it as a sun-stone on a cloudy day, to see Harald as more than a man, even when he acted as less than one. Harald had a vision too, a peaceful, united Norway, strong enough to stand against King Eirik of Sweden, strong enough that its laws would be obeyed, so men like Herlaug could not take revenge with impunity, and so feud need not destroy families and districts.

"A man needs a north star," said Ragnvald slowly. "To steer by. For a long time, I thought mine was taking back Ardal, and then becoming king of my grandfather's district. But—"

"Harald took that away from you," said Oddi.

"Yes," said Ragnvald. "And that made me angry. But it is he, and his vision for Norway, that is my north star. I use what gifts I have for him."

"For yourself," said Oddi sullenly.

"I support Harald for myself, yes, and my family and my friends," said Ragnvald. "I do not want to lose any of those things in his service, but if I have to . . ." Harald's mother, the sorceress Ronhild, had predicted that Ragnvald would give up everything, even his life, for Harald. If Harald was his north star, that prophecy was an ocean beneath his feet, depthless and dark. He had never told anyone that, not even Oddi. The fates were asking him to give up Oddi now. He sighed. "Tell me what you want, Oddbjorn Hakonsson. I owe you much, and I will pay my debt."

"Being your brother was my north star," said Oddi brokenly. "When my father left me with nothing else certain, I had that. I want it back." Oddi looked at him, searching his face again for something Ragnvald felt certain he could not give. "But now I want"—he took a deep breath—"I want nothing from you. I go to Halogaland, and I will come and fight Harald's battles for him, this one last time. I have sworn never to raise my hand against you, and I will not be forsworn."

"I have sworn it too," said Ragnvald. "I will always count myself your friend, even if you do not." He did not trouble to hide the longing in his voice, and hoped that Oddi would answer it.

"Farewell, Ragnvald Half-Drowned," said Oddi. "It is time for you to go to your king."

35

ODDI LEFT NAUSTDAL ON THE SAME DAY AS RAGNVALD, WITH the bulk of Hakon's men, heading north to Halogaland. Heming went back to Tafjord, and Ragnvald departed with Sigurd and Aldi, sailing between the barrier islands. As his ships traveled south, Ragnvald wished that he had ravens like Odin did, who could watch over Oddi and Heming and report back to him.

"We're passing Stavanger Fjord now?" Sigurd asked Ragnvald as they crossed before a gap in the barrier islands, a few days after leaving Aldi and the bulk of their force in Sogn. The mainland, rising to the east, was green and gold in late summer, a patchwork of fields and forests; even outcroppings of bare cliff looked gold in the sunlight. The coastline appeared unbroken, but Ragnvald knew it splintered into a maze of other islands and short fjords, any of which might be mistaken for Stavanger Fjord by an inexperienced navigator.

"Yes," said Ragnvald. "Once King Gudbrand's land. Now Harald has set other kings to guard it."

"Hakon said that it was a rare place for an ambush," said Sigurd. "He pointed out Ker—Kver—Kvernevik. Said Gudbrand should have trapped Harald there."

"Kvernevik," said Ragnvald. "That is the entrance to Haversfjord, which is a bay more than a fjord. It is said that is how Gudbrand's father won his kingship, by luring all the other jarls of Stavanger into a battle there. What else did Hakon say?"

"Hakon said that a hundred ships could hide in the harbor in the middle of that island, and none could see them," said Sigurd, pointing to an island that looked no different from any of the others, low lying and covered with a mix of firs and ash trees. Without Hakon's men around, Sigurd seemed very eager to please Ragnvald, glancing at him frequently to try to read the impression his words made upon him. But he also looked out toward the horizon with a newfound interest and intelligence.

"Kvernevik," said Ragnvald again. "Do you think Solvi and his forces are there now?"

"They might be," said Sigurd. "We are too few to take battle to them, aren't we?"

Ragnvald looked back at the other ship. Yes, they were far too few. This force could raid a farm, or even a small town if they attacked quickly and retreated just as fast. It could not bring war.

"I want to see," said Ragnvald. "I think you may be right and that is where he intends his ambush." Sigurd stood straighter, glowing with pride as Ragnvald gave him the credit. "But I have never been there."

They camped early that night on an island only big enough for a few small households with low hovels, each boasting a few goats and chickens. Ragnvald traded some silver for one of the goats to feed his men, though they would all have to make the bulk of their meal from bread softened in brackish water, as they did on empty islands. These poor householders could not afford to lose much livestock.

The next day, Ragnvald hired a fishing boat from an unwilling fisherman and promised to return it in a few days. The fisherman looked at the handful of silver Ragnvald paid him with suspicion. Silver was not very useful out here on the margin of sea and land.

"I need to go and see for myself," said Ragnvald to Sigurd as the fisherman walked away grumbling. "I can't give Harald good advice if I don't." He tugged off his embroidered tunic and traded it for one of simple homespun from one of his men.

"Should I go with you?" Sigurd asked.

Ragnvald shook his head. Both of them were half a head taller than even a well-grown fisherman would be, having rarely known hunger or illness. One tall fisherman might be overlooked. Two, with the shoulders and wary stance that only battle could teach, would instantly arouse suspicion. He chose Frakki and Malmury to accompany him instead. Frakki was small and slim enough to be mistaken for a boy still, and Malmury was tall for a woman but still short for a warrior.

"What if you are captured?" Sigurd asked. He licked his lips nervously.

"I hope not to be," said Ragnvald. He wished Arnfast were with him. He trusted Arnfast to scout and spy.

"You should send someone else," said Sigurd. "You have to be able to get to Harald and tell him everything you know. He might not listen to me."

"If I do not return, go to Harald," said Ragnvald. "Tell him of this place. I am nearly sure this is where the ambush will be. He should meet up with our allies at"—he peered across the inner waterway toward a small indentation in the coast—"that bay across the water. He will be lured here, I imagine, chasing a small fleet, and then he will run into a mass of Swedish ships, and the ship of every rebel king."

"You will come back, though," said Sigurd.

"Yes," said Ragnvald. He gave Sigurd a grim smile. "Almost certainly."

"Don't go," said Sigurd. "There is no reason you have to be the one to do this. Send someone else."

"I have to. I don't trust anyone else."

"You don't trust me?" Sigurd asked.

"I trust you to go to Harald if I fall. You witnessed Hakon's betrayal and his death. You can tell Harald what he needs to know." He made Sigurd repeat his message and his instructions again, until he was certain that Sigurd could do almost as good a job convincing Harald as Ragnvald himself could do.

He watched small waves cross the sheltered waterway and meet the shoreline on the other side: low green hills, dun-colored beaches that rose to grasses that now looked blue in the twilight. It could be here or it could be anywhere. But Ragnvald had heard of this, the place of Gudbrand's legendary ambush. Solvi would hide some of his ships in the bay, and more outside it to close his trap. He would probably put some men in the woods to help choke off ships at the entrance to Kvernevik. A ship's captain might think he was entering Stavanger Fjord there.

Ragnvald allowed himself a short nap before waking in the middle of the night. It was late enough in the summer now that the sky grew black for a time around midnight. He took the braids out of his hair and rubbed seawater and sand through it, and more into his beard and onto his face. A fisherman would not braid his hair like a warrior. He bid Frakki and Malmury do the same.

They took the fisherman's boat across from their island to the inner archipelago as the sky lightened. It was a nimble little craft that moved swiftly before a steady morning breeze. Ragnvald enjoyed its responsiveness to the steering oar as he guided it through a long right-hand curve into the opening at Kvernevik.

Once they passed through the narrow entrance, a large bay opened up before them. At first glance, the forest that reached down to the shoreline disguised the ships that clustered there. Their sails had been taken down, and the masts looked like bare trees, swaying in a breeze. Ragnvald bade Frakki and Malmury put out a net and pretend to catch fish, while he tightened the sail so the wind would move the boat even with the drag of a net.

When they drew closer to the ships at the far end, Ragnvald could see these were dragon ships, long and lean, with a shallow draft. This bay might have been designed as a trap by crafty Odin himself. Even within its boundaries, jutting points of land provided cover for yet more ships. The narrow entrance to the bay was flanked on both sides by scrub-covered hills, perfect for hiding archers with fire arrows.

Ragnvald thought about how he would spring this trap if he were in Solvi's place: attack Vestfold or Harald's town of Tonsberg—the wealth of merchants and artisans made it a tempting target—then lead Harald in a chase back here. Or let it be known that Gudbrand had made the attack, in which case Harald, advised by Guthorm, who knew the history, could guess where to go. Gudbrand was supposed to have perished at the battle of Vestfold, but Ragnvald had heard tales of him living since then—and if not him then his sons, or someone claiming to be one of them, anything to bring Harald to Stavanger. Harald would see his quarry escape into this passageway and think it was another entrance to Stavanger Fjord and follow.

Harald could turn the trap against Solvi's forces—send a small group of decoy ships, large enough that the rebels would believe it was the whole of the attacking fleet, and then wait. Eventually the ships on the outside, ships meant to close the trap, would do so, and when they did, all would be trapped within. Like Solskel, but on a larger scale. The men on the decoy ships would be in the greatest danger, and these ships could not be empty, they must appear to be the whole force. Well, Harald could usually motivate his men to do foolish things.

"I've seen enough," said Ragnvald. "Pull up the net. We're going back."

Frakki and Malmury brought in the net as Ragnvald turned the boat. The breeze went slack for a moment, then shifted, sending shadows rippling across the water.

"We'll have to row," he said.

A splash made Ragnvald turn his head, and he saw oars from one of the dragon ships hitting the water. At first, the ship hardly moved at all, but then it began to gain on Ragnvald's boat with each pull. In the calm air, Ragnvald's skin sweat and prickled under his homespun tunic. If he was truly a fisherman, would he flee, or try to sell his catch? As long as Solvi did not captain the approaching ship, Ragnvald might still get away.

He motioned for Frakki and Malmury to stop rowing and allow the dragon ship to pull up alongside the boat.

The young captain put his foot up on the gunwale and called down to Ragnvald. "Fisherman, what are you doing here?" he asked. "Did you come to sell us your catch? Why did you turn?" He had auburn hair, skin as smooth as fresh cream, and a studied grace to his movements.

"No catch today," said Ragnvald. Their net had been empty.

The young man narrowed his eyes. "There's always a catch. You wouldn't come in here without one."

"You fish, then," said Ragnvald.

"You don't look like a fisherman," he said. "Or talk like one either." Ragnvald had been trying to talk like old Agi in Geiranger Fjord. "And you don't dress like one. Fishermen don't wear so much clothing on a warm day like today. Or those shoes." The captain smiled, a cruel and satisfied expression that looked strange on his childish face. "I think you should see my king. He will know what to do with you."

Ragnvald had not brought his sword with him, only a dagger shoved, bare, into his belt, and a small ax strapped to his back. More than a fisherman would carry, but little enough that he still felt naked. Possibilities flashed through his mind. Fling down his weapons and swim to shore? He could do that. Unlike most warriors, he had learned to swim as a boy, taught by his stepfather, Olaf, who had laughed at Ragnvald's hatred of cold water. His throat tightened imagining the chill of the water. He had not swum since Solvi's blade, seven years ago. Then, his ability to keep his head in deep water had probably saved his life. Likely neither Frakki nor Malmury knew how to swim, though, and if he left them to be captured by this captain of Solvi's, he did not know what they would say under torture.

A grappling hook landed on Ragnvald's boat. Ragnvald hacked at the lines with an ax, then had to jump to avoid being hit by another flung hook. Men slid down the lines, almost capsizing the small boat when they landed. Frakki drew his dagger, and died choking on a sword blade that one of the attackers shoved through his throat.

Malmury took a slash to the stomach, deep enough to kill her within a few days, if not immediately. Her face wore a look that Ragnvald knew from other battles, for only a deep belly wound made a man—or woman—look sick like that. She threw herself into the bay, choosing to bleed out in the water rather than die of fever a few days later. Ragnvald could not blame her.

It was too late for Ragnvald to jump into the water and swim to safety. This captain would certainly kill him rather than let him escape, and he could not get far enough away to avoid a spear in the back, or worse, a grappling hook through the shoulder. Ragnvald's too-vivid imagination provided him the image and the sensation, the dull thud and growing pain, the tearing of muscle and bone as they hauled him back.

He presented his wrists for the captain to tie them. "What is your name?" the captain asked.

Ragnvald had dirtied himself to look like a commoner, but he had also been a king for seven years, and he knew how to don the authority he had shed, no matter what situation he found himself in. "Ragnvald of Sogn," he said. "The fish were not biting today, but you have still caught one for your master."

"My master?" the captain asked. He touched his chin in the manner of young men everywhere—this beard was new to him; its fullness still needed checking.

"Solvi Klofe," said Ragnvald. "Take me to him."

✛　✛　✛

THE CAPTAIN, WHOSE name was Thorstein, escorted Ragnvald to a camp in the woods, one that had been occupied for some time, Ragnvald thought. The split and sanded logs they used as benches were covered with carvings made by men with too much time on their hands. The bench on which Thorstein bade him sit was decorated with a carving of a woman with an enormous vulva about to receive an equally enormous penis that had two eyes and a snake's forked tongue. Ragnvald almost smiled at the artwork. Men were the same everywhere.

He felt an odd sort of calm, even with his warriors dead. Sigurd had been right to worry that he would not return. If Ragnvald saw him again, he would praise him and reward him for that. If not, Ronhild's prophecy would be satisfied, for Ragnvald would have given his life for Harald. Solvi would not kill him. It was not their *wyrd*.

No one had mistreated him yet. Thorstein's guards had shoved him when they walked to the camp, trying to make him stumble, but Ragnvald could recover himself easily—after all, once he had been agile enough to run on moving oars, and an oafish guard could not so easily humiliate him.

Solvi had aged noticeably since Ragnvald had seen him last. The lines at the corners of his eyes were deeply carved from always looking

out over a shifting ocean. His face was more stern. But when Solvi's
eyes lit upon him, Ragnvald saw something like joy cross his features.
He tamped down the expression so quickly, though, that Ragnvald
wondered if he had seen it, and what it had meant. He greeted Ragnvald with an ironic nod, which Ragnvald returned.

"Ragnvald of Sogn?" Solvi asked. "Yet, we hear you are of Maer, and
today, I see, you are of Rogaland. And I hear you are called Ragnvald
Half-Drowned because of me, so should I call you Ragnvald of the Fjord?"

"Whatever you wish," said Ragnvald. He lifted his tied hands. "As
you see, I am in your power."

"Yes," said Solvi. "And how I have longed for this, yet . . ."

"Yet when you longed for it, did you picture giving me my life
and freedom as a gift to my sister?" Solvi stopped walking toward
him, and Ragnvald continued, trying for an insolent tone, to see if
Solvi could be pushed to anger. "But you did the ill to her, driving her
away, pregnant. You have a fine daughter, by the way. Red-gold hair,
like yours. I think she will be a beauty. When she is older, I will find
a good husband for her, I promise."

Solvi stepped closer to him and slapped him hard across the face, a
blow meant for humiliation, a blow that meant Ragnvald must have
payment for him, gold or blood, or he would be shamed. He had expected that, but not the stinging pain, the ringing in his head that
accompanied it. It had been a long time since anyone had dared to
strike him.

"What are you doing here, Ragnvald Half-Drowned?" Solvi asked.

"Fishing," said Ragnvald. He bared his teeth. He did not mind the
name, it reminded him that he had walked the edge of life and death
before, and did again now.

Solvi hit him again, this time from the other side, a jeweled ring
on his hand slicing a cut across Ragnvald's cheek.

"You still want my face to bear your marks, I can tell," said Ragnvald, working his jaw. He probed his teeth with his tongue to see if
Solvi had loosened them; he was vain of them and hated the thought
of losing one. He had best not smile broadly again. "You have that in
common with your new allies." He nodded at Herlaug, who stood
behind Ragnvald's shoulder, hands clenched.

"Let me have him," said Herlaug. "I will make him talk."

"Yes, I suppose you will," said Solvi, "but how will you know if he tells the truth?"

"Oh, I'll make him speak."

Solvi met Ragnvald's eyes briefly, and something like sympathy flashed between them. "Do you know what Ragnvald told me when he was sixteen, and on his first raiding ship? He said that if he were captured in a raid, he would talk swiftly under torture, and lie swiftly, because then when he told the truth no one would know what to believe."

"So he admits he has no honor," said Herlaug. Ragnvald laughed at that, making Herlaug's disfigured face darken with anger. "I will know the truth," he promised.

"You would not even know what questions to ask," said Solvi. "What should I ask you, Ragnvald? Did you come alone? No, you did not sail a fishing boat from Naustdal to here. Did you meet Hakon? Of course you did, and he is dead now, unless I miss my guess, or you would not have been able to come. Do you know what we do here? I think you must have a guess at that as well. Does Harald know? He will."

"I did not meet Hakon," said Ragnvald truthfully. If he did not speak with care, Solvi would figure out everything Ragnvald did not want him to know, and too quickly. Sigurd would not come to rescue him, but continue on to Harald soon.

"I must have time to think," said Solvi quietly, seeming to speak to himself more than Herlaug. "Tie him tightly and put a double guard on him."

Ragnvald's calmness started to crumble when Solvi gave Herlaug charge of securing him for the night. He feared this boy and his cruelty far more than Solvi. While Herlaug's guards held their swords on Ragnvald, Herlaug retied Ragnvald's hands behind him, and his legs too, around the ankles and again around the knees. Soon Ragnvald's fingers began to tingle and grow numb. A man could lose his hands this way—Ragnvald had seen it. Most often it happened by mischance, but Herlaug might have done it on purpose.

He threw Ragnvald into the clearing where the slaves slept.

Ragnvald crashed into a tent pole and the heavy wool, stinking of fat, fell down over his face. Herlaug tossed some bread after him, and walked away laughing. He was not hungry enough to wriggle around on the ground until he found it—let the squirrels have it tonight. Tomorrow Solvi would feed him as befit a man.

Solvi had placed him in Herlaug's care, though. Ragnvald's belief that Solvi would do him no lasting harm was less strong now. Ragnvald had killed Ulfarr, who had relished carrying out Solvi's cruelest orders. Now he had Herlaug, who would do far worse.

In the middle of the night, Ragnvald pulled himself up to sitting. His arms were tied so that he could not bend them enough to pull himself around and through them. He could only sit on one hip, in an ugly imitation of a woman's coquettish pose, or kneel, which he did not like to do either, though it gave him freedom to flex his wrists until the rope gave him enough slack that blood flooded back into his hands. Solvi would not kill him, not yet. He needed to know what Ragnvald and his allies knew. Solvi suspected Hakon had been killed—could Ragnvald keep that from him? Likely not.

Solvi would want to know if Ragnvald's allies would come looking for him. He had sent Sigurd to bring Harald here, to turn the ambush upon its makers. He had told Heming and Oddi to gather as many forces as they could and come south for the battle to end all battles, a chance to defeat all of Norway's enemies in one place. Everything turned on whether they would do it, if Ragnvald could trust Sigurd, Heming, and Oddi—his stepbrother, and Hakon's sons, all three of whom owed him a debt of vengeance, though Sigurd, at least, had sworn not to pursue his.

If he chose not to trust them, he could convince Solvi that Harald knew of his trap, and if he stayed, Solvi would waste the year's last month of easy sailing in waiting for a battle that would never come. That would risk the least.

Ragnvald flicked a piece of rope with his finger until the end frayed. Yet, yet, yet—if Sigurd brought Harald here, if all the ships and warriors of northern Norway came here, this battle would be decisive. Ragnvald would never have to fight another big battle for Harald, for Norway would be his, and Ragnvald could have his land back.

You make everyone into your *tafl* pieces, Oddi had said to him, bitterly. But Ragnvald was the one who saw the whole board, better than Harald, better than Hakon, certainly better than Hakon's sons. He struggled with his bonds again, and fell over. The soft pine needles hid rocks, one of which bruised his shoulder.

You trust no one, Oddi had also said. But now he must trust each of his allies to do his work. He wondered which plan Oddi would prefer, if he would hate for Ragnvald to be right again, a master *tafl* player winning the game, or if he would hate worse if Ragnvald mistrusted him. He missed Oddi fiercely. They should have been sailing together from Naustdal, and then Oddi would have been the one carrying his message to Harald, not Sigurd.

Sigurd—he trusted Ragnvald, and so did Heming, even when he knew that Ragnvald had helped push Hakon into rebellion. And Harald trusted him even when Ragnvald would no longer fight his battles for him. These were not figures on a *tafl* board, but allies coming together, some reluctantly, for Harald's dream, Ragnvald's vision.

✢   ✢   ✢

SOLVI LEFT RAGNVALD alone for a few days, during which Ragnvald received barely enough water to sustain himself, and little food. He was left to soil himself rather than taken to a latrine, until the slaves in the camp where he had been left gave him a wide berth because of his stench.

He cautioned himself to be patient, but there were moments, when he had to sit in his own shit, or when he smelled the scent of cooking coming from the fires of Solvi's warriors, that he felt no more than an animal, and wanted release from the torment of his body. In his more lucid moments, he wondered if Solvi and Herlaug even knew the misery that their neglect caused.

Then Solvi sent Herlaug, who told him right away that he was not allowed to hurt Ragnvald in any way that would maim or disfigure him. He asked no questions, only beat Ragnvald bloody, blacking both his eyes so they swelled into slits. The thirst when his body tried to heal itself became more painful than any of his bruises and cuts.

Finally, a day or two after the beating, slaves stripped and bathed him, and then clothed him again, under heavy guard, and brought him, hands tied before him, to Solvi's tent. Solvi gave him watered ale, which he had to raise to his mouth with both his hands tied before him. It took all of his restraint not to bolt it down and beg for more. Each sip disappeared into his mouth like water on sand. He had once seen a shipwrecked man die from drinking too much water after being rescued, and so he controlled himself.

"You cannot have come alone," said Solvi. He paced before where Ragnvald sat. "Harald must know that I am here. And now Hakon is dead. I am leaving."

Ragnvald hardly reacted to Solvi's announcement. If Solvi left, that would be the death of Ragnvald's plans, and he would have been captured for naught, but those consequences seemed far distant from the joy of the cool liquid in his mouth. When Ragnvald failed to react to his words, Solvi dashed the cup from his hands. Ragnvald cried out and lunged forward after it. Guards rushed over and hauled him back to his seat.

"I am leaving," Solvi repeated. "What do you say to that?"

"I say that I am still thirsty," said Ragnvald.

Solvi slapped him, sending a bright explosion of pain radiating through Ragnvald's swollen cheek. He moaned and held his hands to his face. How had he been reduced to this whimpering animal so easily, not even by torture but by mere bruises and thirst?

Solvi asked no more questions, so Ragnvald continued staring fixedly at the ground where his cup had landed. His throat worked. Solvi gestured, and a slave brought more ale. He put the cup again into Ragnvald's hands. Ragnvald drank more quickly this time. Let it make his belly ache as long as he drank it before Solvi could deprive him again.

He held his empty cup and tried to slow his breathing. He heard men talking, dicing, complaining about the food and the poor hunting on this small island—and nothing of packing up to leave. Solvi was bluffing, trying to make Ragnvald react. He had been wounded in battle before, and suffered long and painful recoveries, but somehow, being at Solvi's mercy made this pain worse and more frightening. He could not predict what would happen, or resist any attacks.

His disgust with himself, a deep and helpless anger, only made him feel more powerless, quicker to break. The only advantage of his easy crumbling was that he could, perhaps, make Solvi believe he had wrenched a confession from Ragnvald that Harald knew nothing of this place.

Once Ragnvald had drunk his fill, Solvi's guards returned him to his clearing, spread now with new straw that did not stink of his days of pissing and shitting on it. For the following few days, a slave brought him bread and water, and a guard took him to the latrines to relieve himself twice each day. Perhaps Solvi did not ever mean to question him. That would be good enough—the longer they delayed here, the more likely Harald and his allies would come. Solvi need not send out a raiding party to lure them in, only wait. Every day that passed brought Ragnvald closer to victory.

✤ ✤ ✤

HERLAUG KICKED RAGNVALD awake in the middle of the night. "Solvi has given me permission to hurt you," he said.

Ragnvald wished that looking at Herlaug's face did not remind him so much of Jorunn. He wondered if she had found peace in death, knowing that her vengeance had succeeded. Would she now be one of Odin's carrion crows, or did she go to a gentler afterlife?

A guard's torch cast a flickering light that made a ghastly mask of Herlaug's face. Ragnvald stared instead up at the tree branches crossing overhead, the stars jewels between them, set in a velvet sky. Herlaug took hold of one of Ragnvald's fingers, twisting it until it broke with a wet splintering sound Ragnvald felt as much as heard. The past few days' respite had given him enough strength not to scream from the pain, but a few more fingers broken and he would.

"Who knows of this place?" Herlaug asked him.

"I know," said Ragnvald.

Herlaug slapped him across the healing bruises on his face. "Who else knows?"

"Gudbrand, I suppose. Any who have heard the song of his conquest," Ragnvald answered.

Herlaug hit him again. "Who else knows that we are here?"

"I do not know who has seen you, or know the minds of everyone in Norway," said Ragnvald.

"Why are you here?"

"I came to find Solvi, and I did."

Herlaug had more questions for him, more fingers to break. Ragnvald stuck as close to truth in his answers as he could. He did not know who was coming here. He did not know who would rescue him. That much was pure truth. He had chosen to trust men who owed him vengeance, hoping that friendship and loyalty would triumph, but he did not know. He told Herlaug the story he wanted Solvi to hear: that Harald knew nothing, that Ragnvald had sent many scouts from Naustdal, trying to find Solvi's location, in small groups that would be easily overlooked.

He was crying that out, "I do not know, I do not know, I do not know," when Herlaug stopped twisting his middle finger and stood up to walk away from him.

A few days later, Herlaug came to rebreak fingers that had begun to heal, and Ragnvald cried out that Harald knew everything, that every king in Norway knew everything, that they were all coming to destroy the fleet. He did not know if that was true either, but it was satisfying to say in the moment he screamed it out. Herlaug left him alone for a few days while Ragnvald had time to regret what he had done, to feel the shame of it.

✢   ✢   ✢

RAGNVALD'S PAIN EBBED and flowed. He was at his best when he could ride those waves, at sea in a boat with no oars, no steering, no sail, only tossed upon them. When he gave himself up to them, time passed the same way, sometimes fast and sometimes slow. All present, though: no past to regret, no future to fear. It was far worse when he thought of the future and the past, and whether his hands were maimed forever, whether he would hold a sword again, whether his decisions would lead to Harald's death. The worst moments were when Solvi sent someone to make him do something. Stand, eat, piss. Move swollen fingers, or look at them, black and purple and red, fat like sausages ready to burst over a hot fire.

Solvi came to him on a hot afternoon when flies buzzed around Ragnvald's head, and he bore the irritation of their landing on the corners of his mouth rather than suffer from moving. "I thought you were braver than this," said Solvi. "How can I fear Harald when you are the best he has? I thought you would die well."

Am I to die? Ragnvald thought, but did not ask. He would not speak unless Solvi threatened him. Solvi had stayed. Ragnvald had won that, at least.

"You have suffered so little compared with what I suffered as a boy, and yet I could offer you death rather than more pain, and you would take it, I think," he said.

Ragnvald swallowed a few times until he felt he could speak. "I don't care what you think of me," he said. It was the most truthful thing he had said since Solvi captured him.

"No?" Solvi asked, though he did not sound surprised. "You and I are more alike than I had thought."

Perhaps Solvi meant it as an insult, but it gave Ragnvald a strange sort of comfort. Under torture he would have done as Ragnvald did: break easily, like a branch in a gale, rather than let the whole tree topple. It did not hurt to know that. It did not even hurt to imagine Harald knowing of Ragnvald's humiliation. The only thing he feared was Harald's defeat.

36

TONSBERG STANK IN SUMMER. SOMETIMES THE MUD AND SEA-
weed dried out so that the scent only tickled the back of Svanhild's
throat, but then rain came, and released the stench of all the rotten
things from the ground until it rose up, steaming and fetid, and her
stomach heaved. She recognized the sickness of early pregnancy.
When she carried Solvi's children she had grown lethargic and inward facing; Harald's child seemed determined to fill her with fretful
energy.

She became out of breath as she climbed the hill above the town,
walking quickly to stay ahead of her guard. She did not know if that
was because of the pregnancy or because she had become weak in her
new life, a housebound woman with nothing but leisure to occupy
herself. Harald had been called away from Tonsberg to fight deeper
into Vestfold, and the last messenger had said that he had pursued his
enemy Rane into Gautland, which was claimed by Swedish jarls. Harald had been offended that the rich farmers of Vermaland had given
their loyalty to Rane so soon after giving it to him. Vestfold was his
land, had acclaimed him king before any other districts of Norway had
heard his name.

Reports of Harald's victories continued to reach Tonsberg, battles
great and small, shield walls that crumpled quickly when Harald's
forces attacked. Harald had left his uncle Guthorm to watch over her
and Tonsberg, and Guthorm instructed Harald's men Grai and Illugi

to follow her everywhere. She found their company distasteful, and thought they did not like her any better, though they did not try to make her suffer for it, as Ulfarr had. Without Harald, Svanhild worried Grai and Illugi would fall to cruel entertainments, and so she kept watch over them as much as they did her.

She was panting and red-faced when she reached the top of the hill and turned to look back down at the harbor. Puffy white clouds filled the sky, rising up through the air like bubbles in ale. She wondered if a thunderstorm might come this afternoon, when the clouds closed in, watering Tonsberg's fields and turning its streets again to mud. The air had that feeling, even with the heat of the sun and the blue of the sky, a waiting tension. Or perhaps that was her. Rumors had reached them that Hakon had ordered Rane to return to Vestfold in the first place, even that Hakon had allied with the Swedish king. Svanhild wished she were a sorceress, as Harald's mother was, and could cast her awareness out away from herself, over land and sea, to know how Harald fared in Vestfold, how Ragnvald protected Maer, and where Solvi did his raiding. Perhaps Ronhild would teach her, after her child was born.

Svanhild gazed out into the distance, squinting against the brightness. At first, the speck on the horizon seemed like sun in her eyes, but then it resolved to a ship, its sails striped with white and faded red—Ragnvald's colors, though they were the colors of other kings as well. The vessel was a dragon ship, narrow, with an enormous sail, so big that the long ship seemed to fly in the strong wind. She could not hear it from where she stood, but imagined the power of the wind making the mast creak.

She ran back down the hill to Harald's hall, which felt big and empty with most of his warriors gone. Guthorm sat outside, talking with a merchant who had come a few days before, and who had news from Dublin, comings and goings, Irish attacks, the long illness of King Imar, and questions of who would succeed him.

"Women slaves still bring the best prices, young as you can get them," the merchant was saying.

"Our enemies don't usually bring their daughters into battle," Guthorm replied with a laugh, "but I'll see what we can do."

"Young boys are good too, but I have to sell them farther south, usually. Louis the Pious doesn't like that sort of thing in his court. He would pay a lot for a good smith, though."

Svanhild approached. Solvi had dealt in slaves sometimes but preferred smaller cargo, precious stones, silks, and spices. "I saw a ship coming toward Tonsberg," she said to Guthorm. "A dragon ship." She hesitated. "Ragnvald's colors."

"No scouts have come to me," he said.

"My eyesight is better than your scouts'," Svanhild replied. "I think it is friendly, but it may not be." Guthorm still made no move to stand. "I think we should ready men to fight them off if necessary. We have more than enough to repel them on land, and if you send some to man the ships—I think two will be enough—we can keep these forces from escaping if they find the battle goes against them."

"You say it bears Ragnvald's colors and is friendly," said Guthorm. "No need for men to fight."

"I might be wrong," said Svanhild.

"But you have better eyesight than my scouts," said Guthorm, mockingly.

"I'm not certain," said Svanhild.

"If you are frightened, take your women and hide inside." Guthorm laughed.

Svanhild would not do that, and instead she went down to the shore with extra guards to greet the newcomers. Guthorm followed with his own guards though not, Svanhild noted, enough to mount a good defense. Well, she would have to trust her eyesight, and the fact that this ship had brought too few men to attack Tonsberg, well guarded as it was.

She recognized the first man off the ship before her mind could supply his name, and she rushed forward. "Sigurd, brother," she cried, when her tongue caught up with her feet. The only remnant of his boyhood was the hesitant expression on his face. She could not have told why she was so pleased to see him now, grown up into a warrior's shape.

"Svanhild!" he cried. "Is Harald here? I heard you married him. I have—there is too much. I must tell you and Harald what has happened. Ragnvald has been captured. By Solvi, I think!"

Svanhild's stomach twisted on hearing of Ragnvald's capture, and then her heart leaped when Sigurd spoke Solvi's name, even though he was her enemy now, her husband's enemy, and Ragnvald's enemy. He had promised her he would not kill Ragnvald if it was in his power to prevent it.

"He is not here, but you must tell me and—his uncle Guthorm is here," she said. "He is Harald's chief adviser. You must tell us what has happened."

Sigurd was not good at telling a straightforward story, or picking the most important facts to impart, but after Guthorm had made him repeat everything a few times, from his leaving Sogn with Egil, to Ragnvald failing to return from scouting at this bay, Kvernevik at Haversfjord, Svanhild had formed a picture of what had happened.

"I sent one of Ragnvald's ships as a messenger to Oddi and Heming. But I don't know how many allies Solvi has," said Sigurd. "He said he had many in Uppsala: Sulke of Rogaland and his brother Sote, Kjotve the Rich of Adger and his son Thor Haklang . . ." Svanhild remembered meeting some of them at Solvi's side. "But he did not name them all, and—" Sigurd turned to Svanhild, a pleading look on his face that she recognized as the same one he wore when they were children and he wanted her to cover up some wrongdoing. She nodded encouragingly. Sigurd need not worry; he had done well.

"I don't know either," she said in a low voice. She remembered when Ragnvald had been angry with her for holding back what she knew before the battle of Solskel and tried to remember more. They had visited so many lands, and in each one Solvi might have collected an ally. Or he might not. The Moors in Spain would probably not stir from their hot lands, even for Solvi. "Gudbrand and his sons. Nokkve. Rorik of Dorestad. I don't think he could pry Imar out of Dublin. Still, best imagine that every king Harald has ever expelled from Norway will want to fight by his side now."

"And Ragnvald wants us to sail into this trap," said Guthorm. "That is foolishness."

"Ragnvald said this is the chance to defeat them all," said Sigurd breathlessly. "No more little battles, no more little betrayals. Hakon is dead, so they have fewer allies than they were expecting, if they expected all of his men and his sons."

"And Ragnvald believes that Heming will bring those forces to fight for Harald," said Guthorm. "I do not. I would never advise Harald to do this."

"Perhaps that is why he left you here," said Svanhild imperiously. "You would rather let your allies sail into Solvi's trap to be defeated? Harald will be far weaker then. And how will he keep his allies if he does not come to their aid?"

"They are not his allies, they are his subjects," said Guthorm.

"Even more reason to go, then," Svanhild retorted. "He has told me a king's duty is to protect his subjects."

Sigurd swayed on his feet, stumbled, and caught himself. Svanhild looked at him more closely; she had noticed his strength, the way he held himself, a man now, grown into his height, and failed to see the salt dried into the creases of his eyes from long sea travel, the energy that came from nervousness, and covered fatigue.

"You should sleep, brother," she said. Sigurd gave her a little smile in return for the word, which warmed her. She had not realized how lonely she had been since leaving Naustdal until she saw a friendly face, not someone new, or half an enemy, as Guthorm seemed to her. "We should discuss this more in the morning. I have been a poor hostess."

She found a private bed for Sigurd, in a quiet corner, separated from the rest of the hall by heavy hangings. She brought him a ewer of water and a cup in case he became thirsty in the night, and sat down next to him, on the bench where the mattress was laid.

"I do not think Guthorm will send a message to Harald," she said. "Or send the forces we have here at Tonsberg."

"I am tired, Svanhild," he said. "Sister." She smiled fondly at him. Most of her memories of their childhood were of fights between them, of injustices that she had cried about to Ragnvald, at least until Ragnvald had grown up too much to pay attention to her. But Sigurd was familiar, and seemed as pleased to see her as she was to see him. If Solvi killed Ragnvald, Sigurd would be the only true family she had left.

She leaned over and kissed Sigurd's forehead. "Guthorm does not like Ragnvald much. Perhaps he will try to let him fail to spite him. I do not know. You and I can find a better strategy without him."

"I thought you hated me when we were growing up," he said.

"I did sometimes," she said. "But we were children, and never did each other lasting damage."

Sigurd yawned again. "You were so much brighter and faster. My father taunted me that a girl was better than me at everything."

"I think you made me stronger," said Svanhild. Sigurd smiled again, and closed his eyes to sleep.

✝   ✝   ✝

HARALD HAD ORDERED Svanhild to obey Guthorm in all things when he was gone. It had been his final instruction when they stood on the shore saying their good-byes.

"What do you fear I will do?" she had asked.

He touched her face. "I do not want to give you ideas," he replied. "Only—he will keep you safer than you seem willing to keep yourself. I know the tales. You are brave, Svanhild, braver than half my men. But you are not a man, you are a woman who carries my son. A son as bold as you could be the heir to all of Norway."

She knew he meant this to capture her imagination, fill her with the dream that she might one day be like Ronhild, mother of a mighty king, a woman's highest ambition. The mother of a king could wield his power as no one else could.

"You have older sons," said Svanhild. The tide was starting to turn. Harald must leave soon if he did not want his men to spend a hard day rowing.

"My fittest son will be the one who rules my kingdom," Harald replied. Svanhild had a vision of small boys fighting one another, daggers bared, fighting with the animal cruelty of childhood. "We will speak on it more when I return. For now, obey my uncle."

"Do you have minders for all of your wives?" Svanhild asked.

"I have never had a wife before that needed such instruction," he said. He glanced behind him.

"Not even Gyda?"

"She is not my wife yet," said Harald. "I swore to marry her when I had put all of Norway under my rule."

"I hope that is soon," said Svanhild. "You should have more than one wife who does not obey."

"Are you telling me you will not obey my uncle?" Harald asked. He still clasped her forearms and had been stroking them. Now his grip tightened painfully, and she tried to pull away.

"I will obey your uncle if his instructions seem good to me," Svanhild had said. "Let us leave it at that."

She did not ask Guthorm for leave to depart with Sigurd in the morning; she had decided over the night that he would never give it to her, and this way she would not be disobeying Harald. The sea breeze blew her hair back, making her feel cleaner, more purely herself, than she had in a long time, perhaps since walking around her patch of land with Unna and Eystein. She smiled at Sigurd. None would expect them to leave so early, before the sun crested the horizon, when the winds were gentle, and blew in the wrong direction. Sigurd's pilot was competent enough, but chosen more for his knowledge of the Norse coast than for his sailing ability. He did not know how to do what she did now and use a combination of rowing and steering to allow the sail to make the most of the breezes carrying them out of view of Tonsberg before the sun reached its zenith.

With a good wind, it was only a short day's journey to Harald's hall at Vestfold. As she sailed up Oslo Fjord, Svanhild saw the signs of war on the land, burned fields standing next to fields that should have been harvested, rye bowed down by its heavy grains so that soon it would fall and, in the best case, seed the next spring's crop, and in the worst, rot and make all who ate it sick and mad.

At Vestfold, Svanhild counted twenty ships, fifteen with Harald's colors, and five she did not know. The battle was over. Rane could only have hoped to hold Vermaland if Harald ignored him, or if he led Harald into his trap. Rane was dead, though. Svanhild recognized his body as she passed it, huge even in death, his chest three times as high as that of any other body lying on the ground.

Harald sat with his captains around a fire, while under the sound of crackling wood, and the low voices of men talking, Svanhild heard the unmistakable noises of a sick tent filled with the wounded and dying.

"Svanhild, what are you doing here?" Harald asked when he saw her.

Svanhild presented Sigurd, and told him what they knew. "Jarl Rane was supposed to lead you into a trap, but now I see he has not lived to do so."

"You disobeyed me," said Harald.

"I did not ask your uncle's permission," said Svanhild. "He would have let your allies fight on your behalf without the help they should have from you. If you go, you can defeat all of your enemies at once, with all of your allies by your side."

"You disobeyed me."

"I did," said Svanhild. "Divorce me for it if you wish, but go."

✝   ✝   ✝

GUTHORM SAT WITH Harald at their outdoor table at Tonsberg while Svanhild paced around them. Her pregnancy sickness troubled her less if she paced, and it gave vent to her impatience, which would have them already sailing to defeat Solvi.

"I know the spot," said Guthorm slowly. "It is a good place for a trap." She had returned to Tonsberg with Harald and all his forces. He had been almost too angry to speak with her at first, though after talking with Sigurd at length, he was forced to agree that he could not let Ragnvald and Hakon's loyal sons sail into a trap meant for him without going to their defense.

Svanhild used every bit of charm and persuasion she had learned from Vigdis, and then later in Solvi's bed, to soothe Harald's anger with her. It seemed to her, after observing him for a time, that he would have forgiven her more quickly had he not agreed with her urgings. Then she might apologize for being wrong, and he could forgive her that.

On the trip back to Tonsberg, Harald told her what he had learned fighting the Swedish forces. He and King Eirik had tried to make a truce at the home of a wealthy farmer named Ake, who showed his loyalty to Harald by putting him in his newer hall, and sending his young and handsome servants to attend on him, while housing King

Eirik in the older hall, and sending his oldest servants. The require-
ments of hospitality had been satisfied, treating both kings equally,
while Ake demonstrated his clear favor for Harald.

In the middle of the night, King Eirik and his troops departed with
no alliance agreed upon, while Rane led Harald in a chase back to
Vestfold.

"He meant to lure you to Haversfjord, I think," said Svanhild.
Harald had frowned but saw the truth of it.

"You will stay here, uncle," said Harald, after they had made plans
to sail in the morning. "I do not want Tonsberg to go undefended."

"What about your wife?" Guthorm asked.

"What about her?" asked Harald in return. "I asked you to watch
over her, not ignore her counsel."

"She disobeyed me, and she disobeyed you," said Guthorm. "That
is grounds for divorce. As soon as the child is born, you should acknowledge it, and divorce her."

"Her brother is my best adviser," said Harald. "I value his counsel
above all, and I will not insult him by rejecting his sister."

Those words struck Guthorm deeply, Svanhild saw from his sudden pallor. He had been demoted, fully and finally. She wanted to
hear the answer to Harald's question, if he would take her with him
into battle as she had gone often with Solvi, or whether he would
leave her with Guthorm. She thought of suggesting that if Harald
took her with him, she might serve as a hostage of last resort. Solvi
would take her in trade again, she knew that, perhaps to save Ragnvald, perhaps to save Harald himself.

"What are you going to do?" she asked when they lay together
in bed. His anger at his uncle had finally purged most of his anger
against her.

"I have erred in setting my uncle's judgment above yours, I see,"
he replied. "Once I trusted him more than anyone. Now I must trust
you more, and your brother the most." He laughed to himself. "A man
whose judgment I trust more than yours must be wise indeed—so
I need your brother back by my side. I trust my inspirations while
other men think of strategies."

Though grudgingly given, Svanhild still felt a pleasant warmth at the compliment. "Ragnvald is Solvi's captive," she said. "I want to go with you and do what I can to free him."

"What if he does not want to be freed?" he said, jesting, though she felt his tension through where her back rested against his chest. "I recall that you did not want to be freed from Solvi, when he gave you that same choice."

"That was many seasons ago," said Svanhild. "Now I want my brother back, and I want to be by your side. If you prefer an obedient wife, divorce me, and marry someone else. I will make my brother understand."

"I fear for you," said Harald. "My other wives don't rush headlong into danger, carrying my sons."

"It is well I am not your only wife then," she replied, satisfied that she would sail with him the next day.

"What if this is the end of fighting for Norway?" Harald asked as Svanhild began to drift to sleep. "What will I do then?"

"Build your towns, make your kingdoms rich," Svanhild replied. She twined a length of his matted hair around her hand. Broken ends pricked her, and it quickly covered the whole length of her fingers. "Cut your hair."

✝ ✝ ✝

SVANHILD SAILED IN Harald's ship until his convoy reached the small bay Sigurd had described, so close to the entrance to Havers-fjord that Svanhild feared Solvi and his allies would already have scouts watching them. Oddi, Heming, and another thirty ships were already there. Oddi said that they had captured some of Solvi's scouts, tortured them into revealing their pass codes, and replaced them with men of their own. Solvi led too many warriors from too many allies for all of them to know each other.

Harald, Heming, Oddi, and Sigurd agreed on a plan the next morning. Harald had one of Rane's ships, and this would sail into Havers-fjord, with five of Harald's ships in pursuit. Solvi's allies should close in behind them then to trap Harald's forces in the bay and slaughter them, and then the rest of Harald's forces would pursue and better the odds.

"Even with all of Solvi's allies and the forces that King Eirik sent, we have a third again as many men," said Oddi. "It should be enough." His voice had a new hardness to it that Svanhild had not heard before. He spoke with a self-assurance that Ragnvald might have had in his place, and Svanhild felt a touch of loss. She had not seen this in him before, when they were lovers.

After that, nothing remained but to feast and sleep. Men ate and drank as deeply as they could, for the next day would be long. They did not care if they ran through all of their ships' stores, which would do them no good in the afterlife. Svanhild could not sleep either. She lay in a tent by herself, listening to the talk and movement of men. She had not brought a serving woman with her, desiring that no women should suffer for her decisions, but now she wished she had a companion to share her blankets and warmth.

She had come all this way, and now she must get close to the battle. She could spot Solvi's ship among all the chaos. Even if her eyesight failed her in old age, she would always see him more clearly than she saw other men. And Solvi's ship was where she would find Ragnvald.

In the blue light before dawn, she went to Oddi. Harald would try to keep her from this battle, but she knew how to charm Oddi. He would give her a ship.

⊹   ⊹   ⊹

ODDI SAT IN the entrance of his tent with the door flap open, watching the night fade. With Ragnvald gone, the waiting and brooding fell to him. Svanhild made her plea.

"I'm not giving you a ship," said Oddi.

"We can get him back," said Svanhild. "You and me. If you find me a ship."

"Who?" Oddi asked with studied indifference. "Who will we get back?"

"My brother." Svanhild wanted to shake him.

"I don't care about that," said Oddi. She had heard about a rift between them but discounted it. Oddi had been Ragnvald's faithful companion for many years, without, it seemed until now, a moment's doubt.

"I don't believe you," she said. "You are sworn to him."

"Oaths mean less than they used to, I think." He gave her a small smile. "Just ask my father. But do not worry. I am here. I do not mean to betray him."

"But you won't help me get him back?"

"Sigurd told me how he was captured," said Oddi, running his hand through his hair. "If he didn't always insist on proving himself the best, the bravest, the first into danger, and the last to give up his watchfulness . . . then he might leave room for other people to have their moments of glory."

"You think that is why he does it? Because he will not share his glory?" Svanhild put her hands on her hips. She had considered flirting with Oddi to see if that would convince him to do what she asked, but she had always approached Oddi forthrightly before, even when she invited him to her bed.

"Why else?" Oddi asked.

"Because he fears if he does not always risk everything, dare the most, then our stepfather will be right. He will be a worthless coward. He will be less than his father, Eystein, a boaster, with more good tales than good deeds. You are his dearest friend, surely you know this."

"His stepfather is dead," said Oddi dismissively.

"Your father is dead, and yet you want to make a break with Ragnvald to appease him."

"That is different." Oddi looked away.

"It is not at all different. At least Ragnvald's endless struggle with Olaf makes him brave. Yours with your father makes you stupid."

"I thought you came here to seduce me for your ship." Oddi had a note of petulance in his voice.

"I am pregnant," said Svanhild.

"I did not mind last time," said Oddi. He gave her a strained leer that faded when Svanhild scowled at him.

"You don't have enough good pilots," said Svanhild. "I was listening to the discussions. You can put your mediocre ones on the ships lashed together to make the fighting platform—they will have to do little after the ships are tied up. But you will need ships on the outside that are not tied down and can harry the platform. Only the best can steer a ship well enough for that."

"And you are the best," said Oddi doubtfully.

"I sailed with Solvi Hunthiofsson for six years. I have traveled farther than you have ever dreamed, and been in my share of sea battles. How many sea battles have you been in?"

"A few," said Oddi. "Harald prefers to fight on land. But seeing is not the same—"

"Ask Harald's pilot Falki if I am a better sailor than him. Then give me a ship to lead. Tell your men it was Harald's idea, if you prefer, and if Harald questions you, blame me."

That seemed to make him willing to consider Svanhild's offer. "If I do this, no one will know?" he asked.

"I will say that I told you it was Harald's command."

"And what do I get?"

"A grateful queen who owes you a favor," said Svanhild. And she would bring Ragnvald back so they could patch up their friendship. Oddi would owe her more for that than she would him.

<h1 style="text-align:center">37</h1>

THE DAY OF BATTLE DAWNED CLEAR AND HOT. SVANHILD STOOD
at her ship's steering oar, waiting for the signal that Solvi had taken
the bait, and it was time to close the trap upon him. Falki had helped
Oddi to assemble a crew for her ship that would accept her: his friends
and men who had seen her steer before. The crew still looked at her
suspiciously when she came on board, but seemed to like her better
when she began talking to them, finding out what tasks each man
excelled at, and telling them what commands she was likely to call out
during the battle. The more swiftly they put out or brought in oars,
and turned the sail, the more maneuverable the ship would be.

It was a small ship, small enough to be crewed by ten men easily,
and five if necessary. She had twenty. Perfect for quick attacks. She
wanted the sail reefed in and secured by fewer lines than usual because, in close quarters, fast maneuvers and tight turns would make
them most effective. The men murmured appreciatively when Oddi
said that Svanhild had been trained by Solvi Hunthiofsson himself.
The glory that would accrue to all of them if they fought for a woman
captain, and beat the great sea king Solvi, would never be forgotten.

Harald had sent off his decoy ships midmorning, and now, at noon,
the signal—a red banner—waved from the bank at the entrance to the
bay, telling Svanhild it was time. The breezes were fitful enough that
rowing was necessary. Still, she kept the sail up to catch what wind

there was, and steered carefully. If she could spare some of her men's energy for the battle ahead, she would.

The ship in front of her turned and entered the bay, scraping along the shallows in the narrow entrance. As it exited the channel, Svanhild saw that it listed to the right. Beyond the ship, half hidden by the sail, other ships joined the fighting, turning Solvi's trap into a true sea battle. From this far away, they looked to her like toy ships on a pond, and the splashes from men falling into the water hardly seemed real. The ships of Solvi and his allies had surrounded Harald's decoys. Somewhere among them was Solvi himself. Svanhild was certain he would keep Ragnvald close by as a hostage to save his life as a last resort. She could not let herself believe otherwise.

She gave the command to enter the channel. The water flowed faster to the left, so she aimed for that side. This narrow entrance would hardly be deeper than the height of a man, and a ship must navigate carefully to thread that needle.

She saw the sharpened spikes in the water, and steered hard right, calling out, "Only rowers on the left, only on the left!" A moment later and the spikes would have torn out the bottom of her ship. Steer too far right, and she would catch on the shallower ground there. Too close and her ship would sink.

The ship that preceded her heeled over even farther to the right as it filled with water from the holes the spikes had made in the hull. Svanhild had heard of this tactic before for protecting a settlement when no other means were available, but a ship was so precious, representing a fortune in labor, timber, and the knowledge of master craftsmen, that only a desperate foe would attempt this. Solvi was that.

In the battle platform created by Harald's decoys and Solvi's allies, some ships rode much lower than others. At least half of Harald's ships would sink before the day was over. This sea battle already dwarfed any she had seen before, a maze of ships locked together in combat. At this scale, the number and fierceness of warriors and the placement of ships mattered more than wind or quick steering. At best, Svanhild's men could pick away at the outside, help the odds, and try to avoid becoming entangled with the fighting platform.

As Svanhild's ship exited the narrow channel, she yelled back at the ship behind her, "Spikes in the water! Stay to the left! Tell the others." The forecastle man in the prow was too far away for Svanhild to tell if he was shocked to be given instructions by a woman, and Svanhild could not glance back to see if her instructions had been heeded. She must trust, and continue.

The wind moved unpredictably in this sheltered bay, making shadows on the water that tempted Svanhild to chase them, to catch a breeze and spare her men's energy, but she knew she could not. She must reach the battle.

She sailed around the fighting platform, while her men threw lines to those who had fallen into the water but still lived. Svanhild chose one of Solvi's ships at random. Her men threw two grappling hooks to draw them close, and leaped across to kill those waiting at the rear of the fighting. As soon as her men had done their work and returned to her ship, they cut the lines, and she pulled away and found another ship to attack. She kept watch for any ships that might try to do the same to hers, but her oarsmen obeyed her well, switching between rowing and attack, and the small breezes seemed designed to allow her to attack swiftly and pull away again.

She always forgot, until she was in a sea battle again, how slowly they seemed to move, through long lulls while she maneuvered her ship into position, followed by short spasms of violence. She knew too how easy it was to get distracted trying to see the whole battle, or fearing for the safety of her warriors, and in those moments of distraction, battles were won and lost. Svanhild put Oddi, Ragnvald, and Harald out of her mind and concentrated on what she could do: move her warriors to where they could kill Solvi's men, and save Harald's.

A ship that had come loose from the fighting platform began to sink. Svanhild brought her ship around to rescue its crew, taking on fifty men who crowded her decks—among them Sigurd. She had worn her boy's garb, and he did not notice her until she gave some instructions to her rowers. He gave her a surprised grin but otherwise kept his head enough to do as she commanded, and took his men to board one of Solvi's ships as soon as Svanhild brought them close enough to the fighting platform again. She could continue doing this all afternoon, and be an important part of the battle. She might not win the glory that her men wanted, but her presence and success would be sung of, and she would make sure the skalds knew the names of all of her men. She would have to learn them herself, when the battle was over. Still, she wanted to be the one to confront Solvi, not Harald, not Sigurd, and not Hakon's sons. He must know what he had given up in her, and know that she was the cause of his failure today.

When the sun descended close to the treetops, the tide of battle began to turn against Solvi and his allies, even with ten of Harald's ships taking on water and sinking. Harald simply had too many warriors, and Solvi had not expected to be fighting a force that equaled or bettered his. He had been closed in his own trap, again.

Svanhild could not tell his ship from any of the others until she saw one small ship dart out from behind the fighting platform and begin heading for the channel, riding a wind that had come up as if summoned by the gods. That could only be Solvi, making his escape. His allies would never forgive him, and perhaps he did not mean for them to, but if he had Ragnvald with him—and Svanhild was sure that he did—no matter how many men Harald killed, this battle would be a loss.

"Reverse course!" Svanhild ordered her men. They helped her take in the steering oar on this end of the ship, and let down one at the other end. She ran down the length of the ship, leaping over and between the men who stood and turned so they could change the direction of her rowing.

"Pull harder!" she yelled. She wanted to bring the ship into position to catch the wind Solvi was using.

"Why do we flee?" asked one of the men nearest her.

Svanhild scarcely had breath to answer, but she knew how quickly her hold over these men could break—she led them because of Oddi's and Falki's word, and the fact that she had directed them well in battle. They must continue to believe that she knew best, or they would mutiny.

"We are not fleeing," she said. "That ship carries Solvi Hunthiofsson and King Ragnvald. I will stake an arm ring for each of you on it." She was too winded to make her voice heard to all of them. "Pass word along."

Her men increased the strength of their rowing as the news swept down the length of the ship. Her sail caught the wind in the same moment that Solvi lined his ship up to exit through the channel.

"Keep rowing," she called out. She needed every bit of speed. She lined up for the channel well in advance and aimed for the deeper side. The spikes that had done so much damage to ships entering pointed the wrong way to harm hers on the way out. Their ends, now splintered and shattered, only scraped harmlessly along the hull. Svanhild gained on Solvi's ship, forcing it over to the shallower side of the channel, where its keel scraped along the ground and brought it to a halt.

"Grappling hooks," Svanhild commanded. She had her breath back now, and excitement made her blood sparkle. She sang out her commands and her men obeyed her, throwing across hooks of wood with metal tips, and hauling on them until her ship drew closer to Solvi's, freeing both of them from the channel and sending them spinning, locked together, out into the sea between the barrier islands.

Svanhild called out for attack. Her men leaped across the breach. She had not let them fight enough today, and though they had just finished rowing as though possessed by gods, they still attacked with a fury that drove Solvi's men back along the far gunwale and into the water.

"Stop, stop," she heard Solvi's voice call out. "I have a prisoner to trade." Svanhild craned her neck, but she could not see his head, hidden behind the shoulders of taller warriors.

"Do not kill them all," Svanhild commanded her men. "Make prisoners of the rest."

Svanhild let one of her men help her across the gap between gunwales that separated her ship from Solvi's. She stepped slowly, feeling truly like a sea queen, both fragile woman and powerful goddess, as she had felt when she first stepped onto Solvi's ship outside Geiranger Fjord, and made his men into her allies to save her merchant friends. This was even better. She had all the power here.

Her men stepped aside so she could walk between them, toward

Solvi, where he stood, looking at her with longing, his red-gold hair lit by the afternoon sun. Something in her chest softened—she had missed him so much: her beloved, the man who had been nearly as close to her as the child in her womb, who she had known better than she knew herself. For a moment, his betrayal and all his cruel words seemed like a storm long past.

She was not here for him, though, except to defeat him. She was here for Ragnvald, who stood at Solvi's side, a rope binding his wrists before him. He looked half dead. Some of the fingers on his hands were broken, twisted and purple. Angry, livid bruises swelled on his forehead and cheekbone. One of his ears was crusted with blood. And it was his eyes, downcast, then alight with fear and desperate hope when they found Svanhild's, that made her throat grow tight. She supposed Solvi would want her to be grateful that he had left Ragnvald alive, but he had hurt and humiliated him. Ragnvald would rather be dead than endure such shame.

Solvi too looked as thin and worn as bare winter branches. Svanhild clenched her jaw. He had done this to himself, had pushed her from his side, blamed her for Eystein's death, and caused much of the death she had seen today. Harald would never hurt her as he had, because he could not. She did not love him enough.

"Svanhild," said Solvi softly, "it's you." He had so much hope in his voice that her tears for Ragnvald began to spill over. "I have saved Ragnvald for you. I told you I would never kill him. Come with me."

"I am here for my brother Ragnvald, not for you," she said. "You are Harald's prisoner." She looked at Solvi's right hand, which he flexed near his dagger. She should order her men to take him prisoner as well, before he could threaten Ragnvald.

Solvi let go of the rope he held, gave Ragnvald a shove. He stumbled toward Svanhild, and then found his feet and moved gingerly to stand next to her. Solvi reached out toward Svanhild. "Come with me," he said again. "Send Ragnvald back to his king and come with me. We will leave Norway. We still have the whole world besides."

If he had spoken to her like this after Eystein's death, if he had crossed the gap between them rather than widening it, if he had once looked at her like this after Eystein grew sick, they would be together now. Where, Svanhild did not know. In Tafjord's hall, under siege by Harald, or in another foreign court, eating exotic food, lying long abed. It would not have mattered. She would have been by his side.

"I am pregnant with Harald's child. His son," said Svanhild.

Hatred twisted Solvi's features for a moment before his lips curved into a smile. She knew this smile—it contained mischief and cruelty as much as love. "I would raise his son as my own," he said.

"I will not go with you," said Svanhild.

Solvi sneered. "Because Ragnvald will not allow it?"

Ragnvald spoke for the first time, his voice cracked and broken. "Svanhild has earned the right to do what she pleases."

Svanhild crossed a hand over her womb, where Harald's son grew. Would Solvi raise Harald's son as his own? Harald's son would be strong enough to survive their travels, and hard enough to be Solvi's heir.

"Forgive me, Ragnvald," she said.

"Svanhild, don't," he said.

Svanhild ignored him and stepped close to Solvi. She touched his cheek, and that smile faded into a raw expression of longing. "I will let you go," she said, "if you swear by Ran and Njord and all of the nameless gods of wind and sea that you will never seek to reclaim your land or any other land in Norway."

"You will believe my oath?" Solvi asked. The corner of his mouth went up, an ironic smile that tugged at her chest. "Will you come to me, if Harald mistreats you?"

"I will do what seems right," said Svanhild. "That is all."

Svanhild gave Solvi a cup of ale for swearing, and he said the words, meeting her eyes the whole time. He swore by wind and rain, by ships and gods, by his own luck, and by his love for her that he would never seek to reclaim Tafjord or make war on Norway again. "I will have no home until you come to me," he said.

Later, she could hardly remember his words, only the vivid blue of his eyes, and the high color of his cheeks. The smile that held neither joy nor happiness, which he wore like a mask. She took the cup from him and left him with Snorri, Tryggulf, and Thorstein to crew his ship, taking all his other men as prisoners. If a gale came up they would have to cut the lines, for four was far too few to lower the sail. Solvi could find more followers, though. He would survive.

She unbound Ragnvald's hands and ordered her men to help him back into her ship.

"Will Harald be angry with me for letting him go?" Svanhild asked him as Solvi's ship grew smaller behind them. She looked at the men who had obeyed her orders without questioning. They could have stopped her as well, but they had not.

"He might," said Ragnvald. "But as I said, you have earned the right. Do you want me to say it was my doing?"

"No," said Svanhild. "If he cannot forgive me—"

"I will make him forgive you," said Ragnvald. "I do not want you tempted to go back to . . . Solvi. I do not claim to understand it, but I know you—you will never be entirely free of him."

"No," said Svanhild, and now her tears spilled over. "No, I will not."

✛   ✛   ✛

RAGNVALD STAGGERED OVER the benches in Svanhild's ship, trying to lean on her arm without appearing to. After a few steps, he had to sit on one bench to swing himself over to the next, and was breathing heavily by the time he reached the steering oar where she sat, and eased himself down to sit on the ship's floor next to her. Even with his pain and exhaustion, he felt almost euphoric. She had come; Heming, Oddi, and Harald had all come to fight this battle when he needed them most. He rested his hands gently in his lap.

"He may not survive without a real crew," said Ragnvald while he caught his breath.

"He will," said Svanhild grimly. "But he will not attack Norway again."

"How can you be sure of that?"

"He never wanted to," said Svanhild. "He only . . ." She shook her head. "He will miss the dead—he loved Ulfarr. But he will be happier this way."

Solvi would only be happy if Svanhild went with him, Ragnvald knew, but Svanhild must know that as well, and it would do no good to speak of it. Ragnvald had been holding his hurt at bay during the battle, and now that he did not even have others' fighting to distract him, he could feel every cut and bruise, the throb of twisted fingers, the ache of weeks sleeping on hard ground, woken frequently for more abuse, a body made weak by thirst and starvation.

Svanhild's men had killed some of those who had witnessed his shame. Many of the rest were prisoners, and Harald would let Ragnvald kill them if he wanted to. Harald's ships towed Solvi's captured convoy toward the shore. He would take some of Solvi's men as slaves, and hold others for ransom. Ragnvald might ask for those slaves and sacrifice them in thanks to the war gods. Or he might sleep.

⁂

HARALD EMBRACED SVANHILD when he saw her, pulling her close and kissing the top of her head. Then he frowned and held her at arm's length. "What have you done, Svanhild?" he asked.

"I took a ship—said you had given the order," she said. Ragnvald had never seen anyone defy Harald more calmly. Even Hakon had not been that brave. "It was I who noticed the spikes in the channel that sank ten of your ships."

"We're hauling them out," said Harald. "They will be repaired."

"It was I who rescued my brother Ragnvald," Svanhild continued, as if Harald had not spoken. "I promised my men an arm ring each for their bravery, and they have deserved it."

"What of Solvi Hunthiofsson?" asked Oddi. "We cannot find him anywhere."

"He must have been on one of the ships that escaped," said Harald. "Next summer we must find him. He cannot be allowed to live and attack Norway again."

Svanhild's chest rose with a deep breath. She must know that the tale would be told. Too many of her men had seen it. Better to tell Harald now. "I let him go," she said.

The roar of voices drowned out whatever Harald said in answer. He held up a hand and waited for quiet. His face looked as though it had been hewn from stone, set and hard, drained of color. "You let him go?" he repeated.

Ragnvald stepped forward to try to take some of the blame, but

Svanhild stopped him with a raised hand. He was glad to let her take command now.

"He was my husband once," said Svanhild. "He is the father of my daughter. I made him swear in terms he cannot betray that he will trouble Norway no more."

Harald looked as though the triumph of this day, the death of all of Solvi's allies, the victory over even the king of Sweden, had been for naught.

"A woman's kind heart," said Oddi nervously. "Blame me, King Harald, for letting her take a ship. She has the skill, but not the judgment."

"Blame me," said Ragnvald. "I was there and I allowed it to happen."

"No," said Svanhild, quietly, but in a tone that allowed no more argument. "It was my decision. Punish me if you wish. I will not argue it if you wish a divorce. I don't think you will lose my brother if you choose that. I will deserve it."

"If I do, will you go to him?" Harald asked.

Ragnvald saw a shadow cross Svanhild's face. He had never seen anything like the reaction that Svanhild and Solvi had to each other, as if they were one person in two bodies that it offended the gods to keep separate. In his fatigue, he thought that if Svanhild said she would go to Solvi, he would make sure they reached each other. She had rescued Ragnvald and fought a battle for him. She deserved whatever reward she desired.

"I bear your son," said Svanhild finally. "I will not put a weapon against you into that man's hands."

"You do," said Harald. He looked like a boy again, grateful to have been given the opportunity to save face. He spoke loudly, so all of his followers could hear: "My son will have the boldest mother of any woman living. He cannot help but be a warrior king with such parents." He spread his arms for Svanhild, who went to his side. His men cheered before returning to their ale and battle reminiscences.

She was a good queen for him, Ragnvald thought. Both had the sense of ceremony and occasion that drew all eyes. Her answer had been both truthful and politic.

Harald's voice rang out over the crowd again. "Today, with your help, I have made all of Norway my kingdom, your kingdom, our kingdom. All my enemies are dead, save one. But what kind of king would I be if I allowed him to live and threaten us? I swore seven years ago that I would not cut my hair or shave my beard until I had put all of Norway under my rulership, and I say my rule is not complete until Solvi Hunthiofsson is dead. Next summer, we will root him out wherever he is, and spread his entrails over the ground. Who is with me?"

The cheers that sounded told Ragnvald that every man was. He had the excuse of his wounds to do little more than give Harald a weak smile.

During the feast that night Ragnvald sat by a fire, eating slow spoonfuls of porridge fed him by Svanhild. If he ate any faster, he would make himself sick. His hands, throbbing with pain, and itching as they healed misshapen, would not serve him. He could at least move all his fingers, which meant that with the help of a healer, more pain, and hard work, he would hold a sword again. Svanhild had made her tent near his so she could help with anything he needed.

Sigurd spoke of how he had killed Herlaug in the battle, avenging Jorunn, and making Arnfast's family safe. Ragnvald would need to help Harald understand why Hakon's betrayal should be hidden in the songs the skalds made so Harald could keep the honor of his ally. It would let Hakon's sons—Heming and Oddi at least—keep their family's honor as well.

"So it is not done," said Ragnvald to Svanhild when a lull in the stories and toasts allowed him to speak quietly. "I had hoped . . ."

"Harald will not catch Solvi," said Svanhild. "And what do I care if he cuts his hair or not?" She tossed her own hair out of her face. It had come loose from its braid during the day of battle. "It looks wild and handsome this way."

"Who do you think he will drag across the North Sea looking for Solvi?" Ragnvald asked. He had never felt more tired. "I wanted so much for it to be over."

"Harald will not find him," said Svanhild. "And while I am making sure of that, I will also make sure that you have time to build up your kingdom again."

"You believe you will have so much influence?" Ragnvald asked. "I think Harald is angry with you."

"I think Harald will hear the songs they sing of me, and forgive me," said Svanhild. She gave him a conspiratorial smile. "A man can always forgive a woman for being too tenderhearted."

Ragnvald smiled back at her. Tomorrow he must speak to Harald about Sogn, find out who Harald intended to rule all the land that Hakon had claimed, for petty warlords would, even now, be positioning themselves to take power. Tomorrow he must submit to healers who would rebreak his fingers and set them straight. Tonight, though, he let Svanhild fetch him more porridge. On the other side of the bonfire, Harald grinned and gestured, telling the story of his triumph.

He saw Ragnvald watching, and raised his glass. Ragnvald nodded slowly, his shoulder muscles protesting. Harald stood and came over to join him, sitting between him and Svanhild.

"You should not have to rise tonight, even for me. I am glad you are well, my friend." He tugged Svanhild into his lap. "My mother said you would suffer much in service of your vision, my Norway," Harald added.

"I didn't know she told you that," said Ragnvald. It had seemed a secret between him and Ronhild that Harald did not need to learn.

"She did," he said. "You did not fight in this battle, yet I see your hand in everything that occurred." He frowned at Svanhild. "Well, almost everything. I asked you to fight for me again and you have ended my fighting forever, at least on these shores."

"There will always be raiders, squabbles," said Ragnvald. "Do not curse the peace just yet."

"Curse it? I bless it. I have sons who do not know me, and more on the way. I have a kingdom to rule, and the best men to aid me. And you have suffered much. Name your reward and you shall have it."

"Sogn," said Ragnvald. "I want only to return."

"I wanted to give you all of Maer to rule," said Harald. "Heming must go north to Halogaland and secure his rule of his father's land."

"What of Oddi?" Ragnvald asked.

"He does not want to be a king," said Harald.

Ragnvald bowed his head. He would make no more decisions for Oddi.

"Sogn is yours," said Harald. "But perhaps you will let Atli's son guard it for you, while you preserve Maer. If Solvi returns to our shores again, it will be there."

Ragnvald sighed and looked at Oddi across the fire, sitting next to Aldi. Aldi had suffered the most from Ragnvald's plotting—his father, Atli, had fallen by Ragnvald's machinations, and he had deserved better. Let his son hold Sogn while Ragnvald defended Maer from Solvi's old seat. He could live with that. Svanhild, curled in Harald's lap, her eyes closing, lived with a greater sacrifice.

AUTHOR'S NOTE

THE SEA QUEEN IS A WORK OF FICTION THAT TAKES ITS INSPIRA-
tion from "The Saga of Harald Harfagr" in Snorri Sturluson's
Heimskringla, The Saga of the Kings of Norway. *The Sea Queen* incor-
porates more historical events than *The Half-Drowned King*—or at least
events attested to in the *Heimskringla*. Solvi's defeat at the battle of
Solskel and Harald's triumph over all of his enemies at Haversfjord are
considered key moments in the founding of Norway. Hakon and Atli
did indeed find their ends on each other's swords.

However, ninth-century Norway is only beginning to emerge from
myth into written history. Most of the existing sources for the life of
Harald and his contemporaries were written many centuries later.
Ninth-century Norway did not have written language other than
runes, the angular writing found on Viking markers like the Danish
Jelling stones, which were raised in memory of great deeds and departed family. Runes in Viking-age Norway were used for fortune-
telling, as well as marking some religious and other monuments, but
not for historical record keeping.

In the thirteenth century the Icelander Snorri Sturluson, a historian, poet, and politician, would write down the *Heimskringla*, and
many other sagas. The *Heimskringla*, based on oral tradition, almost
certainly has gaps and inaccuracies. Furthermore, many scholars believe that Snorri Sturluson used the saga to make certain implicit arguments about Iceland's political situation at the time, leading him

to highlight some stories and leave out others. The works of Saxo Grammaticus, a twelfth-century Danish historian, and *Historia Norwegiae*, a history of Norway written in the thirteenth century by an anonymous Scandinavian monk, also attest to Harald's conquest of Norway and his reign, while focusing on different aspects of the events than the *Heimskringla*.

In writing *The Sea Queen*, I have used the stories in the *Heimskringla* as a jumping-off point, and also asked myself what might have been the real events behind the stories that Snorri Sturluson and others passed on and recorded. My sources mention Ragnvald, Harald, Svanhild, Solvi, and many others, but I have invented aspects of these figures' relationships—such as Svanhild and Solvi's romantic involvement—and also invented some new characters, like Ragnvald's stepmother, Vigdis, and his man-at-arms Arnfast. Still, those wishing to avoid spoilers for the rest of the trilogy should probably avoid Wikipedia and the *Heimskringla*.

NAMES

Because so many names and name parts are repeated in the history of Harald Fairhair, I've had to make some tough choices. For instance, Ragnvald's brother Sigurd (here I've made him a stepbrother) shares his name with many other Sigurds, including a son of Hakon Grjotgardsson. It would be terribly confusing to have two important characters named Sigurd in a novel, so Hakon's eldest son takes the name of one of his other sons, Heming.

Similarly, the prefix *Ragn-* (meaning "council, wisdom, or power") is found in the names of many characters in Harald's saga. For the sake of clarity, I've used the spelling Ronhild rather than Ragnhild for Harald's mother. I also shortened the name of Ragnvald's betrothed, Ragnhild(a), to Hilda, again for clarity.

Old Norse—similar to modern Scandinavian languages—is an inflected language, meaning it has noun cases. Old Norse names in the nominative case, the case used when the person is the subject of a sentence, end with the suffix -r, so Ragnvald would be Ragnvaldr (sometimes transliterated Ragnvaldur). For ease of pronunciation, in most instances I have omitted the -r suffix, and used more anglicized versions of the names without diacritics, e.g. I use Solvi rather than Sölvi.

SOURCES

Here are a few, but not nearly all, of the books I have found valuable in researching Viking Age Norway and early medieval Europe. This includes works used for researching *The Half-Drowned King* as well. Christie Ward's Viking Answer Lady website, www.vikinganswer lady.com, is also a useful resource.

Bagge, Sverre. *From Viking Stronghold to Christian Kingdom: State Formation in Norway, c. 900–1350.* Museum Tusculanum Press, 2010.

Bauer, Susan Wise. *The History of the Medieval World: From the Conversion of Constantine to the First Crusade.* New York: W. W. Norton, 2010.

Davidson, Hilda Ellis. *Gods and Myths of Northern Europe.* New York: Penguin, 1990.

———. *Roles of the Northern Goddess.* London: Routledge, 2002.

Fitzhugh, William W., and Elisabeth I. Ward, eds. *Vikings: The North Atlantic Saga*, Washington, DC: Smithsonian, 2000.

Foote, Peter G., and David M. Wilson. *The Viking Achievement: The Society and Culture of Early Medieval Scandinavia.* London: Book Club Associates, 1974.

Griffith, Paddy. *The Viking Art of War.* London: Greenhill, 1995.

Hjaltalin, Jon A., and Gilbert Goudie, trans. *The Orkneyinga Saga.* Edinburgh: Edmonston and Douglas, 1873.

Jesch, Judith. *Women in the Viking Age.* Woodbridge, England: Boydell, 1991.

Jochens, Jenny. *Women in Old Norse Society.* Ithaca, NY: Cornell University Press, 1995.

Jones, Gwyn. *A History of the Vikings.* Oxford, England: Oxford University Press, 1984.

Larrington, Carolyne, trans. *The Poetic Edda.* Oxford, England: Oxford University Press, 2014.

Lindow, John. *Norse Mythology: A Guide to Gods, Heroes, Rituals, and Beliefs.* New York: Oxford University Press, 2002.

Short, William R. *Icelanders in the Viking Age: The People of the Sagas.* McFarland and Company, 2010.

Sturluson, Snorri. *Heimskringla; or, The Lives of the Norse Kings.* Translated by Erling Monson. New York: Dover, 1990.

Thurston, Tina L. *Landscapes of Power, Landscapes of Conflict: State Formation in the South Scandinavian Iron Age.* Kluwer Academic Publishers, 2002.

Wells, Peter S. *Barbarians to Angels: The Dark Ages Reconsidered.* New York: W. W. Norton, 2009.

ACKNOWLEDGMENTS

THE SEA QUEEN REPRESENTS THE CONTINUATION OF A LONG process of research, travel, and writing. It owes much to the support of my husband, Seth Miller, my parents, Mark and Karen Hartsuyker, and my sister, Julianna Lower. My early readers, Nicole Cunningham, Laura Brown, and Peng Shepherd, all provided invaluable feedback. Publicist Heather Drucker, marketing director Katie O'Callaghan, publisher Jonathan Burnham, and deputy publisher Doug Jones, as well as Milan Bozic, Patrick Arrasmith, and Shelly Perron, did beautiful work to bring this book out into the world. And finally, my editors, Terry Karten and Clare Smith, shaped this book mightily, as did my agent, Julie Barer. I could not have done it without you.

ABOUT THE AUTHOR

LINNEA HARTSUYKER can trace her family lineage back to the first king of Norway, and this inspired her to write her debut novel, *The Half-Drowned King*, the first book in her trilogy about the Vikings, which was published by Harper-Collins in the United States and internationally in six other countries. *The Half-Drowned King* was an Indie Next and a Barnes & Noble Discover pick, and was named the best historical fiction book of 2017 by the American Library Association. Linnea grew up in the woods outside Ithaca, New York, studied engineering at Cornell University, and later received an MFA in creative writing from New York University.